PERFECT PREY

Are you being hunted?

Consortium Book 2

(937) 408-5742

RICHARD VERRY

ALSO BY RICHARD VERRY

PERFECT PREY

Are you being hunted?

Consortium Book 2

Richard Verry

PERFECT PREY

Are you being hunted?

Consortium Book 2

RICHARD VERRY

Prologue

Across the centuries and around the globe, something evil is out there. Hiding in the shadows, they watch and study the lives around them.

No one knows they exist, not the public, not the authorities, and most especially, not their home countries. They live outside the box on a global scale. They operate beyond the reach of the authorities, always on the hunt for the next perfect prey. This centuries-old organization calls itself—the Consortium.

Even those that work for them don't know the Consortium's real purpose. Most work as hired contractors and agents, believing they are submitting candidates to a global headhunting employment agency. Charged to find the best talent for positions in exotic locations worldwide, they stay vigilant in their search. After all, the Consortium only wants the best talent to meet their needs.

Only a privileged few know the real purpose of its existence. Hidden among the multiple layers within the Consortium, secrecy abounds, and security is paramount. Each hand of the organization knows nothing of the others. Kept isolated from each other are Agents, Researchers, Assassins, Hunters, and Transporters. They operate in complete ignorance of one another. The elite membership of the Consortium prefers it that way.

In the center of the Consortium, only one person knows all. As an elected position, the Chairman is elected for life to oversee the organization's running to satisfy the wants, desires, and needs of the membership. Everyone answers to the Chairman. As long as the Chairman provides the perfect prey at auction, they are happy to let someone take care of the details.

The Consortium is always on the hunt, anxious to acquire new prey and eager to satisfy their bloodthirst. If you are young, beautiful, vulnerable, and alone in the world, then you are their perfect prey. After all, who's going to miss a few thousand culled out of billions each year?

Chapter One

"Good afternoon, Chicagoans, and thank you for joining us on this storm-ravaged day a week before Thanksgiving. I'm Charles Litter."

"And I'm Judy Weston, and this is Channel 3 News at Noon. Before we get to the national news, let's hear from Chief Meteorologist Stacey Pendulum. Stacey, how are things out there?"

"Yes, Judy. Things are ugly out there in the streets of Chicago." The camera had cut to a scene of Stacey standing in Chicago's streets, white with snow blowing sideways, and people and cars struggling to make progress against the blustery conditions. She wore a polar parka. Judy tried hard to keep her face visible to the camera, even as the wind insisted on blowing the fur-trimmed hood over her features. She took it in style, never missing a beat.

"The first major storm of the season has descended on the city, and Chicagoans are taking it all in stride. The windy city residents are no strangers to snowstorms, and they're dealing with it like champs. The snow's been falling now for a couple of hours, and we're predicting that it could last until late into the evening, perhaps even into tomorrow's rush hour. Airlines canceled hundreds of flights, so if you have reservations for the holidays, please check with your ticket agent. On top of that, the wind is stressing the highway department trying to clear the streets so early in the season," Stacy Pendulum reported.

For the next five minutes of airtime, Stacey described the winter storm that had descended over the city. After giving the standard weather report, she carried on and interviewed people in the streets, either helping others or just enjoying the first significant snow of the season.

"People are out here helping out, as we expect from our citizens. If you look behind me, you'll see some helping a stranded driver..."

However, one driver didn't care for the storm nor the road congestion. The driver only cared about one thing. That was how fast she could get to the hospital, where her sister dealt with a life-threatening issue.

Blowing the horn in frustration, Rachel pounded on her steering wheel after turning off the radio. "Come on, damn it. I've got to get to the hospital. Move it, people. MOVE IT!" Staring out into the falling snow-swept aside by her windshield wipers, Rachel Ladensen yelled out in frustration to no one in particular. "Fuck! I've been inching along for forty minutes now, and I've only made it, what – seven blocks from home! I still have a long way to get to the hospital."

Rachel had reason to worry. Not for herself, but she was concerned for her sister Heather, who had been readmitted to the hospital early this morning. She hated herself for turning off her phone overnight. She had decided to sleep in after a night of carousing, drinking, and a pickup. He had left her bed in the wee hours of the morning long before the storm hit, leaving her relaxed and satiated. She needed sleep and turned off her phone, not expecting anything to happen. Then at breakfast at around ten this morning, she turned it back on and discovered dozens of messages from her parents. Heather had relapsed and was transported to the hospital. The prognosis wasn't good.

"Fuck!" she yelled again, angry not at anyone in particular. "Of all days …"

Slowly, Rachel made slow progress as she inched her way closer to her destination. Well over an hour later than she intended, she pulled her car into the hospital parking garage. After putting the parking slip on her dashboard, she ran towards the elevators that would take her to the hospital lobby. Fifteen minutes later, out of breath, she ran into Heather's room.

"Heather, I'm so sorry, I…I tried to get here sooner. I…oh, I'm just sorry. That's all."

"Don't sweat it, Rach, it's all right. It's not like I'm going anywhere anytime soon." Heather replied in a calming tone intended to lower Rachel's stress levels. It worked. Rachel's exasperation settled down. Worry painted itself across her face, replacing the anxious anger at herself she felt earlier.

"How are you?"

"I'm fine. It'll be alright. I know it."

Turning towards her parents, she gave each of them a hug while saying, "Hi Mom, Dad. I'm sorry I missed your calls. I shouldn't have turned off my phone."

"It's fine, dear," her mom answered. "You're here now. That's all that matters."

Looking over at Heather, though intending for anyone in the room to answer, Rachel asked: "How are you really?"

"Fine, at least for right now."

"Come on, Heather. You wouldn't be here if that were all." Rachel insisted.

"Dear, Heather's right. She's fine right now, at least for the moment." Dad reassured her.

"Well, what happened?" Rachel insisted.

"Hon, early this morning, she had a bad relapse, and it got quite painful. Her body felt like it was on fire, and bruises appeared all over her torso and legs. We thought it best to get her to the hospital as quickly as possible. So, we packed her in the car, and they admitted her. She's on some pretty good painkillers, but that won't last very long."

Over the next couple of minutes, he related what had happened and how they got Heather to the hospital. He went into some detail as Rachel held Heather's hand, the one with the IV stuck in the back of her hand. Heather smiled back, somewhat comforted by the touch.

Heather had always been the family's calming influence while Rachel fretted at the littlest things. Having Rachel here, her sister and best friend, was all Heather required. Now she could give back to Rachel and ease her fears and calm her nerves. She always knew what Rachel needed before even Rachel knew.

"And, what's going to happen next," Rachel asked.

"Well, we're waiting for the Doctor to come in and tell us. The nurses tell us that he will be here in the next hour or so. As you can see, your timing is excellent."

"Well, that damn snow didn't make things any better," Rachel complained.

"Sweetie, you're here now. That's all that matters." Mom reassured her.

Calming down, Rachel eventually sat down in the side chair and continued to hold Heather's hand. Mom stood on the other side of the bed, stroking her child's face, sliding stray hairs from her eyes. Over the next hour or so, they talked, dancing around why they were all gathered. Every so often, a nurse would stop by to check on Heather and take her vitals. Two minutes later, the nurse left, giving the room back to the worried family.

Presently, they all heard a knock at the door. Turning towards the interruption, the family noted that it was Heather's oncologist, Dr. Yung. He was the Doctor overseeing her case ever since she was diagnosed with leukemia eighteen months ago.

"Good afternoon, everyone. I'm sorry to keep you waiting. I wanted to get the results of the latest tests before I came to see you. I wanted you to know what I know."

"And the word is…." Heather's dad trailed off.

Walking up to Heather, he stopped at her bedside and looked her right in the eye. "Heather, I'm sorry. The word is not good. The cancer is accelerating, and everything we've done to date is not working. I'm sorry, but unless we can find a suitable bone marrow donor, that is our only option."

"So, Doctor, you're telling me that we need to find a suitable donor that matches my profile and soon. Once we find that donor, they must be willing to donate some of their bone marrow. If we get past that hurdle, you must kill all of my existing marrow and replace it with the donors'. Then, after all that, the marrow has to take and grow. If all of that happens, then I might have a chance of surviving this."

"That's about right, Heather. I'm sorry."

"That's a lot of ifs, Doctor."

"Yes, my dear. It is. I'm sorry, but that's our only hope at this point."

"Next, you're going to tell me that even if the marrow takes, it might still not work, and I might still die anyway."

"Yes, Heather, there is a good chance of that happening as well. I'm sorry."

"So, what happens next?" Heather's dad asked.

"Well, we need to find a suitable donor. That's first on the list."

"And how would you go about doing that?" He asked.

"We check the donor list. But first, we need to update Heather's profile for comparison. I have already ordered the necessary tests. We took what we needed this morning. However, we'd like to do workups on the three of you." The Doctor said, looking at the family. "Familial matches will provide the best chance of success."

Rachel was proud to note that both her mom and dad agreed, as she hurriedly did. "When can we do that?" Rachel asked, anxious to get started right away.

"If you like, we can schedule those this evening. I must warn you; you will feel some discomfort when we extract the tissue samples." The Doctor confirmed.

"Anything, Doctor, we don't mind," Rachel answered for the three of them.

"Alright, assuming we get the samples tonight, we will have the results by morning, and we'll know if any of you would be a candidate."

"What happens then?" Rachel's mom asked.

"Well, first off, you must be prepared that none of you are a match. In that case, we go to the donor directory and look for a comparable match. However, assuming one of you is a match, we would then do a deeper investigation to confirm you could be a donor. That will entail taking a sample of your marrow from your hip to do the workup. Extracting the sample will hurt, and you will be in some pain. We will try to numb the area, but we will need to drill into the bone itself to get to the marrow."

"And then?" her dad asked.

"Assuming you are a match, we would then schedule the transplant as soon as possible. The longer we wait, the weaker Heather will become, and the less likely the procedure will work."

"Then what are we waiting for? Let's get started," her dad affirmed.

Looking at Heather, the Doctor asked her directly, "Are you willing to accept the marrow donation. There is some risk to the donor and significant risk to you."

"Doctor, what other choice do I have? I'll be dead soon if I don't."

"That's true." Dr. Yung replied. "What about the donor? There is some risk to them, though not as much as you."

"Doctor, that is their choice, and I will accept their decision."

"Good, I'll get the paperwork started. A nurse will be in shortly to have you all sign the necessary releases."

Looking back at Heather, "Don't worry. We'll find the right donor and get you well. You'll be celebrating the holidays at home with family and friends."

"Thank you, Doctor," Heather said a bit weakly, who then turned and left the room.

With both Rachel and her mom holding Heather's hands, "It'll be alright. You see."

"I hope," Heather said, her voice trailing off in fatigue. Several yawns followed, and Heather fought to keep her eyes open.

"You get some sleep, dear. You've had a rough day." Mom said.

"I guess you're right," Heather mumbled, who closed her eyes, and a moment later, she was asleep.

Whispering, Rachel offered her mother the side chair while she and her dad leaned against the windowsill. Instantly, she felt the cold outside pass through the window and touch her back. She shivered, hoping it wasn't a bad sign for things to come.

***

Taking turns and one by one, Rachel and her parents went down to phlebotomy and gave their tissue samples. Upon return, all three camped out in Heather's room so that they would be there when the results came in. Despite the hour, since none of them seem hungry, they skipped dinner. Of the four of them, only Heather appeared to get a decent night's sleep, only interrupted when a nurse came in to do a vitals check. Since all seemed well, they let her rest.

As for the other three, they took turns napping in the chair. About two a.m., the nurse's station offered them all the coffee from their pot. Rachel's dad thanked them and offered to chip in for the coffee. They politely declined. He just nodded his gratitude and returned to his daughter's room; his shoulders slumped over with obvious emotional pain written all over his body.

Moving to the lounge on the floor where Heather's room was, Rachel and her father talked well into the wee hours of the morning. Dad was comforting, but Rachel couldn't shake the feeling of dread and loss. She felt sure that Heather wasn't going to find a match and would be dead by the holidays. Dad held her and let Rachel cry in his lap. It didn't seem to help much, but Rachel was grateful for the kindness. The despair she felt went beyond anything she had ever felt. It crippled her.

"Dad, I'm not sure what I'm going to do without her," she lamented to her father.

"Honey, it's going to be alright. You'll see." He comforted his only other daughter, stroking the back of her head while smoothing her hair with his fingers.

"I know, Dad, but I get this feeling of dread. I'm not sure I can handle it. What if none of us is a match, and they don't find anyone on the registry."

"Have faith, Honey. They'll find a match. Hopefully, one of us, and if not, they will be someone on the registry who is a match. It'll all work out."

"But Dad, what if all the matches on the registry are out of town and unreachable? She'll die. I can't deal with that."

"Sweetheart, you are one of the strongest people I know. You'll get through this. Please have faith. You must trust that God has a plan for her and us."

"I hope so, Dad…I hope so."

Eventually, Rachel fell into a restless sleep on her father's lap. At one point, her mother came out to check on the two of them, and seeing her daughter finally asleep, she whispered "Good" to her mate. "Are you all good?"

Dad nodded, yes.

"Okay," her mom whispered and went back to sit with Heather, her tears welling up in her eyes. It was a long night.

***

Dread evident in their sunken eyes; they were barely awake when Dr. Yung returned to Heather's room at around six in the morning. Instantly they became alert to hear the news.

"What's the good word?" Rachel's father asked.

"There's good news. While you and your wife are not a match, Rachel is a possible candidate."

Erupting in mild cheers, Dr. Yung held up his hands in front of him to stop them.

"Listen, while it's good news, we still don't know if Rachel is a donor match for Heather, only that she is a possible match."

Turning towards Rachel, "The next step in finding out is we need to take you downstairs to a sterile extraction room and take a bit of your bone marrow for testing."

"Anything doctor, anything. I'm ready. Can we go now?"

Smiling, the Doctor continued after the interruption.

"Rachel, do you mind if we step outside?"

"Uh, oh, okay. Sure."

Stepping out into the hallway, Doctor Yung continued.

"Rachel, I wanted to talk to you privately. Heather has little choice. However, there are risks to you. You do have a choice. You will have to deal with long-term effects while you heal. I want to make sure you understand the risks without distraction or undue influence from your family. Even if you turn out to be a match, if you don't want to go through with this, I can tell them that you're not compatible."

"Doctor, I don't care about all that. All I care about is Heather. That is all that matters. If I have to deal with some pain, or whatever it is you're worried about, I can handle it. I just want to help Heather.

"Good. I know you're anxious. Anticipating your answer, I've already started the paperwork and reserving the room. Are you sure you want to go through with this? Extracting the sample is going to be painful. If you are a tissue match, then it will be even worse."

"Yes, Doctor. I understand anything for Heather. She's my sister and best friend. She would do the same for me." Rachel retorted.

"Okay then, stay close. I'm cutting some hospital rules to get this done so quickly since time is of the essence."

"Yes, Doctor, yes. I'll be right here."

Satisfied with Rachel's responses, the two of them returned to Heather's room.

The Doctor gripped Rachel on both shoulders and said, "It'll be alright. Heather will get better, even quicker, with you helping her. Stay positive. Heather has a strong advocate on her side."

"Yes, I will. Thanks."

Walking over to her sister, Rachel looked down at Heather. Managing a hint of a smile, filled with emotion, she said. "See, you're going to be alright."

Heather managed to give her a weak smile before closing her eyes. Minutes later, she fell into a restless sleep as Rachel rested her hand on her arm. They came for Rachel a short time afterward. After kissing her sister goodbye, she reluctantly left her bedside to see if she could become Heather's hero.

***

Several days later, on Black Friday, Rachel was sitting uncomfortably next to her sister, engaged in soft conversation with Heather. They were alone and spoke of things only two sisters know. It's not like they were twins, Rachel was a year and a half older than Heather, but they grew up together. In most respects, they were twins. They did everything together. By the time Rachel became a woman, she had failed to leave Heather behind. Instead, she helped Heather progress through her transition to womanhood. They double-dated, they hung out, and even went to the same college. When it came time to move out, they shared an apartment to save money. Decent living accommodations in the city of Chicago are expensive. They even left the other alone when there was a proverbial sock on the door to their bedrooms.

Rachel looked after her younger sister, hoping to protect her from the evils of the world. Try as she might, she could not protect her from the scourge of leukemia ravaging her body. Hoping for a miracle, the girl's disease pained her in ways that she could not understand. All she knew was, black and blue bruises tinged in ugly yellow blotches covered her body, while tears in her eyes seemed to take up permanent residence, adding to the black look of death in the sockets around her eyes. Overall, her skin looked pale and yellowish, tinged with blue. If Rachel didn't know better, she'd swear that her sister looked like some alien from another planet.

"Rachel, look at me," Heather said, breaking her reverie. Slowly looking up at her face, Rachel returned to the here and now.

"Rachel, it's going to be alright. You're going to be a match and save my sorry ass."

"And what if I'm not Heather? What if there's no match on the registry. You'll die, and I'll be all alone."

"So, I die, and you'll go on, strong and giving as ever. I'll be there with you in your heart. I'm okay with all this. I love you, Rach. You must know this." After a pause to gather her strength, "I'm good with this, whatever happens."

"Heather, I love you too. I just have this feeling of dread that no matter what happens here, something bad is going to happen. I don't know what I'd do without you. You're more than just my little sister. You're my best friend. You're supposed to be my maid of honor at my wedding."

"Shuud up! What wedding? Have you been holding out on me? Did you meet someone I don't know about?" Heather chastised her older sister.

"Whoa there, kiddo, no one yet, I will meet someone one day, and when I do, I will want you there."

"Okay, fair enough. I'll be your maid of honor if you'll be mine."

"Deal!"

The sound of a knock at the door interrupted their conversation.

"Hey, Doctor. Have you got news for us?"

"Yes, I do. Are your parents here?"

"No, they'll be along in a bit. They went home to clean up and change clothes."

"Oh, is that the smell I sense from down the hallway?" The Doctor teased.

Used to such taunts, the girls smiled at the joke. They needed a bit of relief, so they were in a charitable mood, despite the circumstances. Doctor Yung watched in amusement, content to see the two of them putting on a stoic front in these dire times. It didn't take long for the two of them to return their concentration on the good Doctor.

"Ladies, I have good news. Rachel, you're a match. As close to a perfect match as we could hope."

"Wow, see Rachel," Heather began, "I told you it would all work out."

"Yes, you did, Heather." Turning to the Doctor, "I'm ready. When can we get started?"

"I must reiterate the risks with you. The paperwork goes over them in detail. Shall we proceed?"

"Doctor, I'm ready, and I understand. Heather does too, don't you?" She said, looking over at the bedridden girl.

"Yes," Heather said weakly.

"Should I do something now to get ready?"

"Sleep, Rachel, get some rest. You're going to need it." The Doctor replied, who then went on to describe the details of the procedure. Ten minutes later, with everyone satisfied, he exited the room to get things rolling.

Jumping up in glee, Rachel grabbed both Heather's hands and exclaimed. "You're going to be alright. This is the best present ever. You're going to get better."

"Yes, Rach, thanks to you. If you don't mind, though, I need to rest. I'm feeling drained, and honestly, I hurt all over."

"Oh, sure," Rachel said, gently placing her sister's arms back down, careful not to hurt her. "You sleep now. I'm here if you need me."

"Thanks…" she said, her voice trailing off to almost nothing. A moment later, Heather was asleep.

After looking at her sister sleeping restlessly, Rachel stepped out of the room and called home. Mom answered, and Rachel happily gave her the good news. A short time later, both her parents arrived at the hospital to await the next stage of Heather's recovery, scheduled to happen on Monday. Everyone except for Heather was anxious to get started as soon as possible. Last week, time dragged on wearing a dark cloak. Now, time still dragged on but with a shawl lined with hope and good cheer.

***

A month later, the entire family celebrated Christmas at home. Heather was home, recovering. The bruising on her body was fading, with a healthy pinkish color returning to her skin. As Dad had iterated, the best present of the season was Heather back home. It was a happy time for all of them. When New Year's rolled around, for the first time in a very long time, Heather drank the champagne toast, albeit it was barely more than a sip, but she was able to add to the good cheer.

About half-past midnight, Heather found Rachel staring out the window, lost in her thoughts.

"What's up, Rach?" she asked.

"I don't know, Heather. I'm glad and all that you're getting better. I still have this sense of foreboding. I don't like it. It feels like a dark cloud is still hovering over us, and I can't see why that would be."

"While things can still go wrong with my recovery, I won't let that bother me. Let's just be happy I'm here today. Just think, I made it to the New Year. Let's just put the past behind us and move forward, day by day. Alright?"

"You're right, Heather. It's probably nothing, one day at a time. Got it, hey, I forgot to tell you. I met a guy!"

"You did? Spill it, girl. I want to hear all the details."

"Well, he's a radiologist at the hospital."

"A doctor, wow! When you go for it, you go for it. What's he like?"

"Well, he's …" For the next half hour, the two sisters talked and joked like old times. For a brief moment in time, they put the troubles of the past year aside.

Mom and Dad watched them from a distance, smiling in remembrance of better days of yore. The Doctor's prognosis report on Heather was excellent. He was confident that Heather would make a full recovery and live a regular life.

The outlook on Rachel was positive as well. There were no signs of lasting after-effects from the donation. As long as Rachel took care of herself, he felt that there would be no lingering effects to worry over. All in all, the coming year was looking good to them, something to help them forget the pain and anguish of the past year. Neither of them would argue that the past year sucked.

Returning to their guests, they all joined in the celebration of Heather's recovery. Pouring new rounds for everyone, laughter and good spirits filled the room. The top-shelf liquor helped as well.

"Everyone, may I have your attention." Dad started. When he felt he had them, he continued, "Please, raise your glass. Here's to the New Year. We have Heather back, and that alone is my special gift from God for the coming year. Here's to Heather and her continued recovery."

Chapter Two

"Avril, do you remember where this door leads to?"

"Yes, Sir. It's the door to your office."

"And what is my rule regarding my office?"

"Sir, that I may never enter it."

"Correct," he said as he left her side and walked up to the door. Turning towards her, he commanded. "Come here."

"Sir?"

"I said, come here."

"Yes, Sir," Avril answered and began approaching him as he stood in front of the door.

A couple of steps away from the door, Avril started feeling a tingling sensation around her neck. Her collar was warning her to stop. However, Sir had not told her to stop, so Avril continued her cautious advance. Another step later, and she began feeling as if thousands of ants were walking all around her neck. They even seemed to crawl across her neck and down her spine. It was terrifying. Taking another hesitant step closer, the sensations around her neck intensified. The ants were now biting and stinging her. She stopped her approach.

"Why did you stop?"

"It hurts, Sir," Avril answered, a look of distress and fear appearing on her face.

"Nevertheless, I require you to come closer and stand next to me."

"Yes, Sir."

Sliding a foot forward, Avril extended a foot and tentatively transferred her weight to the extended foot, and pulled the other next to her. Sharp stabbing pain replaced the stinging ants, shooting through her neck and into the center of her brain. Unable to stop herself, she cried out in distress, her face distorted and scrunched up.

"Sir, it really hurts. Must I?"

"Avril, do not make me ask you again."

"Yes, Sir, I'll try," she answered, not realizing that she only had one more step to go.

"Trying is not an option. You will stand next to me. Failure to stand next to me will earn you a severe punishment for disobedience." Sir answered, a look of contentment on his face, though Avril didn't notice it. She felt nothing but the unbearable pain of a pinball rebounding inside her skull. Trying to ignore her discomfort, she turned her attention to the task.

Briefly closing her eyes, she saw what appeared as thousands of fireflies darting to-and-fro on the inside of her eyelids. In other circumstances, it would be a beautiful display of light and color. Now, however, it was just another warning of certain death from her collar.

Edging forward, one tentative inch by inch, Avril moved closer to him, the trigger to her agony and near-certain death. Somehow, she managed to slide up next to him, to cry and whimper in her distress. Her knees threatened to buckle, sending her crashing to the floor. The fireflies disappeared, replaced by exploding stars and knives slashing inside her head. Her knees buckled, and she slid to the floor. Lifted to his chest, Avril let go and expressed her agony in the way she knew he liked, with screams. Too distraught to notice the smile of pleasure on his face, she buried her head in this chest and broke down in tears and anguish.

She didn't notice his hand stroking the back of her head, soothing her.

After an inappreciable length of time, he picked her up and carried her to her private quarters, setting her down on her sofa. Sitting down beside her, he positioned himself so that he could rest her tortured head on his lap. Giving her time to recover, he just sat there and waited, lightly stroking her head and combing her hair with his fingers.

As her pain subsided, Avril mumbled, "Why, Sir? Why must you hurt me so bad?"

"Avril, it is who I am. I cannot change that. It is in my nature."

"Sir, do you feed off of my pain and anguish?"

"Hmmm, an intriguing question. I guess in a way I do. I never really thought about it before. We'll talk about it later. Right now, rest. You will have a headache for the remainder of the day. By tomorrow and after a good night's sleep, it will subside, and then we can continue your training."

"Sir, you know I expect a commensurate pleasure to offset the agony I just suffered?"

"And you will. I will reward you with that tomorrow."

"Yes, Sir. Thank you, Sir."

Avril rested, comforted by the gentle stroking of his hand on her head. In so many ways, she didn't understand him nor understood his need to see her suffer the way she did. She didn't get his desire to punish, torture, and kill the women he possessed. Oh, sure, she accepted it, only she didn't comprehend it. What choice did she have? Despite their agreement, she remained his property. He owned her, and he would never let her go.

Without a shadow of a doubt she knew, that part of him ruled his behavior. Their agreement came second to his need to make others suffer. Even though she had chosen to accept his dominance over her with the promise that he would never kill her, she knew that one day, he would kill her. In one final stroke, he would end her suffering. She was at a loss as to finding a way to prevent it. Escape would be apparent, but that too seemed an insurmountable mountain to climb. However, she maintained her resolve to find a way to die of old age.

"You understand, Avril, that had you stepped any closer to the threshold of my office, you would have been rendered unconscious?"

"Yes, Sir. However, it might have been worth it to stop the agony I felt."

"Avril, you might be right. I remind you that dropping unconscious at the door would not have stopped the collar from hurting you. Too much time under its influence would have resulted in irreparable harm to you. You would be useless to me."

"Sir, I thought we agreed that you would never kill me or do irreparable harm to me."

"Ah, and there's the thing. In this case, I would not be killing you or doing irreparable harm to you. You would have done that to yourself, choosing to suffer the collar to its extreme. In this case, I conducted the test in a moderated session. Had you fallen unconscious, I was there to take you from harm's way. I might not be able to if you tested your boundaries on your own."

"I see, Sir. A subtle distinction and one that I have trouble accepting. I did not put the collar around my neck. Even though I have accepted it and chosen to wear your collar, it is – not my doing that it can and does harm me."

"And isn't it? I am not the one choosing to test the collar to its extreme. I am not the one deciding to press forward until I fall unconscious. Aren't you making those decisions?"

"Yes, Sir. I see your point. Part of me doesn't agree. It feels wrong. That's the only way I can express it right now. When I get my wits back and can think straight, maybe then I can articulate my thoughts so that you can understand. Right now, my headache is overwhelming my ability to think straight. It's so bad that, well, I am on the verge of screaming, even though I know you love hearing me suffer. I am having trouble – articulating my thoughts. Something that I was about to say, suddenly disappears and I am – well, I can't remember what I was about to say."

"You said a part of you feels that way. What about the other part?"

"Sir, logic agrees with you. You make an interesting point. However, right now, I can't seem to wrap my thoughts around the conversation. Plus, I'm sleepy. All I want to do is go to bed and sleep. Despite resting comfortably on your lap, I need to rest and recover. It would be helpful if I could lie down in bed."

"Go lie down. Dinner will be ready in a few hours. We'll talk more over food."

"Yes, Sir. Thank you, Sir." Avril responded, getting up and sliding into bed. It didn't matter to her that he just stood there, watching the look of pain on her face as she pulled the covers over her body, struggling to unsnag the covers caught on her heels. She just closed her eyes and tried to smother her headache. The pain behind her eyes was excruciating; she never heard the door close behind him as she drifted off to sleep.

Refreshed and feeling better, Avril walked down the stairs to meet Sir for dinner. She found him in the lounge, where he took her the day of her first group sexual experience. He was reading from his data tablet.

"Good evening, Sir," she greeted and took her usual kneeling pose in front of him, hands clasped behind her back, and waited.

Without acknowledging her entrance or respectful greeting, he continued to review the information on his tablet. She watched him intently, curious as to what he was reading. She had learned a long time ago; he would share what he felt she should know. For all she knew, he could have been looking at porn, though that was not likely. Frankly, he shared little with her since her capture. She didn't even know who the president in her home country was. As much as she wanted to know, her curiosity often resulted in painful, disciplinary action. Instead, she knelt, keeping her back straight and eyes front.

Several minutes later, Sir looked up at her. "Good evening Avril. How did you sleep? Do you feel better?"

"Thank you, Sir. I am feeling much better. I think I was asleep even before you left the room."

"Yes, you were. I enjoyed watching you sleep. As pained as you looked getting into bed, it was quite the opposite after you fell off. Your entire body seemed to soften and relax. It's a sight that I'll never grow tired of seeing."

Nodding, Avril kept quiet.

"Hungry?"

"Yes, Sir."

Reaching out to take her hand, "Good, let's have dinner."

Letting him help her up, Avril faced him as he reached in and kissed her. She returned the kiss, allowing him to probe his tongue behind her lips. Of all the issues surrounding her captivity, his kisses weren't one of them. She certainly enjoyed his kisses. Despite his cruelty, when he kissed her, her blood boiled and heat radiated throughout her body. She returned his passion.

Breaking off, "Whew!" he whispered.

Smiling, she nodded ever so slightly. She knew that kissing Sir to her fullest potential was one way to keep herself alive for another day.

After taking her arm in his, he escorted her to the intimate dining room.

Approaching the table, he held her chair out for her, and she sat down. A moment later, he joined her, taking a chair to her left.

"I think you're going to like the meal I had prepared for you."

"Sir, as you know, I have yet to be disappointed in the meals you prepare."

"Except for those you used to get through the food alcove during your first year with me."

"Well, Sir, now that you bring it up. Those meals weren't the tastiest," she said, noticing but not acknowledging the serving girl who walked into the room. After all this time, she had stopped seeing that everyone was nude. In this case, however, in addition to her black training heels, she was wearing a black bow tie over her collar and one of those lacy black serving crowns trimmed out in red roses on her head. She stood next to the serving buffet and took one of the mandatory poses, hands behind her back, one heeled foot in front of the other, and waited until needed.

"Nor were they intended to. However, the meals were sufficient to keep you healthy. Now, would you like a drink?"

"Yes, Sir. I would."

"Do you have anything in mind? Feel free to order anything you'd like, including an alcoholic drink."

"Thank you, Sir. How about a vodka martini, very dry, with extra olives?"

Snapping his fingers, he said, "Done."

Immediately, the serving girl approached the table. "Vodka martini straight up, very dry with extra olives for the lady. I'll have my usual single malt on the rocks. Make it a double."

"Very good, Sir," the serving girl acknowledged and turned to the bar to make the drinks.

"While we wait for the drinks, tell me about this afternoon from your perspective."

"Sir, if I understand you correctly, you want me to relate the events of going to your office?"

"Yes, Avril, but not necessarily the event itself, but your experience approaching the door."

Gulping, Avril thought about it a moment. She was about to open her mouth to respond when the serving girl returned with their drinks. Grateful for the interruption, Avril used it to collect her thoughts.

In the meantime, Sir raised his glass, indicating he wanted to say a toast. Lifting her own, she noted the martini glass glistened from floating ice crystals, indicative that the vodka was at just the right temperature. Just the way she liked it.

"Here's to you, my lovely and exciting Avril. You never cease to amaze me. I am very proud of you."

Surprised by the toast, Avril looked back, dumbfounded and speechless. She didn't know what to say. Smiling gratefully, she looked into his eyes and smiled. After tilting her glass towards him, the two of them drank deeply. Avril watched him as he swirled the scotch across his tongue before swallowing. As for herself, the vodka didn't stay long in her mouth, quickly letting it flow down her throat. Instantly, she felt its warmth explode through her body. A sense of calm fell over her. It was not often that he allowed her alcohol, so she intended to savor this surprising drink.

"You were about to say?" he said, as the serving girl took her position next to the serving buffet and waited.

"Oh, Yes, Sir, about this afternoon," she began, evident he was listening intently. "As we approached your door, I will admit, I was scared."

She paused to see if he would interject a comment, as he so often did. Taking a departure from his usual behavior, he remained silent and looked at her intently. The strength of his concrete stare made her uncomfortable. From his body language and the intensity of his gaze, his unspoken demand to share her feelings was palpable with every passing second. She didn't want to share some of her reactions. Yet she knew he wasn't going to let her off the hook either.

"I … ah … saw that door frame and knew what was about to happen. I didn't want to approach it."

More to bolster her confidence than for any other reason, she took another sip of her martini.

"Sir, why did you make me?" Avril continued.

"Don't deflect. I might answer your question later. Right now, I want you to relate the experience from your point of view. Describing your impressions is something you have done for me in the past. You know you can do it."

"Yes, Sir. I get that," she replied, struggling with her thoughts and discomfort. "He's going to make me say it, isn't he?" she asked herself, careful not to vocalize the question. Staring down at her glass, she absently twirled her hair around her fingers. "Please, no. I don't want to do this," she said again in her head.

Glancing up, maintaining he focused on her.

"No, he's not going to let it go. Fuck." She mentally resolved to answer him.

"Ah, well, I remember seeing you framed in the doorway, telling me to come to you. I don't remember the exact words, but I do recall that you were commanding me to come to you."

Pausing once more, she continued. "I remember feeling as if I was frozen in place, unable to move. Then, I remembered staring at the door frame, petrified as to moving closer. However, the tone of your insistence cut through that."

Avril paused again, taking a sip of her cocktail.

"I remember walking over to you. That was when I felt my collar reacting."

For the first time, Sir interrupted. "It was more like an inch at a time. You barely moved your feet forward, but I was proud of you. You moved, knowing what was going to happen."

"Thank you, Sir. Though at the time, it felt like I was taking full steps forward. When I first felt the collar, it was just a soft tingling sensation, nothing at all that upsetting. However, moving closer, the tingling became ... well, I'm not sure how to describe it. It felt like hundreds of ants crawling around my neck. Then, as I approached even closer, I felt like hundreds of fire ants were stinging me, setting my neck on fire."

Taking a deep, cleansing breath, she went on. "At that point, I remember starting to back away. In fact, I was willing myself to back off, except that my feet didn't move. For some reason, I couldn't move backward. I could only move forward. I think it was because I knew you would be upset with me if I didn't obey your command."

"And...." Sir said, leading her on.

"Eventually, I moved closer, slower as I recall." Sir nodded but did not interrupt. "The closer I got, the more the stinging burning around my neck got. It seemed worse than anything I've ever felt from you in the past."

"Tell me, are you still scared of it?"

"Oh Yes, Sir, very much so."

"Fascinating! Thank you for sharing. It's good information. Relating your feelings as you have, helps me learn more about you."

"Sir, if I may, I would have thought that by now, you knew everything about me and what makes me tick."

"Ah, the human psyche has too many facets for any one person to learn, even in an entire lifetime. I'm happy to keep learning more about you."

Staring at her nearly empty martini glass, Avril asked herself. "Was that a compliment?"

"I don't want him to learn more about me. In other ways, yes, I do. Hmmm, I am resolved not to spend the rest of my life as his property. I can never even let him know that, either by voice or body language. I need to stop dwelling on it, especially when I'm in his presence."

"Easier said than done," she lamented to herself.

"Sir, I must say I'm flattered by your desire to learn more about me." Avril deflected, as saying something close to the truth was the easiest way to lie.

"But?" he interrupted.

"I like ... uh, oh," caught off guard by the interruption. "Well, yes, I do have some reservations about your desire to learn all there is about me."

"That's understandable, but why?"

"Sir, I, well, I don't rightly know. Even though I agreed to stay with you and accept your ownership over me, there are times I struggle with the concept. I've always believed that it is wrong to own people. Your claim to me contradicts that. I indeed agreed, but ultimately, I feel that it is just not right. I can't control that feeling. I can't even seem to manage it. It just happens. I don't seem to have any command over my emotions. I don't understand, but I am trying to reconcile them."

"Avril, my pet, I can appreciate your conflicts. Now, I don't know if I can help you resolve your feelings, but perhaps I can give you a bit of wisdom. Feelings just are. They appear and disappear on a whim, and we humans cannot control them. We can only deal with them as they happen. Does that make sense?"

"Hmmm, well Sir, I don't know, maybe."

"Merely accept those feelings and emotions just are. You scream in pain when I hurt you. You also scream in joy when I pleasure you. Can you make those screams happen on command? Of course, you can. But those are not real. They don't come from your gut, your inner soul, so to speak. I want the ones I demand, come from a part of you that you can't control. I ask you to work on accepting them. After you accept them, you can work on dealing with them. It will take time, and in this case, it could take years. I understand your conflict with my ownership of you. I contend that your base feeling of humans owning humans is fundamentally wrong. The practice of owning people goes back over ten thousand years, perhaps more. Maybe if you look at the paradox from that perspective, you can figure out how to reconcile your conflict."

"Sir, I will take your console and reflect upon it. You make a point that I had not considered. Sir, perhaps if I could have access to the net so that I can research the question, would that be something?"

"Oh, so you're now turning the conversation around. My answer is no. I will not grant you access to the net, nor any other form of communication from the outside. You will learn from what I offer you, nothing else. Have you forgotten the appropriate rule in the rulebook? However, since you are a special case. Should you ever become a member of the Consortium, that may change. I will not make a promise that I cannot keep. You will have to wait and see."

Looking up and maintaining eye contact, "Yes, Sir. I understand. You're correct. I should have remembered the rule and not made the request. I submit myself to punishment."

"As right as you should. Come over here," he instructed, pushing his chair out from the table.

Avril left her chair, and when Sir patted his lap, she bent over and draped herself face down on his lap. In no time, she felt the wallop of his hand on her bare ass as he spanked her. As hard as the spanking was, she didn't feel the need to cry out. She had become used to them, even though they hurt. Gripping the chair legs, she weathered the spanking as he turned her bottom a bright red. Counting off the strikes, he stopped when the count reached twenty-five.

Getting up, "Thank you, Sir, for my well-deserved punishment," Avril confirmed. Standing in her standing pose, she held her hands clasped behind her back, feeling the heat still radiating from her ass.

"It's good to get past the punishments quickly so we can move on. I've forgotten about the infraction."

"Thank you, Sir. It was an honor to submit to your punishment."

"You may resume your seat," he said to her, snapping his fingers to the serving girl, "Another round."

"Yes, Sir, coming right up." The serving girl replied, turning to the beverage bar.

Avril, gingerly sitting down before pulling her chair up to the table, rested her hands on her lap. "Sir, thanks for the extra drink."

"Think nothing of it. I'm pressing you to reveal yourself and some of your most intimate feelings."

Nodding, Avril lowered her gaze and waited.

"As I recall, you were relating your feelings as you stepped up to my office door."

"Yes, Sir. Let me see. I remember the agony of the fire ants, the only way I know how to describe the sensation of stinging and biting. It felt as if they were burrowing into my very flesh and driving their assault directly into my brain. I don't remember how long it took before I collapsed, but it felt like hours."

"More like a couple of seconds."

"Then, as I recall, I collapsed, and while falling, you caught me, Sir."

"Yes, that's right. What do you recall after that?"

"After that, why blissful nothingness," Avril paused, allowing the serving girl to set a fresh drink in front of her. Taking a sip, relishing the renewed warmth and delightful taste, she continued. "The next thing I remember is waking up, lying on the sofa with my head on your lap."

"Oh," she added, nearly shouting, "I remember, there was that massive headache. I almost cried out from that alone, resting there as you petted me."

"On a scale of zero to ten, with ten meaning screaming as if you were burning to death, how do you rate the headache?"

"Are you kidding me, Sir? A ten, that's what it was."

"But you weren't screaming in agony. At best, you were moaning a bit. How can you rate it a ten?"

"Yes, I guess you're right, Sir. Make it an eight though it could have been a nine. It sure felt like I was on the edge of screaming. Maybe it was because I was resting on your lap, and you were comforting me. Otherwise, it might just as well be higher."

"That makes sense. What, if anything, did you get from the incident?"

"Sir, that I will never approach one of those agonizing exits. And that afterward, you eased my discomfort. Aftercare, I presume?"

"Yes, anything else?"

"You are cruel, Sir. You enjoyed watching me crumble in pain like that."

"Yes, I did, but you already knew that."

"Still, it is one thing to suffer your torment in the playspace and quite another to feel your torment in other ways."

"So that you remember, you are mine. I own you, and I will do with you as I please."

"Yes, Sir. I understand."

"Avril, understanding is not required. Acceptance is. Do you accept my ownership over you?"

"Sir, as I said earlier, I'm working on that."

"Good. Now, let's eat."

Chapter Three

The belt of the treadmill mesmerized me. Staring at the seam in the belt captured my interest. Several times, I caught myself counting the number of times it flew by under my feet.

Walking the treadmill was one of the few personal pleasures available to me that connected me to my old life as a marathon runner. Whenever the opportunity arose to work out, I always took to the treadmill to satisfy my need to use my legs.

I still miss it. Ever since Sir took me from my home and my former life, I'm stuck to doing no better than running in high-heels on the treadmill. Let me tell you, running with spikes on my feet is not all that pleasurable. I'd prefer running shoes over heels any day.

I need to feel my hair clump up on the back of my neck, running past the crowds cheering me on, and the endorphins running through my body. I would almost kill to get that sensation back. Hmmm, come to think of it, I might have to do just that to escape this gilded cage I'm locked within.

Just when I was getting good, finishing in the top ten in the Boston and New York City Marathons, I was stolen and sold into a forced life of servitude, pain, and suffering. Granted, I am well fed, enjoy a healthy sex life, and want for little. The one thing I yearn for is the one thing denied me, my freedom.

Freedom, in my old life, I was blissfully unaware of how precious my freedom was. Sure, I had issues at work, like the crappy boss who used me and kept me from advancing in my career. Then, while I lived in a decent New York City apartment, that was only possible by inheriting it after the death of my parents. I still miss them, especially Daddy. But it was my life. Whether I made mistakes or not, I was in control of my destiny. That was something, wasn't it? Now, Sir has taken my freedom away from me, and I have no control over my future. Sir dictates what will happen to me, including killing me one day.

Of course, the treadmill does little to satisfy my desire to run. Sir maintained his requirement that I wear my stiletto heels at all times, including when I work out. Running in them was impossible. The best I could do was to program the treadmill to move no faster than a brisk walk. The slow pace annoyed me to no end.

Thankfully, he frequently replaces them. I have several pairs, all identical, that I rotate, so I don't get an infection from wearing the same footwear too much.

My only relief comes when I bathe or swim. That means that the moment I exit the shower or bathtub, I quickly dry myself off, and before even hanging up the wet towel, I slip on my heels and buckle them to my feet. Otherwise, Sir insists on punishing me if he catches me without them. Not that he doesn't have the opportunity to punish me, he does. But I learned a long time ago that his punishments are far worse than continually wearing the shoes. There is one advantage, though, wearing them has strengthened and toned my calves. In my entire life, my legs never looked so good.

I used to be able to sit down when putting them on. It was maybe six months ago that he required me to stand up, slip my feet into them, and then bend over to buckle them around my ankles. He tells me that it is to make sure I maintain my flexibility. I think he just likes to see me stick out my naked ass at him and exhibit my unveiled pussy for him to poke if the urge takes hold of him. Not that I mind that much. Being fucked by him is always a pleasure. It's all the other stuff he does to me or makes me do, which is the issue.

Even when I try to run hard and fast, the high spikes on the bottoms of my feet force me to slow down. But I make do. When Sir first granted me access to the treadmill, I soon realized that I would break an ankle. Of course, he warned me that should I do so, he would severely punish me for my failure to comply with his rule. Breaking an ankle would limit his ability to take his screams from me and could just as quickly find me dead.

I've gotten somewhat accustomed to his painful punishments, but I still suffer, writhing in pain for days afterward. Take that time a few weeks back when he tested my collar outside his office door. That day, I honestly thought that I was going to die. The agony I felt in my neck and head almost drove me to madness. If he hadn't caught me as I slumped under the anguish of it all, I suppose the collar would have continued to torment me, even in my unconsciousness, until I died. At least with our play sessions in the dungeon, he will hurt me, but Sir also makes me happy. When he punishes me, it just hurts. I try to avoid them as much as possible.

"Huh, I stopped counting the seams in the treadmill," I realized. "Oh well. At least the mileage counter on the console is still keeping track. Look at that. When I last looked, the display read twelve miles. Now it reads twenty. Where did the time go? No matter, there's only eight more to go."

I returned to my reverie, staring out the window at the world around me. It was springtime when I agreed to that awful choice. My options were limited. I would either die a horrible, painful, and immediate death, which in my mind was the equivalent of committing suicide, or I could suffer the occasional punishing sessions. In return, I could live and enjoy comparable pleasure offsetting the agonies I suffered.

It was an impossible choice, but somehow, I made it. I'm not even sure why I did it. All I had to do was refuse to answer, and he would have ended my misery, once and for all. But noooo, I had to open my big mouth and agreed to live. Will God ever forgive me?

Now, it is late autumn, and the leaves are turning colors. Most have already fallen to the ground. I can't see too many of them because of all the pine trees, but it gives me a sense of the changing seasons.

"I wonder, is it Halloween yet, or did I miss yet another holiday?" I muttered softly under my breath. "Actually, should I even care? I doubt I'll see home again."

My thoughts were running rampant, and I let them wander.

Sir does enjoy some holidays, though I still can't figure out what they are. It's almost as if he makes them up. I can't make sense of them. The last one seemed to have a harvest theme to them, and the celebration before that was in summer. There were often other smaller parties and only a small, intimate number of his friends in between these occasions.

At these get-togethers, I am usually the centerpiece of their carnal needs. Always, they used me in ways that served their sexual and sometimes sadistic needs. Often, I accommodate more than one cock at a time until I was pleasantly sore all over. By the time the morning arrives, I am exhausted with cum dripping from my ass and pussy, slowly drying to a white, crusty frosting smeared all over my body. I've never had so many orgasms in a single night as I have at these parties. I don't understand it all, but I am certainly not complaining.

I have to admit the parties are fun. Until I came to live with Sir, I had never had multiple sexual partners at the same time. During these parties, I was the focal point throughout the event. It didn't matter whether they shared cocktails before dinner, during, or afterward during the post-dinner entertainment; I was the topic of conversation and pleasure. I know that if I ever get out of this predicament, I will lament the loss of these experiences.

"Oh, dear, I lost track of the miles again. I'm over thirty miles. Umm, that was hypnotizing."

Stepping off the treadmill, I grabbed the gym towel and wiped the sweaty sheen from my body. I was looking forward to slipping into the hot tub and enjoying a few moments out of my heels. Walking over to the nearby jet tub, I removed my shoes and carefully stepped into the hot water. The thermostat read forty, which I had learned meant about one hundred four degrees. It would feel fantastic at that temperature but limit my soaking time to less than twenty minutes, more if I felt faint or lightheaded. Sir wouldn't like it if I overdid my soak. I turned on the jets.

Settling down in the hot, bubbling water, I found a strategically placed jet and leaned up against it. The vigorous stream of water massaged my upper back and shoulders, easing my aches and pains and feeling oh so good. Even my breasts felt lighter, as they seemed to float above the surface, my nipples poking through the bubbles. It felt nice, taking a bit of their weight off my shoulders. Closing my eyes, I wanted the water to soak away my troubles, even those that I could do nothing about.

Leaning my head back, I rested it against the sidewall and let my mind wander.

Thinking about my situation, I still wanted to find a way to escape, free from him and the Consortium. I didn't know how to do it. One way or another, they would search and find me, return me to him, and he would take out his disappointment on my flesh. Without a doubt, I knew he would kill me but not until after I suffered long and hard by his hands. There would be no way easy out. He would punish me hard and in the most awful and gruesome ways. I've seen what he's done to other women. I would suffer in worse ways than what they all endured, combined.

While I've grown to deal with his punishments, that would not do, not at all.

I know. Take, for example, what happened after I gave Sir my answer to that awful decision. Sure, he took me to his bed, and in a charming, loving way, made love to me all night long. Never once had I slept, and never once did he demand that I pleasure him. No, his emphasis was on satisfying me. Of course, I made sure he felt good in the process. Both of us climaxed several times but what he did to me exceeded anything I offered him.

I swear I experienced a single climax that seemed to go on much of the night. There was no letup, no slacking off. No, he had me in a state that if it weren't for the bed, I would have collapsed in a heap on the floor. As it was, we needed fresh bed linens before the night was over. I never knew I could get so wet and ejaculate volumes of my juices. Still, I did, soaking the sheets by the time he let up.

Through it all, I lost all sense of time and even of my body. It was all lost to me.

It was the next night that I paid for my pleasure. He took me to the play dungeon, after which I experienced a compensating level of pain and anguish. He strapped me to an overhead pipe and chained my legs to them on nearby posts, spreading them wide and leaving me completely exposed and vulnerable from attack. I was spread eagle, as I have come to think of the position, and unable to move much. He whipped me mercilessly. He even broke several whippy bamboo canes across my legs and torso. Man, do those ever hurt.

He attached electrical wires to me, some on my privates, others on my already tender nipples, and others, well, let's honestly say in particularly sensitive areas already burning from his earlier torment. After he wired me up to an unknown device, he sat back, and like some orchestra conductor, played his instruments by shocking me in various ways, orchestrating multiple movements of the symphony playing on the stereo in the background to my screaming.

He wanted my screams, and he got them. I don't remember much of that night after the electrical play started, but I remember being surprised that I hadn't died during the ordeal. I passed out somewhere along the way, waking hours later and, for all I knew, days later.

When I came to my senses, I noticed he was still sitting there, classical music deep with organ bass tones playing in the background. He reached for the confounded device, and before I could yell NO, he activated the machine, and I again screamed. How long this went on, and how many times he resumed his torture after each intermission of blissful lapses into unconsciousness, I have no idea.

What I do remember is finally waking up in my bed, agonizing from raw wounds resting against the rough fabric of my bedsheets, a material I knew to be silk.

He never considered giving me painkillers, or at least something to dull the pain. No, I had to suffer for days, lasting into weeks as my wounds healed. I remember inspecting my body at one point, horrified to find that my entire body, from my neck to my feet, was covered in ugly welts, burns, and bleeding wounds.

In the en-suite, I found cream for my burns and bandages for my wounds. Next to them, I saw instructions for their use, and over the next week or two, I changed the dressings and soothed my burns with the cream every four hours or so. I still didn't have a clock to know what four hours represented, so I performed the activity as soon as I woke up and before going to sleep in the evening. During the times in between, I may have napped for only minutes or days. I had no idea. I just tended to my wounds until they healed.

I suspect it took a month or more before they disappeared. Since then, I was the object of Sir's torment several more times, making me think he needed my screams every other month or so.

I didn't see him much after these sessions. I know that he left me alone for at least a week afterward and disappeared from the estate during these times. I presumed he went to attend to Consortium business, but he never shared that information with me. I was just glad to be left alone. As enjoyable as the pleasure he gives me is, I still can't wrap my head around the idea that pleasure is suitable compensation for the torment I suffer.

"I need to get out of here and away from him." I almost vocalized as I got out of the hot tub and made my way to my favorite chaise lounge flanking the swimming pool, and stretched out after putting my heels back on.

"But how?"

"If I escape, they would track me down. So, if I escape, I would need to ensure that they can't find me. But where shall I hide? From what Sir has told me, they have operatives all over the world. There is nowhere I could hide. They would still find me. I believe him. I have no doubt, and I accept his statement as fact. If the Consortium has been around for over a thousand years, they must be powerful enough to avoid detection that entire time."

"So, the question in need of an answer is, how do I prevent them from finding me? How would I do that?"

I've given that question a lot of thought over the months since that fateful day. All these months later, the solution continues to elude me.

"How can I escape and still stay out? How can I stay clear of the Consortium for the rest of my life and live a good life? How can I live and die at a ripe old age? How, indeed!"

Chapter Four

"Good morning Sir."

"Good morning, anything to report?" The Chairman asked, stopping by his secretary's desk before stepping into his office.

"No, Sir. All's quiet. I'm reviewing the overnight reports from the various departments. So far, there's nothing significant to report."

"Good, I'll be in my office reviewing the latest batches of candidates for approval. I presume that all the candidates presented have passed our background checks and requirements for submission?"

"Yes, Sir."

"Good. I had no doubt that would be the case. How are your wife and kids?"

"Very well, Sir. They're doing fine. Thank you for asking."

"And your girlfriends, not all are doing all that well, I presume?"

The secretary laughed a bit before responding. "You presume correctly. All three are in the holding cells below. One is particularly sweet. She's a painslut for sure. She practically laughs at me when I beat her. Playing with her is fun. It's becoming more and more difficult to get a real scream out of her."

"If you need any advice on the situation, I give you leave to ask. What about the others?"

"Thank you, Sir. If the need arises, I will. I still have a few more tricks up my sleeve for that one. As for the other two, I'm still breaking in one, and the other, well, she's a welcome stress relief. She knows how to fuck, that's for sure."

"Isn't life grand?" the Chairman asked, before tapping the secretary's desk and walking into his office, closing the door behind him.

He went to the coffee bar as the first order of business and poured himself a cup of espresso; very hot, dark, and bitter, just how he liked it. He also dished up a small bowl of fresh fruit from around the world and carried the coffee and fruit over to a small, intimate table next to a window. Picking up one of the international newspapers, he began reading. An hour later, and after the second cup of espresso, he finished perusing papers from around the world. The newspapers were from major metropolitan centers in France, Germany, Sweden, and Saudi Arabia. Getting up, he debated whether to get another cup of coffee but decided to wait until later. Staring out the window, he took in the scene before him. He loved the view. He considered his estate as one of his most treasured possessions.

Turning, becoming anxious to review the latest batch of candidates, he went to his desk, sat down, logged onto his secure laptop. The laptop was connected to a closed, highly secure, encrypted network, available to only the highest members of the Consortium. No internet connections to the outside world were allowed. Their cyber division worked very hard to maintain its security and hid its presence from the global network agencies worldwide. They were well aware that the international agencies routinely trolled the 'dark web' or the 'black web.' They avoided those networks like the plague. That was one sure way to gain unwanted attention.

All data coming into the network came via 'sneaker-net' and thoroughly screened and scanned at various stages in isolation before being admitted into their private network. No outbound communications were allowed – ever. And while they've never needed to use it, there was a failsafe system to destroy all data by merely failing to reset the self-destruct regularly.

The critical information was always hand-delivered, in person.

Reaching for the keyboard, the Chairman called up the records of the first candidate. Looking at the counter on the screen, he remarked to himself.

"Ouch, this is going to be a long day."

He wasn't bothered by the fact that with a click of his mouse, he would determine the fate of one-hundred seventy-nine humans around the world. Would they live their lives in obscurity or be culled for the amusement of the Consortium and their membership?

As the morning changed to afternoon, he canceled several candidates, sending them off into blissful ignorance, never knowing just how close they came to becoming fodder for the torturous pleasures of others. Despite the organization's cost to research these candidates, he deleted their records, knowing full well that there was more to picking the right prey than just for others' amusement.

He tagged another half dozen as a potential sacrificial lamb, marking them for slaughter during training as an example to the other, more profitable candidates. He accepted several dozen more for pickup, flagging a few for himself. These had the potential to meet his needs. He would circle back later to look deeper into their records.

About a half of the way through the list, he stumbled upon a candidate that caught his eye.

Jenni Palos was a gorgeous, petite girl with short blonde hair and perky tits. According to the reports, she was astonishing in bed, capable of fucking and climaxing several times a night with multiple partners. One of her partners reported she seemed to roll one climax into another over an hour without a break. She seemed to love recreational sex, much more so than most girls, and she considered it fun. The file summarized her as a true hedonist.

He dug deeper into her file, curious to see what he would find. She was a college student in her second year at school. Her grades were good, and she worked as a sex worker to help make ends meet. She was paying her way through college, intriguing him. Her family seemed disinterested in her wellbeing. According to the file, she fended for herself for most of her childhood while her parents did their own thing. She even went away for weeks at a time on holiday without informing them of her whereabouts. They didn't seem to mind or care.

"Hmm, that should make it easy to pick her up without too much fuss," he said thoughtfully to himself.

He then delved into her finances. She wasn't well off. However, her activities as a sex worker kept her bank balance nicely topped off. She wasn't wealthy, but she had enough in the bank to keep her going for some time. He then checked her spending habits. What he found intrigued him more.

Unlike most women of her age, she spent frugally. She didn't buy into the latest fad, nor did she feel the need to collect every purse, wristwatch, iPhone, sunglasses, outfit, or shiny object on the market. No, instead, she bought with a purpose. Take shoes, for example. She only bought the best, preferring comfortable elegance over an array of uncomfortable shoes. While she had something for any occasion, he liked noting that she wore the best stilettos when it came to dress-wear, even commissioning two custom-made pairs. He smiled when he read that. He decided that when they took her, the pickup team would also pick them up.

What he found most enticing of all was her resilience to overcome challenges, both mental and physical.

"That could be useful, especially in Avril's training." He once again mumbled thoughtfully.

He flagged her as his. Of course, she would still have to survive training and auction, but he would not have a problem buying this one out from under the others.

"No, you know what?" he said out loud. "Fuck it! I'll pay the special-order fee. I'll not allow the guards in the training facility to mess this one up." He clicked the appropriate button, flagging her as already sold, setting the wheels in motion to pick her up at the earliest opportunity.

Leaning back in his chair, the Chairman rubbed his hands together, anticipating a new challenging opportunity. Smiling, he got up to stretch his legs and ended up looking out his windows overlooking his favorite views.

"Come," he responded when he heard the knock on his office door.

"Chairman, sorry to bother you."

"Yes, what is it?"

"Sir, we've received a special order. One that I thought you should know about."

"What's so special about it?"

After answering his question, the Consortium Director and Chairman closed his eyes, shutting out the world before him through his floor to ceiling windows. To any casual observer, the Chairman was visibly disturbed.

"Close the door," he commanded his underling.

"Yes, Sir."

"Hmmm, him ...?"

"Yes, Sir. He claims it is quite urgent."

"When it comes to him, they're all urgent."

"Yes, Sir. I agree. However, in this case, it may be warranted."

"How so?"

"Sir, he needs a new heart. He's dying, and time is short."

"Why doesn't he use the global registry like everyone else?"

"As I understand it, Sir, they've denied him entry to the list. As the report documents, his proclivities and eccentricities contributed to his failing heart."

"So, he wants us to come to his rescue, give him a few more years while destroying his new heart, at the expense of someone else."

The secretary only smiled in agreement. He continued to stand there, waiting for the Director to mull over his decision.

"Did our medical unit confirm the diagnosis?"

"Yes, Sir. I made certain of that before I brought the request to you. We've treated him for his heart condition for some time now."

"Damn. I knew he wasn't feeling well. I just didn't know the extent. Do we have anything in inventory?"

"No, Sir. Not at present. However, we do have a candidate that is still in the vetting process, which appears to be a perfect tissue match."

"Really? If we haven't finished vetting the candidate, how do we know whether they have a suitable heart for transplant?"

"An interesting story, Sir, the candidate already went through tissue type matching. It seems her sister needed a bone marrow transplant, and the doctors typed her to see if she was a suitable donor."

"A woman?"

"Yes, Sir."

"Is she pretty?"

"Sir, she is your type."

"Hmmm, that's too bad. Did she save her sister?"

"As of the last report, the sister was doing well, recovering nicely."

"Leukemia, I presume?"

"Yes, Sir."

"How did she come to our attention?"

"In a hospital, Sir..."

"Why do we have an agent in a hospital? We don't take defectives."

"Yes, Sir. We don't. However, our agent just happened to be training at Westgate General Cancer Center in the lab research department and stumbled upon her tissue match procedure purely by accident. Otherwise, she would not have come to our attention."

"Too bad, for her, I mean. Crap. Allegedly, there was something in the lab report that stood out to alert her to our attention."

"Supposedly, Sir."

"Alright, you say that medical has approved the tissue match."

"Yes, Sir. At least as best as can be determined with the records we accessed. Of course, if you authorize the request, we will perform our private tests and confirm before performing the transplant."

"Yes, that makes sense. How far along are we with the vetting?"

"To be honest, Sir, I would like more time to confirm the candidacy. We only learned of her existence a couple of weeks ago, and we're just getting started with her background check. There are still many unknowns with this one, and taking her may be risky."

"Yet, if we don't, we'll lose a valuable member. Pain in the ass member, but a valuable member nonetheless."

"It appears so, Sir."

Staring out of his window, the Director pondered the question for a time. Then turning towards his desk, he picked up the phone and dialed a number. When medical answered, expecting his call, they confirmed all that his secretary told him. The member was in dire need of a new heart. The only one available was still beating in the candidate just entering the vetting system. Unless the member received a new heart soon, he would most likely die within the week.

Hanging up, the Director returned to his window and stared out once again to a world he wasn't seeing.

"We should let him die," he said rhetorically.

"Sir, you should know that he is willing to pay four times the going rate for the special order."

"I should charge him ten times the amount. Teach him a lesson on the cost of gluttony and excessiveness." the director snapped. "Alright, but charge him five times the rate, and he picks up all medical costs. So, help me, if he causes us problems, I will take the heart back and show it still beating after I cut it out and hold it up for him to see. It should make for some interesting final moments."

"Also, arrange for the surviving sister to get a fully paid Ivy League college scholarship to compensate her for the loss of her sister. I'm sure one of our alumni members can make that happen, anonymously, of course. Charge that cost back to the member as well."

"Yes, Sir," the underling responded.

"Pick her up, but not until after four days. I want the background checks to be as thorough as can be in such a short time. Call in favors and accelerate the process, whatever it takes to get it done. I want to know as much as possible about the girl and her family before we pick her up. We can always cancel if it is too dangerous. Even afterward, we can make it look like an accident, but we can't do even that once we take the heart. You have three days to complete the checks."

"I also want to see the girl before we cut her open." The Chairman added. "I want to see for myself who we are about to sacrifice to save a costly but valuable member."

"Yes, Sir. I will arrange it. Assuming we proceed, you will need to be back here five days from now. They plan on doing the transplant within forty-eight hours of pickup. That makes the timing very tight for the member."

"That will be too bad for him. I'm not going to jeopardize the organization to get him a heart. He brought this on himself. He could have taken better care of his body. Let him sweat it out. It'll do him good. If he dies before we harvest, we can add her to inventory or return her home unharmed if necessary."

"Very good, Sir, I'll get right on it."

"Also, I want her other organs harvested and sold on the black market. We might as well get some good out of this."

"I'll make sure we do, Sir."

"You know, of course, this goes against every rule and procedure we have to safeguard the integrity of the Consortium."

"Yes, Sir. I do."

"If we make a mistake on this one, cull the wrong person, we risk exposure and ultimately the destruction of our lifestyle and our community."

Nodding, the secretary affirmed the Director's assessment. A moment later, the Director waved his hand in dismissal, and he made a discreet exit.

"For the good of the Consortium, I should let him die." The Director muttered.

The secretary wisely stood mute.

Speaking to no one, staring out the window, the Director grumbled. "He had better be worth it. As it is, I'm going to make sure he knows he owes me."

Leaving his office, he remarked to his secretary, "I'll be down in holding. I need to work off a little stress."

"Yes, Sir. Shall I alert the guards to prepare one for you?"

"No, that's alright. I want to inspect them first. I may do nothing or much more. It all depends on what I find that interests me. If I find one, I'll prepare her myself for the short life she has ahead of her."

"Very good, Sir," he said as the Director made his way to the elevator to take him down into the subterranean levels.

Chapter Five

"Wow! That was fucking awesome," he said as he stood up and scanned for his trousers.

"I'm glad you liked it. I loved being with you. I don't have many clients that can do that to me." Jenni said as she rolled over onto her side, watching the john retrieve his clothes and start to dress.

"Same here," he said, looking past her. "Holy shit, the bed is soaked."

"Yes, lovely, isn't it? You're hot, in case you didn't know. That must account for the mess."

"Why, thank you. I think you're pretty hot yourself." The john said as he gathered up his clothes and started putting them back on.

In the meantime, Jenni stretched out on the bed, displaying her feline feminine lines for him. Her torso pulled tight, her breasts seemed to float on her chest, flattened but for her nipples standing firm and proud.

"Nice!" the john complimented her as she continued the sexy, enticing stretch.

Pointing her toes, she seemed to grow several inches as she stretched. With her arms over her head, she smiled back at the compliment. Relaxing and gently caressing one of her breasts, she continued to watch him.

Snatching his necktie, Jenni jumped off the bed and tied it for him, periodically flicking her eyes up at him. As she finished, he wrapped his arms around her narrow waist and pulled her close. Leaning in, he kissed her one final time, caressing her bare ass cheeks and cupping a breast in the process. His kiss returned; he slapped her on the ass, loud and hard enough that it left a mild pink impression on the otherwise pristine flesh.

"Ouch," Jenni replied, mocking a twinge of pain from the injury.

"Next week?" the john asked.

"Sure, same time?" Jenni said, picking up her clothes and putting them on. It didn't take long, as all she wore was a thong, short skirt, tank top, and a pair of super high-heel sandals.

"Yes. Say, can I contact you directly, without going through the agency?"

"I'm sorry. That is not allowed. You are not my client, but rather the agency. That would not be right."

"Yes, I thought so. Okay, until next week," the john said, palming several bills in her hand before walking her to the door. "I'm looking forward to next time," he said after one last brief kiss and opened the door.

"Me too!" she replied as she stepped through the door and walked down the hall towards the elevator. Along the way, she looked at the bills and smiled before stuffing them in her purse. A few minutes later, she was in the back seat of her driver's car.

"Did everything go okay?" the driver asked her as Jenni settled in and put on her seatbelt. Leaning back in, content that her shift was over, she could go home. She settled into the deep upholstery of the seat and closed her eyes. She was ready for bed and getting a good night's rest.

"Yes," she said softly.

"Good, are you up for another appointment? We're rather short-handed today, and a special client called up asking for a go. You're the only one available at the moment."

Sighing, but knowing that she had it within her to earn a bit more money, she said, "Sure, why not. Anything I need to know about?"

"Nope, same old, should be a standard session. Just make the client happy. Can you do that?"

"Sure," Jenni answered.

"Good girl. We'll be there shortly. It's a private house in the hills."

"Whatever," she responded absentmindedly, closing her eyes and leaning back into the plush leather interior.

Inside, the driver smiled, knowing full well what was about to occur. They had been cultivating this one for months now, and he wanted a go at her first.

Jenni began reflecting absentmindedly on her life. There was nothing specific bothering her. She just let her mind wander. Mind-wandering or 'wool-gathering' was a common occurrence during her downtimes. This time, she slipped into thinking about her home life. There were days when she missed her parents. They were nice and all but seemed not to care what she did or where she was.

Both of her parents seemed more interested in their lives and keeping up with their friends and neighbors. It was one reason why they bought a house in a nice neighborhood in Morristown, NJ. They lived paycheck to paycheck, and even once, cleaned out her savings account to pay the monthly expenses on which they were seriously behind. To her, they always seemed to be one step ahead of foreclosure. For their friends, they spent money lavishly on parties and alcohol. For their daughter, they did squat, nothing, nada. What the fuck was that? In all honesty, she preferred to live in a smaller house and have them involved in her life. They couldn't even help her with college. She had to find the scholarships, and she still had to find a way to pay for her room and board. Fucking for cash earned her enough to handle it. It soon led to stripping at a club and picking up johns in her freshman year.

It was fun and all, but she was scared all the time. She didn't want to be arrested or assaulted during a pickup. It was scary. So, she quit and struggled the second half of the year. When the school year ended, she looked at the bill she needed to pay to register for the coming year. She didn't know where she'd get the money.

A girlfriend stepped in and showed her how to get it. By July, she earned enough at the escort agency to pay off her freshman year. Her clients loved her five-foot-one petite tanned body with blonde hair and natural perky tits that made her a commodity they craved. She had all the business she could handle, and her bank balance was growing. The best part was she discovered that she loved sex; the more, the better. She loved it so much that she doubted she would ever lock herself down to a single person by getting married.

The job even brought in enough money that Jenni could indulge in her favorite passion of high-heels and skimpy bikinis. Since she was a young girl, she loved wearing mommy's shoes. On her seventh birthday, Mom gave her her first pair. She loved them instantly, and she'd been wearing them ever since. When she wasn't, even barefoot around the pool in one of her skimpy bikinis, she walked as if her feet were wearing them, up on her tiptoes, heels high off the ground. She loved the looks of desire from guys when she walked past them.

After several moments lost in her thoughts, her mind slipped to her course load. She had a major test coming up in English Lit, and she wasn't ready for it. This job in her second year of college was great and all, but she didn't want to do this after college. Earning her degree and a career were her goals in life. To her, job and school were double-edged swords. However, she needed both to move ahead in the world. But she had to admit. It was better than picking up johns in hotel bars. This way, she had a driver and security guard to take her around to some very wealthy clients. Perhaps, one day, she could leverage their connections for the future.

Arriving at her destination, she looked at what looked like an ordinary, modern cape-style house, one of the thousands built on the area's rolling hills. It was a contemporary and straightforward home sporting stucco siding and large, expansive windows. Except for the one light she could see past the front door and driveway lights, it was otherwise dark. Getting out of the car, she walked up, followed by the driver who was right behind her. As was commonplace, the driver followed, ensuring she was at the right address and was safely inside.

However, instead of ringing the doorbell, the driver pulled out a door key, unlocked it, and opened the door.

"Oh, you're my client?" she asked in mild surprise.

"Yes," he said. "I hope you don't mind. I apologize for the deception. I intend on paying for the privilege."

"No, it's okay, you're alright. In fact, this will be no charge. You could have just asked me. I like you, and you've been very kind to me. Besides, you smell good, and your breath smells sweet, unlike some of my clients. Thanks for watching out for me. I appreciate knowing that there's someone there if I get into trouble."

"That's me. Thanks. I appreciate it. Are you sure you won't let me pay you?" he queried, confident that she would say no. He led her to the bedroom. After they each stripped off their clothes, she came up to him and knelt in front of him.

Taking him into her mouth, she swallowed him deeply, thanking him properly for safeguarding her well-being. Her sucking teased him into a fury as she held him off from cumming several times, burying him into the dark recesses behind her lips. When she got him to a point where she felt he could not hold off any longer, she stood up and stood on tip-toes and kissed him firmly with an open mouth.

Breaking the kiss, he said, "Wow, you're a champion at that."

"Thank you," Jenni said with a sly smile. She knew how well she had gotten at sucking guys off. There were all different kinds of blowjobs, and she knew just which one her driver would like. Her intuition was correct. He was delighted.

Leading him to the bed, she first sat down and scooched back, leaving her bottom just on the edge of the bed. Leaning back, she stretched her legs up and wide, tipping her pointed high-heel shoes towards the ceiling. She smiled at him between her open legs. Those scrumptious legs spread wide, she saw him admire the prize she knew he so desperately wanted and she was about to give.

Smiling at her, he walked up to her and began stroking the inside of her legs with his fingertips. Starting at her knees, he worked his way to her well-heeled feet. He climbed onto the bed and settled between her knees. Moving his fingers upwards, he stroked the inside of her thighs, heading towards his prize. As he did so, the head of his cock danced against the door to her womanhood, teasing the two of them into a flushed, heated excitement. He felt the heat of the object of his desire reaching out to him.

"For a girl who's been fucking all night, you're still in heat, ready to go again."

"You got it, big boy. I'm ready. Give it to me."

"It's coming, Jenni. Just hang on."

Sliding his hands up and down her legs, they got closer and closer to the prize on each descent. He moved slowly, sometimes lightly touching her with the pads of his fingers. At other times, he lightly scratched her with his fingernails as he dragged them up and down the inside of her thighs and calves. She ooh'd and aah'd on each transition. He took his time with this one. He knew he had all the time in the world. She wasn't going anywhere.

By now, she supported her legs with her hands behind her knees. Her wide-open legs were straight as boards, showing off the treasure resting between them. Jenni was anxious to get on with it and stick it in her already. She was hot to trot and ready for the real action.

"Shhh! My lovely, I'm getting there." He softly whispered, a sly smile on his face as he read her body language.

Between panting breaths, she answered. "I know. It's just that this is so good, and I don't want you to stop. Though, I so want you inside me. I want to feel your cock filling me up."

"So, it's working."

"Oh, yes, it's working. I can't wait for the next stage. You torment me in such nice, wonderful ways. Your touch is … I don't know … delightful."

"I'm glad you like it."

"Hmmm," was her only response, laying her head back down on the bed. He smiled and continued stroking her legs, adding light, flickering kisses to his repertoire. He didn't know whether she was lying to him, trying to get it over with, or was she genuinely enjoying herself. Honestly, he didn't mind. She was his for the taking, and after that, well, she would wish that she had cared better.

"My God, this man is good." Jenni thought to herself. "He knows what he's doing and knows how to please a woman. I can learn a lot from him. Oooh, that's good," she expressed in her head, no longer able to concentrate on anything other than what his fingers were doing.

By the time he was slowly circling her pussy, she was flushed all over with a lovely pink color underneath a shimmery moist sheen. She was breathing heavily. She was more than ready for him. With Jenni lying in front of him, he prepared to stab her with his cock.

She reached for it as if to guide it into her.

"Shhh! No, I'll do it. Only now, you keep holding onto your legs," he commanded her. She liked him in control.

Her hands returned to holding the inside of her knees without complaint. Grasping his instrument of pleasure, he stepped in closer. Sliding his cock against her womanhood, he threaded its head between her labia, teasing her. Sliding cock along his sensitive underside, he painted her clit with long smooth strokes, enticing the hood to recede and reveal the precious center of her sex.

"Wow!" she mumbled softly, rolling her back to give him better access. Slowly, with smooth but firm strokes, he continued varnishing her pussy and clit.

"It does feel nice," he responded.

"Yes … it does. Don't … stop … oh, please …" she murmured in delight, trailing off at the end.

He stroked her for a minute or more. She couldn't tell how long. She did note that, at times, his strokes were rhythmic, long, slow, and steady. At other times, they were chaotic, shifting in length, speed, and pressure against her pussy. It was glorious. She was in heaven.

Then he paused, long enough for her to begin wondering what he was doing. Opening her eyes, she looked up at him with questions in her gaze.

"Ah, you're back. I want your complete attention for this."

"Yes, Sir, whatever you say!"

Smiling, he teased her one more time, positioning the head of his cock between her labia, knocking on the door to her inner sanctum. Holding back just a bit, he didn't make her wait for long. In one smooth motion, he slid into her, stabbing her with his manhood as deep-seated as he could. She gasped in breathless delight.

Breathless and yet not; she screamed as pleasure consumed her body, separating her from the world around her.

"Oooh," she screamed again and again.

He let his cock sit firmly planted inside her for a minute, his balls resting cheerfully against her. She wallowed in the joy of a cock that wasn't paying for the honor of fucking her. Without a doubt, she appreciated that he took care of her and wanted to return the favor. After a bit, he slowly began withdrawing before pushing back inside.

Hmmm…" she drawled as her bliss began to fade a notch. "That's soooo … nice!"

"Glad you like it. I'm pretty happy myself."

"Don't let me stop you," she retorted.

The driver began fucking her harder, driving into her harder and faster, now slapping his balls against her body. Jenni's breathing became short and rapid. A subtle sheen of sweat slickened her body, and her feminine, musky scent filled the room, screaming for more and harder.

"That's it, honey. That's how I like it." Jenni gasped out between her rapidly building breaths.

Pounding her, driving her deeper into the mattress, the driver picked up speed and strength in his penetrations. He could feel her heat penetrate his cockhead. He felt the friction of his thrusting warming the length of him. He smiled at her as veins seemed to push out from alongside his neck. Slapping her butt hard with his balls, she relished the pounding punishment by pushing back at him in time with his strokes. He climbed on top of her and pounded inside her.

Reaching in between her legs, and he grabbed her breasts and played with her nipples. No doubt about it, those nips sat on milky smooth utters whose skin was baby smooth. Stoking them, one side and the other, he allowed the rock-hard nipples to play across his palm, enjoying the path they took investigating his hand. Little shivers of joy seemed to leap from her nipples and slice into him. Playing with them, he wanted to dig his fingers deep into her breasts, his knuckles white as they grasped the behind the flesh, holding them to her body. It was as if he wanted to rip those silky, smooth utters from her body. With all his willpower, he resisted and held back. He was confident that someone else would pay to have that pleasure.

Lost in her world of pleasure and lust, Jenni knew nothing of his thoughts. He just looked down at her and smiled. She was so far gone that she didn't even notice his malicious smile.

Little by little, she slid closer and closer to the headboard. Nearly pulling out, he grabbed her by the ankles and pushed them above his head, settling her calves on each of his shoulders. Plowing away as he fucked her, Jenni's eyelids closed even more tightly, embracing the building ecstasy in her body about to be released, the second of the night.

Her feet pointed towards the ceiling; the driver pushed them over so that her ankles kissed each of her ears. While doing so, he pulled out and slid the underside of his cock over her pussy and clit. Sliding his slick member across her clit, revealed from its protective hood, she arched her back and took a deep, rapturous breath and held it. Pursing her lipstick coated lips, she wallowed in the gentle stroking, thoroughly enjoying the waves of pleasure coursing throughout her body.

Pulling back, almost teasing her further, he slid his cockhead down a notch and positioned it right against her anus. After a pregnant moment, he opened her up, sliding smoothly into her ass, filling it with his cock. Once again, in one smooth motion, he dove deep into her, squashing his balls against her butt. He felt her bear down on him, squeezing him, gripping him, as if to prevent him from withdrawing. She was tight, alright, and that made it all the better.

"Oh, yes, I like that. What took you so long, babe?"

"Oh, just enjoying myself. Are you ready for the finale?"

"Oh, yes. Please, do me, make me cum. Fuck me hard!" She demanded.

Fucking her hard, practically pile driving into her as fast as he could, he felt her heat and scent build to ever-climbing heights.

"Oh, yes! – Oh, fucking God … yes, yes … YES!" she suddenly screamed out and went all silent, her breath taken away by the orgasm raging through her rigid body. He was right behind her, shooting his cum deep into her rectum. He watched her disappear, her eyes rolling up into her head. She faded into her little world of orgasmic, blissful ecstasy.

He loved watching them cum. He wished he could get so lost in his climaxes, not that it bothered him, of course. Women just seemed to enjoy orgasms in such manners he couldn't imagine. However, he cherished his version of bliss. His climax was moments away. That would more than make up for it.

A minute later, he withdrew but kept a finger on the pulse of her clit and orgasm, preventing her from coming down from her pleasure. He was careful to touch her gently, knowing that her clit was hypersensitive. He knew he could just as quickly lose her, her orgasm crashing to a halt in sharp pain, rather than fall gently, enjoying the pleasurable moment in time.

Leaning forward, he kissed her on the lips while reaching under one of the pillows, where he secured a Taser to the bottom of the headboard. She kissed him back, transferring her lust to him as best as she could.

"That was sweet, Jenni. I liked that, watching you cum like that," he whispered.

"Hmmm," she responded in kind, her eyes closed as she relished the sensations captivating her.

"Now, goodnight, sweetheart," he breathed softly.

Removing his lips from hers, he gave her one last caress on the cheek. She still had that thoroughly fucked smile on her face when he touched the Taser to the side of her neck and activated it. Instantly, her eyes shot wide open in disbelief, her body going rigid. A moment later, she was out like a light, the electricity leaping from the device and shorting out her brain.

Sliding off her, he took a moment to peruse the unconscious woman lying before him. She was beautiful, no doubt about it. In some ways, it was a shame that, in all likelihood, she'd be dead before the year was out if she even lasted that long.

Sitting down on the edge of the bed, he fondled her milky white breasts, pinching and pulling her nipples in the process. With his other hand, he opened the bedside table and pulled out an injection kit, filled with a series of single-use needles. Wrapping a rubber tourniquet around her upper arm, he slapped the inside of her elbow, revealing a suitable vein. Selecting one of the syringes already prepared with the correct dosage for a woman her size and weight, he injected her. She'd sleep for at least a day.

Putting his instruments away, he went to the closet and pulled out a black bag, similar to one a doctor would use for house calls. From it, he extracted several lengths of rope and a leather mouth gag. The gag was of the kind that entirely covered her mouth and protruded behind her teeth, compressing her tongue. The mouth gag might not be necessary, but it was proven to keep her quiet. He went about the task of gagging and binding her, followed by bagging her clothing and purse, minus her tip money, of course. She wouldn't ever again need money. He even bagged his clothing. He wrapped her in the bedsheets and dumped her on the floor. He left her shoes on; as even unconscious, she indeed looked fabulous in them. There was no need to leave her DNA anywhere in his house.

After showering and putting on a clean set of clothing, he remade the bed with a fresh set of sheets. Looking around and satisfied that he left nothing of hers behind, he carried her to the house's attached garage. Inside was a commercial delivery van loaded up with various boxes as if prepared for a delivery run. The logo on the truck's side was of a well-known delivery service in the area, though the vehicle wasn't in their inventory. He packed Jenni in a similar box, along with an oxygen canister set to release the life-giving gas slowly. Satisfied she would survive transport, he sealed her in the box. He doubted she would need it, but it was better to be safe than sorry. After all, they wouldn't like it if he delivered her dead.

Loading her into the van, he added other, ordinary-looking freight and boxes. Driving off as if nothing was wrong, he was merely making the day's deliveries. Yet, only one delivery interested him. The rest, well, they may be useful the next time.

Chapter Six

"Would you girls like another round? It's on me," the bartender casually offered Misty and her new friend, Susan.

Looking over at drinking buddy, Misty answered, "Sure, why not?"

Smiling back, the bartender walked down the length of the bar to begin preparing their drinks.

"He shure … is cute," Susan mentioned, slurring her words. She already had one too many drinks, but what the hell, she wasn't driving. Her hotel was just down the boardwalk.

"He certainly is," Misty replied, "I wouldn't mind him tapping my ass."

"Now that … whose say that I wouldn't … mind a goes at that as well."

"Then he's all yours, Susan. I've got other plans."

"What … plans?" she asked as their drinks materialized in front of them.

"Two martinis extra dry, one dirty and one with a twist." He said as he placed them in front of them. Then, looking at Susan, he said, "This is your last one, honey."

"Ah, pooh," Susan said with a mock pout, her dreamy eyes gazing at the tall, muscular bartender with the square jaw and day-old scruff.

"Just enjoy this one but make it last."

However, instead of walking away, the bartender stayed, staring right at their bikini tops, barely containing the sweet delights contained within. The two girls glanced at him and then at each other, knowing there was always a price to pay for free drinks. They let him look down their cleavage.

"Say, what are you two doing later?"

"Oh, nutin special," Susan slurred. "Whatcha doing?"

Misty stayed quiet. As cute as the guy was, she had a modeling gig later. One, she couldn't be drunk for it, and two, she needed her sex drive to be at its strongest. Modeling, whether simple nude shots or fucking on camera, was hard work, and she needed to be in top form. The pre-gig drinks just made it easier for her to loosen up and follow directions.

"Well, I was hoping to hook up after my shift. I'm free in a couple of hours," he said.

"Sorry, I'm tied up the rest of the day after this. I got a gig to work. Susan here, though, she's available. Aren't you, sweetie?"

"Shure am! I'm available, ah, available right now for a little action in the back. Youse knows what I mean."

"You know what. You're too drunk. I'll think I'll pass." The bartender said, after taking another long, hard stare at Misty's tits and moving off.

"Prick!" Susan mumbled. "Whoose does he think he is, telling me I'm too ... too drunk."

"My poor Susan, he may be right. You are drunk."

"Yeah? So what? I could drink you under ... uh ... under ... the table."

"You're right. You can," taking a sip of her martini before sliding off the barstool.

She got stuck a little, her bikini bottom sliding a bit to the side, revealing just a bit too much. Straightening up, making sure to flash the bartender as she did so, she thanked him again for the drink. He nodded and smiled at her, knowing that his time with this girl would come soon enough, assuming she graced one of his barstools again. Besides, even if she didn't, there were plenty more like her.

"Hey, I got to go. See you around, alright?" Misty said, downing the rest of her martini in a single gulp.

"Alright girrrl, see ya around," Susan replied, obviously drunk and slurring her words.

Misty turned and walked down the boardwalk, knowing all the while that the bartender continued to stare as she swung her hips back and forth on her heels and swaying her long silvery blonde hair across her back. Flicking a bit of hair off her ear, she turned her head and blew a kiss to the bartender.

"Hmmm, maybe later, I'll come back for a taste of that man. He sure was cute." She said to herself. "I gotta be careful that Susan isn't there. She was nice and all, but I don't like drunks."

Taking her time, as she was already going to be early for the modeling session, Misty took in the sights. The sights being eligible men that might help her achieve her goals. Finding a man to marry and keep her in the money was all she cared about these days. She didn't think she would have much trouble finding him. She took care of herself, ate right, and maintained what she considered a perfect figure.

She was nineteen, five-foot-four, one-hundred ten pounds, with a fantastic figure, including her fabulous big tits sporting nipples that only the thickest of bras could hide. She never wore those kinds of bras anyway. She liked the looks that men gave her when they first noticed her tits before looking into her eyes. In the bright sunlight, the shadows under her nipples made them stand out all the more. Men appreciated them, and she was too much of an exhibitionist to deny them the pleasure.

Passing the shops, bars, and numerous hotels, she kept a lookout for potential mates. She wanted to find a rich whale, one that spent lavishly to keep her in style. While she found many wealthy men, who showered her with gifts since sixteen, she had still yet to hang onto one. Now at twenty, she wanted more. So far, all she got was either a night or two, maybe a month or so, and then they moved on. After a while, she had learned why. The men she had dated were not looking to settle down. They weren't looking for the right girl, but any girl who would lie back and spread her legs for them. They were looking for a brief stint with which to mark their bedposts. Once they had their conquest, they didn't need or want her anymore. With nothing to give them, they found a new girl to take her place.

She was a bit more discriminating.

Sure, she would lie down with a man, but these days, if they didn't have something of value to offer her, she played hard to get. She learned that the chase was even more valuable than using her to mark their bedpost. It gave her time to learn more about them and find ways to offer them what they needed and not just what they wanted. Today's gig was one of those steps towards that goal.

The years of learning how to have sex gave her an insatiable appetite for the sheets. If she wasn't fucking a man, she was using her vibrator, usually daily, to get off. Thankfully, she wouldn't need her bedside table friend today. Today's gig was undoubtedly going to get her off. She was looking forward to the euphoric episode that would last the evening and into the night.

"Oh, yeah, it's going to be fun."

Turning down one of the hundreds of streets dead-ending at the boardwalk, Misty walked along, passing numerous people walking towards the beach, hoping to find a spot to spread out their blankets and catch some rays. She rarely spent time sunbathing on the beach. It was too public, and the nearest nude beach wasn't within walking distance. Instead, she preferred sunbathing naked in her backyard. These days, tan lines were not in vogue with the photographers. They wanted pure, clean, uninterrupted lines along her body.

After passing a couple of blocks, she arrived at the studio and walked in.

"Hey, you're early," the photographer remarked. "Pleased to see you Misty, I'll be right with you."

"Yeah, well, take your time. I got an early start, and it just felt like the right thing to do.

"It's all good. I'm just setting up now. Since you're early, why don't we start with some shots just of you in your finest? Then later, when your partner shows up, we'll move on to some more explicit scenes. How does that sound?"

"Perfect. Does that mean I'll get paid for a double?"

"A double, ah, sure. I guess that will be alright."

"Well, we did contract for just the single session, didn't we?" Misty asked.

"Yes, you're right. We did. Well, then, we best hurry and get started. Randal won't be here for at least another couple of hours. That will give us a lot of time for the singles."

"Randal, is that his name, the guy that I'll be fucking?"

"Yep, that's him. He's got a great build and a better face. You'll like him. I've got some ideas for shots that will make you squirm."

"Just no anal, I don't do anal," she reminded him.

"Gotcha, you don't need to worry. You know, it pays better."

"Yes, I know, maybe someday, just not today."

"Fair enough. Did you bring any changes in clothing, or do you need to use my wardrobe?"

"I brought some things. They're here in my handbag."

"Hmmm, that can't be much. They're not wrinkled, are they? That won't look good in the photos."

"Well, I don't think they are. It's just some lingerie and swimsuits and such. I'll fix them if they are wrinkled. As you said, they won't look good in the photos if they were."

"That's a good girl. Let me finish up. In the meantime, fix your makeup. I would like to see you touch up your cheekbones. Put on some eyeshadow and eyeliner with gobs of mascara as well. I want your eyes to pop. Just don't overdo the shadow. It's your eyes that I want to use to draw people in."

"You mean, you don't want my tits to do that?"

Laughing, he said. "Well, tits first, then eyes. Okay?"

Joining in the laughter, Misty said, "Okay."

"After that, find a pair of tight jeans and put them on. Don't worry. You won't be wearing them long. I want to start the session with you slowly peeling them off, alright?"

"Got it, jean peeling, then spread 'em."

"That's the spirit. Now, get going. I should be ready in fifteen minutes."

"I'll be ready."

"In the meantime, read over the model release and sign it. I'll also need a copy of your identification for the files. Your photo session will be worthless unless you sign that, and you won't get paid.

"Consider it done."

"Good."

With that, Misty went one way in the studio while her photographer went another. Under the studio's hot lights, Misty posed for him throughout the next couple of hours, following his directions, giving him the shots he wanted. She was a pro at this, having posed several dozen times for nude modeling sessions for the past couple of years.

She had made a lot of good contacts in the business, and it paid the rent. Living in Santa Monica, housing was her highest monthly bill. As for the rest, bikinis, skimpy shorts, and tops didn't cost all that much. Even food wasn't much of a problem. Her modeling sessions forced her to eat light, and her dates paid for most of what she did eat. Beyond that, it was her shoes. She had a passion for heels, having worn them regularly since she was six. In fact, she found it hard to walk barefoot or in flats. On more than one occasion, someone would ask her why she walked on her tiptoes around the pool. Her usual answer was, "I like to." Her bone structure had grown using her heels as a pattern for their shape. Being a size five with high arches and curvy, slender feet, she loved how she looked in heels. Besides, the whales she sought favored the look.

Later, when Randal arrived, she was more than ready to do the duo session with him. He was more than cute and gorgeous. He was strong and well-built, but not like a bodybuilder. He had a square, angular face, broad shoulders, and an enormous dick. Throughout the night, they fucked in many exciting poses. Keeping him hard for several hours and the shots taken wasn't much of a problem. He had a remarkable recovery, capable of resuming their photo session after short rest breaks while they reset the scene.

The cum shots turned out fantastic. Randal came three or four times during the session, coating her body with the gooey milky substance. He even tasted good. Somewhat unusual for a photoshoot of this type, he came inside her mouth. Viewers typically wanted to see cum exploding from dicks. Cumming inside her mouth prevented this. Only by holding it without swallowing, allowing it to leak from the sides of her mouth, did the photographer get the shots he needed. Fortunately, his cum tasted good, with a salty-bittersweet flavor she had come to relish over the years.

Eventually, they all tired, and the session ended. Misty took her time dressing, enjoying the conversation with the two of them. The photographer was easy to talk to, and after Randal left, Misty decided she had one last lay in her. Showing her appreciation for the night's work, Misty knelt in front of the photographer and took him into her mouth.

"That's not necessary, you know," he said.

Sucking him deeply into her mouth, she garbled. "Shhh!!! I'm busy. Just be quiet and enjoy it."

After blowing him, swallowing him deep into her mouth for several minutes, she pulled down his pants. As he took off his shirt, Misty led him to the bed, already smelling of sex, and pushed him down. Straddling him, she placed him against her pussy and lowered her body, driving him deep into her inner being.

"Ah, that feels so good," she whispered, leaning over and kissing him on the mouth. Encouraged, the photographer began stroking her, alternating between hard and fast with soft and soothing.

Misty came several more times that night, easily slipping into orgasmic pleasure without the choreographed positions. Eventually, somewhere just before dawn, the two fell into a deep sleep, Misty spooned by her lover.

***

Shortly before noon the next day, they woke up and pleasured each other one last time. When finished, Misty dressed and went home to shower and sleep some more.

The photographer packed up his equipment, filed the photos on his computer storage array, and then opened a file. Typing in Misty's details, along with her id, model contract, and rights assignments to the photos, he added them to her photo session file. He did one other thing. He zipped up the entire folder, photos, and documentation and copied them to a particular flash drive he had hidden away. The unique flash drive included an encryption algorithm that hid the data from prying eyes.

When the data finished copying, he picked up the phone, dialed a number by heart, and waited. He hung up when the line answered. On the other end, the phone system recorded the connection and set a series of events in motion. He made the drop on the following day, turning over the flash drive to his contact, and receiving a replacement. Later that day, he found his payment deposited into his bank account. If he never heard from her again, he knew that they offered her that exotic job, traveling the world. Otherwise, she'd show up at his door also, and he'd redo the shoot, apologizing that he had lost the photos from the first session along with her contact information.

Within a week, Misty's investigation began. The research and background checks were well underway. A team of hunters was assigned to study her, watch her, and bed her. After they completed all the background checks and investigations, they forwarded her candidate file onto the Consortium. Shortly after that, the Chairman approved her admittance into the fold. Several weeks later, they scheduled her pickup date, and a substantial bonus mysteriously appeared in the photographer's bank account.

The photographer smiled, knowing exactly where the money came from, as he photographed yet another sweet little thing, whose photos also may never appear in print or on the web. Now he could afford to buy that fast action camera.

Looking into the viewfinder, he focused the lens on the new girl's face, took several portrait shots, and then moved onto those fabulous naked tits. Life as an erotic nude photographer was grand.

Chapter Seven

Her rental car pulling into the hotel parking lot, Rachel searched for an available spot, hopefully, close to the main door. The conference was nearing an end, and she was anxious to get through what she presumed would be a dreary day of lectures. Rachel had hoped to book a room in the same hotel as the conference, but by the time she signed up, there wasn't a vacancy. She even tried to find a room at the Hilton but had to settle on the DoubleTree a couple of miles away. It was nice enough, but the Hilton would have at least supplied a comfortable bed and with suburb sheets.

"Ah, there's a spot," she muttered to herself, pulling in and shutting down the engine. After taking a brief look in the mirror to check her makeup, she stepped out, retrieved her purse and briefcase, and went inside.

After finding her usual seat at a table, Rachel deposited her bag and purse before turning towards the refreshment table. Selecting a delicious-looking pastry and making herself a cup of coffee, she sat down and waited for the conference to resume.

"I hope that this turns out to be worthwhile. So far, I'm disappointed. It's been a waste of my time." Rachel thought as she began her second cup of coffee. Minutes later, the conference leader resumed her place at the podium and started speaking.

By lunchtime, Rachel was tired of sitting. Her ass hurt, and her legs felt cramped. They had only given the attendees a single ten-minute break mid-morning, which she gratefully used to take care of her bodily needs. Two cups of coffee had played havoc with her bladder, and yet, she needed a third to try and stay awake as they lectured her on material she already knew.

Sitting at a table with her lunch of a cold salad of field greens and Ahi Tuna, she leaned back and rubbed her eyes.

"So, how's the conference going for you?" one of the attendees asked her.

"Well enough," she answered him, unwilling to say just what she thought about it. Her boss had insisted on her going. She agreed more to keep him happy and the chance to get out of the office for a while on the company's dime.

"I already know much of the material. Still, I'm learning some insights into the behaviors of a market under stress.

"Ah, you're getting that too! So am I. I'm learning so much from this conference. I ...." the attendee droned on, as Rachel tuned him out, only giving him the occasional 'aha.' To be honest, she wished he would shut up or turn his attention to someone else. She was tired, and he didn't interest her at all. She was hoping she would find someone more interesting to spend the night with.

***

As the conference day ended, her lunch companion approached her and asked her out.

"I'm sorry. I already have a previous engagement." Rachel said, lying through her teeth.

"Ah, that's too bad. Well then, until tomorrow," he said, turning away in search of new prey to share the evening, and perhaps, bed them as well.

"Fucking idiot," Rachel mumbled to herself as she walked past him and out the door on the way to her car.

Returning to her room at the DoubleTree, she quickly stripped and put on her workout clothes, a loose t-shirt, comfortable gym shorts, and sneakers. Combing her hair with her fingers, she wrapped a sweatband around her head. Putting on her earbuds and playing her favorite mix from her phone, she grabbed a gym towel and made for the hotel's workout room.

An hour later, her skin flushed and radiant from the workout, she returned to her room, stripped, and jumped into a hot shower. Clean and refreshed, she laid down naked on the bed for a bit, allowing her hair to dry in the towel. Turning on the national news, she was disturbed to find out that yet, another lone gunman sprayed bullets from an automatic weapon, mowing down dozens of shoppers in a busy shopping mall.

"What is happening to my country?" she asked herself. "If it's not all this political intrigue, it's the weather trying to kill us all, and now, we have yet another massive shooting, massacring innocent people."

Disgusted, Rachel turned off the television dressed for the evening, hoping to find some happiness out of this day.

***

With the help of the hotel desk, Rachel found this rather good Tuscan restaurant within walking distance. After enjoying a rather good red wine with her Sicilian style calamari, she dined on Chicken Piccata and grilled asparagus. The food was delicious, and the wine even better. After dinner, she took a chair at the bar and began conversations with the patrons who bought her drinks in the hope of taking her home.

She thought about it. She could use a good lay, and she wasn't attached to anyone in particular at home. She had considered one rather dashing gentleman until he saddled up close to her, and she could smell his breath.

"I'm not sleeping with anyone whose breath is that bad," she decided, keeping her opinion to herself. "Too bad, he sure was a looker."

In the end, and not far from midnight, she decided she needed sleep more than a good lay, so she left, brushing off the guys who still had high hopes for sleeping with her. Strolling, with a bit of a wobble, she made it back to her hotel. By now, she looked forward to getting out of her heels, stripping off her clothes, and climbing into bed.

Walking into the hotel lobby, she briefly glanced at the desk, noting that no one was there now.

"Guess they're in the backroom," she speculated as she made her way to the elevator.

Stabbing the call button, she waited. Staring absently, another woman came up behind her and poked the call button again.

"Stupid woman, can't you see it's already lit?" Rachel thought to herself. "It's not going to make the elevator car come any faster by pressing the button again and again."

Soon enough, the elevator doors opened, beckoning them to enter. The woman behind her pushed her aside and jumped in, pulling her large suitcase behind her. Shaking her head, Rachel followed and pressed the fourth-floor button, ignoring the lit twelfth-floor button.

"Well, at least we're not on the same floor," Rachel thought.

As the doors closed, Rachel could almost feel the woman hovering behind her, as if to invade her personal space. She considered turning towards her to tell her to back off. Just then, the elevator slowed and stopped at her floor.

Whispering a sigh of relief, Rachel approached the door. As it opened, she almost ran into a man attempting to step onboard. As she backed away to avoid the collision, something touched the back of her neck, and pain immediately scrambled her brains, and everything went dark.

What she didn't know was that the woman Tasered her, knocking her unconscious. As she fell, the man caught her in his arms and stepped into the elevator car. As the doors closed, the woman laid the luggage bag on the car floor and opened it. The man expertly folded Rachel into the suitcase. Even before the elevator got to the sixth floor, they closed and sealed the suitcase lid, trapping Rachel inside it.

Smiling to each other, the man and the woman stepped off the elevator on the twelfth floor and calmly walked to their room, nonchalantly dragging the suitcase behind them. After entering, they deposited the bag on the bed and opened it.

Checking Rachel's vital signs, they were pleased to note that everything was normal and that Rachel suffered little effect from the sudden electrical surge into her skull. Not that it mattered, they weren't interested in her brain.

"You have the sedative ready?" the man asked the woman.

"Yes, just give me a moment," she answered as she opened a drawer and withdrew a syringe kit.

"Let's see now. With her weight and body build, this should be just right." the woman said as she filled the syringe with a strong sedative. She stuck her arm, making sure she found a suitable vein to transport the drug quickly throughout her system.

"She'll be sleeping for hours," he said.

"Good, you got her room all cleared up?"

"Yes, housekeeping will find it as if she slept well and checked out early tomorrow morning. We have an associate who looks like her taking her place on her flight to Chicago. They'll collect her luggage, take an Uber home, and deposit it at her place. When they finally notice her missing, they will assume she disappeared somewhere in Chicago, rather than in this dismal city."

"Good. We have time, care to make it enjoyable?"

"Sure, why not. Transport won't be here for at least an hour," he said, taking the woman in his arms. After kissing her, he slowly slid the strap of her dress off her shoulders, and it dropped to the floor.

Picking her up, he tossed her on the bed, alongside Rachel, still folded in the suitcase, though the case remained open.

The woman looked over at the sleeping girl as the man pulled her panties down.

"Ahhh, beautiful," he commented, staring at the treasure between his companion's legs.

"Shhh," she responded, sitting up so that she could help him undress, as he kicked off his shoes. Freeing his cock, she took him in her mouth, sucking him to a raging erection. His cock head purple with engorged blood, she looked up at him. Then looking at the unconscious Rachel lying alongside her, she leaned back, spread her legs, and guided him inside her. As he fucked her, the woman kept looking over at the peaceful face of Rachel, folded in the suitcase, knowing that the girl's life was about to change forever. She didn't know what they wanted with the girl, and she didn't want to know. They paid her well to do these missions and to keep her mouth shut. She came in a magnificent orgasm staring into the face of the poor Rachel. She liked cumming, staring at the faces of her captured prey. Her partner mauled her breasts in near unison and expelled his seed all across her belly.

Dressed and cleaned up, the man closed the lid on the suitcase, dropped it to the floor, and raised the travel handle. Together, the man and woman left, pulling the loaded luggage behind them.

Getting on the elevator, they kissed one more time as the car dropped to the lobby. Walking calmly out the door, arm in arm, they stepped up to a waiting limousine. The driver placed the suitcase into the trunk as the couple climbed into the back. As the driver closed the trunk lid, the couple leaned in and kissed, his hand stroking the insides of her leg, slowly sliding upwards. They never felt the limousine pull away on its way to the airport.

After about forty minutes, the limo pulled onto the airport grounds and right into a hanger. The door closing behind them, the car stopped off to the side of a plane, standing ready to depart. The driver immediately jumped out and held the door open, allowing the man to exit. Straightening her dress, the woman let her partner help her from the limousine. They were met by an attendant, who walked with them to the trunk of the vehicle. The driver pulled the suitcase from the back and resumed his place behind the limo wheel.

After the driver was out of hearing range, the attendant asked. "Is she in there?"

"Of course."

"Good. Take her inside." The attendant commanded. The man grabbed the suitcase handle and dragged Rachel inside a room off to the side of the hanger. The other two followed him inside and locked the door behind them. Laying the suitcase on its back, the man opened the case and flipped the top open.

"Hmmm, she's pretty, too bad." The attendant said. "Get her ready."

"Yes, Ma'am," the couple responded.

Pulling Rachel out of the suitcase, they began stripping her. In short order, she was lying naked on the ground. Meanwhile, the attendant rolled out a clear acrylic box, a coffin's size and shape. Parking it alongside Rachel's body, the couple dropped her into the box. The attendant lowered the cover over the top, and the man began welding it shut with a heat gun. As he worked his way around the lid, his woman companion rolled over a device and hooked up two hoses to the box, providing a constant supply of air, mixed with a sedative to keep Rachel quiet and, more importantly, alive.

After checking the top and air hose seals, the attendant said. "You're dismissed. We will deposit the payments into your accounts within the hour."

"Thank you, Ma'am." A minute later, they were back in the limousine, rolling out of the hanger.

The attendant looked down at her prize, a bit of sorrow in her tone. "Oh, dearie, what did you ever do to get caught up in all this. Such a shame," she finished, "such a shame for such a beautiful girl."

After covering the acrylic box with an opaque black cloth, she walked over to a desk and pressed an intercom button.

"The package is ready," she spoke into the microphone. "Load it up."

"Yes, Ma'am," came the scratchy reply through the speaker.

A pair of husky men walked into the room and began rolling the cloth-covered box out to the plane. They were paid well enough not to look under the drape or ask questions. Arriving, they put the acrylic crate into the private jet's cargo hold. Making sure to secure the cargo, they left, closing the cargo hold door behind them. A member of the onboard flight crew removed the black cloth, hooked up the air supply hoses, and turned on the system, ensuring a positive airflow into the box. Satisfied, they returned to the main cabin.

Minutes later, the hangar doors opened, and the jet rolled out onto the tarmac. Almost no time at all, the jet plane lifted off and attacked the sky, climbing high and heading east. It would be hours before it touched the ground again, well outside the States, landing on an airfield where no one asked questions about the plane's origin or its cargo.

Chapter Eight

"Robert, the view is spectacular," Lara exclaimed, excited by the panorama surrounding them.

"Yes, it is, hon. Look at how those mountains seem to rise above the clouds, almost as if nothing is supporting them."

"It is fantastic. You're right, of course. It does seem like they are floating on the clouds. Just look at the colors revealed in the sunlight. The minuscule air droplets make them look like jewels."

"Beautiful, there's no doubt about it."

Lara and Robert stood together, staring at the beauty that Mother Nature saw fit to show them. His arm wrapped around her waist, held her tight to his side, while hers loosely wrapped around his back, slowly receding before cupping his ass. Responding in kind, he dropped his hand inside her shorts and returned the gesture. Lara smiled up at him before returning her gaze to the landscape before them.

They were an item, traveling together across Europe without a care in the world. The entire sum of their worldly possession packed in their backpacks, now lying on the ground behind them. It was enough that they had each other. Lara was born in Switzerland so hiking the mountains around her home was natural for her. Robert was Austrian, so he was comfortable with hiking in the region.

They met a few years ago in a coffee bar. To that point, Robert was comfortable initiating conversations with random people, girls in particular. However, when Robert spied the girl who he later found was named Lara, he stopped looking. Then, after taking her to bed, he knew that she was the one.

It helped that she was a medium frame woman with long brown hair and sported small tits that barely filled out a 'B' cup. They were a perfect size, capable of filling his open mouth as he sucked on them. If they were any bigger, he would be unable to accomplish the feat, which would disappoint him. More importantly, she had responsive nipples, growing tall and hard for him either by touching them or, even better, looking at them poking back at him under her tee. To him, she was gorgeous, beautiful, and glorious in bed. Why she had fallen for him bewildered him to this day; without a doubt, he had gotten the better deal.

Lara wasn't shy about being approached by guys. She looked good, knew it, and appreciated the looks that guys gave her as she walked past them. She wasn't a tease by any stretch of the imagination. She was just particular about the guys she returned their interest. That day and out of the blue, a guy approached her and offered to pay for her coffee. She would out of hand, usually reject such an offer, but when she turned and saw the guy, she instantly fell for him. To her, he was gorgeous. He had a long angular face framed by long dirty blonde hair that reached the top of his broad shoulders, topping a well-built frame. He was wearing hiking shorts, which showed off his thick, sturdy legs. In an instant, a flash of desire flooded her brain as she imagined her legs wrapped around him as he pummeled her with his dick.

After accepting his offer, they sat at a sidewalk table and talked for hours. Neither had anywhere pressing to go, and he absentmindedly blew off a connection with another girl he met yesterday. That one was history, and Lara was his future.

On the following day, after sharing breakfast, they meandered around the countryside, getting to know each other better. It turned out that they shared much of the same interests. He was from Austria and her, Switzerland. They were practically neighbors. Neither one of them cared about possessions, owning homes, and working at meaningless jobs. Instead, they were free spirits, taking them where the wind blew, not knowing, nor caring where they bedded down for the night. After that first day, they never slept alone nor with someone else. They were an item.

After several months together, they decided to travel the continent, working odd jobs along the way to pay for food. When money was tight, they lived off the land, hunting meat from the forest, picking fruit from the trees, and digging up edible greens from the fields. They wanted nothing except for each other.

Occasionally, they would go into town, spend an evening surrounded by people or get medical attention as needed. At one point, Lara got pregnant. Knowing that a child would inhibit their free lifestyle and after a brief, uncomplicated discussion, she aborted the pregnancy. After that, they took better precautions to keep her childless as they traveled around the continent.

Unknown to either of them, fate stepped in, and someone at the clinic forwarded her contact to the Consortium. Months later, Lara got the sense that someone was tracking them. Robert dismissed her concern. Lara, trusting him, forgot all about it.

In fact, a handful of people were rotating in and out, tracking them, watching their every move. There was a high demand for couples in their mid-twenties, athletically built and beautiful together. Here were such a pair and easy culling. Though there were still unknowns about them, especially with their sexual concourse, their observations indicated that they routinely enjoy lively sexual escapades, indoors and out. It seemed to the hunters that given an opportunity, they would each take time out to enjoy a tryst before moving on, picking up where they left off.

Over time, they uncovered both of their full backgrounds, from where they were born until now. Neither had any family to speak of and had chosen a life together. They were easy pickings.

After making love in front of nature's splendor, Robert and Lara went about making camp. Setting up the small, two-person nylon tent, they unpacked a pair of warm sleeping bags, zipped them together, and laid their nest inside the tent. Preparing a campfire, they watched the sun dip in the sky, slowly disappearing behind the mountains. By the time darkness set in, their only light had come from the fire, adding to the warmth they had shared.

After eating their evening meal, they sat around the fire, enjoying the stillness of the night. As the fire died down, they laid back and enjoyed the spectacle of stars that revealed themselves dancing across the visible panorama. The Milky Way stretched a roadway across the sky, and they each shared their stories about favorite stars and constellations. Robert loved that about Lara. She could come up with such amazing, fanciful stories, made up on the fly. They were both ludicrous and utterly believable. When they couldn't stop yawning, they crawled into the tent and fell asleep in each other's arms. The feel and warmth of each other's bodies, lying chest to chest, gave them instant comfort and relaxation. Tomorrow promised to be another day in paradise, just the two of them together in their journey through life.

The moon setting just below the horizon, total darkness descended across their camp. Only the stars flying across the sky gave them any light whatsoever. A silent helicopter dropped a pair of lines in a field not far away, and four shadowy figures slid to the ground. Getting their bearings and putting on their night vision glasses, they slowly crept up the grade to the clearing on top of the mountain where their prize awaited them.

As the cloaked figures approached the camp, they slowed and carefully inspected their surroundings. Sure enough, the heat of two individuals radiated through the walls of the tent. Scanning left and right, they detected no other heat signatures, giving away the presence of other humans or wildlife.

Cautiously approaching the tent, the leader waved his arms to order his men to fan out. Then, pulling a small canister from his pocket, he attached a hose and nozzle to it. Feeding it through a small opening in the zipper, he opened the valve of the canister. Within minutes, he filled the interior of the tent with a gas, rendering the subject's unconscious.

Waiting five minutes to be sure they were out, the leader then opened the tent flaps, allowing the anesthetic gas to escape. Reaching in, he pulled them out, still cocooned in their sleeping bag. As he did so, the other men in the raiding party broke camp, scattering the remains of their campfire, and packed up all of Robert and Lara's belongings.

Radioing the chopper, it appeared silently overhead and dropped to the ground. After depositing the couple and their gear into the aircraft, the raiding party climbed aboard. Within sixty seconds of touchdown, the helicopter was back in the air, leaving not a trace of Robert or Lara on the ground. It was as if the earth opened up and swallowed everything whole. Five minutes after that, each of the couple had been stripped, bound, and gagged. The whole operation took less than fifteen minutes.

Within the hour, they would be unloaded at the airport and transported to parts unknown. Neither the pilot nor the hunters wanted to know what happened to their prey after delivering their cargo. It was none of their business, and they all were very well paid not to ask questions.

Chapter Nine

Sunlight streamed through the floor-to-ceiling windows filling Avril's room full of light. The late afternoon sun was no longer straight above but at an angle, drawing shadows across the lawn. Avril stood looking out at the panoramic view below. It's a scene she saw almost every day but denied her. In of itself, it pained her to stare out the window. If she could have anything, it would be to walk out in the open, free to enjoy the grass and trees, and going anywhere she pleased.

The beautiful landscape, slowly transitioning from winter to spring, was breathtaking. The sun was shining as the last vestiges of winter snow gave way to early spring flowers. She loved looking out over the fields and mountains in the distance. Her enjoyment diminished only by her inability to feel the grass beneath her feet or feeling the sun directly touching her skin.

Avril stood there for several minutes, savoring a cup of spiced chai with milk, lost in her reverie. She appreciated learning that one thing from him. All her life, she always had lemon with her tea. He had introduced her to using milk. At first, she resisted assuming she wouldn't like it. How wrong she discovered. Now, after all these months, she wouldn't think of drinking it any other way.

Her thoughts weren't on anything in particular. She merely let them wander as she stared out over the lawn and the trees beyond.

"It's a beautiful day, isn't it?" Avril heard behind her, breaking her out of her reverie.

"Yes, Sir, it is." She answered him before slowly turning to face him.

"I'll bet you wish you could go out there."

"Honestly, Sir. Yes, I do."

"In time, my dear, in time. In the meantime, you look ravishing this afternoon. Did you finish your workout in the gym? You look glowing."

"Yes, Sir, and showered as well."

As Avril finished her tea and put down the empty cup on a nearby table, the two approached each other. Halfway across the room, he stopped, but she continued coming closer.

"Avril, my dear, you are, without a doubt, beautiful. I could eat you up."

"Thank you, Sir," she replied, a smile on her face and her eyes lighting up. "Shall I lie down on the bed and let you indulge yourself?"

"Hmmm, don't tempt me."

"Never, Sir, I'm yours, and you can do with me as you please."

"Come here, you minx," he said, taking her in his arms. "To see you, hold you, my chest tightens. I can feel my heart pounding with excitement. I find it hard to keep my hands off you."

Avril seemed to melt into his arms. She may be his property, but she had also come to enjoy his compliments. Pleased, she found that she could melt in his arms and get lost staring into his deep green eyes. Something about him entranced her. While he could be cruel and sadistic, he also had a tenderness about him, which he often shared with her. In all the times she had watched him with his other girls, she had never seen that tenderness with them. It seemed that he reserved it for her.

Looking up into his dreamy eyes, she waited. In under a second, a spark of electricity leapt across the span just before their lips touched each other. Moaning, she fervently returned his kiss as he probed the inside of her mouth with his tongue. Opening her mouth more, she accepted his tapering flame of desire intruding into hers. Feeling his chest against hers, she held him tight, feeling his excitement grow against her thighs. Her juices began to flow, and now more than ever, she was ready for him. All because of a kiss!

"Whew," he exclaimed, breaking off.

Still holding her around the waist, he kept her close, pelvis to pelvis. "You certainly know how to keep my interest, my dear."

"Thank you, Sir. I think," she started, "oh, I didn't mean it like that. It's just well; I don't know. I know you complimented me, and I meant to stop there. The 'I think' wasn't necessary."

"Avril, it's alright. I get it. Now, even after all this time, you're still adjusting to your new life with me in my home."

"I suppose, Sir. You're probably right. Just the same, I didn't mean it the way it came out."

"I understand. However, I didn't come in here to hold you for a moment. I came in here to ask you to come with me. I have something to show you."

"Sir?"

"But now that I have you in my arms, that can wait a minute. You're hot and ready for me. I intend not to let that get by me." He finished as he swooped her into his arms and carried her over to the bed.

Tossing her on her back, he began unbuttoning his shirt. A moment later, he threw it across the floor and was already working on his trousers.

"Here, let me get that, Sir." Avril offered, sitting up and undoing his belt.

In no time at all, his slacks had joined the shirt, and Avril leaned back. After spreading her legs with her knees up high, he climbed on top of her. Reaching for her breasts, Sir grabbed each of them in his hands as his fingers dug in, mauling them. Leaning over her as he held on, he maneuvered his lips to meet hers. Just as their parted lips reconnected, the head of his cock found its target.

"Don't be gentle, Sir." she moaned between excited moans. "Right now, I need you hard and heavy."

Sir didn't say a word but answered her in the only way she needed to know. Without a doubt, he got the message, responding in kind. Driving his hard, thick erection, he buried himself to the hilt, grinding his pelvis against hers in the process.

Sucking in a deep, cleansing breath, Avril lost control, arched her back, and pushed back on him, trying to get every millimeter of him deep inside her.

"Oh, Yes, Sir." Avril muttered in a slow, heated breath, "that's what I need."

Putting all the strength he could, he held himself inside her, as far as he could go, and ground his body on top of hers. She rewarded him with a growl, low and intensive, wallowing in the joy of the moment.

After letting her get accustomed to his invasion, he lifted off her ever so slowly. Before he withdrew, leaving no more than an inch of his cock inside her, he rammed back down, reasserting his presence in her cunt.

He established a rhythm, bouncing up and down, driving into her as he pressed her body into the soft mattress. She screamed in joy, cumming with the smallest of orgasms in the process.

Pounding – driving – crushing – bouncing – without abandon, he slammed into her, filling her, pushing her every button. Avril's eyes closed, but behind them, they rolled up into the back of her head.

With their lips smashed together, his cock driving into her hard, Avril reached around his back and dug her fingers into him, not caring if she hurt him or not. Later she would discover that she left deep scratch marks, some of which welled up with blood sealing the wound. All she knew now was that she was his, his manhood taking her, his hands mangling her tits, as he asserted his ownership of her.

"Sir ... I ... ah, I ... may I ... cum?" she asked.

"Yes, my dear, cum for me. Cum for me now!"

As he finished, his tone firmly demanded she must do as commanded. An observer might have thought he growled his permission rather than just firmly saying it. Whether he did or not, Avril hadn't noticed. She hadn't heard anything after he said 'yes.'

With the answer Avril needed, pleasure overwhelmed her, and the world around disappeared. All that remained was the sense of his lips on hers and his cock driving deep into her. In the height of her climax, except for the cock buried inside her, she lost all sensation of him. She felt as if she was falling over a cliff with nothing to support her.

In those moments, she had no sense of her body. He split her wide open. Nothing seemed to support her, not even the bed. All she felt was an all-encompassing sense of pleasure exploding in every cell of her body, derived from the heat of the head of his cock to her innermost region. She stopped breathing for the longest time. Breathing didn't matter to her anymore. Only the explosion of raw pleasure ripping through her body mattered.

In the final stages of her orgasm, her fingers stretched out, her nails splayed and touching nothing but air. But she could feel his erection expanding before driving one last time into her. She could almost feel his cum splatter against her cervix. It was this final feeling that overwhelmed her, and the world around her went a dark gray before she passed out.

***

"Oh, I see you're back with me."

"Yes, – Sir," Avril responded weakly.

"Good, but you scared me. You've never passed out during sex before."

Avril almost couldn't hear him. He seemed so far away. "Sir, I ... ah, what did you ... say?"

"Never mind, my dear. I'm just glad you're alright. Did you enjoy yourself?"

"Oh, Yes, Sir." she dreamily answered but with a definite air of excitement. She was still wallowing in the aftermath of her climax.

Lying there, underneath him, Sir was still on top of her. She could still feel him inside her, though his erection was weakening. Avril tried to lift her weighty arms and stroke his body. Either she was too weak, or they were too heavy, she failed. Her arms fell back on the bed alongside her. She couldn't move them, no matter how hard she tried.

"Sir – I feel so – weak."

"Shhh, my dear, yes, I seem to have found your breaking point."

It took a moment for Avril to figure out what he meant by that but eventually, she nodded her agreement.

"That was wonderful, Sir. I … well, I feel fulfilled, more than I think I ever have. Thank you, Sir."

"You're welcome, my dear. I feel grand as well. I don't think anyone had ever throttled my cock as you did when you climaxed. It was very satisfying and very, very intoxicating."

"I'm glad, Sir," Avril whispered weakly, her eyes still closed.

Feeling content, his full weight on her, Avril liked the feeling of him lying down on top of her, pressing her firmly into the mattress. Reluctantly and feeling a sense of loss, he slipped out.

"Oh, Sir…" she said with a distinct air of regret.

"Shhh, it's alright," he assured her as she opened her eyes and looked up at him.

She smiled when his face came into focus. Her breathing labored; he lifted his upper body off to allow her to breathe more easily. As he did so, he took a hand and caressed the side of her face, combing some unruly hair away off her face. She couldn't help but smile at the tenderness of his touch.

Settling back, she enjoyed the moment, wishing it could go on indefinitely. Maybe she fell asleep and perhaps not. However, when she next opened her eyes, it was apparent that some time had passed. Sir was no longer lying on top of her, and except for herself, her bed was empty. Leaning up on her elbows, she looked around the room.

"Ah, there he is," she thought to herself when she found him in his chair in her room.

"How do you feel?" he asked when he noticed her propped up on her elbows.

"Wonderful Sir, missing you though, how long was I out?"

"Not long, Avril. I needed to use the facilities. You looked so peaceful that I didn't want to disturb you."

"Speaking of facilities, Sir, I need to use them." Throwing the sheet covering her, "when did that get there?" she wondered. Avril got up and hurried to the on-suite. A few minutes later, she returned and stood by his side. "May I sit?" she queried.

"By all means."

Avril sat on his lap, positioning herself so that she could feel his cock against the underside of her thighs. Wiggling a bit to ensure firm contact, she draped an arm around the back of his neck and leaned in and kissed him. He kissed her back, adding more passion than she expected. As he kissed her, he took a free hand and cupped one of her breasts, gently massaging them in his fingers. Avril moaned, her body enjoying the moment.

Breaking off from the kiss but leaving his hand where it was, Sir said, "Now for why I am here. Not that the respite wasn't wonderful. It was. I do love fucking you."

Avril wanted to ask, "Even more than your other girls?" but knew better of it. Instead, she added, "Thank you, Sir. You're not too bad yourself. You can fuck me that way anytime."

"Well, later, perhaps. Right now, I have something to show you. She's been waiting for a long time."

"She? You mean, you have a new submissive waiting for me, Sir?"

"Yes, I do. She's cute and very malleable. You should have no trouble dominating her."

"Sir, what can you share with me about her?"

"I'll give you the once over, the same as what any of the membership knew when she went up for auction. She's a petite five-foot-four bi-sexual, one-hundred twenty-one pounds, with silvery blonde hair. She was an aspiring model who happened upon the wrong photographer, nineteen if I remember correctly.

He did take some beautiful shots of her in a nude modeling session, and the follow-up investigation revealed she was a wild one in bed. In fact, fucking either men or women seem to be her favorite past-time. I can attest that she's got a great body and knows how to use it. She is from Southern California and lived most of her adult life living in bikinis and hanging out at the beach. She was on the prowl for a whale to marry and set her up for life."

"Sir, it seems to me she got two out of three of her wishes."

Laughing at the thought, "I suppose you're right since I have no intention of marrying her. I hadn't thought about that before. That's funny. I intend care of her for the rest of her life, and I am, to a degree, a whale."

"That's true, Sir. Thank you for my gift."

"Then, as soon as we get dressed, we'll go, and I'll introduce you to her."

"We, Sir?"

"Yes, Avril, we. In your closet, you'll find a pair of black leather pants and a black vest. Leave the vest unbuttoned. You may put them on, along with a pair of your favorite crystal earrings and necklace. The blue of your heels will look splendid with the black leather."

"Oh, thank you, Sir." Avril squealed, jumping up from his lap and running to the walk-in closet.

"You have ten minutes to get ready. Don't be late, or you'll be suffering the fate I have in store for your new sub."

"Sir," she spoke loudly from the closet, "what's her name?"

"Her name? Uh, wait a minute while I think."

"Oh, that's right, her name is Misty, Misty Ciwells."

"Misty, um? Well, let's see if her name fits her."

Exactly seven minutes later, Avril strutted out of her closet, wearing her outfit.

"Oh, Sir, the outfit is wonderful. The leather is so soft it almost feels like a second skin."

Staring at her, awed by the beautiful vision standing before him, Avril watched him suck in a breath, holding it as he appreciated her. The leather pants held tight to her body. Looking in the mirror, Avril could see the outline of her camel toe at the top of her thighs. She had never seen that vision before, not having worn panties in years. The vest covered her but didn't. As instructed, she left it unbuttoned, but she doubted that it would remain in place unless there were a strong wind it covered her breasts and yet not.

***

"Now, Avril, before we go in there and meet your new submissive, remember, you own her. She is yours to control, command, and dominate. You have ultimate power over her life and, more importantly, her death. Make sure she knows it. You can do whatever you want to her, but remember, too little control is just as bad as too much control. You must read her, her body language, her stance, her attitude towards you. She will tell you, not in words, what she needs to control her."

"I understand, Sir. I remember your training."

"Don't get cocky. In your previous training, I was there. The subject knew I was there and likely responded to my dominance. This will be your first solo session, so you will not have that advantage."

Avril nodded. "Yes, Sir."

"Remember your training, have confidence in yourself, and you'll do fine. Make me proud."

"Sir, have you had your honor with her yet?"

"You mean, have I fucked her yet?"

"Yes, Sir."

"Be clear in your questions. I will not have you dancing around the actual words you mean to ask."

"Yes, Sir, I understand."

"No, I have not fucked her. At the proper time, I expect you to offer her to me. Then I'll take my time teaching her that as cruel you can be to her. I can be worse."

"Yes, I see how we can use that to our mutual advantage, Sir."

Reaching for the doorknob, Avril was about to open the door when she was interrupted.

"I'll be watching you on the monitor."

"Yes, Sir. Thank you, Sir."

Holding her head high and pushing her shoulders back, Avril opened the door and met her new test.

The room was similar in layout to the one she spent the night chained to the wall after that first disastrous dinner party almost two years ago. The memory was still vivid in her mind. She decided to use that to her advantage.

Misty stood in the center of the room. A series of spotlights all around her left little to hide behind. She was up against a wooden post, her hands and arms chained with shackles high above her head. As customary for new purchases, except for wearing her training heels, Misty was naked. Sir was correct. She was a petite thing. Her long blonde hair draping her back and shoulders reminded her of slow-moving water sliding over rocks and boulders in a stream.

Avril assumed she had been standing there quite some time, given that her session with Sir delayed her entrance to introduce herself to her new submissive. Her head hung down, her chin resting on her body. Although the door opened, she failed to look up or appear curious about who entered the room.

Closing the door behind her, Avril walked deeper into the room. Approaching the girl, she stopped in front of her and stared. Misty didn't look up, even though Avril could tell that the girl was aware of her presence. Walking around her, Avril slowly took in the body hanging from the chains. The shackles around her wrists supported much of the girl's weight, left her feet barely touching the floor.

As Avril walked around her, she noted that except for the new nipple rings, her body seemed to be untouched or abused. Of course, that was about to change as Sir expected her to torment and abuse the poor girl.

Completing her circuit around the girl, Avril stood once again in front of the girl and studied the body. She was alive but holding back. Avril took her time, evaluating what she observed. Suddenly, the answer came to her.

Stepping up, Avril slapped her hard on the face, whipping the girl's head around.

"You will look at me when I come into the room. Is that understood?"

Tears were whelming up in the girl's eyes; Misty merely looked back at Avril. No acknowledgment or agreement in her body language.

Immediately, Avril slapped her again, across her cheek. Misty's head snapped around and back against the post. The blow had so much energy that the girl's head bounced against the column.

"I said, you will look at me when I come into the room. Is that understood?" Avril snapped severely.

Tears were now flowing down her cheeks. Misty paused before nodding. Then, from somewhere deep, she angrily yelled.

"Who the fuck are you? What right do you have to hold me here?"

She was about to continue her rant of questions when Avril silenced her with another slap to the face.

"Who gave you permission to speak, bitch." Avril interrupted.

"Let me tell you what you are and why you're here. But first, the rules. You will not speak unless given permission. You will do as I say, without delay, or suffer the consequences."

"What the hell does that mean, suffer the consequences." Misty interrupted before having to deal with another stinging slap to her face. The crack of the back of her head against the post echoed throughout the room.

"Ooowwww," she yelled.

"I told you, bitch, you may not speak unless given permission. Now, as I was saying, you will not speak. You will do exactly what I tell you. You will offer not a single complaint. While you are here, you will suffer as you have never suffered before. While you will suffer, that will be nothing compared to what I will do to you should you break my rules."

Misty, her damp cheeks a bright red from the slapping, just glared back.

"Good," Avril stated matter of factly. "Now, to continue, you belong to me. I paid for you, and now I own you. You are my property to do as I please. Your old life, as you knew it, is over. This is your new home, and you will never leave here, at least alive. When I finish with you, after I have wrung from you every last scream, every last beg for mercy, your last bit of resistance, I will kill you. Now, do you understand me?"

After a long pause where Misty kept her mouth shut but looked back with an air of disbelief and bewilderment, Avril continued.

"I will beat you, torment you, and make you suffer in unimaginable ways. You're here at my pleasure. I will also fuck you, give you pleasure, and allow others to fuck you. I may even allow others to beat and torment you if I tire of you. In other words, I will be the giver of pain and pleasure, my pleasure, your pain. If you fail to do as I tell you, your agony will be even worse."

Wide-eyed in fear, Misty kept her mouth shut. Avril glared at the girl.

"Good," Avril said. "Now, you may ask a single question."

"What do you mean, I'm yours? I'm no one's property. Unchain me. You can't own people. That's illegal."

Misty barely got the last comment out before Avril backhanded her across the face."

"I said, you may ask one question. I said nothing about permitting you to say anything else." With that, she slapped Misty across the face again.

Misty was visibly crying now, her chest heaving as tears flowed out of her eyes and down her face.

"I told you, bitch, you belong to me, bought and paid. You are mine to do with as I please. You were allowed a single question. You violated that order, and you suffered the consequences. From here on out, any further violation of my orders will incur my wrath. From now on, I will not ask you whether you heard me. I am presuming you not only heard me; you understand my orders."

Avril balled up her fist and punched her, connecting across her jaw. The snap of her head loudly reported around the room. She followed up with another punch to her gut. Unable to double over, all Misty could do was pull her knees up and heaved, trying to process the blows. With the wind knocked out of her, it took her a long time before she was able to gather her first breath after the punch to her gut. Avril turned her back on the girl and walked away.

Strolling over to a nearby wall, sat a table, upon which rested various crops and canes. Avril casually dragged her fingers across the toys before stopping. Looking down, she picked up her favorite. It was a flexible cane made of natural bamboo. Swishing it back and forth, it sang as it cut through the air.

Returning to her property, Avril showed her the cane, whipping it back and forth.

"Now, you will learn that disobeying me will bring you unprecedented anguish upon your body."

Avril gave her half a second to process her statement before swinging hard. She landed the length of the cane across her midsection, just below her ribcage. Misty screamed as she tried to double over in pain. Her arms strung up high over her head; she was unable to bend over. Instead, she tried again to draw her knees up. In her weakened state, she couldn't do much more than lift them a mere foot or two.

As the pain of the strike resolved itself, Avril landed another one on her belly, lower than before. The girl screamed again, receiving another blow to her lower torso, just below her belly button. Unable to stop crying, Misty twisted back and forth in a failed attempt to shield her body from the caning.

Avril continued to rain blows against the girl's torso, working up and down her abdomen from just below her breasts to just above her pubic region. It didn't take long before she was stripped with nasty welts crisscrossing her torso among a field of bright red skin.

Working her way downward, Avril began adding bright red stripes to the fronts of both of Misty's thighs, crisscrossing them in intricate cross stitch patterns a dressmaker would find delightful. By this time, Misty was too weak to fight off the onslaught to resist.

However, she wasn't out of it so much that she still cried and screamed. During the punishing training, Avril made sure Misty knew just what it felt like to feel the cane right on her pubis and pussy. She was rewarded with the most heartfelt scream of all as Misty took a brief moment to react to the caning direct to her pussy. Avril could feel her Sir's smile from the monitor.

To finish her off, she landed half a dozen stripes across her tits, turning them into a roadmap of pain and anguish.

Finished, Avril stood back and looked at the girl. Admiring the scene, she contemplated what she had just done. In her old life, doing what she had just done would have been unimaginable. Today, she took it upon herself to target and intentionally hurt this girl. Her only mistake was to get noticed by the Consortium.

"What am I doing?" She thought to herself. "More importantly, what have I become?"

Directing her comments to the whimpering girl, Avril spoke sharply to the balling and exhausted Misty. "Reflect on your painful lesson. I expect that there will be many more such lessons before you finally get the message. The sooner you accept you are mine to do with as I please, well, the easier it will go for you."

Done, for now, Avril returned the cane to the table and walked out of the room, leaving the suffering Misty to feel her pain and anguish all alone.

Chapter Ten

Blackness slowly gave way to awareness. As reality returned, Rachel sensed something was wrong … really, really, wrong. For the moment, she kept her eyes closed; her head and neck hurt like hell. She had the worst headache in the back of her head. It was massive, pounding away inside her skull.

"What the hell happened?" was her first thought.

Listening carefully, she knew she wasn't in her hotel room. She couldn't remember even getting there. The last thing she could recall was walking into her hotel and making her way to the elevators. Try as she might, she couldn't remember even getting on the elevator to take her room.

"What happened?" she repeated to herself.

Smart enough to realize all was not right; she continued to listen hard. Off in the distance, likely in another room, she heard the muffled sounds of people talking. Only she couldn't make out what they were saying.

Very carefully, she tried to move an arm, surprised that it wouldn't budge. Testing both arms, she sensed that they were held in place by straps. After determining the same for her legs, she moved on to trying to figure out what happened and where she was.

For a long time, all she did was listen, reaching out into the world around her to get a sense of where she was. As the fog of her unconsciousness faded, she sensed wires and tubes draped across her body.

"Am I in a hospital?" she wondered. "What happened to me? How did I get here?"

Figuring she was alone, she carefully opened her eyes. As they slowly came into focus, she looked around. Sure enough, she was in a hospital room.

"Did something happen to me? Was I injured in an accident? Why am I strapped down?"

Questions raced through her mind as she tried to get a sense of what was going on. Looking down at her arms, she confirmed that someone strapped her down to the bed. The odd thing was, she was naked, bare ass to the wind, without as much as a sheet covering her. Looking down towards her feet, she discovered that she was held down by several straps, around her neck and across her waist, thighs, and ankles.

Straps made of thick canvas, the kind used for straight-jackets, bound her arms and wrists to the side of her body. Her legs and feet were similarly secured to the bed's side rails, leaving her legs spread wide open. Whoever strapped her to this bed had unfettered access to her privates. Feeling vulnerable and exposed in her nudity, she shivered.

"What the fuck?" she muttered a bit out loud.

At that moment, she realized that she wasn't alone as she surmised. As she uttered her frustration, out of sight, someone sat up and left the room. For a brief instant, she watched the back of a woman in a nurse's uniform walk out the door.

"Hey!" Rachel exclaimed, "Come back. I want to know what happened to me."

The nurse didn't acknowledge her and left. In a last-ditch effort to get answers, Rachel tried one more thing. "Hey! I need to go to the bathroom." The door closed behind the nurse, leaving her entirely alone.

Screaming in frustration, Rachel pleaded for someone to come back and release her, or at least tell her what was going on. No one came.

With her neck still sore and her throat hoarse, she laid back, fuming at her situation, realizing that there was nothing she could do about it. Strapped down as she was, unable to move more than a finger or toe, she was helpless. She failed at each attempt to test the strength of her straps. All she got out of it was choking, the neck strap tightening around her neck amid her struggles. Only by surrendering to the bindings did the neck strap relax enough to allow her to breathe normally.

A long time later, the door to her room opened. Turning towards the door, Rachel watched a man in a dark charcoal grey suit with a shimmery grey tie walk in. In other circumstances, Rachel would have given him a second look.

"Please, can you tell me what's going on?" Rachel pleaded.

She got no reply. The man stood there, looking her over.

"Can I at least get a sheet over me? I'm cold."

Again, her query was left unnoticed. The man just stood there, looking at her. From Rachel's point of view, he seemed to study her, moving slowly up from her feet, up her legs, over her torso before settling on her face. He seemed to ignore her nakedness but instead focused on her. In a way, it was kind of eerie, yet, he appeared to sympathize over her situation.

"Who are you?" she asked, rather calmly notwithstanding her situation.

"What am I doing here? Was I injured and in need of medical attention?"

All her questions went unanswered.

"Why am I here?" she asked.

"Because I want you here," he said.

Then, he said the strangest thing.

"I'm sorry," and walked out the door, leaving her alone once again.

Screaming expletives until she was hoarse, she stared at the ceiling and resumed her crying.

A few minutes after that, a nurse returned and inserted a needle into the back of her hand. Hanging an IV bag, the nurse adjusted the drip to ensure a nice steady flow into her vein.

"What's going on?" Rachel asked to deaf ears.

Turning, the nurse reached for the tray containing syringes, tubes, and other items. Rachel watched as she drew blood and filled a variety of test tubes. A small chunk of her flesh was also taken from her hip and added to the filled test tubes resting on the medical tray. Before leaving, the nurse injected more medication into the IV line.

"Why?" Rachel managed to say before she fell asleep.

***

Over the next day or so, Rachel laid there, strapped to the hospital bed and unable to move. At some point, she realized that she must be wearing a catheter as she never once needed to get up and use the bathroom. Soon enough, a nurse came in and exchanged her Foley bag, confirming her suspicions. Never once did anyone speak to her, reassure her, or let her know what was going on. They continued to keep her in the dark.

She was poked and prodded for hours. They took her blood pressure, temperature, and other vitals before leaving. None of it hurt that much, but it was a severe breach of privacy. She had long since stopped being concerned about her nakedness. Several times a day, and more often than it seemed necessary to Rachel, they took more blood, filling a host of new test tubes.

"Vampires," she muttered to them, "fucking vampires."

They ignored her and went about their business, whatever that might be. Every so often, she would ask them, "Would someone please tell me what's going on?" She gave up, hoping to get an answer.

All she could do was lie there without so much as a bedsheet to cover her. She stared at the ceiling, shivering, troubled by what they intended to do with her.

At what seemed like early morning, someone came in and injected a medication into her saline drip. Minutes later, she drifted off, unconscious to the activities around her.

***

Waking, Rachel panicked. There was a tube down her throat. A machine was now breathing for her. She could feel her chest rise and fall as air alternately inflating and deflating her lungs. She also discovered a tube stuck down her nostril and an IV stuck in her arm with a couple of different bags of fluid seeping into her bloodstream. It took a while before she calmed down.

"What the fuck now?" she ineffectually tried to yell.

In response, a nurse came in and injected Rachel with something. Minutes later, her body relaxed from the mild sedative.

The nurse left, replaced by another one dressed in scrubs and carrying a tray. The nurse began washing her. Paying specific attention to her chest, the nurse cleaned her entire body. When she finished, the nurse smeared her chest with a smelly yellowish substance.

"Iodine," Rachel guessed as the nurse went about her business. It was about then that someone dressed as a surgeon entered the room.

After reviewing her physical state, the surgeon snapped his fingers, and a pair of orderlies entered the room. Unlocking the wheels to her bed, they rolled her out of the door and down a long hallway. Arriving at their destination, she was transferred to a stainless-steel table, making sure she was tightly strapped down and immobilized.

Leaving, she heard the orderlies tell the doctor that she was ready. He nodded as they disappeared out the door as he continued going about his business. What business he had in mind; Rachel was at a loss to figure out. Slowly, she felt the sedative wear off as her body became more responsive to her mental commands. The machine was still breathing for her, and the tube down her nose was doing something else, what it was, she didn't know. The doctor eventually left, leaving her alone.

Listening carefully, Rachel could hear noises and all sorts of activities in the next room. She couldn't tell what was happening, but she knew that for her, whatever it was, wasn't good. Except for the man in the grey suit, not one soul has spoken to her. All she knows is that the man told her he was sorry.

"Sorry? Sorry for what?"

Lying there, naked on the cold steel table, she prayed that everything would turn out alright in the end. Somehow, she didn't think it would. After maybe about twenty minutes, a pair of nurses entered the room in full surgical gear. Unlocking the wheels of her table, they rolled her through a set of double doors and left her staring up at a blinding overhead light.

After a few minutes to get used to the glare, she was able to take in her new surroundings. Looking around, she noticed an unconscious older man on an operating table. A surgeon was working on him. His chest was cut open, and his ribs spread wide. Elbow deep in blood, the surgeon had his arms inside the man's chest, working carefully. Various wires, hoses, and tubes snaked all around the man. Like her, a breathing tube was down his throat as a machine breathed for him. Another device with hoses attached to it had a red liquid flowing through it. Was that blood? It was impossible to tell whether the man was dead or not. All she could figure out was that he must be alive as a series of machines kept emitting a variety of rhythmic sounds.

"What the hell?" she thought to herself.

In full-face mask and surgical gear, a different doctor approached her table and stared down at Rachel. She recognized a man's look, appreciating the naked body of a beautiful young girl strapped to the table. Behind the surgical mask, Rachel swore he was smiling. The revolting look made her nauseous. Stroking her body and inserting a finger up her pussy, he played with her before moving to her breasts and giving them firm repetitive squeezes.

"Are you ready for us to begin?" he asked the doctor elbow deep in the elderly man's chest.

"Yes, ready. You may begin. Just leave the final extraction to me. It has to be just right."

"Certainly," her surgeon replied, stripping off his outer layer of gloves and replacing them with a fresh pair the nurse was holding out for him.

"Oh, my God," Rachel realized. "They are going to take my organs and give them to that guy. Oh shit! They're going to kill me."

Speaking to his support people, her surgeon said. "Okay, let's begin."

One of the nurses approached, pushing a rolling cart filled with various stainless-steel tools, all individually wrapped in sterile plastic. The second nurse rolled over another stainless-steel table containing a pair of containers, sitting in an ice water bath.

With fear in her eyes, Rachel pleaded to the surgeon, "Please, don't do this."

Picking up a scalpel, he answered her with a nasty smile. Eyes wide open, she screamed past the tube down her throat as he took a handful of a boob and began slicing under it. Though the physical pain was excruciating, the anguish she felt from her breast's loss was worse. A minute later, the grinning surgeon held it high in his hands where she could see it, lovingly caressing the softening nipple.

"Oh, my God, please, no!" she tried screaming past the tube down her throat. Tears fell from her eyes, drenching her cheeks and dripping onto the table.

Dropping the severed breast onto one of the surgical trays, the surgeon walked around to the other side of the table and grasped her remaining breast, pulling it sharply up from her torso. Rachel screamed again as the scalpel made its incision under the organ and began cutting it free. In no time at all, the surgeon held it high. He sneered like the predator he was, hoping to get a rise out of her. He succeeded.

Crying profusely, Rachel refused to look at her severed breast, trying not to envision the bastard gruesomely caressing it. Irreverently, he dropped it to join the first one on the tray. A nurse took them, her precious girls now cleaved from her chest, and retired from the room. Tears spilled from her eyes at an ever-increasing rate.

In her anguish, Rachel heard the surgeon say, "Now, we get to the good stuff."

Opening her eyes in terror, she saw the surgeon pick up a long-curved scalpel and sliced her chest open. Starting just below her neck, he cut a long incision down, around her navel, stopping just below her mound.

Rachel screamed as he opened her up, scarcely noticing the festive look in his eyes.

"She screams just lovely, doesn't she?" her surgeon asked the other surgeon working on the older man.

"Yes, she does," he replied, undistracted in his work. "Remember, don't sedate her. We need it untainted by introduced chemicals."

"Oh, I wouldn't dream of sedating her. I rather enjoy seeing her beg for her life through her screams."

"Yes, I figured. So that you know, I am almost ready."

"I'll be ready when you are, my friend."

"Good."

Rachel felt each slice of the blade, cutting and separating her flesh from her rib cage. Unperturbed in her agony, her surgeon carefully sliced and pulled her meat and muscle over to the side. Soon, he exposed the white bone of her rib cage.

With her chest wall tissue out of the way, the surgeon put down the scalpel and picked up a tool that looked like a set of bolt cutters. Grasping the ends of the long handles, the surgeon positioned the cutter's business end over one of her ribs and squeezed it closed. The crunch of bone-breaking shot through her as she nearly sprang up and off the table.

Rachel screamed louder than ever. The excruciating pain was worse than ever, more so than at the loss of her precious breasts. Rachel almost lost consciousness from the harrowing agony.

"Oh, yes. This one appreciates my work." Her surgeon roared in response to her suffering.

Working his way around the sides of her torso, the surgeon methodically cut each rib, one by one. With each crunch of bone, each snap of another rib-bone, Rachel rewarded him with another bloodcurdling shriek. Rachel knew that she was about to die. It would be an unbearable, horrendous death. One she wouldn't wish upon her worst enemy.

"Well, I now have an enemy that might justify such a death." She abruptly realized.

"Okay, that's the last one. The sternum is ready for removal." Rachel heard him say. To whom she didn't care. Even though he had finished cutting her ribs, the painful memory remained as she suffered.

Grasping a new scalpel, the surgeon cut away the last remaining tendrils from her ribs and lifted them free from her body. Tossing it aside, he scanned inside her chest and again, began slicing. Closing her eyes, she refused to watch him work. Though she still ached all over, her misery came from his prior work. Now, with his hands deep inside her chest, she felt nothing. She wasn't numb to his work. Instead, it was something different. Something she couldn't quite figure out.

Opening her eyes in anger, she watched him slice through the protective membrane protecting her organs, granting him in-depth access to her chest cavity. He freed her lungs in minutes and lifted them from her chest, moving them off to the side. Fascinated, she watched the machine inflate them, sending life-giving oxygen to the rest of her body.

He soon smiled, and reaching into her gapping chest and caressed her innards. Bent over and enjoying the sight, he twisted his head in her direction and said, "You have a beautiful, healthy heart, beating ever so perfectly."

Rachel would have screamed if she was able to. However, no air passed by her vocal cords, vibrating them into the nightmarish screech she would have preferred.

"Ready?" Her killer asked towards the other table.

"In a minute, we're almost ready. Are you having fun over there?"

"You bet. I've never cut a living, beating heart from a body before. Now that I am holding it in my hand, I can feel the pulsations as it pumps blood. It's surprisingly warm to the touch, and it just, well, it feels great holding it."

"Well, don't get used to it. I'm about to come over there and get it. It has to be done just right and match up with the void this dead one is leaving behind."

"Well, take your time. I'm sure our girl here would appreciate as much time as she has left to enjoy the moment."

A couple of minutes later, Rachel succumbed as they cut her still-beating heart from her body.

Her last thoughts ended with, "I hope they kill you all, you fucking bastards."

Chapter Eleven

The Chairman was reviewing the financial reports for the last quarter. After scanning over page after page of fiscal data on the activities, he leaned back and smiled. He was delighted at the strong positive numbers, which added his excitement to the upcoming auction tomorrow. Rubbing his hands together, he relished the thought of what tomorrow would bring. He was confident that not only would the membership leave happy with their purchases, but they would also be talking about the new entertainment he prepared for months to come.

"Our business is certainly lucrative," he said under his breath. "Profits are growing at record levels. The members are going to be very pleased when we release our quarterly dividends."

Reaching for his cup of coffee on his desk, he had just taken a sip when he heard a knock on his office door.

"Come!"

"Sorry to bother you, Sir. However, we've just received a special order from one of our members."

"Yes, well, you know what to do with special orders. Process it."

"Yes, Sir, I do. However, this one will need your attention."

"What's so special about it?" the Chairman asked.

"Well, Sir. That's just it. This member is requesting that we acquire for him a prepubescent child between ten and fourteen. He doesn't care whether it is male or female, just that it must be prepubescent."

"What!" the Chairman snapped. "He knows that we don't deal in that, under any circumstances. We only deal with people of legal age. That's where we draw the line. Tell him no. We won't take the order."

"That's precisely it, Sir. I've already told him that. He knows our policy full well but insists that we take this one. He asked to speak to you."

"Who is it?"

After getting the name, the Chairman responded. "He's an idiot. I'm not sure I ever liked him, and now, I know I don't."

"Yes, Sir. I agree."

"Alright, put him on."

"Yes, Sir. I'll transfer him right away," as the bearer of this unfortunate request turned and closed the door behind him. The Chairman barely had time to reflect upon this unusual request when his phone rang.

"Explain yourself," the Chairman roared with a heavy hint of annoyance in his tone.

"Good morning Mr. Chairman. I am fully aware of the restriction, yet, I am asking, as a favor to you and the Consortium, to please accept my order."

"You know full well that we cannot. The by-laws of our charter specifically prohibit the acquisition of anyone under the age of eighteen. And now, you are asking for a child. A child who hasn't yet tasted what it's like to experience the grander things in life."

"Yes, Mr. Chairman. I understand. Nevertheless, I am asking. I have my reasons."

"What are those reasons?" the Chairman began to say but stopped himself. "No, don't tell me. I don't want to know."

"Fair enough, I am still requesting that you fill my order. I am willing to quadruple the special-order fee."

"What you're asking for is … well, it's beyond belief. I should charge you ten times the normal special-order fee."

"If that is what is necessary to fulfill my order, then I'll pay it."

"That's quite a substantial sum."

"Yes, I know, and it will make quite a dent in my accounts. Alright, I agree. I'll pay ten times the amount."

"And if I still refuse, what will you do?"

"To be frank, Mr. Chairman, then I'll have to use my resources to acquire the merchandise on my own."

"Certainly, you know that is specifically forbidden."

"I do, and frankly, I didn't intend to tell you that, but the need is great, and I elected to try through approved channels."

"Alright, let me think about this. It will take at least a week to put this together. I sincerely doubt our inventory database has any record of anything that will meet your order. Can't you amend your order to one that has just turned eighteen?"

"No, Sir. I apologize, but I can't. I need a prepubescent boy or girl.

Which I don't care? So long as they are between the ages of ten to twelve."

"You make me sick, you know. Just the idea of what your intentions are turns my stomach."

"Yes, Sir. I understand. Nevertheless …"

"You want me to agree to this."

"Yes, Sir. I do."

"Give me a week. I'll get back to you," rudely disconnecting the call.

Dialing another number by heart on his private, secure line, the Chairman waited as the phone on the other end rang.

"Yes," he heard.

"I have an assignment for you. I'll transmit the details to you in the normal fashion. However, please note, this is for a current member. It must look like an accident, and you have four days to complete the job. There must be no mistakes and completed on the first attempt. He will not allow us to make a second. You have four days to complete the assignment."

"Four days, consider it done. I'll get back to you when completed."

"Very good," he finished, hanging up the phone.

His mind racing with heavy dark thoughts, "who the fuck does he think he is, placing an order for a damn child. It's revolting."

The day ruined; he rang for the underling who alerted him to the order. Upon answering, the Chairman said. "I've taken care of the order. Do not mention this order to anyone else. Which reminds me, who else knows of this order?"

"No one, Sir. The member was good enough to bypass channels and come directly to me."

"Well, that's something then."

May I presume that we will not be fulfilling it?"

"I'm still thinking about it."

"Sir, you're not considering it, are you?"

"I haven't decided. I told him I needed a week to look into it. By then, I hope the member will have come to his senses."

"Yes, Sir. I understand."

By the tone of his response, the Chairmen presumed that his meaning was clear. The member would not live to see the order fulfilled.

"Yes, I assumed you would," he added as he disconnected the call.

Leaning back in his chair, he smacked the desk with his fist, yelling out, "Idiot!"

Closing up the files, he stomped out of the room on his way to the gym. He needed to work out his emotions. Then, if the gym didn't relieve some of the anger raging through him, perhaps some playtime in the dungeon with the prey would alleviate his wrath.

"The fucking idiot!" he exclaimed as he walked into the changing room and stripped.

Chapter Twelve

Standing, Avril stared blankly at those gathered around. There were dozens of them, almost all of whom she didn't know. She assumed they were people from the company, the same company where her parents worked. The funny thing was, none of them seemed upset. She had been frantic. Now, all she felt was pain mixed with anguish. The death of her parents floored her. They were such a big part of her life, and now they were dead. She didn't know what she was going to do without them.

Their body language implied not sadness but relief, even happiness. Her parents spent half her life, teaching her how to read body language. It seemed contradictory to the reasons for the gathering. She didn't know how she was going to get through this day. She didn't know how to get past the next month, or years for that matter.

Their attitudes perplexed her. Besides, just who the fuck were they?

"Mom, Dad, why did you have to go and die on me?" Avril bemoaned. "I don't know what I am going to do. These people, these people pretend to be your friends, mourning your loss. I can see it. These fuckers are happy in their fabricated mourning. Mom and Dad, they weren't your friends. They're glad you're dead. What did you ever see in any of them?"

"Why did you have to go and leave me? Why, Daddy? Why?"

Abdicating to her sadness, she looked up at the trees, sunlight glittering through the leaves casting migrating shadows on the ground. In the lingering mid-morning dew, the leaves seemed to sparkle. They were sparkling with life and joy. It was almost as if her parents were trying to send her a message from the beyond. Whatever it was, she wasn't getting the memo. Her heart was too torn up to feel their touch, a graze that briefly stroked her cheeks. Staring past the leaves, she took in the blue and inviting sky. She wished they were flying through the air on her way to her. She knew they had already floated away from her.

Her despair soared by the second. Her gut felt empty and hollow. At the same time, it felt solid. She ignored the paradox; her pain consumed her. She felt dead inside and out. Only her feet keeping her upright indicated that she was still among the living.

Not wanting to look, she forced herself to look downward, settling her gaze upon the two coffins, disappearing into the hole in the ground, a cavity from which they would never return, where they would rest until the end of time.

The first sported dark walnut trimmed out in brass. Her father resting inside, it slowly sank, dwindling in size as it faded from view. He would be happy having his precious wood holding him close, just as his downtown office had been in life.

A second coffin was decked out in angel white glossy metal and trimmed out in brushed nickel, dropping in time with her fathers. She picked the package as it most closely aligned with the memory of her parents. To Avril, she was an angel and daddy's little girl.

"Daddy!" she cried in her head, not wanting to give these assholes around her the satisfaction of seeing her cry. She didn't notice her mascara running with the tears falling from her eyes, painting her cheeks black.

"Daddy, please don't leave me."

He didn't answer, of course, she knew he wouldn't. Her heart was a different matter. She wanted him to respond so much that she felt her knees buckle ever so slightly. Staring at the walnut lid, she envisioned her father reaching his hand out to her. She caught herself from reaching back.

"Avril."

Somewhere in the back of her mind, she sensed that the priest was trying to get her attention.

"Well, fuck him. I don't want to talk to him." She decided. "He's a prick. Let him wait for me. Oh, God, what am I ever going to do?" she cried out in her head, not wanting to take her eyes off her parents, now situated in the dirt.

"Avril?" she heard again, not knowing or caring what came next. Looking up at the priest, she stared past him, unseeing him. "What the hell do you want?" She reflected. "Can't you leave me alone?"

"Avril?"

"Would you care to say a few words?" she thought she heard him say. "Fuck no. I don't want to say a few words. I want them back. That's what I want."

"Avril?"

"WHAT?" her yelling, bouncing around inside her head.

The priest faded in the distance while she stared at the coffin lids just visible over the edge of the graves.

"Avril?" she heard with a note of concern from the tone.

"Concern?" she thought. "These fucking assholes didn't care about her. They only cared that her parents were dead and they could all make more money with them gone."

"Avril!" She heard again, only this time, from far away but suddenly racing towards her.

"Are you alright?" She heard again, only this time, realizing that she had been dreaming. Sir was trying to wake her. Her dream fading, she opened her watery eyes.

"Are you okay? You were crying in your sleep."

Looking through moist eyes, unable to focus, she tied to answer through a sore throat.

"Yes, Sir. Sorry. I was dreaming."

"That much I figured, about what? What made you so sad that you cried in your sleep?"

"Sir, ah, well, the dream is fading, but I was dreaming about the death of my parents."

"Tell me about it."

"Yes, Sir. Though I would rather not if that is alright with you."

"No, it's not alright. Tell me."

"Yes, Sir. Please just bear with me. My throat is very sore, and I'm hoarse. Even now, I'm struggling. It hurts to talk, after all that went on last night."

"Well, I'm not surprised. You did exercise your vocal cords during our session. We'll do something about that over food. In the meantime, tell me about your dream."

"Yes, Sir. Well, it was a dream about the burial of my parents. I remember the day, but not because I remember what happened. I remember it from how I felt. I was standing at the foot of the coffins, just as they lowered them into the ground. I was surrounded by dozens of people, almost all of whom I didn't know or cared to know. I assume my parents worked with them."

She paused for a bit as if to collect her thoughts.

"The funny thing was, none seemed saddened by their death. They almost seemed happy about it. They seemed to believe with them gone, there were openings for advancement and making more money. They already had more than they could spend, and yet, they wanted more. I remember thinking at the time; they were greedy sons of bitches."

Avril paused again, staring at the ceiling above their bed. A bed she often shared with Sir since that fateful day when she made her hated decision. While she accepted her situation, she hated it as well. She still didn't have a choice in how her life progressed. He continued to tell her what to do, when to do it, and punish her if she didn't live up to his expectations.

It all might have been better if he listed every one of his expectations in the rule book. While there were hundreds of rules laid out in the book, Avril had come to learn that it wasn't all that comprehensive. Frankly, he expected more things from her not specified in the rule book. In so many ways, she hated him for making her decide her fate. She hated that he had made her choose to live or die, and to live, she had to learn and do despicable things.

"And?" she heard, breaking her out of her daydream.

"Oh, yes, I got lost in my thoughts." She croaked, adding "Sir" only after she realized she had left it off. No need for any additional punishment.

"Apparently. Go on, please."

"Surrounded by these awful, greedy people, I couldn't look at them. Not wanting to look at their coffins dropping into the ground, I looked upwards. I saw sunlight streaming through the trees. It was almost as if my parents were speaking to me, the light sparkling through water droplets. At the time, I couldn't hear the message. I only remember feeling their presence. In the dream, I think I finally started hearing the message. Only, I still can't seem to decipher it. I only know it filled me with pain and anguish, and the sunlight seemed to give me joy and hope."

"So why were you crying?"

Rolling onto her side, supporting her head on her bent arm, she tried to focus on him. With her other arm, absently caressing her tortured breast, she answered.

"I miss them, Sir. After all these years, I still miss them. At the time, I didn't know how I was going to live without them. I thought I might die. Even now, I still think that I can't live without them. We were close, and they taught me so much. I miss them, that's all. Standing there at the gravesite, amongst those strangers, they were the only ones I truly loved. Everyone else, well, they didn't seem to matter."

"I am sorry for your loss." Sir told her. "However, you do know that there is someone who does care for you."

Giving a half-hearted smile, Avril looked into his eyes. "Yes, Sir. I do."

"Good, then get up. Breakfast will be ready in thirty minutes. Don't be late."

"Yes, Sir," she said, throwing the covers from her legs. Giving him a show, she slowly rotated her body, swinging her heels over the side of the bed, and stood up. Sliding up to him, she reached out and passionately kissed him.

"Whew!" He replied, after being released from her embrace. "After all this time, I still love your kisses."

"Thank you, Sir. I'll be ready on time. In the private dining room, I presume." Avril said, strolling to her room and en-suite.

"Yes, Avril, and Avril?"

Turning towards him, she waited.

"My marks look lovely on you."

"Thank you, Sir. I trust you will have that pleasure for days to come." She said, resuming her progress to her room.

Sir watched her disappear as she stepped through the doorway from his room on the way to hers. As her ass vanished from view, stripped with his caning marks, he felt his chest tighten, in awe. Soon, he figured, he would know whether she was the one, the one to carry on his future.

Stepping into her en-suite, Avril first took the opportunity to look at herself in the full-length mirror, postponing her much needed bladder relief. Rotating back and forth as someone getting ready for a date, she inspected the damage. Sir striped her body last night, leaving his imprints all over her chest and torso, as well as her back, bottom, and legs. The marks left dark red complaints of raised welts that seemed to float over her skin. Dragging her fingertips across them, she recalled every impact, resulting in either horrified screams or lasting whimpers.

However, as she caressed the welts, she also recalled the tenderness he had shown her, stroking her with a bit of rabbit fur, cooling the injuries. After he finished caning her, he used a soothing cream on her welts to heal and soothe their heat. It was a surprising concern for her well-being. Usually, he left her to recover on their own, suffering alone. As the evening progressed, he touched her in all sorts of places, and not necessarily in her erogenous zones, further embellishing her pleasure. She knew he eventually fucked her, but she didn't remember the acts. She only remembered the joy as she went over an orgasmic cliff and soared to ever-higher heights of ecstasy.

Recalling the session as she relieved herself, she was at a loss about reconciling the two sides of the experience. In one case, she felt agonies that would have been enough to kill her before her taking. In the other circumstance, she relished what Sir did to her, asking for more even as the night turned into morning.

With the pressing business resolved, Avril removed her heels, started the shower, and jumped in. Instantly, she regretted not checking the temperature. Even warm, the heat cut through the welts, causing her to yelp.

Adjusting the taps to a cooler temperature, she finished washing and shampooing her hair. Not wasting time, she finished quickly, dried her hair, and redressed, putting on her super-high heels sporting the three crystals she earned all those months ago. Since then, he had not deemed her worthy of a new gem. There were days that she wondered what she would have to do to earn a fourth. Often enough, she didn't want to know.

After putting on her makeup, making sure not to cover or embellish his marks, she carefully checked the results. Satisfied, she hurried back to Sir's room and made the bed. She stepped into the dining room with time to spare, stopping inside the door frame and taking a sexy pose, modeling for him.

Chapter Thirteen

A nothing blackness enveloped her as she slowly recovered from the electricity scrambling of her brain. She felt a vague sense of moment as darkness slowly dissolved into a grey mist. Shadows seem to bounce around in her field of vision, yet, these shadows remain unresolved. They were blurs. She sensed them but right now, it was difficult to focus on them. Besides, she was tired. It was taking all of her effort to concentrate. Closing her eyes, she returned to her blissful state of unconsciousness.

***

The next time she sensed something, she was in the midst of an incredible dream. She was lying in bed, a man satisfying her. She sensed his need as he planted his mouth between her wide-open legs and lapped her pussy with relish. It didn't take long before she felt her rocking in time with his oral attention. In her dream, she sensed her building passion, hoping he would soon penetrate her and bring her the ecstasy she craved.

As she dreamt, he sat up and positioned himself between her legs.

"Ah," she dreamed, "he's about to fuck me. I can feel his heat. I can feel my need."

As he leaned forward, she yearned for his shaft to find its target, her mouth opened with a breathless need.

"Yes, there he is, coming over, on top of me. Just about there, big boy. Give it to me!"

Suddenly, pain shot through her, nudging her from her dream. Her head was on fire, the pain awful. Lightning jumped around in her head and behind her eyelids. Her skull felt like it was about to explode.

"Oh, no!" Jenni screamed, suddenly waking up and forcefully sitting up.

Her head whacked against an obstruction, preventing her from sitting up. It fell back on whatever it was that she was lying.

"Ow!" "Ow!" "Ow!" she yelled over and over again.

Reaching up with her hand, she rubbed it where she hit her head. It was tender, but there's no bump, just a massive headache. In thinking about it, the trouble was there before she hurt her head—no doubt about it.

***

Opening her eyes, she looked about, seeing an out of focus world around her. Everything was a bit blurry.

"Oh, God, it stinks. What the hell is that smell?" she asked no one in particular.

Reaching up carefully with her hands, she touched the obstruction above her head. It was smooth and felt like her bathtub at home. It was transparent, as she could make out shapes around her. Forms she could not identify were all around her. She decided to worry about that later.

"What the hell? Where the hell am I?"

Frantically, she started flailing her hands about, feeling the acrylic all around her. Eventually, she realized it was a box. She was inside a box.

"What the fuck?"

Sealed in, it was nearly the size of her body. There was no room to move about, sit up, or even scratch between her toes if she needed to. It was small, just big enough to keep her.

"A box? A container?" she realized. "What the hell happened to me?"

Bouncing her head back and forth, looking up, down, and sideways, it was all the same. All around her, solid plastic walls closed in around her. Not to make matters worse, but it was moving, and she was riding along with it, inside this thing, this box.

She felt it tilt forward, backward, and even sideways at times. Not drastically but enough so that she felt nauseous at the movement. Nausea compounded her headache, and she felt her gut retch. Swallowing hard, she managed to keep it down, hopefully for good.

That was when she realized she was naked, from head to foot. She wasn't wearing a stitch of clothing. Clawing with her painted nails, she tried finding an edge that she could use to open the damned box. After several minutes of trying without success, she dropped, exhausted at the effort.

Besides, there was this severe headache, and her body's desire to retch, threatening to dump the entire contents of her stomach to – where?

"Oh my God, please don't let me throw up?"

A minute or so later that is just what happened. The box suddenly bounced a bit more than usual, and Jenni's stomach decided it was time to leap for her throat. Turning her body as best as she could onto her side, she retched, bringing bile and burning acid up her throat and out of her mouth. It sprayed the inside of the box, smearing the transparent plastic, and even worse, smelling up her small enclosure even more. Just the smell seemed to propel her into more retching.

Spitting the rest of the nasty fluid from her mouth, she suddenly wished for water to wash the inside of her mouth and throat of the burning acid. Making spit as best as she could, she used it to coat the inside of her mouth and spit it out to her side.

Groaning, "Oh, God. What is going on here? Where am I?" she asked herself repeatedly.

Leaning back and closing her eyes, she hoped and wished this was all a dream.

"Nope, it was not a dream. This is real, and I am in big trouble."

Over the next half hour or so, she tried to kick at the plastic enclosure. There was nothing to be said, nor was there any progress in her efforts. All she got was a sore ankle when she accidentally hit her foot at an odd angle. She did, however, find a pair of one-inch holes near her feet. Feeling them with her toes, she could almost feel the air movement from them. She figured out that these kept her alive and allowed her to breathe. Right now, though, she was too distraught to think about them much at all.

Resigned, all she could do now was to lie back and wait until something happened. What that might be, was beyond her. All she knew was she was powerless, trapped inside this plastic box, inside a moving vehicle. From the low drone of engines, she thought it might be a plane. A truck or train didn't make that sound. Coupled with the occasional bouncing and sliding left or right, it had to be a plane.

"Oh, God, where am I being taken?" she pleaded to no one.

What was worse, she had to pee. "How long could I hold it?"

***

Hours later, staring at the plastic shroud above her and trying to sleep, time passed slowly. She tried to whittle away the time by figuring out what to do when she got out of her acrylic prison. She spent much of it squeezing her knees together, trying to hold her bladder. Eventually, nature won out, and now she was swimming in a pool of her piss, swaying back and forth, getting into her hair, and coating her entire body. Since then, having relieved herself once, it didn't matter how many more times she let it flow when the urge presented itself. After all, how much worse was it going to get?

So far, she didn't know what she was going to do. Jenni also tried humming some of the tunes her mother sang to her when she was a little girl. She found that hard because as much as she wanted to get out from underneath her tyranny and live on her own, she missed those sweet moments of tenderness her mother deigned upon her little girl. Tears fell from her eyes.

***

A jarring bounced her up, almost hitting her head on the top of the box. As she recovered, Jenni realized that the plane had just landed, and the roar of the engines assaulted her ears, braking as it slowed down. Her body slid to the bottom of the box. It took all her effort to keep from being squeezed into a tight little ball and drowning in her bodily fluids sloshing around her.

Several minutes later, the plane rolled to a stop, and the engines stopped. A blissful silence enveloped her, which did not come as a relief. Instead, Jenni anxiously began looking around her. Except for loud clanking every so often, presumably the plan's doors opening, nothing happened that directly affected her.

For the longest time, she laid there, wondering what was to come. The answer remained elusive for what felt like hours. As she set out to wait, she detected a sweet, aromatic scent in the air she was breathing. Grateful for the relief from the stench of her own body, she allowed herself a small smile. In moments, everything went dark and quiet.

Waking once more, she cautiously opened her eyes. The scene outside the box had changed.

"Huh?" she thought to herself. "Where am I now? Did I fall asleep? But … how could I. That's all I've done all these hours in this damn box."

Jenni continued to wonder what the hell was going on. Once again, she resigned herself to wait until they, whoever they were, let her out of the box. Looking around, she appeared to be in a large, brightly lit, tiled room.

Metal pipes were sticking out of the walls with what might be metal versions of a lily. They were high on both sides of her. She estimated that they were well above her head should she be standing against the wall, "A shower room?" she wondered.

She noticed what seemed to be a garden hose coiled up at the end of the long room behind her head. That was when she saw the door. A man was standing in it. Then she noticed the shadow covering her eyes. Looking at its source, she noticed the woman with long red hair looking down at her.

The woman was stunning. Except for a pair of high heels, she was as naked as she was. On second thought, she wasn't just stunning. She was gorgeous. Her long red hair stood out against her pale skin and tapered down to a stunning pair of cobalt blue stilettos. If there was one thing Jenni knew, she knew her shoes, and the pair this broad was wearing was unmistakably custom-made and very expensive.

However, the woman did not capture her interest very long. Standing next to her was a man. It was evident to Jenni that he was the one in charge. The woman stood submissively beside him and was intently listening as he spoke to her.

Jenni could not hear what they said, but eventually, she realized that the man was giving the woman instructions. Her hypothesis was confirmed a couple of minutes later when the woman left only to return shoeless. In her hand, she held a tool in two hands, almost as if she didn't know what to do with it. However, that was not the case. Stepping up to the plastic box, the woman placed the tool against the corners and activated it.

Instantly, a radiant heat emanated from the tool, and the seam between the wall and the top parted. As the woman worked, Jenni could tell from her face's crunching that she smelled Jenni's body odors. Jenni figured that she must have gotten used to the smell, but this new woman tried hard not to breathe as she worked her way around the top of the box.

When she returned to where she had started, the woman lifted the box lid and laid it off to the side. Jenni immediately tried to jump up and run. However, her body failed her. She found her legs weak and barely capable of supporting her weight. Running was indeed out of the question.

"STOP!" Jenni heard screaming at her.

Surprising her, it didn't come from the man. He stood mute. No, instead, it came from the woman, a woman such as her. In shock, she looked over at her in disbelief. That was when she noticed two things about the woman. First, piercing her nipples were metal rings. Jenni had seen nipple piercings before, but never ones that seemed to have no beginning nor endpoints. It looked to her as a continuous loop of metal, without start and end. Later, as she showered, she reflected upon the rings wondering how that was possible.

The other thing she noticed was a ring of more metal encircling her neck. It looked like solid white gold. Somehow, Jenni didn't believe that and assumed that it was something else.

"Get out." The woman commanded her with an air of authority.

Nodding, Jenni carefully stepped out of the box and stood there on wobbly knees. "Damn, what's the matter with me?" she asked herself. "Why am I so unsteady standing here?"

She didn't have too much time to ponder the question. The woman shoved her to the wall and made her stand under one of the showerheads.

"Wash," she spoke harshly to her as the barely warm water flowed down from the showerhead.

Looking over at the wall, she noticed a bar of soap and a scrub brush.

"Do a good job, or I'll do it for you," she said, pointing to the rough scrub brush.

Nodding, Jenni picked up the soap and began washing the dirt and grime from her body. She worked quickly, but when she thought she finished, the woman snapped.

"I said, wash!" Her tone and inflection reinforced that the woman was not happy with Jenni's washing techniques.

"Alright, alright," Jenni yelled back, only to be rewarded with a backhand across her face. Jenni was stunned and fell to the shower floor.

"Get up, and wash. Do not speak unless I permit you to speak. Do not make me repeat myself."

Jenni was about to retort, as she rubbed her hand against her bruised cheek, but thought better of it. Nodding, she slowly stood up and resumed the washing. Thinking she was clean when looking over at the bitch, she knew that this woman disagreed with her. She continued washing.

"Now, wash that grimy hair of yours and make it shine," the woman said, handing her a bottle of shampoo.

Later, when she was finally allowed to stop washing, the woman told her. "Listen, bitch, you now belong to me, and I belong to him." she started, indicating the man standing in the doorway. "Therefore, you belong to him. Anything he tells you to do, anything, you do it. Just as anything I tell you to do, you do it. Nod, do not speak if you understand."

Wide-eyed in disbelief, Jenni stood mute.

"I asked you if you understand. Do you? Do not make me ask again."

Jenni nodded, if ever so slightly.

"Good, now that we have that straight, I want you to know, you will never return to the life you left behind. You will never return to that world. You now belong to me, bought, and paid. Do not question me. Do not question him. You will refer to him only as Sir and to me as Ma'am. Every time you speak to either of us, you will add our titles to your response. Do I make myself clear?"

Jenni didn't quite comprehend what the woman was saying to her, and she took too long to nod. Her delay rewarded her with another backhand against her cheek, and she crashed to the floor once again.

"Stand up, bitch. Hmmm, perhaps that will be your new name from now on. I'll have to think about it. Bitch, hmmm, I like it. Until I come up with a better one, that will be your name from now on. Now, I said, stand up bitch."

Deferring to the woman, Jenni looked down at the shower tiles on the floor and slowly stood up.

"Now bitch, nod if you understand. You are now my property. I will use or abuse as I see fit."

Jenni slowly nodded, though she almost opened her mouth in retort. She snapped it closed.

"Good bitch, you're learning. Slowly, of course, but I'll make sure you comply. If not, your time on this planet will be short – very short indeed."

Jenni almost couldn't believe her ears. "Would she kill me if I didn't comply? Oh, shit."

"Ah, I see you just realized the ramifications of any disobedience. Yes bitch, if you resist, if you complain, if you try to escape, I will kill you. The sooner you accept that the better off your life will be."

Jenni stood mute, a furious stare drilling holes into the woman's eyes.

"Now, come with me. It's time to finish your entry into this house. After that, I will begin your orientation into what we expect of you in the coming days and weeks, assuming you last that long."

As the woman walked towards the door, the man stood aside. He then handed her a wand of some sort, with two small metal prongs on its end. It looked nasty, for sure.

Chapter Fourteen

Drying last night's dishes, concern for her sister occupied Heather's mind. She had been off all day, bothered by a dark, nagging sensation. The hole she felt deep inside her belly felt heavy, almost as she had a brick sitting in her gut. She didn't like the feeling, that was for sure. She couldn't get it out of her system. Something was wrong, and she didn't know what it was.

Heather had left her a couple of messages, but so far, Rachel hadn't called back. She wished Rachel would call back. It was unlike her not to call her. They spoke every day, especially since she had saved her life with the gift of bone marrow. That was indeed a gift from God, and Heather knew in every cell of her body, she could never thank her enough for her gift of life. Lying in her hospital bed, she had sworn to cherish her sister, to love, be there, and protect her with her life if necessary. Before her transplant, she had taken her big sister for granted, no longer. Since that day, they talked every day and saw each other as much as possible. Her precious gift gave her life, and she intended to honor the gift she could never repay.

As she put the last of the dishes away, a cold chill suddenly raced through her body. Goosebumps instantly popped up and down her arms. She shivered, and the glass she was holding bounced off the counter and crashed onto the floor. Glass shards scattered all around. Something was wrong. Something was terribly wrong with Rachel, and she was in trouble. Heather knew it. Somehow, she knew something was wrong but didn't know how or what to do about it.

Picking up the phone, ignoring the broken glass at her feet, she dialed Rachel's number. It rang several times before going to voicemail, yet again.

"Rachel, call me. Please, I'm worried. Is everything alright? I feel something is wrong. Call me back, right away, alright?"

Putting the phone down, Heather then picked it up again and texted.

[Heather] Rachel, where are you? Are you alright? I'm worried. Call ME!

After she put the phone back down, she turned and leaned against the counter, deep in worried thought. She felt it. Something was wrong.

Not knowing what to do, she cleaned up the broken glass, plugged her phone in to charge, and went to bed. Tossing all night long, she didn't get much rest. Usually, she could sleep soundly, unaware of her surroundings, and not remembering her dreams until the alarm woke her the next morning. Not this night, instead her dreams were filled with night terrors and screams. She felt a painful ache in her chest and anger spewing from her thoughts.

Heather had been awake for at least an hour when the sun began to peek above the horizon. Her mind racing with worry; she was unable to sleep. Her night terrors left an indelible impression upon her mood. Getting up, she took care of business in the bathroom, but not before checking her phone to see if an overnight message had come in … still nothing.

Feeling clean and her bladder empty, but not refreshed, she got dressed and checked her phone for the umpteenth time this morning, hoping that something had come in, but still nothing.

Determined, she got her purse and keys. "Alright, enough is enough. I'm going over there." Heather mumbled to herself. Rushing out the door, she hurried to her car. Throwing her purse onto the passenger seat of the car, she climbed in and got behind the wheel. A minute later, she was racing down the street on her way to Rachels.

Half a block behind her, a black sedan pulled out from a side street and followed at a discreet distance.

Heather, oblivious to everything around her, hurried on to her sisters, determined to find Rachel and ease the ache in her gut. Every time she came to a stoplight, she banged on the steering wheel, frustrated at the delay. One time, Heather almost ran a red light, judging that there was enough time to beat the yellow before it changed. At the last moment, realizing she wouldn't make it, she slammed on the brake, stopping just in the nick of time.

Five minutes later, she pulled up at Rachel's apartment building and raced inside. The black sedan parked nearby but far enough away to remain unobserved. The occupant picked up a phone and reported in, asking for instructions.

Racing inside, Heather knocked incessantly on Rachel's door, rapping as loudly as she could. Without waiting for a response, she took out her key to Rachel's apartment and unlocked the door. Stepping in, she called out Rachel's name.

"Rachel! Are you here?"

"Rachel?" she cried out louder.

Turning on the lights, she walked about the apartment, looking for her sister. It was soon apparent that the apartment was empty. Nothing seemed out of place. The bed was unkempt and seemingly slept in. Her luggage from the trip rested on the floor to one side. Checking the bags, she figured that Rachel hadn't unpacked yet. All of her things were still folded neatly inside the suitcase, and the carry-on bag looked like she opened and emptied much of it. All in all, everything seemed reasonable to her.

"Okay, she got home, alright. She did say she had finished for the day on her business trip and was looking forward to returning home. So, it appears she made it back. That confirms the text message I got from her indicating that she arrived safely and went straight to bed.

Looking around, she didn't find her purse or phone, so apparently, she had those with her. Nothing seemed out of place. It just seemed to her that Rachel got home, crawled into bed, and fell asleep. Then, after waking, she got up, dressed, and went out. She even had her dirty travel clothes in the hamper. It all looked normal to her.

"How come then, she didn't call me the next day or return my calls?" she wondered.

Looking around for a note, she found none. Nor did she find Rachel's purse or phone. Nothing seemed out of place, and yet, something was wrong. Heather knew it. She just knew it.

Bewildered, Heather sat down on the living room sofa, not knowing what to do. Reflecting on the past two days, she discovered nothing that stood out that gave her any indication of something might be wrong. But her gut was telling her otherwise. Staring aimlessly around the room, Heather couldn't get the feeling of dread sitting in the pit of her stomach.

After a half-hour, she got up, found the notepad on Rachel's kitchen counter, and wrote a note to contact her as soon as possible. Heading for the door, she turned and looked back before shaking her head and locking the door behind her. Her head down, her hands stuffed in her pockets, she made her way back to her car.

Reaching into her purse, she pulled out her phone and called Rachel's number. Once again, she got no answer, going to voicemail after several rings. Leaving a panicking message, she then sent off a text message, more to ease her growing panic.

"Okay, Heather." She asked herself. "Where would she go first thing in the morning? Did she have to go to work today? No. This was Sunday. She flew in Friday night, and they didn't expect her at work until Monday. So, where would she go on a Sunday morning? Breakfast perhaps? Without me? I suppose it's possible, but come on, we haven't seen each other in a week. Going out for breakfast would have been a perfect time to reconnect."

Looking around, she didn't see Rachel's car, giving further evidence that she had gone out. Driving off, she still didn't notice the black sedan following well back behind her. Heather headed to their favorite breakfast place. Twenty minutes later, she drove into the parking lot but didn't see her car. Undaunted, she went inside and looked around. Disappointed, Heather started to leave when one of the servers asked if she wanted a table.

"Ah, no, thank you. Actually, I was looking for my sister. Have you seen her today?"

"Rachel? Ah, no. I haven't. Sorry. Is anything wrong?"

"Honestly, I don't know. Thank you. If you see her, would you please ask her to give me a call?"

"Sure, hun. I sure will."

Returning to her car, Heather went to the next three restaurants they tended to frequent, all with the same results. No one had seen her sister.

"So now what," Heather asked herself, picking up her phone and calling Rachel's number only to be disappointed once again.

Dropping her forehead onto the back of her hands clutching the top of the steering wheel, Heather seemed to break down just a bit more, concern shifting into the realm of worry and terror.

"Where are you, Rachel?"

Off in the distance, a car sat idling, the soft whisper of exhaust barely visible exiting the tailpipe. Sitting behind the wheel, the driver picked up a phone, dialed a number, and put it to her ear.

"Subject is searching for her sister. She's made the rounds of numerous restaurants, not staying to eat, but rather talking briefly to the staff, and leaving minutes later."

"Stay on her and report anything significant. Don't let her see you. We'll send backup to alternate surveillance. You are team lead."

"I understand."

"Backup will report to you within the hour."

"Very good. Is there anything else?"

"Stay out of sight and unobserved. Report anything significant or out of the ordinary."

"Will do," she added as she disconnected the call and replaced her phone in her jacket pocket.

Staring at the subject, she couldn't help but feel sorry for the girl. Her efforts were for naught. She was on the snatch team and knew that the sister was half a world away by now, never to return. It was curious why they selected this particular girl for the taking. Tasking her with taking that girl was out of character from other subjects. She didn't get it, but then again, they didn't pay her to speculate. They paid her well to do as they asked and not ask questions.

Usually, those she took were alone in the world, without family or friends worrying about their disappearance. This girl seemed to have connections. In the last twenty-four hours, she had discovered that Rachel was part of a loving, intimate family. Not only that, they were a well-connected, influential family. Her father was a big-wig in the American government, with ties to the Justice Department. Her gut told her that taking the girl had been a risky venture. She hoped it was worth the risk. She could only trust her superiors that it was.

Noticing that the sister was backing out of her parking space, she readied herself to follow. Where she would go next, she wondered.

Chapter Fifteen

Sitting in her room, at her drawing table, Avril was working on a new portrait. The composition was of Sir and herself. She's naked as usual, and he was standing behind her, a hand conveniently resting on her shoulder, caressing her neck. It's a bit of subtle symbolism that one day, she will die by his hands. Hopefully, it's subtle enough that he won't get to see it. Even if he does, she knows it won't matter. He may even like it better because of the imagery.

"Avril, attend me."

"Yes, Sir," Avril answered, her introspection broken by the interruption. Standing, she briefly looked at the portrait before turning towards her owner.

Following him out of the door, he led her to the main level. Stopping at the door that led to the lower levels, he turned to her.

"Avril, there is a new arrival. I acquired this one, especially for you. Unlike Misty, this one will be yours to care for, torment, take your pleasure from, and ultimately kill. Do you understand?"

"Yes, Sir, I understand."

"Good. Her name is Jenni. Unlike you, she did not go through the training facility. She has not had the pleasure of the guard's orientation, gotten her nipples pierced, or watched someone die as a demonstration of their power. I had her transported directly to me, and now I give her to you."

Avril nodded; not sure she wanted the girl.

"Look, you wanted to become a member. We negotiated a contract, and you're going to live up to it. It's the next step towards achieving your goal."

"Yes, Sir, I understand." Avril nodded.

"The girl is still secured in the box. When you go in there, you will cut her loose, get her cleaned up, and then orient her to her new role. That means heels, nipple rings, and of course, her collar. You will give her all of them, explain the rules, and keep her in line. Then, before you leave her in her cell, you will make sure she understands who the boss is, just as it happened to you. Got it?"

"Yes, Sir, I'm to clean her up and orient her. I will make sure she knows to wear the heels at all times, and I will be welding her nipple rings into place and putting her collar on her neck."

"And then?"

"I will teach her a lesson, her first painful one."

"We understand each other."

"Sir, if I may?"

"Go ahead."

"The collar, Sir, I don't know how it works," she asked. "How do I secure it around her neck?"

"Avril, that's an excellent question. I will give you the collar at the appropriate time. It is self-locking. Just snap it into place, and it is permanently locked. As soon as it snaps into place, it activates and connects to the house and my security system. That is all you need to know. Does that answer your question?"

"Yes, Sir, thank you, Sir."

"Ready?"

"Yes, Sir."

And with that, Sir turned and opened the door. Walking down into the depths under the estate, Sir turned to the unpleasant end of the hallway and away from her original living quarters. He led her to the large shower/killing room. The wet room made it easier to clean up blood and guts after he killed his victims. She had the dubious honor of hosing the place down in recent months.

As they walked, Avril thought about her time back at the training facility. It was her first prison after they took her, but Sir had referred to it as such. She hated her time there, as well as every moment since. As cruel and sadistic Sir was, those guards were pure evil. They took real joy in hurting those that went through the facility. Jenni was fortunate to be spared that time of fear, pain, and torment.

For Avril, her time there was less about the pain and more about the fear. Her vivid memories did little to dull the feelings still flowing every cell in her body. Her nightmares consumed her nights, as do her recollections throughout the day. She was glad that poor Jenni had avoided that fate but saddened that instead of a bunch of nameless guards abusing her, she would be the one, the only one to hurt this poor girl.

"Avril?"

It took a moment for Avril to realize that Sir was trying to get her attention.

"Oh, sorry, Sir, I was preparing myself," she covered.

"After you …"

"Yes, Sir," she answered and stepped into the wet room.

The room was brightly lit, with light from all sides leaving little opportunity to hide in the shadows. The box in the middle drew her eyes immediately. There was little else to capture her attention. She had seen the room often enough, and scrubbing blood from the tile joints revolted her.

Dumb to it all, all she could do was focus on the girl secured in the box. Two hoses still connected it to a nearby wall, providing fresh air to the sleeping girl. From experience, she knew that the air pumped into the plastic crate could be tainted with a mild anesthetic to keep the occupant quiet and subdued. Avril stood there a bit, studying the unfortunate girl. The trouble was, if it weren't Jenni, it would have been someone else.

Studying the scene, memories of her own experience in the box hit Avril. She remembered waking up in a near panic. Others around her indeed panicked, and her gut convulsed. She felt as if a circus was doing somersaults in her belly. Her knees felt weak, and she almost slipped to the floor. The feelings of helplessness nearly overwhelmed her.

She needed to take control of herself. "Come on, Avril. Steady now," she told herself. Taking a deep breath, one that she didn't care whether Sir noticed or not, she threw her shoulders back, emitting an authoritative posture of confidence.

"She's for me, Sir?" Avril commented. "She's beautiful."

"Yes, my dear Avril. She's all yours. Enjoy yourself."

"Thank you, Sir."

"You remember what to do?"

"Yes, Sir," she said before walking over to the box and stealing a look. Walking around the sleeping girl, she studied her carefully. She was short and small and weighed almost nothing. Her long blonde hair was her most prominent feature. She was filthy, of course, but Avril expected that. She had streaks of mascara and dried tears down her cheeks. She was lying in a pool of body fluids. Avril wondered how long she laid in that foul crate.

Unsurprisingly, the girl had woken up at some point and panicked. The scrapes on her knuckles confirmed her suspicions. Unconscious, the girl's features looked peaceful. Avril knew that would soon change. By the end, nightmares would consume the girl's dreams. Only her death would resolve that.

After disconnecting the hoses, she stood watch, waiting for her to wake up. A few minutes later, the girl stirred. A moment later, she opened her eyes and began looking around. She quickly found Sir standing by the door. However, Sir would not stand for having the girl focus on him. Instead, he wanted the girl to focus on Avril, to bond, so to speak with her. With a slight shake of her head, she stepped forward. Immediately, Jenni turned and looked at her. Concern written all over Jenni's face; it softened ever so slightly when she saw Avril.

It didn't take long to free her from the box, and almost immediately, she tried to bolt for the door. In her weakened state, the girl's legs failed her, and she fell back into the box, splashing in her piss. After leading the woman to the shower, she had her wash. However, she talked back to her, forcing Avril to take back control immediately. Backhanding her across the face, Jenni dropped to the floor, rubbing her bruised cheek. In that single moment, Jenni knew that she didn't have a friend in Avril.

After she cleaned herself up, Avril began her job of orienting Jenni to her new life. Using her experiences at the training facility, she started breaking in the girl. Directing Jenni to walk past Sir into the next room, she had her sit down on a stable, rough wooden chair.

"Do you understand that I now own you?" Avril barked. Inside she was a mess, but outwardly, it was the only way, so she kept her composure. Jenni nodded.

"Stay," Avril commanded.

Taking the new collar sitting on a nearby table, Avril fingered it, wishing she didn't have to put the terrible device around the girl's neck. Memories of her collar snapping around her throat flooded her thoughts. The meaning of the thing, the pain it could cause, the agony she felt, and the symbolism it represented filled her with a hate she never thought she would ever feel.

Fingering this simple piece of metal, she rolled it between her fingertips. Tossing it in her hand, she knew what she had to do. Resolved, she stood behind the girl, placed the collar around her neck, and snapped it into position.

"Do you know what this means? This collar I've put around your neck?" she asked after walking around to face the unfortunate woman.

Jenni shook her head.

"It's a collar. It represents your life. It also signifies that I own you. It binds you to me and this house. Should you try to escape and manage to make it to a door or window, this collar will activate. If you're lucky, it will only immobilize you. If you're not, well, you won't live to realize it. It will kill you with an electrical shock, powerful enough to kill a cow. You, bitch, are my cow to serve my needs and my desires. I own you, and I will do with you as I please. Is that understood?"

Jenni was now crying. "Please, don't kill me. Just let me go. I won't tell anyone. Please. I promise."

After another backhand across the mouth, "What did I tell you about speaking out of turn? Did I permit you to speak?" Avril demanded.

The girl's head was resting on her chest, tears streaming down her cheeks and landing on the tops of her breasts. She shook her head.

"That's right. I didn't. You won't live long if you continue to misbehave."

Standing back, Avril walked around to the girl's back and composed herself. She knew that she couldn't let Jenni see her softer side. The side that prayed that it would soon all be over. She needed to compose herself for what was to come.

Walking around to her side, she squatted down, and using the straps attached to the chair, secured the girl to the heavy chair. After strapping down her legs, arms, and lap, Avril pulled over the wheeled cart with the piercing needles, rings, forceps, and welding torch.

Picking up the forceps, Avril grabbed a nipple and clamped it between its jaws. Jenni looked down at what she was doing and then started to whimper. She began to open her mouth to beg, but a quick look from Avril shut her down.

Pulling the forceps, stretching her nipple and breast out and away from the girl's body, she took a needle and shoved it through, punching a neat hole. The girl yelled.

"Oh, it's not that bad. You want bad? You'll soon get that." Avril taunted.

Threading the ring through the hole, she repeated the process with the other nipple. Then, using a pair of pliers, she closed the gap and welded them closed. Jenni screamed. Avril knew precisely why. The memory of the burning heat searing her tender flesh was still fresh in her mind. With a cup of ice, she cooled the red-hot metal by placing it against her inflamed breast. Before long, the girl's crying slowed to a whimpering.

Standing upright, Avril pushed the table away, where it rolled to a stop near the wall.

"Keep them clean while they heal, simple soap and water four times a day until I tell you differently. You get me?"

Unstrapping the girl as she nodded her agreement, Avril grabbed her by the arm and walked her out the door. Sir followed behind. In no time at all, Jenni was in her cell, having read the note on her mattress, wearing her training heels, and sporting several new welts on her ass from the belting Avril had just given her. Leaving her alone, Avril returned to Sir's side for his analysis of the events.

"Very well done, my dear Avril, you may have what it takes to gain membership. However, I did notice a couple of times where you were hiding your true emotions. You don't like what you're doing to the girl, do you? Don't answer that. I know you didn't. You're torn and conflicted. You'll work it out and join the Consortium, or you will continue as my property, to do with as I please. You're choice."

Avril nodded, "Yes, Sir. I understand."

"I'll do better. It's just that I have never done this on my own, without you guiding me, training me. I don't know if I can do it."

"Well, you'll figure it out, one way or another. From my perspective, I see it within you to do it. Once you get past your first kill, it will get easier."

"Kill Sir?"

"Yes, Avril, you must kill before they consider you as a candidate for membership. Whether it's this girl or another one, you must do it. Besides, you know as well as I do that one way or another, Jenni will die. Just as the rest of the stable of prey dies, either by my hands or yours."

"Yes, Sir, I get that."

"I know you do. Now, should we have a bit of dinner before you take your privilege with this new one? You best take it tonight because tomorrow, I'll be taking my privilege, and she may not be in any condition afterward to attend to your needs."

"Sir, you wish to fuck her or hurt her?"

"Well, fuck her for sure. Hurting her will come later."

"Yes, I see. Sir, I think it would be best to work up an appetite before dinner. I wouldn't want dinner to slow me down."

"Brilliant, Avril. That's just what I would do. I'll leave you to it. Besides, I have one of my new acquisitions to break in before dinner. Any toys you need are in the cabinet over there. Just make sure she's properly secured at all times, not that she's going anywhere. You might want to make sure she knows just what that collar of hers can do."

"Yes, Sir, my thoughts exactly. How much time do I have to play with her?"

"Oh, three or four hours or so would be sufficient, I should think. All night if you want, I'm going to take her tomorrow. Make sure she knows you're giving her to me for the night. I'll let you know when I'm ready."

"Very good Sir, I'll see you tomorrow then."

Avril turned towards her prey for the night. She stood there many minutes staring at the girl. Jenni stood mute, an air of defiance in her posture mixed with disbelief and fear. The red marks from the earlier slapping still apparent on her face and chest, Jenni glared back at Avril. In many ways, Avril felt sorry for the girl. No one knew better than her what was to be Jenni's fate. There is no chance of escape for her, no chance whatsoever to regain her innocence and resume her old life. That, unfortunately, had already been taken from her forever, impossible to reclaim.

"So, you're going to kill me."

After a quick tilt of her head, Avril said. "Seems that way. I am sorry. I wish it weren't necessary."

"Why?"

"I've been asking that very question for two years now."

"Is that how long you've been here? I noticed you're wearing a collar similar to the one you put around my neck, and rings in your nipples are exactly like those you put into mine. That fucking hurt, you know."

"Oh, I know very well just how much it hurts. I assure you. This is just the beginning."

"Who is he?"

"He? He's your owner and master. He bought and paid for you. However, he transferred your ownership to me. In payment, he will take his pleasure from you."

"How?"

"How? Well, you're not going to like it."

"I don't like it now."

"Yes, I get your meaning. Well, it's like this. Sir will take his pleasure from your body."

"You mean he's going to fuck me?"

"Fuck you. Yes, but that is only a small part of the pleasure he will take from you. Fucking you is the easy part. The other pleasures he will take from you will be very different. You won't like it."

At that moment, the two women could hear the blood-curdling screams of another woman through the cell walls.

"Do you hear that?" Avril asked. "That is the kind of pleasure he will take from you. Blood-curdling screams of pain, anguish, and torment are his thing. He lives to hear his victims scream before he kills them. You and I are just one in a long string of victims he and his cronies take each year for their pleasures."

"And yet, you still live."

"I still wonder about that myself. I think Sir is in love with me."

"Really?" Jenni remarked in disbelief like some teenager.

Avril shrugged her shoulders. "Hmmm, yes, I don't know for certain, but it does seem that way. Still, I am his captive, just as you are."

"Has he taken his pleasure from you? I mean, has he made you scream in pain?"

"Oh, yes. So many times, I thought I was going to die. I've also seen him kill, first hand. He's brutal, but he can be tender as well."

"Tender? Really?"

"Oh, yes, his lovemaking skills were beyond compare. Before they took me, I slept with my fair share of men. None are in his league. Even before he came to love me, he was a powerful lover, capable of bringing me to such heights. Afterward, well, let's just say, I am overwhelmed and unable to stand for hours. My legs are shaky, and my body sings with a song that lasts for days."

"Hmmm … still, he's a brute. He tortures and kills people for sport."

"Oh, yes, that he does, quite regularly in fact. The one he's with right now will probably not survive to the morning."

"Oh," Jenni remarked under her breath. "Hey, did you have to strike me?"

"Yes, and I will hit you again and harder. I may even be the one that kills you."

"You?"

"Yes, Jenni, me … he's training me. I think he wants me to partner up with him, to be his companion and consort. I've negotiated an agreement that he will submit my application to join his Consortium as a full member."

"Wait, Consortium? There are more like him?"

"Oh, yes, at least a dozen that I have personally met. From what I have been able to figure out, there are at least a hundred full members and tens of thousands of operatives worldwide. They take thousands of people each year for their personal agendas, killing all of them a short time after taking them."

"Thousands? Each year?"

"Yes."

"All dead?"

"Almost all, some survive for a time acting as servants, but they never return to their old lives. Eventually, they, too, are killed."

"As you will too someday …"

"Yes, I expect so."

"So, what's next?"

"Next?" Avril responded. "Why, you fuck me, of course. You might as well enjoy it because tomorrow, you'll scream. Soon after that, you will die."

"And there's no escape, no way to get out of here?"

"Not that I can find, and I've been trying. As best as I can figure out, if you follow his rules to the letter, suffer, and survive his punishments, the longer you stay alive, as slim the odds are, there is a chance. All I can tell you is never to give up, never surrender. Suffer his torments and survive. He likes strong, determined women. The longer you give him that, the longer you will live."

"Then, I might as well as enjoy myself tonight, because tomorrow I may die. I will certainly suffer. I might as well have a happy memory to help me through it." Jenni said, smiling coyly.

"That's the spirit," Avril said. "But before we do, there's one thing you need to know. That's no ordinary collar around your neck. That's a shock collar, and I have the trigger." She said, opening the hand, showing the girl the small device with a single button on it. Her thumb hovered over it.

Jenni stared at it as Avril continued. "You should also know that this trigger only works on your collar. It will not affect mine. Not only that, every door and every window in this complex will trigger your collar merely by approaching it. Get to close, and it will cripple you with extreme pain. You will wish you were dead as your brain fries through electrocution. If you don't understand, you're about to."

As she finished her statement, she pressed the button, and Jenni screamed and fell to the ground. Her screams silenced as she hit the ground, as the collared took her breath away. Her hands clawed at her throat; her fingers curled under the collar trying to rip it from her neck. On her knees and supported on her elbows, she leaned forward, writhing in agony. Avril stood nearby, watching, knowing that Sir expected her to give her the maximum dose as a lesson in the girl's situation's futility. In short order, Jenni collapsed on the floor, lying on her side, her fingers still wrapped around the collar.

Soon enough, Jenni's writhing slowed to twitching. Avril relented and took her thumb off the button. Jenni slowly relaxed and began breathing again, perspiration instantly covering her body. After a minute, she uttered under her breath but intentionally loud enough for Avril to hear.

"You bitch." Jenni breathed with a venom that only someone in extreme pain could muster.

"You'll say much worse in the weeks to come. Now get up and fuck me. As you said, it's time for pleasure before tomorrow's fun begins."

"Whatever you say, slut."

"Ah, you say the nicest things."

Chapter Sixteen

He stood on the corner, watching the tanned, enticing girls in thongs and string bikinis walk by. He was waiting for his wife and kids to join him for a day of relaxation in the sun. Looking at the talent so close only served to tease his desires in taking one and fuck the shit out of them before killing them. One particular girl, barely eighteen and most likely on a school break, caught his eye. His lust taking over, his head filled with an image of standing behind her, fucking that pretty, tight little ass grabbing what could hardly be called tits. In his fantasy, he cut her throat as he came, spewing blood across the sands of the beach. Feeling the stirrings in his crotch starting to show, he smiled before turning away and took a sip of his drink.

His thoughts turned to yesterday when he arrived in Oahu. His body was tight and full of knots. He needed to get away, and after a difficult couple of months, he decided to take the family to the beach.

Yesterday, they climbed into his private jet and flew to Honolulu, Hawaii, arriving too late to hit the surf. After checking into his favorite five-star hotel and settling into their room overlooking Waikiki Beach, they made their way to the nearby steakhouse, Dukes. Palming a C-note into the hands of the hostess, she seated them at the perfect table overlooking the sands and surf. As the sun set over the horizon, he failed to see the beauty of the sunset. Instead, his attention focused on the pretty young things frolicking in the sand.

Sipping a Mai-Tai, he never heard his wife ask him, "Sweetheart, thank you. I appreciate you taking the time from your work to give us this time together."

"Hun, did you hear me?" she asked him, breaking him out of his fantasy of fucking one of those exquisite young things playing in the sands.

"Huh? Oh, I'm sorry, staring at the sunset. I got lost in my thoughts."

"It is beautiful, isn't it?" She asked.

"The sun, yes, it is." He covered, not interested in the sunset at all.

Diverting his wife from his real interest, he took another drink of rum in his Mai-Tai. Seeing that he was about to finish his cocktail, he signaled his waiter for another round. By the time it arrived, he had finished his first and was anxious to start the next. He knew from experience. He would drink several of these toxic drinks by the time the night was over. After that, he would collapse on the bed in his room, not interested at all in fucking his wife with the perfect body and lustful disposition. No, he wasn't interested in fucking her at all.

"Hun, please slow down," she asked, indicating his drink. "I would like to enjoy this night with you."

"Yes, dear, I'll try. It's just that I don't get to drink these wonderful Mai-Tai's very often. This place makes the best. I don't know how they make them or where I'm drinking them. Maybe it's because we're on the shores of Waikiki Beach, overlooking the Pacific Ocean."

"I understand dear, I do. There's plenty of time to enjoy your drink. I am looking forward to sharing some quality time, just the two of us."

"Oh? What about the kids?" he asked.

"Sweetheart, they'll be sleeping in the next room. We'll have all night together to get reacquainted. I ordered a bottle of champagne as a nightcap."

"How thoughtful, Dom, I presume?"

"Of course, dear, nothing but the best for you."

He nodded to himself, believing she felt too comfortable spending his money. If anyone was going to blow it, it was up to him. It might be about time to get rid of her and move on to a new filly.

"Okay, dear. I'll take it easy. Say, where's that waitress with our appetizers? I should eat something while I drink these Mai-Tais."

"Dear, they don't call them waitresses any longer. They call them servers now."

"Well, it's an abomination. What's more, they should dress the part, none of these button-down shirts and slacks. Here on the beach in Waikiki, they should be wearing grass skirts and not much else. Anything more is despicable and an insult to their gender."

"Sweetheart, I love you, but you need to get with the times. Today, it's all about gender equality and all."

"Well, it's still an abomination. Women should dress like women and not like a man, that's all I'm saying."

"Yes, dear," she answered him, resigned to recognize that she would never change his mind.

In the meantime, he returned to staring out over the sands, watching the young things walk around, the older ones with a drink in their hands and skimpy bikinis on their bottoms. They were nice to look at, but now that it was past dinner time, the ones he was most interested in had left the sands, presumably to return to their rooms and their parents. All he could think about was having one of those for dinner. Shaking his head, he looked at his wife, uncertain how to deal with this aging twenty-something, and picked up his drink. Thankfully, their appetizers were arriving, much to his kids' delight and a welcome break in the discussion.

He, of course, and to no one's surprise, ordered baked French onion soup. Digging into the delicious sweet broth, mixed with onion and cheeses, he savored the flavors coating his tongue. In the back of his mind, as enjoyable as the soup was, he preferred tasting the juices of his favorite young things. Male or female, he didn't care. They always satisfied his hunger in ways food could never do.

After sopping up the broth's residue with a piece of Italian bread and scraping the sides of any remaining cheese welded to the outside of the crock, he pushed it aside and signaled for another Mai-Tai. It was delivered just before his porterhouse steak, rare with a side of vegetables he would never eat. Nope, it was the steak he was interested in and nothing else.

Later, after wandering the streets of Waikiki, he dreaded going back to their room. He had no interest whatsoever in fucking his wife. The bottle of Dom waiting for them told him what she wanted in no uncertain terms. Resigned, he closed the door to their room, walked over to the champagne, and popped the cork. Better to get this over.

Pouring a glass and downing it, he poured two glasses and handed one over to her.

"Cheers," he toasted without excitement.

"Cheers," she toasted back before sliding up to him, wrapping her arms around his neck and kissing him deeply. Hanging onto him, she seemed to weigh him down, almost as if to pull him towards the bed.

Relinquishing control, he let her lead him to the bed, undoing his belt as they covered the distance. When his legs hit the edge of the bed, he sat down and leaned back. Putting down the champagne, she pulled him out of his pants and took him into her mouth.

"Nice, hun," he whispered, loud enough for her to hear. He could almost feel her smile while still wrapped around his girth.

In the back of her mind, he was thinking of something else. "Well, she's still got the oral skills; I give her that." He reminded himself as he watched his cock disappear into the deep recesses of her mouth. It will buy her another month or so."

After blowing his load and watching the mandatory swallow, he stood up and allowed her to remove the rest of his clothes. After taking off her own, she pulled back the covers and draped herself on the sheets. Taking a fresh gulp of the champagne, he joined her. Taking ownership of her body, he lost his earlier reservations and took her with heated passion. Taking the pill certainly helped in that, but cumming again was frustrating. No matter how much he possesses her body, fucking that pussy that had birthed two babies had opened her up enough to give him little friction and, therefore, little satisfaction.

"Don't worry about it, sweetie. You're doing just fine." She said to him, her voice trailing off as she swam in a lake of pleasure.

Having enough, he withdrew and stroked his cock, knowing precisely what it would take to shoot his cum all over her body. Using his free hand, he grabbed her hair and pulled her head close to him. She might as well satisfy him, he thought, as he shot his load all over her face, which dripped down onto her chest. He smiled at the image of his juicy white cum spewed over her eyes, nostrils, and her chin. It would please him even more if she snorted, breathing in his cum and suffocating her. His happy smirk grew two more sizes.

Looking down, he stared at her milky white breasts glistening with his ejaculate. He smiled, feeling her submissiveness in wanting to please him. He knew that she could never please him the way he wanted and needed. No, she was too old. One day soon, he would trade her in for a younger model, a much younger model.

Collapsing alongside her, he rolled over to go to sleep. Of course, she had other ideas and wanted to kiss and cuddle, needing a bit of aftercare to put the seal on their lovemaking.

"Go clean yourself up," he commanded her, not seeing nor caring about the pool of tears welling up in her eyes.

By the time she returned from the bathroom, he had rolled over with his back to her, fast asleep. He never noticed that she sat on the side of the bed for a long time, her tears replacing the cum on her chest. Seeing the nearly full bottle of champagne and his half-full glass as well, she drank it all, not caring about a morning headache that was sure to follow.

***

The next morning found them on the beach after breakfast. The kids played in the surf, and his wife lounged on the chaise, reading one stupid magazine after another. Undeterred, he watched the talent all around him, drooling at the imagery of taking one after another and having his way with them. Of course, some filled out those tops, nearly falling out of their cups. They were nice too, but right now, he wasn't all that interested in them either. Still, they were better than his wife lying next to him.

Watching all of those pretty young things was giving him an erection. Of course, he didn't mind, but he could be arrested for dealing with it out on the beach. That was one Consortium rule that he followed to the fullest, never doing anything that would lead to an arrest.

"I'm going for a swim," he announced to his wife.

"Have a good time," she answered him without looking up at his retreating figure, also not looking back.

Walking into the surf, the warm water did little to shrink his growing erection.

"All the better," he thought as he swam out beyond the rest of the swimmers.

Eventually, he reached a point where he stopped, and treading water, pulled his cock out and began stroking it. Fantasizing about all of those pretty young things hanging out at the beach brought him quickly to full erection. He loved watching them run back and forth from the edge of the water, using their sand buckets to pick up load after load of sand and water and return to their sandcastles.

Not that he cared about their enterprise. Instead, he was interested in seeing them squat down, spreading their luscious legs and flashing their assets at him. Stroking faster, he fantasized, taking them, forcing him on them, watching his erection disappear inside those tight little holes.

Still treading water, nearing the culmination of his stroking, he closed his eyes in final moments. Just as he was about to spew his seed, he felt something touch his ankles. Caring more about his pleasure, he ignored the sensation and focused on his cock nearing its explosion.

A second later, he felt something clamp down on both his ankles and pull him down. Just as his pleasure reverie broke, he disappeared under the surface. As soon as his head submerged, something grabbed him around his chest from behind and pulled him deeper under the water.

Thrashing now, trying hard to extricate himself and swim back to the surface, he panicked. His mouth opened wide as he tried to shout. Instead of his screams escaping, water flooded his mouth and into his airways. He struggled to survive as water filled his lungs. The firm grasp his attackers had on him pulled him deeper underwater. Air bubbles began escaping from his mouth and nose as water pressure squeezed his chest.

Desperate to breathe, he watched the bright light shining above the surface grew darker. He continued to sink as his two attackers dragged him deeper and deeper.

His chest was burning, and in desperate need of air, his autonomic body functions took over. Mouth opening, his body forced him to breathe in the warm Pacific Ocean waters. A minute later, he went limp and died. His body drifted to the bottom, his cock still resting above the waistband on his swim trunks.

His two attackers swam off, content in a job well done. Minutes later, they surfaced near their dive boat, climbed aboard, and took out a couple of beers. Starting the engine, they moved off at a leisurely pace typical for the area's long-time residents. Soon they were out of range and out of danger.

It took over an hour before his wife missed him. It took another couple of hours before his body surfaced, and someone found it. Later, at the coroner's inquest, his death was ruled as accidental, probably from loss of conscience when he ejaculated amid his climax. The coroner found semen residue in his urethra.

Even though his wife cried for his death, she didn't mourn him. She now had his money, and she was free of him and his despicable desires. No, she was grateful the world was rid of yet another predator. Besides, now she was free to find a new man, better suited to her needs. After all, now that she had his money, she could afford to be picky.

Chapter Seventeen

Sir was already seated at the time, drinking a cup of tea with milk. Looking up over the teacup's rim, he smiled at the show Avril presented him. With one hand high, leaning into the doorframe, and another cocked on her hip, she crossed her legs at the knees and modeled for him. She pirouetted and presented her back to him, knowing that he was scanning up and down, gazing at his marks left on her body. He smiled.

"Very nice, very nice indeed, they look lovely on you."

"Thank you, Sir. It is my pleasure to be able to display them for you. I presume you like them?"

"Very much so. I only wish that there was someone I could show them to."

"The household staff, Sir?"

"Oh, they don't count, my dear. I mean one of my friends. I must schedule a dinner party soon, and then I can properly show you off."

Instantly, images of previous sessions flooded her mind. Some were good, in fact, very good. There were also painful reminders of past dinner parties. Sir made her the center of attention during many of his parties, enticing the attendees to savor her body sexually or torment her in various excruciating ways. The latter were memories she'd rather forget, but every time he brought up the specter of a dinner party, she unconsciously shivered inside, knowing that it could only go one of two ways.

She wasn't sure if she could ever fully accept her status here, but she had given her word. Her word was still something of value, even if only to herself.

Gulping a bit, trying hard to hide her nervousness Avril said, "Yes, Sir. I'm looking forward to it."

"Come in, Avril."

Turning back, she sashayed over to him, bent over, and kissed him. Inside, she smiled when he gently squeezed one of her breasts. For some reason, they didn't hurt as he did so, despite having suffered his vicious passions the night before, leaving various welts and bruises on them.

Her body aching, she craved a couple of Ibuprofen to ease her pains as she carefully sat down. She gave up wishing for them long ago. Sir made it clear that any form of painkiller was never allowed. He wanted his prey to continue to suffer even after he finished torturing them.

After taking her seat, she waited for permission to pour her tea. After a minute or so, with a flip of the hand, her owner indicated his consent. Pouring her tea and adding honey, she took her first sip of the hot liquid. Sitting back, she savored the flavor coating her tongue. While she was usually a coffee person, the tea with honey soothed her raw throat. He had taught her the subtleties of drinking tea and had come to appreciate its value.

"Tell me about last night. Not what I did to you, but rather, how you felt throughout the session."

"Good morning Sir. Or should I say good afternoon?"

"Afternoon it is."

"Good afternoon then, Sir. I'm not sure how to explain how I feel about the session. As usual, it started nice, almost as a tender kiss. I felt warm and comfortable being with you."

"And then?"

"And then, after you warmed my skin, which by the way, was an interesting use of the floggers. Sir, the way you progressed, hitting me using different kinds of floggers, each having different weights and heaviness to their fronds. In many ways, it was quite pleasant, and I liked the attention you gave me. Even when you hit me hard enough to make me yelp, I didn't want you to stop."

"What else?"

"It's … well, Sir, I don't quite know. I seem to remember you striking me from all sides, both my front and back, and high and low, on my chest and back while making sure you flogged my legs, thighs, and calves."

"Yet, there was more, wasn't there? What made you forget about what I was doing to you?"

"Sir?"

"Think about, Avril. There you were strung up and exposed from all sides. Your arms and legs were spread wide, almost to the point where you were barely able to stand on the balls of your feet, giving me unrestricted access to your pussy. You were completely powerless to do anything to shield yourself during my onslaught."

"Oh, Yes, Sir. Now I remember. It's foggy, and I only remember the beginning. But I do remember this. At first, you stood in front of me and swung one of your heaviest floggers in an upwards motion striking me right on my pussy. That hurt … a lot."

"Yes, I suppose it did. And yet …" he trailed off.

"Huh? Hmmm, oh, that's right. It was when you moved behind me and flogged my pussy. As I recall, the flogger smacked me right on my clitoris. But instead of it being painful, it felt wonderful. I remember wanting more of the same, and I didn't want you to stop. I don't remember much after that until I came too when you shifted to whipping me with the single tail."

"Yes, I remember that moment. You finally gave yourself completely over to me the moment. You were conscious and still able to stand on your own, but you had let the world around you fade, to live in the moment of just the two of us and the flogger making you cum again and again. It's going to take some doing to clean that flogger. You don't know it, but you soaked it with your juices to the point that it will need reconditioning. Which, by the way, you will clean tomorrow. I've shown you how to take care of my toys. You will need to give this one extra special care when you do your chores."

"Yes, Sir, that won't be a problem. Which flogger was that, may I ask?"

"Oh, my favorite, the one with the corset handle."

"Oh, that one, Sir, yes, that is a nice flogger and my favorite. The fronds are so soft and yet so firm when you swing it. I'll be sure to take special care of that one. I especially like how the handle has the lacing along its length like a corset. Tell me, Sir, does that help in holding it as you swing it?"

"Indeed, it does. Be sure to do a good job with reconditioning it. Its fronds are anything but soft right now. Tell me about the single tail."

"Well, Sir. It was unmistakably different from what you were doing when you flogged me. As I came out of that initial state, I felt what seemed like little bites nipping at my body. As I became more and more aware of you, I felt the nips become stings, and eventually, the stings became something worse. I don't know how to describe it. I only remember the strikes getting harder and harder after that. My body was on fire. That's what I remember the most."

"That was when I was taking my pleasure from you, rather than giving you all the pleasure. I needed to feel your screams and shifting to the single tail, which allowed me to transition you from your orgasmic rapture subspace experience to a different kind of subspace, one built on pain as opposed to pleasure."

"Yes, Sir, I do recall disappearing again. But before I did, I remember every single strike of the whip on my body, and most especially on my nipples and pussy. Sir, that fucking whip hurt."

"I'm sure it did. I don't always use it that way with you, but this time, I did. However, it did allow you to transition once again into subspace. At the same time, it gave me the serenity I needed to join you."

"I get that, Sir. I've come to accept that the pain is a transition to joyous rapture and necessary to achieve that experience for each of us. I only wish getting there wasn't so painful."

"Avril, you wouldn't transition at all if it weren't so painful. Do you know of Newton's Third Law?

"Um, Sir, is that the one about acceleration?"

"Sorry, no. That's his second law; acceleration is proportional to the net force applied to the object. His third law is 'for every action, there is an equal and opposite reaction.'"

"Oh, Yes, Sir, that's right."

"Relate to me the third law as it applies to our discussion."

"Hmmm," Avril thought about it for a minute.

"Sir, if I understand your reference, you mean that for me to enjoy such rapturous subspace, I must also endure an equivalent level of misery."

"There you have it, Avril."

"Yes, Sir, I don't remember much from that point on. What I do recall is that I screamed. That first touch of the whip sliced through me as if you were slicing me with a sword. With everything you've done to me, I didn't think anything could hurt me any worse. I was wrong."

"And I assure you, you'll feel worse in the future. I'm just starting with you. There is much yet I wish to experience with you."

"Yes, Sir, until last night, I had stopped believing that was possible. What you did to me, well, let's just say, I thought I was going to die."

"And did you?"

"Did I what, Sir?"

"Die, of course."

"Ah, No, Sir, I didn't. I just thought I would. After that, I'm not sure what you did to me. I don't remember. Looking at my marks in the shower, I think you might have also used a cane on me."

"Several, I broke a few in the process. It felt good breaking them over your body."

"Anyway, Sir, all I remember from then on, from one moment to the next, I jumped from pain to pleasure. I have to admit. I didn't feel the earlier pleasures. However, later on, I could feel your fingers inside me, stroking me, tickling my G-spot, and making me cum. The funny thing is, I don't remember much of the pain and agony. I do remember the highs that the pleasure you gave me made me feel. It was almost as if that each segment fed off the next, each enhancing the one to come."

"Amazing how that happens."

"It is, Sir. I remember how I began yearning for the pain, just so that I could feel the pleasure. At some point, I know I fell into a euphoric state, unable to escape, not wanting to escape."

"I wish you could have seen yourself. You were there, inside your body. At the same time, you seemed outside yourself, savoring your emotions, drifting, and floating above yourself. I could see that you had disappeared from even yourself. You were still with me, yet, you weren't. Your eyes rolled inside your head, and your ears stopped hearing me. I talked to you the whole time, and you never once responded."

"I seem to remember hearing your voice, that is. I don't recall what you said to me. I only remember hearing the tone of your voice, soothing me, and helping me."

"I did. I'm glad you remember that. For my part, I alternated whipping and caning you while finger fucking you. You screamed in pleasure much more than screaming in pain. I loved watching you and hearing your squeals. You indeed are something else, my dear. You told me back in the bedroom; you didn't know how you would live without your parents. I'm not sure I can live without seeing you in such states. Sitting there, at the table, you're beautiful. Under my touch, and while you're in that state, you're radiant. I've never seen such beauty in all my life. Between your marks, your skin tones, and the look on your face, you positively glow."

"Thank you, Sir. I do feel something like that. And you're right; I do feel something more than beautiful. I know I feel radiant, but I feel something more. I'm not sure how to describe it."

"There are no words for that kind of radiance I see in you."

"No, Sir, I don't suppose there are."

"Are you afraid of suffering under my hand?"

"Yes, Sir, I'm not sure I can ever get away from that. However, I think I can handle it."

"Good, I knew you could."

"I just wish it didn't hurt so much, Sir."

"Avril, the pain is in your head. You can control it and turn it to your advantage or not. It's up to you. Your back doesn't feel pain. Rather, nerve endings transmit the impulses to your brain, leaving it to decide what to do with them. In most people, the brain processes the sensations as pain, causing you to react. To most animals, humans included, it's a message to move away, run if you must, from the cause of the injury. However, many people know how to process the sensations, turning them into something positive. With you, I hope to train you to process them into pleasure. It's one reason why I ask you to kiss me when I twist and pull your nipples as if I'm about to tear them from your body."

"Sir, in some respects, I can do that. However, I can't kiss you when you whip me or stand outside myself as I suffer your torment."

"And yet, I ask again, did you die?"

"No, Sir. I didn't. I just felt like I was."

"In time, my dear, in time."

"If I live that long," Avril thought to herself.

Dishing up some of the soft scrambled eggs in the serving tray, Avril started a new topic.

"Sir, if I may, I have a question, several in fact."

"You may ask," he responded, giving her permission to ask her questions.

"Sir, what is the status of my membership application to the Consortium?"

"Avril, I told you, your application would take time."

"Yes, Sir, I understand that. It's been many months now, and I'm wondering what might be going on. I don't even know if the application was submitted. Sir, I don't mean to pry, but I did agree to accept your proposal to explore experiences such as last night. In exchange, you would support and promote my membership application to the Consortium."

"Are you suggesting that I am not living up to my part in the agreement?"

"Oh, No, Sir, I wouldn't presume to suggest that."

"Ah, but you might be thinking about it. Come now, be honest."

"Yes, Sir, the thought had crossed my mind."

"You must be patient in these matters. I told you that the Consortium would not look kindly to your application."

"Yes, Sir, I get that. What I don't get is that since then, you've not shared with me on its progress."

"Avril, I'm surprised. I thought you would have asked about your application long before this. What took you so long? In my experience, women don't generally wait that long."

"Sir, I'm surprised. What made you think that I would presume to interrogate you?"

"Ah, so now you're interrogating me," he said, smiling as he looked at her.

"No, Sir," smiling back at him. "I wouldn't dare think such a thing."

"I'm sure you wouldn't. Still, you would like to know what is going on with your membership application."

"Sir, if it would be convenient?"

"As it so happens, I had intended to bring this up on my own, after lunch, that is. Before I get to that, does your throat feel better?"

"Yes, Sir, the tea helped a lot."

"You sound better. Your voice is not as hoarse as it was earlier."

"Thank you, Sir," she answered and sat back and paused, well aware that his eyes were stuck on her. Watching them slide up and down her body, she waited, feeling a bit of control over him. Little by little, she was figuring out how to get what she wanted from him. Just one more little advancement into that knowledge base she was slowly building. After some time perusing her, he finally spoke.

"Avril, I will tell you this, I did propose your application to the executive committee. It has not yet been submitted to the general membership. There are still many things that need resolving before that happens."

"Thank you, Sir. What things?"

"Well, first off, you caused quite the uproar over your request."

"Not unexpected, was it, Sir?"

"No, it was not. Nor will it stop at the executive membership. Once the application goes for a vote among the membership, there will be more. By then, there should be enough evidence to quench their outrage."

"So, what's next?"

"Avril, you are learning and gaining experience with your training, but there is still much you must do to get you to the point where you can be a peer among the membership."

"Sir, you know I am anxious to learn from you and handle myself with my girls."

"Yes, I can see that. You are making progress."

"Sir, since you first started training me, I've learned how to handle a flogger, whip, and various other instruments of pleasure and pain. I've learned about human anatomy, learning what makes a body tick. I've studied where the various pressure points are, along with the various erogenous zones. I was surprised to learn that there are so many of them."

"Fascinating, isn't it?"

"Yes, Sir, I've even learned to inflict pain and punishment upon my subjects, slowly coming to enjoy the sensations I feel as I cause their misery."

"And yet, you still haven't taken the next step."

"Sir, I don't understand. Aren't you pleased with my progress?"

"Yes, Avril, I am. Your progress is right in line with what I expected. That's not the issue. I'm still wondering whether you can go all the way with what you must do to prove yourself worthy. There are plenty of subjects under your control, and yet, you've not taken any of them down."

"Down, Sir? I don't get you."

"Avril, what is the one thing that I do to prey that you have yet to do?"

Avril didn't answer him right away, convinced that he was referring to the one task in torturing her subjects, the one thing that would prove that she could be a dominant, a sadist like her owner. She dreaded this requirement. She put it off as long as possible. Was it time to step up?

"Sir, I don't quite know what you're saying."

"Avril, you're deflecting. I won't have that. You know precisely what I mean. You've seen me with my subjects. You know my level of cruelty. You know what ultimately happens to the bulk of my lineup."

"Sir?"

"Avril, we've talked about this. It's time to step up."

"By step up, if I understand you correctly, you are waiting for me to … to, ah, well, you know."

"Avril, stop twisting your hair around your finger. You know what I mean. I want you to say it. I will not say it for you. You must say it, in your own words, using your voice."

Avril sat there, staring at her empty lunch plate. She didn't want to say what he wanted her to say. First, it embarrassed her to even think of it. Second, she didn't want to do it. Logically, she knew she had to, but emotionally, it was the last thing in the world she wanted to do. It was one thing to dominate another person, torture and torment them. She even started feeling a kind of exhilaration in causing them pain. She knew Sir well enough. He wasn't going to let her continue without taking the final, ultimate step in their agony.

"Sir … it's really difficult for me," she begged, grasping more of her hair and began twisting it around her finger. Realizing what she was doing, she let go of her hair and put her hands on the table.

Sir kept quiet, forcing her to resume the conversation.

Avril continued to stare at her plate. Pushing it aside and clearing the place setting from her dirty silverware, she absently brushed crumbs while still twirling her hair in her fingers. She didn't want to say the words. She'd sooner talk about having sex in public in the middle of Times Square in N.Y.C., on display for millions to see, then say what Sir wanted her to admit.

The silence between them grew thick. Persistent as ever, Sir stared at her, waiting for her to speak, to say what she must say. Still, he sat in silence, unrelenting, and waited for her. It was maddening.

"Sir, please don't make me."

Deafened by his silence, she knew, deep inside, that he would sit there, make her sit there, forever until she said the word. Still, she held back, hoping that God would give her a way out. So far, none seemed evident.

Silently to herself, she prayed, "Please, God. I've suffered so much, trying to stay within your rules. If there was ever a time, please help me now. I don't want to do this."

As she prayed, she briefly looked up at Sir, seeing that he wasn't backing down. If there was any saving grace in this, he was patient, letting her deal with her demons. Still, his face spoke a language of stern determination. He wasn't going to back down, not at all.

"Bastard," she thought.

Hanging on to the silence, she fought with herself not to say the words. She was failing, and he was winning, and they both knew it.

"Sir?"

He remained silent and just returned her look.

"Please?"

"Fuck, were his lips glued shut?" she lamented inside her head.

For once, the comfortable silence between them failed her, transformed into a most uncomfortable silence.

"Sir, you want … you want me to finish it."

"Yes, Avril, I do. However, you must say the words. Two little words are all you need to say."

"Two?"

"Yes, Avril, two, I'm not going to say them for you. Feel free to tell them your way, two or thirty. It doesn't matter. You must say them."

"Yes, Sir."

Once again, she held off, hoping beyond hope, to avoid saying them. His unrelenting demand weighed heavily upon her shoulders.

"Sir, I don't want to."

"And still, you must. I require you to say them. It would make our agreement null and void if you don't."

"Sir! you wouldn't."

"I would. It is all dependent upon what you do, here and now."

"That's unfair."

"Is it? Think about it. You got me to make the concession. To satisfy your end of the bargain, you must make this choice. You must say the words, and then, carry them out, and soon. Otherwise, I cannot help you achieve your goal."

"Sir, why did I ever decide to do this bargain?"

"Good question, I don't know. You surprised me by asking. However, you did, and now it's time to put up."

"Sir, can I have more time?"

"You don't need more time. You need to do this, and soon. You are ready. I know you are. Are you ready to do this? Use your words and tell me. I remind you; I won't say them myself. It is for you to say them."

Another uncomfortable silence enveloped the two of them, though Avril wasn't sure Sir found it uncomfortable. She knew he would out-wait her."

"Yes, Sir, I understand."

Avril paused for some more time. She had little idea how long this exchange of silence had been going on, and in many ways, she had wished that she had kept her initial question to herself. It felt like hours since this uncomfortable silence between them began, and yet, it probably was only seconds, if barely minutes.

After more lingering silence, she took a deep breath and spoke softly. "You're telling me it's time that I kill one."

"Bravo, my dear. Bravo. I'm proud of you. You said the words. Yes, it is time that you kill one, without any help or encouragement from me. When you do, I will observe. Two executive committee members will also observe via CCTV so that there can be no hint of collaboration to fix the results. They will inspect the body before and after the deed, to ensure there is no duplicity involved."

"Someone will be watching?" Avril asked, horrified that others would see her kill someone.

"Yes, Avril, you have to understand. In the entire history of the Consortium, prey has never once applied for membership in our ranks. Your request is unprecedented. Frankly, the committee is dubious of your true intentions. I can't say I blame them. It took me several days to stand back and work out your request. In some ways, I still don't understand it. When I first tagged you, I never thought you would have gone in this direction. I suppose it is partly my fault, telling you that I saw dominant tendencies within you."

"Never? I assumed that it was rare, but never?"

"Yes, Avril, never, you have a long, uphill battle, and even if you adhere to all of the membership requirements tossed your way, you may still never prevail. The committee may order me to kill you, despite our agreement, and I would be honor-bound to do it. My commitment to them supersedes the one I have with you."

"I understand, Sir. As powerful as you are in the Consortium, you are not the end-all on how it's run."

"I'm glad you understand that. Your death will come hard to me, and I will struggle. I've come to appreciate your presence in my life. I would miss you."

"Sir, I think that is the nicest thing you have ever said to me."

He smiled at her, allowing the meat of the statement to sink in.

"Avril, I believe you are ready. Are you?"

"No, Sir. I don't think I am."

"Yet, you are. I know you are. You know the anatomy, you know what it will take, and you've practiced on cadavers. You've cut them open and studied them from the insides. You've seen what it takes to kill my prey. You've seen me kill my subjects in countless ways. You're ready, whether you believe it or not."

"Yes, Sir, if you say so, I guess so."

"Avril, it's not a matter of guessing so. I believe you are ready. You must believe it as well. If you don't believe, you will not be able to do the deed when the time comes. Once you make your first kill, the next will be easier, and the next even more so. Killing will become a part of you."

"... Ah ... killing again?" she said, gulping.

"Yes, Avril, the committee will not be satisfied with just one. They will insist that you take more lives before they agree to submit your application to the general membership for a vote."

"Um, yes ... I understand, Sir."

"In the cells, I have set aside several subjects with which you can use for your first test kill, for that is what it is. We are testing your willingness to do as they do, to kill indiscriminately, and for the pleasure of killing."

"I get it, Sir. I do."

"Then, shall I schedule it?"

"How soon?"

"You could get it done as early as tonight."

"So soon?"

"Yes, Avril, the committee will not tolerate any delays. They are already getting impatient having your application remain on the agenda time and time again."

"Yes, Sir, will you choose the subject for me?"

"No, Avril. You must do that. It's part of the ritual. You pick your prey, amuse yourself with them, toy, and torment them, and then, when you tire of them, you kill them and move on."

"Yes, Sir, I get it. It's just that; it's so soon. I don't know if I can be ready for it tonight."

"If you set your mind to it, you'll be ready. Better to get it over with as soon as possible, rather than let it consume you beforehand. Shall I set it up for this evening?"

"I … Sir, I need more time. Soon, I promise, within the month. I want to review my subjects and choose how I want to do it."

"Avril, I'm not surprised. I had hoped you would jump right into it, but I thought the odds were against a quick move in that direction. Alright, I'll give you the time. Just don't take too long. I will admit, I am interested in who you choose and how you will kill her. You'll find that killing prey is not hard once you commit. Getting there takes effort. Killing prey is not all that difficult, and it gets easier after the first one."

"Prey, is that all we are to you?"

"For most of my purchases, yes, though there are exceptions. You are one. There are others."

"Really? Will I get to meet them?"

"You've already met some, at least in passing. I'll introduce more in time."

"The house staff?"

"Some are, but not most of them. I'm assigning you the duty to oversee the responsibilities of the house staff, starting today. By serving, most get to live longer by cooking and cleaning, but eventually, I kill them too. Yet, in serving me, they tend to forget that their efforts to serve this house will not change the fact that their lives are mine to take. You know I like killing. I enjoy seeing them sweat, hoping I'll spare them. The look on their faces when they realize that their suffering was for naught enthralls me. The moment is priceless. That disheartened look, mixed with tears and cries, encourages me to want to do it again. If I could do it multiple times to the same prey, that would be even better. As it is, I have to hold the feelings in my chest until the next time."

"I'm not sure I will ever see it that way."

"No, you will find your way and embrace it. In the meantime, go over your stable and review your inventory. Make your selection, or selections if you wish to do more than one. One bit of guidance I can give you. I believe you have four training subjects in your barn right now. If there is one that bores you or can offer you little to your training, choose that one. If they can offer you advancement and training, then leave them for later. There's plenty of time to kill them all. Besides, there will be others to replace them."

"Yes, Sir, I understand. I'm inclined to choose that bleach blonde from California, Misty, but I want to look them over again. I'll decide within a few days. Then, I choose the method of her death."

"I agree with you. You have reached the end of the road with that one. If it wasn't for the fact that you were using her as a training object, she'd been dead a long time ago. If it is any consolation, you allowed her to live a lot longer than I would have. Frankly, she's a selfish, self-centered bitch who wouldn't give the time of day to someone who couldn't advance her goals. I despise that kind of girl."

"Yes, Sir, I had realized that myself. Besides, she's almost comatose most of the time as it is."

"Well, I suggest you plan her end, toy, and torture her before you kill her. Take time to set up the scene. Let me know when you are ready a day in advance. I will need to make a couple of calls. After all, it wouldn't do to have you kill her without your witnesses. But don't worry about them. You'll not see them."

"I understand, Sir. If it were okay with you, I would like to play with her before I … I, um, kill her."

"Certainly, feel free to do whatever you wish. Misty's not going anywhere."

Eyes downcast, Avril thought about the task ahead of her. She didn't relish the idea of killing a fellow human, but feeling trapped, it was inevitable. She knew that to escape, joining the Consortium was a necessary evil to accomplish her goal. And if she needed to kill someone to do that, she only hoped God would forgive her. A plan was starting to formulate in the back of her mind, but she knew she was still a long way from coming to terms with it.

"Avril, one more thing, I know I told you that you could plan on how to kill her, but I, in this case, I will decide the manner of her death. For your first kill, you are to use a special knife that I have prepared for you. I want you to cut her throat and then use the knife to cut her head off. How you do that is up to you. Cutting her throat is for your benefit. Cutting her head off is for the witnesses' benefit. There must be no doubt that she's dead and who did the deed."

Gulping again, she looked over at him and nodded. "Yes, Sir, may I go now?"

After a couple of moments, he nodded, releasing her. Avril made a beeline for the door and back to her room, barely able to contain her breakfast from coming back up before she made it to her room and the bathroom. Even so, after she recovered, she needed to clean the floor as well as the bowl.

Chapter Eighteen

Jenni woke up feeling relaxed and well-rested. Last night was a dream in many respects. Sleeping with a woman was a first for her, despite the circumstances. Lying on the thin mattress, she kept her eyes closed to keep the pleasure of the previous evening fresh in her thoughts, keeping the reality of what was to come in the back of her mind.

She wanted to keep the feeling of calm, supple litheness for as long as she could. She didn't know what time it was. Frankly, she didn't care. All she wanted to do was stay in bed as long as she could and enjoy the moment.

A warm surge warmed between her legs as she laid there. Reaching down, she touched herself, feeling heat still radiating from her engorged pussy lips. Yup, she was still wet. Last night was incredible, and apparently, her body wanted more. She knew it was unlikely, but she would relish it as much as she could.

Replaying the evening, she worked hard to commit it to memory. From the moment that she buried her face into Avril's crotch, tasting a woman's salty pussy juices for the first time, she felt the heated passion of another woman's legs wrapped around her head. When Avril began munching on her pussy before fucking her with the strap-on, she lost a bit of herself as she gave in to the sexual freedom of lying with another woman. She had never fucked another woman before and now wondered why she had ever resisted. Now she knew what she had missed all these years.

Still, she had the one encounter, and it would have to do. Memorizing the experience was her mission now. It would have to do, and it would help keep her alive. Rubbing her clit as she went over the scenes, she felt her body respond, slowly building to an orgasm. It warmed her heart and her soul.

As she approached her climax, the door to her cell suddenly opened, and he stood there.

"STOP!" Sir commanded.

Quickly, she withdrew her hand from between her legs and sat up, pulling the thin blanket up over her breasts, covering herself.

"Didn't Avril go over the rules with you?" He snapped at her.

"Ummm …" Jenni started to answer.

"Don't answer that. It was rhetorical. Get up."

Jenni started to stand up, dragging the blanket with her, intending to keep it wrapped up around her body, covering her nakedness.

"Leave it. From now on, you will remain naked for me at all times. You're never to cover yourself. That includes putting your hands over your breasts or groin, ever. Do you understand?"

"Yes," Jenni said, dropping the blanket on the bed and standing up alongside it.

"Where are your shoes?"

"Over there," she said, pointing to them sitting on the floor near the wall.

"Why?"

"Huh?"

"Why are you not wearing them?"

"I don't understand. I was in bed."

"That's no excuse."

"I'm sorry. I don't understand. Are you saying that I should have been wearing them in bed?"

"That's precisely what I expect. You are to wear them day and night. You may only take them off to bathe. Once out, you will put them back on immediately, and then you may finish drying. I never want to catch you not wearing them, ever. That is also one of my cardinal rules. That was on the card left on your bed."

"That doesn't make sense. Wearing heels to bed, I mean."

"I don't care what you think. It's what you will do. And that brings me to a second point. You are to call me 'Sir.' Every time you talk to me, you will use my title. Again, there are no exceptions. Additionally, you are not to ask questions or speak out of turn. You do as I ask or suffer at my discretion. Otherwise, you stay quiet. The only time I want to hear from you is when I want you to scream in pain. And trust me, you will scream. If I want you to talk, I will give you specific permission to do so. Nod if you understand me."

Jenni nodded.

"Now, go use the bathroom, and be right quick about it."

Nodding her thanks, Jenni turned to go, but he stopped her in her tracks.

"Are you forgetting something?"

Jenni turned and looked back at Sir. Realizing her mistake, she picked up the heels, sat down on the edge of the bed, and put them on. When done, she stood up and waited, pointing with a single finger requesting his permission to go to the bathroom.

"Go."

Grateful, Jenni almost ran to the bathroom. Since there was no door to close in the cell, Jenni sat down on the toilet and let it go. A minute later, she cleaned herself up, stood up, and flushed. After washing her hands, she quickly made her way back to her cell and stood before Sir.

"Now, you're wondering why it is and how you came to be here. Let's just say that you came to my attention. I liked what I saw and decided that I wanted you. After that, it was a simple matter of picking you up and bringing you to my home. Now you belong to me. I bought and paid for you. I own you, and I will do with you as I please. You will never leave here. You also heard last night that you will also die here, either by my hands or Avril's. You cannot avoid your fate. Nor can you escape, despite what Avril told you. Neither will she escape, but she has resolved that issue and promised to stop trying. But like you, she will die one day, here in this house and by my hands. Now, I give you permission to talk and ask a single question. Don't test my patience."

"By what right do you think you can kidnap people up off the streets and take them for your perverted pleasures, to maim and kill us? I demand that you let me go."

"Demand to let you go! You are in no position to demand anything, and as for what right? What right does a lion have to stalk and kill an antelope? Girl, I am the hunter, and you are the prey. I've caught you, and now you will suffer and die by my hands. It's a practice that has been going on since the beginning of time and built into our DNA."

"It's wrong, and it's immoral," Jenni complained.

"You are mistaken. You are prey. It's neither wrong nor immoral. Do you think the lion thinks it's wrong or immoral? No, it doesn't. Do you think the antelope thinks it is wrong to be prey, to die by the claws and fangs of a hunter? No, it doesn't. Does it try to avoid its fate? It does, and it comes up with ingenious ways to protect itself. Still, the lion will eventually get its way, taking down its prey sooner or later, just as I have taken you down."

"And now you will enjoy the spoils of your hunt?"

"Oh, yes, starting right now." Sir said as he unbuckled his belt and pulled it free from his trousers. "Enough talk. Permission to speak rescinded. You've also asked more than a single question, and not once did you use my title in your statements to me. Those infractions earned you a punishment. I warned you, and now you will receive the consequences of your behavior. Now face the bed and bend over, face on the bed and your arms over your head."

Gulping, Jenni turned and faced the bed. She leaned over and planted her face on the mattress, extending her arms to the far side of the bed. Clenching her ass cheeks, she waited for the first painful strike of the belt on her ass. It happened quickly, and she clenched her jaw shut, hoping to contain the yell that tried to escape her mouth, even as her ass cheek screamed in agony. Without time to process the first hit, a second landed on her other ass cheek, forcing her to grit her teeth even harder from the resulting burn. Two more quick strikes followed before he gave her body a chance to process what was happening to it.

With tears filling her eyelids and leaking down their edges, Jenni was finally able to take a couple of deep breaths. The flames burning through her ass raged as she tried desperately to deal with the belting.

"Spread your legs apart. I want to see all of you." He commanded her.

She slowly wiggled her feet with difficulty until her legs were far enough apart to satisfy his demand. She knew the exact moment when she had achieved his goal as she felt the brunt of his belt hitting her ass right on top of one of his previous strikes. Unable to contain her agony, she screamed as loudly as possible. Later, when she reflected upon the moment, she had no recollection of screaming at all. She just remembered her inflamed backside taking the brute force of the belt, compressing her flesh and striking fire in her already tortured derriere.

Again and again, he struck her, targeting different parts of her body and not particularly caring to miss certain private parts between her legs. The strikes to her ass hurt like hell. However, the belting to her pussy elicited sheer agony throughout her body. The thunder strokes penetrated her inner core and shot to her brain faster than a bullet. They were pure agony and the exact reciprocal of the most awesome sex one could ever experience. She thought she was going to die right then and there.

Throughout the beating, Sir would take periodic pauses to let the painful lessons sink in and let her wallow in the anguish of the moment. Sometimes he would make her cry and scream until she had little left to let out before resuming. Other times, he would continue his beating even before she could catch more than a couple of breaths.

It wasn't until she stopped feeling the strikes that he took a long pause before speaking again.

***

"Turn over and lie face up."

Ever so slowly, she rolled over onto her back, her inflamed ass barely on the edge of the bed, her feet planted on the floor.

"Keep those legs spread far apart and knees wide. As I said, I want to see all of you. Don't let me catch you trying to close your knees together."

Jenni nodded ever so slightly and complied, spreading her knees as wide as she could manage, opening a passage for his belt straight to her groin. She knew what was about to come, and there was nothing she could do about it.

The first strike came above her pussy, just above her clit, and right on her pubis mons. She doubled over, her shoulders lifting off the bed in agony. But she was proud of herself; she kept her knees apart, according to his instructions. She still maintained some level of control.

When it came, the next hit came right on her clit, and she screamed once again. Involuntarily, her knees started to close before she stopped them and opened them once again.

"Good," he praised her before hitting her again, this time right below her belly button. He followed up with two more strikes, one on either side of the inside of her thighs, just below her pussy. Unable to contain herself, she lifted her legs, raising her feet off the floor, and closed her legs in a futile attempt to protect herself from his onslaught. Jenni couldn't see him, but he just smiled.

"Put them down and keep them spread."

Jenni didn't hear him, only heard garbled noises. The pounding of her heart and an ocean of pain crashing inside of her skull is all she knew.

"I said, put them down, and keep them spread." Sir commanded.

Slowly, her legs resumed their position on the floor, her red-hot pussy open and glared back at Sir.

"That's better. Now, just a few more, shall we?"

With that, he took the belt and pummeled her tits again and again. He made a clinical approach to hitting the soft, malleable flesh, watching the waves rippling back and forth like a stone dropping in a bucket of water. All the while, Jenni yelled out with each hit, barely able to deal with the painful injury to her body.

He didn't stop pummeling her until he sensed that she was becoming immune to his touch. She was crying profusely now, a behavior that calmed his savagery. Standing back, admiring his work, he replaced his belt around his waist and made for the door. Before exiting, he gave her one last instruction.

"Avril will be in tomorrow to begin your training and teach you all about the rules. Pay close attention. Learning them will help you survive here."

With that, he closed and locked the door behind him. He reveled in recalling the brutality of the beating he had just given Jenni. While his darker side was satisfied, his tented trousers betrayed his unresolved lust. Turning, he made his way down the hall and stood before another door. Unlocking it, he opened it and stepped in to find another one of his property, kneeling for him in the expected spot, waiting for him.

Closing the door behind him, he looked at the beautiful girl, kneeling in perfect submission before him. Seeing them submitting to him never ceased to fill him with wonder. Satisfied with his dominance over her, he stepped up and placed his crotch right in front of her face.

"Open," he commanded as he drew down his zipper.

Chapter Nineteen

Sir led Avril to the same wing of the house where he showed her the dead girl that was nearly sliced in half as she strangled to death all those months ago. The memory of that first time she saw what he was truly capable of still burned in the back of her mind. Every time she entered this room, she searched for traces of the girl's blood. There had been plenty of it, seeing how her body was partially sliced in half starting at her groin. She didn't see any, but it didn't stop her from looking every time she came in here. Still, she didn't want to know.

In the center of the room rested a small cage made up of thick steel bars. In some respects, it reminded her of a dog kennel, about three by three by four feet in size. The cage rested on wheels, giving it mobility.

Inside was a woman, tightly compressed to fit into the cage. Folded over, on her knees and bent over, with her forearms stretched out in front, the girl's body filled the entire interior. Avril was uncertain as to how she had fit into such a small space. The position reminded her of a feral cat stalking its kill. However, this woman wasn't hunting. She was the captured prey. The look on her face reinforced the resentment of being folded and locked in a cage.

Wide canvas straps strategically secured to the bars held her firmly in place. Straps held her hips, chest, and underarms to the top of the cage. Other straps fastened her arms and legs to the bottom and sides of the cage. The soft tissue of her body squeezed between the openings of the bars. Her breasts dangled underneath her, swaying to-and-fro at the slightest movement. Her knees were spread apart, each one touching the side of the cage, leaving her genitalia exposed.

She was vulnerable, and Sir had taken advantage of the situation. On a nearby table rested various items – his toys.

"Sir, that's Jenni."

"Yes, that's right. After the evening you two had together last week, I thought it time to start testing her. I'm curious to see how well she'll hold up under your tutelage."

"Tutelage, Sir?"

"Yes, Avril, it didn't escape me that you advised her that the best way to escape was to persevere, suffer my torment, and stay alive. So now, we're going to see whether she has the nerve to do exactly that. We will see whether she has the will to overcome whatever tests we throw at her and survive. I'm going to try and break her, and you're going to give her hope to stay alive. Together, we're going to test her and see how long she will go along with our play until she finally gives up."

"And when she does, Sir."

"She will die, of course."

"Of course, Sir."

Picking up the first toy, Avril recognized it as an anal hook similar to the one he commonly used on her. However, this hook did not have a ball on its end. Instead, it was made with a single length of steel, with a sizable open bend at one end and a smaller eye-hook on the other. She had an idea of what was coming.

"Look at me," he commanded the caged girl. With difficulty, she managed to tilt her head up and raise her eyes to him. To Avril, the look was a cross between defiance and resignation, with it leaning more towards the latter.

"Do you know what this is?" he asked the girl.

"No," she uttered weakly.

"It's a hook, and you're going to wear it."

A puzzled look appeared on the girl's face. Sir just smiled back, squatted down in front of her, and lightly stroked the underside of her chin. If she could have recoiled, Avril did not doubt that she would have. Firmly strapped to the cage as she was, all she could do was to close her eyes.

"Open your eyes and look at me." Sir commanded.

Slowly she opened her eyes, but Avril was uncertain whether she looked at him or through him. It didn't matter. He stared back at her—his gaze drilling holes into the back of her retinas.

"You're going to wear this, and I'm going to enjoy watching you squirm as I stuff it up into your ass."

It took a moment, but she eventually understood what he had just told her.

"Why…why are you doing this? Why am I here?"

"You haven't figured that out yet? You're here because I want you here. You're here to please me. You belong to me. I will do with you whatever I want, and whatever pleases me. Right now, it pleases me to shove this up your ass, but first, there is something I need to do.

Standing up, he looked over at Avril kneeling nearby and motioned 'come here.' Rising, Avril walked over.

"Get the harness," he said, indicating the full head leather harness resting on the toy table.

Returning with it, he told Avril, "Put it on her and make sure it's tight. I want no slippage."

"Yes, Sir."

Squatting down in front of the girl, Avril slipped the harness between the bars. Inserting the stainless-steel ring into the girl's mouth, forcing her jaw wide open, Avril placed the leather straps over the girl's head. She went about the task to buckle it on tight, making sure that she fitted just as Sir wanted it. When finished, she backed away and stood at attention, her hands crossed behind her back. Immediately, Jenni began drooling.

Sir stepped forward and checked her work. Satisfied, Sir turned toward Avril and said, "Good."

Using that universal finger motion towards Avril, she joined him behind the caged girl. Walking around, Sir squirted some lube on the short end of the hook and handed it to Avril.

"Put it in," he told her.

"Gladly, Sir."

Smearing some of the lube dripping from the hook onto her finger, Avril stepped up behind the girl's upraised rear end. Reaching into the cage, Avril first began circling the girl's anus with her finger, lightly touching and lovingly stroking it. In response, Avril could feel the orifice pucker up as if to protect itself.

Undaunted, Avril circled her finger closer and closer before settling on the center of the aperture. Avril could feel the tension in the girl's body, trying to prevent what she certainly knew was about to happen. After a long pause, Avril pushed. Despite Jenni's feeble resistance, once penetrated, the lube made it easy for Avril to bury her finger entirely in her ass. The girl groaned, guttural sounds escaping her throat and passing through the ring gag in her mouth.

After a moment, allowing the anal sphincter to clamp back down on her finger, Avril starting flexing the digit inside the rectum. Avril could hear the girl uttering sounds, though the ring gag prevented words from forming.

Avril found the experience remarkably intriguing and strangely curious. She could feel the concentric rings as she probed the girl's rectum. Next, she started finger fucking her ass, ensuring that she coated the entire length she could reach with the lube.

"Having fun?" Sir asked her.

"Ah, actually, Yes, Sir."

"And, how does it feel about having your finger up someone's ass?"

"Powerful, Sir … I feel powerful and dirty at the same time. I don't know how to describe what I'm feeling at the moment, but I do know I like it."

"Yes, I expected that. In the course of your training, you will learn many things that you've never been exposed to before. This is just one of many new experiences for you."

Her finger still buried in the girl's ass; Avril didn't know how to respond, so she just smiled. So, she remained silent and continued finger fucking the girl, fascinated by the experience.

"Here," Avril heard him say.

Looking over at him, he was handing her the lube. Having her other hand occupied with the hook, she placed it on the top of the cage, and gratefully took the bottle and squirted more of the lube on her hand. Focusing her attention on the finger in the girl's ass, Avril inserted a second finger into the girl. Stretching her further, she resumed her finger fucking, now with two fingers.

Grunts and moans began escaping from the girl's gagged mouth. It seemed to Avril that the girl was now getting into enjoying the sensations. Her body seemed to rock in time with Avril's driving fingers. After studying the girl's body for a time, Avril was sure of it. The girl was helping her finger fuck her ass, pushing backward to Avril, crushing her ass cheeks against the bars of the cage. Both of them experienced the pleasant sharing together.

Using a bit more lube, Avril positioned the third finger alongside the two already in her ass and pushed. There was a bit more resistance as the sphincter struggled to accept the new invader, but Avril and the lube won out. In no time at all, Avril had three of her fingers buried deep inside the girl, who by now was moaning in obvious delight.

As Avril pressed her three fingers inside, she could feel the sphincter relax, each time with a little less resistance to the intrusion. Withdrawing her fingers, Avril could feel the orifice close up around her fingers, sealing the passage behind them. Not to be, Avril pushed them back inside, opening the hole once again, driving just a bit deeper on each thrust.

"How do you feel?" Sir asked Avril.

"Nice, Sir. I don't know how to explain it, but I am enjoying fucking the bitch's ass. She's coming around, and instead of resisting me, she is participating. Her body is demanding that I fuck her ass."

"Yes, I see that as well. A trick, if you want the girl to cum, use your thumb, and play with her clit as you fuck her ass. At the same time, press your fingers towards her vaginal wall. The separation between the vagina and the rectum is paper-thin and packed with numerous nerve endings. That will heighten her pleasure and give you control over her. Besides, it gives you something else to do as you play with your toys."

"Yes, Sir," Avril chimed back as she followed his instruction.

"Then, as she approaches orgasm, you can slow down or stop the clitoral stimulation, thereby preventing her from cumming. Simultaneously, you can still finger fuck her ass, playing with her, controlling her."

"Yes, Sir, I see what you mean. Now that I think about it, I recall you doing the same to me."

"That's right. That's just one way to exert your control over your subject. Now go ahead and finish your pleasure but don't let her cum. She hasn't earned the privilege yet."

"Yes, Sir, thank you, Sir," Avril responded as she continued to finger fuck the girl and occasionally play with her clit. It didn't take long before Avril decided to see if she could get a fourth finger up her ass. Folding her hand over, she pulled out just enough to add her pinky and push. Just like that, her hand slipped in, right up to her knuckles.

"How about that?" surprise evident in Avril's thoughts.

She resolved to investigate this phenomenon further.

"Would she be able to get her entire hand up the girl's ass? Maybe, time would tell."

Avril could feel the girl's growing excitement just through her body language, and she learned how to control the building pressure to climax. It didn't take long before Avril felt she could no longer stop the girl from cumming. She began to be worried that the girl would cum, and she couldn't prevent it.

"Take the hook and put it in her." Sir commanded.

Thankfully, Avril reached up with one hand and grabbed the hook still sitting on the top of the cage. Positioning it alongside and spreading her fingers and not too gently, she inserted the cold steel, planting it deep into her ass in one smooth stroke. Avril could feel the sphincter working hard to accommodate the additional intrusion with four fingers and a metal shaft sharing space in the girl's rectum.

Mission accomplished, Avril resumed her finger fucking, sliding inside the girl's ass following the path of the hook. As she played with Jenni's ass, she spread her fingers, feeling the rectum walls and learning how it responded to her touch. It didn't take long before the girl's climax began growing again. Using the techniques Sir taught her, she controlled the girl's passion bringing her to the brink before drawing her back from the ecstasy the girl desired.

Avril suddenly withdrew her fingers, and the sphincter sealed itself around the hook. Instantly, the girl's building climax retreated, and she groaned with annoyance through the ring in her mouth.

"Perfect," Sir said to Avril. "See, you do have the makings of being a Dominant. You weren't gentle with her either as you put that in her. I wish you could have seen her expression change from near climax to outright surprise and disappointment when you suddenly pulled out. It was spectacular."

"Thank you, Sir. I surprised myself. I was so into the moment that it felt like the right thing to do."

"Do you think you were still able to control her pleasure at that moment?"

"Honestly, Sir, I think I was losing control of her, and she was about to cum."

"To cum without your permission, I take it."

"Yes, Sir, that's exactly it. I was worried that she would go ahead and cum. As you taught me, I would be annoyed that she went ahead and did it anyway."

"And that's why I'm training you. Commanding someone to not cum without permission is not enough. As a dominant, you must learn when and how to control your subjects, preventing them from coming by reading their body language and then positioning yourself to grant permission at just the right moment. You will have failed if you have not anticipated their threshold of pleasure and taken the right actions to control it. As a dominant, you are the director of the action, and it is up to you to control how it will turn out. Cumming without your permission is a testament to your failure, not theirs. Either way, they will suffer the consequence and the punishment for your faltering. Does that make sense?"

"Sir, I don't know. I will have to think about it."

"You do that. Of course, if you intended to punish her anyway, then this might be a time to let it happen and then dish out your punishment. You are still in control and did not fail in your task. In that case, I would have allowed her to have her orgasm, and then as she gave in to it, stripped her of it and severely punished her."

"I see that Sir, it kind of makes sense. Would it be fair to say that experience will guide and help me decide just what to do in these situations?"

"Yes, it will. In the meantime, tie the hook off to the top of the head harness. Make sure it's nice and tight, making sure she's looking straight ahead and can't tilt her head down."

"Yes, Sir," Avril replied, standing up and wiping her fingers clean with the nearby towel.

Picking up a length of cord lying on the table, Avril looped the cording through the eye-hook of the hook and stretched it up to the D-ring sewn into the top of the harness encapsulating the girl's head. Pulling the cord tight, she opened her ass up and forced the girl's head against the top of the cage, planting her face against the front bars. When she had the girl in the position where she thought Sir wanted her, she tied it off.

"Nice!" he said, plucking the cord as if it were a guitar string. It vibrated nicely, confirming that Avril tied it off correctly. "Now, it's time to complete the setup. Bring me that black dildo there on the table."

"Yes, Sir," Avril responded as she turned towards the table. Looking down at the variety of toys remaining, Avril was unsure how much more they could do to the girl. Part of her wondered whether she wanted to find out, and part of her was excited to find out. With a smirk on her face, she reached down and picked up the dildo. Reaching for the lube, she was interrupted.

"You won't need that. Just bring it here."

"Yes, Sir," she responded, putting down the lube. Returning to Sir, she started to hand him the dildo when he said.

"Put it in her mouth." He told her, interrupting her attempt to pass off the dildo.

Surprised by the order, Avril looked down at the dildo and studied it. It was long and thick, barely small enough to fit through the ring gag the girl was wearing. It was shaped just like a cock, with a head and simulated veining along its entire length. Like many real dicks, it curved slightly and flattened somewhat from side to side. A bracket with a swiveling joint was attached to the base end. It took Avril a moment to figure out how to use the bracket. A minute later, she figured it out.

Looking up at Sir with a questioning look, all he said was, "Go ahead."

Nodding, Avril moved to the front of the girl in the cage and squatted down. Taking the dildo in her hand, she placed it inside the hoop of the ring gag and started pushing it past the drool dripping from her mouth. The girl tried to prevent her with her tongue. However, Avril was persistent, and the dildo slipped freely through the ring gag and into the girl's mouth.

Tears welled up in the girl's eyes, and she began gagging, involuntarily retching against the intrusion sliding towards her throat. Ignoring the girl's gagging reflex, Avril continued pushing until it was well into her mouth and pressing up against the back of her throat.

Looking straight into the teary eyes of the girl, Avril whispered, "Don't panic. Just relax. You can do this. I know you can."

Avril wasn't sure if the girl heard her. Ejecting the object in her mouth seemed to be her only desire. Tears streamed down her cheeks, and her face was turning red. The girl started to heave, vomit threatening to explode from her gut. However, since she only had water to drink over the past couple of days, there was nothing in her stomach to expel.

"Relax," Avril encouraged, in a soothing, comforting tone. "You can do this."

Using Avril's free hand, she caressed the side of the girl's cheek, trying to calm the girl. Maybe it was the dildo resting on top of the girl's tongue or something else, but her drooling picked up and shifted from a slow drip to a steady stream leaking out of her mouth. It took a moment, but the girl seemed to find strength in Avril's soothing words and relaxed. Her throat opened up, and the dildo appeared to rest comfortably on the back of the girl's tongue. Slowly, the girl's body settled down, and Jenni looked back with watery, bloodshot eyes. Even her drooling began slowing to a mild inconvenience, pooling beneath her on the floor under the cage.

"Good. See, I told you that you could do this. Well done!" Avril whispered to the girl.

With the dildo fully inserted, Avril looked back up to Sir, her eyes questioning.

"Continue."

"Yes, Sir, however, will she be alright like this? I don't want her to die, at least not yet. I want to learn more about using this one."

"She'll be fine. You need to trust me. And if not, there is more stock to replace her."

"Yes, Sir," Avril answered.

Avril seated the dildo to the cage bar right in front of the girl's nose and clamped it down using the attached bracket. With both ends of the dildo firmly secured into the girl's mouth, it wasn't going anywhere.

"Good. Now come and look. Isn't she beautiful, all trussed up like that?"

"Yes, Sir, I see what you mean." Avril responded, noting that the girl's bloodshot eyes seemed to follow her around, with a questioning look of 'how could you do this to me?'

Sir wrapped an arm around Avril's waist and pulled her close. Together and for the next several minutes, the two of them gazed down at the gagged, nearly choking girl locked in the cramped cage.

He directed Avril to the toys and picked up a long metal rod with a red dildo attached to one end. Handing it to Avril, who took it in hand, he squatted down behind the girl. Reaching into the cage, he parted the lips of her labia with his fingers, indicating to Avril just where to put it. Bending over and leaning in, Avril positioned the dildo against her engorged lips and pushed. The dildo slipped in effortlessly, the girl still wet from the earlier play.

"All the way," he said.

Nodding, Avril carefully pushed the dildo in until she felt resistance from the back of her unyielding vagina. Holding it steady, she looked up at Sir for further direction.

"Clamp it to the bar like you did in front." He told her, handing her the necessary bracket. She inserted the rod onto the clamp and attached it to the cage, adjusting it before tightening it down. However, before she could finish, he said.

"Push the dildo in a bit further. Make sure it is solidly seated. Push her body forward if you must, but don't force it into her cervix. I want it tight against the back of her vaginal wall. She shouldn't be able to move back and forth."

"Yes, Sir, I understand."

Standing up, she put a hand on the girl's tailbone and pushed her forward. Jenni gagged as the dildo in her mouth slipped deeper towards her throat. Simultaneously, she pressed the dildo further into the girl right up to the hilt, clamping the rod in place.

"Good, very good," Sir said, ignoring the sounds of distress escaping from the girl's lips.

"What do you think?" He asked Avril.

"Sir, she looks beautiful, all trussed up like that," she started. "However, aren't you worried that the red dildo might break through her vaginal wall?" she finished, trailing off her words as she spoke them.

"And …?" He asked, trailing off as if to say, 'so what if it did.'

"Well, Sir. She's in a very precarious and dangerous position. She could die like that?"

"How so?"

"Well, assuming she had something to bring up in her stomach, she could vomit and choke to death."

"Anything else?"

"She could still choke to death, unable to breathe if that dildo slips down her throat much further."

"Very good, anything else?"

"Yes, Sir, the hook in her ass could rupture her rectum or colon and, if left untreated, would poison her."

"Very true, anything else?"

"Yes, Sir, the dildo in her pussy, well, it's in there very deep. I suppose it could puncture the wall of her vagina and enter her abdominal cavity, leaving her vagina unprotected from bacteria lying in wait."

"Very true, what else?"

Considering she had used up the observations she already tabulated, she had to think about it. She assumed that Sir knew that there was more, but she hadn't figured it out yet. Then, it occurred to her.

"Sir, if that dildo in her pussy ruptured her vaginal canal, I presume she could also bleed to death. And not just the dildos but the hook could also result in an uncontrolled bleed."

"Excellent, Avril, just what I was looking for. Would you agree that the straps used to support her body in the cage help keep her from hurting herself? It's not perfect, and if she panics, she most certainly will die. In short, this is an example of predicament bondage, only in this case, the predicament isn't how to prevent her from injury and death but how to stay alive. I want to see how long she can manage to stay like this. I'm hoping she can last at least three days. If she makes it, we will release her and allow her to recover. Then we'll give her a new challenge."

"Sir, should we be saying this in front of her? What if she hears us and understands our intent for her?"

"All the better, Avril, it's good that she can hear us. I want her to hear. With experience, you will learn why. Like you, I don't tell my captives everything, but I've always spoken my mind when I wanted to. In this case, I want her to hear us. I want her to know that, together, we will do this to her."

"It looks uncomfortable, Sir."

"When have you known me to care about my property's comfort?"

"Ah, now that you mention it, never Sir."

"That's right, never. Your existence, her continued existence, is at my pleasure. Soon it will be at your pleasure, to do with them as you please."

"If you study her further, you'll notice that while she is experiencing discomfort, she is not in any real pain. Nothing we've done so far is painful to her body. You, of all people, know full well what constitutes real pain. What we've done is nothing of the sort. If she can relax and overcome her fears, she will be fine. If not, and she panics, then she will likely die. It's her choice, and consequently, the second aspect of the predicament. If she stays completely still, calm and relaxed, she will survive the ordeal. If she thrashes about, she will die. It's that simple, and it's all up to her. We are giving her the power to live or die. And the nice thing is, we didn't kill her. She will have done it to herself."

"Yes, Sir, I see what you mean."

"Okay, now. Grab hold of the cage and push her into the next room."

"Alright, Sir, frankly, I'm excited to see what happens. Will she survive the predicament?"

Following Sir, Avril got behind the cage and carefully pushed slowly across the floor. Careful to not jar the cage, she rolled it into the adjoining room. It was a large shower room with showerheads everywhere and water taps located strategically on every wall. In addition to the rain heads peppering the ceiling, it even had a water spigot hanging overhead. A narrow stainless-steel grate surrounded the space, draining water and other bodily fluids from the enclosure. If it were in anywhere else, Avril figured it could comfortably handle a dozen people showering simultaneously.

The lighting in the room was different from the darkness of the other room. Here, bright, diffused lighting illuminated a softly rotating kaleidoscope of color broadcasting on the room's nearly white tile. There was no overhead lighting; just side lighting meant to instill an intimate atmosphere.

"Put her in the center of the room." Sir told Avril. Standing up on her heels, she confidently stood up and looked at the girl."

"May I, Sir?" indicating a desire to walk around the girl and study her with the air of majesty.

"Absolutely."

Her heels clicking softly on the hard surface of the tiled floor, Avril slowly circled the cage, studying the girl from every angle. At times, she squatted down to get a closer look, and at times, reached in, stroking the girl's skin. Once, she even stuck a finger into the girl's ass, joining the metal hook, stretching the sphincter once more.

As she examined the girl, she couldn't help notice that Sir was studying her. Undeterred, Avril continued her examination of the restrained girl. Standing up and finally turning towards Sir, he said.

"Tell me what you're feeling right this minute."

"Hmmm, Sir, there is a lot I am feeling. I'm not sure I will be able to describe it all."

"Just do the best that you can."

"Yes, Sir, well, I'm excited, of course."

"How so?"

"Besides a growing wetness, I'm feeling warm, as if there is something in my gut. It's not a knot, but a growing pressure that seems to be growing larger, almost as if it's a sun coming to life, radiating heat and light outwards. Yes, that part of it. It's heat that is slowly growing, just below and behind my sternum."

"Interesting, go on."

"Well, Sir, there is a part of me that wants to be that girl. To have a dick up my pussy, down my throat, and another in my ass steadily like that. I wanted to understand what it was like to be unable to move, unable to resist, feeling vulnerable, and exposed. Seeing her like that excites me. I'd like to try it."

"Well, I can put you in a cage like hers and let you both spend the next three days together."

"Would you, Sir? I know, only if it pleases you to do so, it will please me. Besides, the experience will teach me how to understand and direct my future submissives."

"Very well then, let's do it; I've got plenty of those cages in stock. I'll get one and set it up. You stay here and watch over our pretty one. I'm sure you're dripping wet at the prospect of being trussed up."

"Yes, Sir, thank you. I am." Avril answered without averting her gaze from the girl. Sir stepped out of the room, leaving Avril to stand watch over the girl.

The girl looked back at Avril and, with her eyes, spoke, "Are you crazy? Why would you do this?"

"Maybe I am," Avril said to Jenni. "However, I know I will not die, and this will be an easy assignment for me. I've suffered far worse than this. Doing it alongside you should give you the strength and determination to survive, knowing that I will survive this ordeal. Don't worry. If you don't panic and remain calm, you won't die. I promise you that."

Avril reached inside the cage and caressed the damp cheek of the caged girl as she talked to her. Stroking lightly, as if she were a lover, Avril continued to comfort the girl, stroking her cheek.

"Relax," Avril whispered to her, "you'll get through this. We'll be doing it together. If I can do it, then so can you."

Jenni slowly closed her eyes in resignation.

"Good. The more you do as he says, the easier it will be for you."

Avril was still squatting in front of the girl when Sir called out to her.

"Ready. Come here."

"Yes, Sir, on my way."

Standing up, "Remember, stay calm, and you'll be fine." she said and turned to the door. "I'll be right back."

Walking into the other room, Avril approached another cage. It was resting in the center of the room, with its top open. Stepping in, heels and all, Avril folded herself as she remembered the other girl was and prepared for a long three days. Fortunately for her, her last meal was many hours ago, and she had lots of practice controlling her gag reflex.

Sir first strapped her legs wide apart to the bars on the side, as he had done with Jenni. Her toes extended beyond the end of the cage. She realized her heels gave her some protection from the raw edges of the cage.

After he restrained her legs, she bent over, and Sir did the same to her arms. In moments, her forearms stretched out in front of her alongside the edge of the cage.

Standing over her, Sir lowered the top onto her back, compressing her body into the small space. Using a few more straps, he secured her around the chest and hips, cinching them tight to the top of the cage. Resting on her knees with her legs spread apart and her head lowered between her outstretched arms, she felt exposed and vulnerable in this humble position. Still, it wasn't too bad. She had posed like this for Sir often during her stay in his estate, only never in a tiny cage.

As Avril prepared herself, she thought. "In many respects, this isn't bad. I can relax, supported as I am by the restraints. It was a peculiar position but not all that uncomfortable. I have, after all, endured worse situations. Still, three days dealing with a dildo up my pussy, down my throat, and a hook up my ass, will be hard, no doubt about it," she continued.

"Avril, your ass is not as virginal as hers. Do you want the hook straight-up, or would you like a little stimulation first?"

"Sir, whatever way it pleases you. However, I'd welcome a bit of titillation if that is alright." Avril answered.

"I'll do the fingers first, and maybe more. Your willingness to endure this test pleases me to no end, and I would like to send you on with something to remember as the days slowly progress. Don't underestimate this test. It will be arduous for you, more so for your companion. You know this, but you have never performed a test this long of a duration. It may seem easy to you now, but in six, twelve, eighteen, twenty-four hours from now, it will feel like a month. Three days will feel like an eternity."

"Yes, Sir, I get that. Still, I have to know for myself how it will feel. Besides, I know that I will not die from this test and that you will be watching out for me."

"Yes, Avril, I will, but that doesn't mean you won't die. You will have the same constraints as that one. Your advantage is that you know you can do this. Frankly, I doubt that one has the same conviction."

He said as he began coating her ass with lube. A moment later, he penetrated her, stuffing first one, then two, then three, and finally four fingers up her rectum, stretching her, coating her, and opening her up.

"Push back your ass," he commanded.

She complied as best as she could in the circumstances. She felt Sir press his cock head against her upraised ass and push, easily penetrating her. In one smooth motion, he buried himself into her rectum and slapped his balls against her vagina. Feeling him slide inside her, she couldn't help but close her eyes and enjoy the full feeling of having his cock inside her. He still impressed her by his stamina, fucking her from behind as he had done so many times before. Her body responded, accustomed to his presence and feeling her body flushed, sexual excitement quickly built up inside her. She gave in to the delight emanating from her ass and allowed her climax to build. It didn't take long before she asked the most crucial question of the day.

"Sir, may I cum?"

"Wait," he replied quietly.

Avril expected his answer and struggled to stave off the building climax. She asked, again and again. Each time he denied her. Her lust building, she clamped down with her sphincter muscles as if to grab his erection and keep him from pulling out. With the lube, it was a losing battle. He effortlessly slipped from her grasp before ramming back hard into her.

She asked again, begging for the release, and received the expected denial. Determined to obey, she focused on her bindings, the coming

days, and Sir's beautiful, delightful cock stroking her rectum. She felt
him put a hand on the small of her back, directing her to remain firmly
planted against the bars of the cage. She pushed back, and he pushed
harder into her. She could feel his legs bouncing against her ass with his
balls slapping her pussy. It was becoming too much to hold off. Her
body pleaded for its release.

"Please … Sir. May I cum!" she begged, this time a bit more
insistently.

"Soon, Avril, very soon," he answered.

"Yes, Sir, but I don't think I can hold off any longer."

"Hold it. You'll be releasing it any time now." He emphatically
affirmed.

"Yes, Sir." she groaned and dropped her head. He drove into her
again. Focusing on the cock up her ass, she realized that it seemed to
grow hotter and thicker.

"Yes," she thought to herself. "He's ready. He's about to cum."
Bearing down on her pleasure, she massaged it and prepared herself for
her release. It wasn't long before she knew, without a doubt, they were
both ready for the coming climax.

"Sir … please … may I cum … now?" She managed to squawk.

"Cum now for me now," Sir commanded.

To be honest, she didn't hear all of it. After the word 'cum,' all she
felt was releasing the stored built-up pleasure, exploding within her.
Clasping his hands gripping her pelvis, Sir unloaded inside her rectum.

"Deeper Sir, deeper … Shoot it into me," she muttered to herself
amid their combined climaxes.

Her eyes glazed over and rolled up into the back of her head. She
disappeared into a fog. All that existed was her pleasure and his
pulsating cock. She stopped breathing on her own, holding her breath as
the pleasure waves rolled back and forth along the entire length of her
body. Time slowed, even as the rocking and pulsation of his cock inside
her remained constant. How long she held her breath remained
unknown to her. As long as he stayed stuffed up her ass, she didn't care.
She was happy, comforted by his presence deep inside her.

Another massive orgasm blossomed, riding on top of the first one.
Focusing on Sir's intrusion, a third one erupted and spread about her
body, without giving her a chance to recover from the previous one.
And still, she held her breath, unable and unwilling to take in the air that

kept her body alive. She drove her thoughts even deeper into the waves of her euphoria, willing it to stay with her. Determined to retain her blissful happiness, she held it tight to her body and soul.

When she felt him start to withdraw, she felt the immediate loss. Faced with the imminent end to her ecstasy, she gave in and admitted defeat. She wasn't ready to return to the real world, but he was a necessary component of her pleasure. Then he drove back inside her, pulling her hips tightly against him. Within that split second, just as she had given up, her orgasm exploded, pushing her to an even greater height of euphoria.

Immersing in the pool of desire, she focused on him. She failed, feeling only his presence inside her, enticing her to wallow in her sea of rapture. Though she couldn't see him, she witnessed the memory of his eyes on fire as he fucked her. Once again, he withdrew just a bit before thrusting once more into her, his pulsating cock trying to eject his last bit of cum held in reserve.

Her body pushed back, demanding to breathe. She didn't want to disturb the wonderful, delightful experience of just the two of them. She held it off as long as she could, bathing in the pleasure still raging through her. She didn't want to take a breath, interrupting the flow of joy traveling about each cell in her body.

Eventually, her lungs won out and forced open an airway to take a deep breath. "Fuck," she thought to herself. "I didn't want to do that."

Evicted from the moment her lungs urgently sucked in as much air as possible, knowing full well that she might force the organ closed for business. Her lungs were correct. Once again, she held her breath, this time trying desperately to hold onto the dissipating pleasure.

As her climax subsided, she focused on his wondrous cock inside her. "Oh, damn, he's lost his erection, and he's pulling out," she realized.

Giving in to the inevitable and instantly regretting her decision, she opened her mouth and began inhaling several rapid, deep breaths before slipping into a regular breathing pattern.

Depleted but still wanting more, she waited for his next move. Unsurprised by what followed, he slipped the cold hard steel of the hook into her ass. After experiencing the hot thick cock inside her, this thing was the exact opposite, cold and unforgiving.

"Something to look forward to over the next three days," Sir told her as he fastened the leather harness over her head and the ring gag in her mouth. Avril closed her eyes and drank in the memory of her ecstasy still seething throughout her body.

Minutes later, she found herself stuffed with a dildo deep in her mouth and another one firmly in her pussy. She felt like she was stuffed, trussed, and ready for a Thanksgiving Day dinner where she would be the roasted turkey, served up for the diners.

Squatting down in front of her when he finished, he said. "That's my girl. You look fantastic. I am going to enjoy watching you over you these next few days. I don't think I've seen you look as beautiful as you do at this moment. Don't let anyone tell you otherwise."

Avril could only smile back at him with her eyes. Moments later, he wheeled her into the wet room where he positioned both cages so that each woman could look at each other. Avril thought it interesting that he placed her to see past the girl and at the door beyond. Seeing the door was an advantage the other girl did not have. She would know when Sir stepped through the doorway.

Smiling inside, Sir departed, turning off the cascade of light falling across the walls. Replacing it was a small, low-intensity spotlight that illuminated a small circle of light between them, a night light of sorts. The night light allowed each other to see the other, but beyond that, not much else.

Avril relaxed as much as she could, allowing her upper teeth to rest on the dildo in her mouth. The position stretched her ass a bit, but that was okay. She was confident that the hook wasn't going to perforate her.

"It will be interesting to see whether or not Jenni survives." Unable to do much about it, she put it out of her mind.

Closing her eyes, she envisioned the subspace she had only recently exited. Moments later, the world around her disappeared, and her mind slipped away. Before dropping off, Avril thought, "if I can keep this up, this ordeal will go fast."

Avril remained in her altered state for several hours. She might have even fallen asleep. She came back to reality when her bladder demanded attention. Knowing full well it would be a long three days, Avril didn't give it another thought and released her stream. By the time she finished, she had realized that little splashed the inside of her thighs.

"Well, that's a relief," she added to herself.

Looking up at the girl in front of her, she realized the girl's eyes questioned whether it was okay to empty her bladder. Avril nodded her answer, and a moment later, another stream added to the pool below them, adding to the reek of urine permeating the room.

Avril looked at the eyes before her, seeing the relief and gratitude of an empty bladder. Avril felt the same way but wondered what the girl was thinking. "Maybe one day, she'll tell me." Keeping her body relaxed, she slipped off to sleep, hoping it was a long one.

Some hours later, she awoke to the awful smell of excrement. Looking up, the eyes of the girl in front of her said, "Sorry."

No matter, Avril figured she would be doing the same before long. Thinking about it, Avril realized that the hook might block some of it, but eventually, her need dealt with the steel occupying her rectum and ejected the mass onto the floor. Trying to see underneath the girl, Avril got a good view of the dirt pile under her. Closing her eyes once again, Avril was determined never to look in that direction ever again.

When Avril next came too, she noticed that Jenni had closed her eyes. Maybe she was sleeping or unconscious. Which? She had no idea.

Closing her eyes once again and defying her willpower, sleep failed her. Instead, her mind reeled with various thoughts and questions, some related to her current predicament and others not. Unable to drift off, she inspected her surroundings.

Her eyes adjusted to the darkness allowed her to see the walls lined with white subway tiles. The floor, a mosaic of ceramic tile set in a design that went from light in the middle to dark around the walls, made for an interesting effect. She was unsure what revealed the different colors and patterns. She resolved to figure it out one day after she was released.

Since she couldn't move her head much, she settled on studying her playmate. She had near perfect tanned skin and blonde hair. "Did she come from a warm climate?" she wondered. "Was she a virgin before being picked up?" she added. "I have a host of questions. I wish I knew more, and even if I did, would I want to know?"

She had long light lashes, which implied that she was a natural blonde, possibly of Scandinavian descent, Norwegian perhaps? It was fun guessing and building a background around the girl, even if it wasn't right. It did help pass the time.

"Was her family also blonde? Were they looking for her? Well, they would never find her, of that she had no doubt whatsoever."

The girl's hair was knotted and gnarly as if she hadn't washed it in a long time. Little wonders if she spent a couple of weeks in the training center before being auctioned off to Sir. In all likelihood, she didn't experience the unpleasant reception she lived through. Since Jenni didn't go through the auction, that meant that Sir tagged her right from the start and shipped her here immediately. As such, they probably caged Jenni right after arriving at the training center, in one of the many small cells set aside for his purchased playthings.

"Playthings for torture before slaughter," she shivered at the inadvertent pun, feeling lucky that she hadn't met that fate.

"Well, I haven't yet, but that doesn't mean I won't," she revised her thinking.

Avril stared at the girl in front of her, dreaming up scenarios of what she and Sir would do to Jenni. Over the next couple of days, various ideas congealed into realistic plans she would discuss with Sir to see what he thought. In the meantime, it was time to redouble her efforts to get through this ordeal. Sir was correct. Strapped and skewered for days was a lot harder than she thought it would be.

Suddenly, Jenni's eyes flew open, and she began coughing in panic. Fighting her bindings, afraid and hysterical, struggling against the invaders to her every orifice, Avril could see the girl was doomed if she couldn't calm down. Jenni's bloodshot eyes, spilling tears, jerked about as if to escape from her puny prison. In horror, Avril watched Jenni lose her grip on sanity and tear her body to shreds. The smell of iron in the air implied that in her struggles, Jenni tore open a wound. She only hoped it wasn't too severe.

Hoping to help, Avril tried to make a noise loud enough to capture her attention. It was as if the look of extreme fear in her wide-open eyes prevented her from noticing anything else. Looking at the girl, Avril could almost drill her stare beyond the eyelids and into her inner self. Jenni struggled vigorously, fighting her bindings and only making her situation worse. If she didn't calm down, the girl would indeed die right in front of Avril. All Avril could do was to calm the girl by taking an air of peaceful composure.

Maybe that worked, or perhaps it was something else, fatigue perhaps, but soon the girl relaxed. Moments later, she was breathing normally, at least as one could breathe with a dildo stuffed in your mouth. It helped to sit back on the hook, thereby making it somewhat easier to draw breath.

Eventually, Jenni looked back at her with watery, bloodshot eyes, in a way that told Avril, 'Thanks.'

Avril slowly blinked. 'You're welcome.'

Over what seemed like the next several hours, Avril watched the girl, trying to instill confidence. She could be wrong, but she figured the girl was getting the message as she seemed to imply the same back at her with her body language. Between meaningful looks between them, Avril thought about her new life.

Since they took her, even now, she struggled to accept her new situation. She didn't want it, but unless she could do something about it, she complied. She still wanted to escape, but three things stood in the way. First, escape seemed impossible. Imprisoned in a house with booby-trapped entrances would cause immeasurable pain and death should she try to traverse those portals.

The second dealt with a promise made not to try to escape. For Avril, keeping promises was a badge of honor. She couldn't remember a time when she had violated an oath. Still, though, it would be nice to return to her old life, whatever that may be.

The third and most likely, the hardest to circumvent was what to do after escaping. No doubt, Sir and his cronies in the Consortium would come after her and return her to his house of horror, capped off with a drawn-out excruciating death.

Deep down, she knew what the Consortium was doing was wrong. Nonetheless, they persisted. From what Sir told her, they had existed for a thousand years.

"Unbelievable," she thought incredulously. "If that were true, then how was it possible to finally end this brutality among the masses? Could everyday people be the root problem?"

"Sir was right. Who was going to miss a few thousand people from among seven billion? I'm the perfect example. I have no one who might still be looking for me. My parents are dead. God rest their souls. Even if I dropped off the face of the earth, who would look for me? If anyone did, would they give up after a couple of months? I don't honestly know."

Avril knew she had lots of time to ponder the question. She had a total of three days of alone time with nothing to occupy her mind.

"Hmmm, I wonder just how long I've been here like this. Has it been more than a day? There's just no way of telling. Sir loves to screw with time among his victims."

Just as the thought crossed her mind, the lights in the room suddenly blinded her. She had gotten so used to the darkness, the light seemed like a blinding sun, scorching her retinas. Squeezing her eyelids closed, Avril waited to allow them to adjust.

"Hello, my lovelies. How are you this morning?" Sir cheerfully called out as he came into view.

Of course, all Avril could do was squeeze her eyes and then blink in response.

"Are you both still here?" he redundantly asked.

Avril could only think, "Yep, still here," as she looked at the girl in front of her, also exhibiting signs of distress from the blinding light.

"It's been twelve hours, time to clean you up. You must be feeling filthy, and I can see why." He spoke.

Snapping his fingers, another one of his kept women entered the room and started hooking up a hose to one of the water-taps around the room.

Avril couldn't believe her ears. "It's only been twelve hours, really?"

Sir must have seen the look on her face because he immediately answered her. "Yes, only twelve hours. I hope you had a pleasant night."

"Shit!" Avril thought.

A minute or so later, Sir's attendant hosed them both down. Thankfully, the warm water felt good. The woman even pointed the water nozzle at her backside and made sure she cleaned Avril inside and out. Sir just stood there and watched the slave work, directing her when she missed a spot or two. When finished, to his satisfaction, she coiled up the hose and took a kneeling position near the door. It was just what Avril would have done if she were in her shoes.

"My shoes! Oh, God, my shoes. They're soaked. Are they ruined?" she suddenly realized.

Of course, there was no way for her to find out until after he freed her from her predicament. While she did love these shoes for their comfort and elegance, she knew that Sir would replace them if they were damaged.

Sir moved over to stand between them. Stroking Avril's head, he first spoke to Avril's companion, Jenni.

"You're doing well so far. I noted that you had a panic attack a few hours ago, which did not surprise me. You should know, the wagering to see how long you both last is quite vigorous. Most are betting that you'll both die by tomorrow evening."

Stopping to let that sink in a moment, Sir continued.

"If my Avril weren't here to help instill confidence in you, I would have bet that you would have died long before that. Even with Avril's help, nearly all the bets have you dying," directing his final comments to Jenni.

Turning towards Avril, he continued, "As for you, most of the bets have you failing this challenge, outlasting her but dying in the end. I, on the other hand, am betting you both survive."

Sir stroked the back of Avril's head before turning back towards Jenni.

"You know that you owe your life to my Avril. Without her, the bets had you dying after a day or so. Without her assistance, I was skeptical and figured you had a fifty-fifty chance to make it through. She is helping you. I'm not sure why she volunteered, but I don't doubt that she will survive this. Take comfort in the knowledge that Avril is here with you, suffering alongside you, feeling your pain and discomfort. You should be grateful for her assistance. If you do survive this, I expect you to give her the respect she deserves."

Turning his attention to Avril, "You should be aware that the betting is against you. I plan on proving them wrong. My money on you. I know you won't let me down."

Avril blinked her acknowledgment, thinking, 'Wow, I thought that they would have learned by now. I'm not going anywhere. At least until I can do something about it.'

Giving Avril a comforting pat followed up with a smack on her ass, Sir turned and left, turning the lights off as he went. Once again, darkness fell upon them. Even the nightlight disappeared. So dark was the room, Avril couldn't see the nose in front of her face. The girl before her vanished as if she never existed.

"Shit, it's going to be a long two and a half days," Avril uttered to herself inside her mind. "He did warn me, but still, I had no idea."

Chapter Twenty

Waking, Lara felt disoriented, uncertain about what had happened to her. The last thing she remembered, she was safely cradled in the arms of Robert, holding her tight as they slept on top of a mountain. It had been a beautiful night, capped off by a loving embrace as the two of them made love under the spectacular expanse of stars and the Milky Way.

Fighting a massive headache, she opened her eyes. She knew at once she wasn't in the tent on top of the mountain. More importantly, Robert was nowhere nearby. Sealed inside a clear plastic crate, she was naked and alone. Pounding at her enclosure, she started screaming. At first, it was for help to get her out of here. Eventually, her cries for help transformed into ones of anger and finally despair.

"Robert, where are you?" she lamented as tears seeped from her eyes and coated her cheeks. In her anguish, she wanted to turn over onto her side and curl up into a ball. The box she was in was too small even to let her do that. All she could do was lie there, on her back, and cry.

Sometime later, after draining the last of her tears, she realized that she wasn't alone. Looking past the clear plastic of her box, she noticed other people lying in clear plastic boxes all around her for the first time. Some were not moving, while others were pounding away at their prisons. Still, others were looking wildly at their surroundings, as if to find out what was going on.

Straining, Lara tried to see if Robert was in one of the other boxes. She couldn't find him. Part of her wanted to know if he was here, with her, even if locked away in a separate crate. Part of her hoped he wasn't somewhere out there and that he was looking for her. That somehow, Robert escaped and was searching for her. It was her only hope to get free.

Nearly exhausted in her search, she gave up and stared at the top of her enclosure. Closing her eyes, she tried to divest herself of her fear and relax. Only then did she realize that she, like the rest of the people in their boxes, were on a plane, flying to some unknown destination.

"Where are you taking me?" she screamed, not expecting an answer. She wasn't disappointed, as no solution presented itself.

Lying there, with nothing to do, she closed her eyes again and tried to sleep. It escaped her, and she drifted in and out of a semi-state of awareness, not understanding nor caring what was to come. She felt powerless, alone, and frightened.

"Oh, my Robert, where are you?"

Hours later, the plane began descending, and soon, it touched down. Slowly taxiing down the runway, the aircraft soon came to a halt.

"Maybe now I'll find out what the hell is going on," Lara muttered.

About a half-hour later, she noted activity among the piled-up boxes. A door to the plane opened, filling the darkish space with a blinding light. Shutting out the painful assault to her retinas, Lara intently listened until her eyes finally acclimated.

Looking through her transparent box, she watched men and women unload the boxes, one by one, and cart them off the plane. Soon enough, they came for her, and as she slid around the inside of her crate, she pounded on the sides, trying to get their attention to let her out.

They ignored her. After carrying her off the plane, they rudely dumped her inside the cargo box of a truck and walked off. Before long, they filled it with many naked bodies in transparent crates stacked all around her. Above her, she stared at the bare ass of a woman who hadn't been able to hold her bladder. She sloshed around in a pool of her piss. Shortly after the truck gate closed, the truck rolled off to parts unknown.

After traveling for a couple of hours, some of it over bumpy terrain and nearly giving her a bloody nose, the truck came to a stop. Soon, everyone was unloaded, stacked onto rolling carts, and pushed into what looked like a warehouse. After the doors closed, they cut her out of her crate.

Immediately, she yelled. "What the fuck? Who the hell are you?"

That was about all she could scream at them as they backhanded her across her mouth. In an instant, she was silenced and taken away by goons on either forearm. They led her to a station where a man carrying a chain approached her and clipped it to her collar.

It was only then that she noticed the collar around her neck. "What the fuck?" she snapped.

Instantly she felt excruciating pain in her head. Doubling over, she nearly fell to the floor, stopped by the two men holding her by each arm.

Laughing at her misery, they led her into another room. The room appeared to be a communal shower. Several of the people from the boxes were already there, standing under a showerhead.

Looking around, she searched for Robert, hoping not to find him. Scanning, she ignored the naked bodies, focusing only on the men. Mostly they were all women, chained under the showerheads, but there were some men. Skipping over the women, she looked for her Robert.

"Robert!" she yelled, and a man at the far end turned towards her.

"Lara. Is that you?"

Instantly, she was glad and dismayed that she had found her beau as any hope for rescue drained down the shower grates.

"Quiet. No talking." A burly man spoke sharply from the doorway.

Looking at Robert, Lara could see the look of an apology for getting her into this mess. Lara shook her head back as if to say, "Don't, it's not your fault."

In time, the guards finished bringing the last of the people from the boxes. Another man stepped in and began talking to the group. She didn't pay much attention. The gist of his speech was apparent. They were now theirs, prisoners to be cleaned up and put into cells. They were to do as they were told or suffer the consequences.

To reinforce their commands, a guard walked along the length of them, singling out a man, thankfully not Robert, and punched him right in the solar plexus. Instantly, the man fell to his knees, nearly strangling from the chain attached to the collar around his neck.

A minute later, the shower heads came on, and warm water drenched them. Taking the soap, Lara washed. Looking about, she could see some of the captives squatting, doing a dump. Not needing to follow suit, she did need, however, to relieve her bursting bladder. Unembarrassed, she let her pee mix with the brown and soapy water on their way to the drains.

Not knowing when she would get the next opportunity to shower, Lara made sure she thoroughly washed and spent extra time on her hair. As she scrubbed, she noticed another woman across from her, not doing a particularly good job of it. Before long, a pair of guards, wearing only shorts, stopped in front of the girl. The next thing she knew, the guards were roughly washing the girl with stiff brushes, turning her skin raw. They weren't done with her yet. They pulled out their erections and brutally fucked her, simultaneously penetrating her ass and vagina.

After violating her until she was nearly dead, they dropped her to the floor, where she choked on the chain locked to the wall above her.

Whispering, Lara said. "Get up. You'll die like that."

"So," the girl whispered back, "maybe it is better that way."

"Shhh! Don't say that." Lara whispered back as a guard snapped. "No talking."

Turning and dropping her head, Lara stared at the shower wall and finished washing her hair.

With the water shut off, guards led them out of the shower room one by one. Leading Lara through the doorway, they directed her to a station where a burly guard grabbed her and held her arms behind her back.

Another guard approached her with a pair of forceps and a thick needle. She tried to back away, but the guard held her steady. Unable to move, Lara watched the other man grasp her nipple, clamp forceps over it, and shove the needle through it. Gritting her teeth in her discomfort, she watched him thread a metal hoop through the hole. Then he did the same to her other nipple.

She didn't realize they hadn't finished. With the two ends of the hoop nearly touching each other, they welded the two ends together.

She doubled over and screamed in pain as the heat immediately seared her tender nipple, cauterizing the wound. Held firmly by the guard behind her, the other man repeated the welding to the hoop through her second nipple. Her screams turned to whimpers as the scorching metal transmitted agonizing fire throughout her breasts.

"Keep them clean, wash them often with soap and water. Failure will result in severe punishment."

She heard the words, but they didn't quite register. Her only thoughts dealt with the agony of her breasts.

"My, you're a pretty one," a guard said as he took hold of her and led her away.

Soon enough, he dumped her in a prison cell. Closing and walking away, he laughed at her agony. Looking about, she sat down on a bunk, barely big enough to let her stretch out. At the back was a small sink and toilet. The cell was scarcely four feet by six feet in length. The area was so small that pacing back and forth was impossible.

Lara was about to lean back and lie down when she noticed a piece of paper on the skimpy pillow. Written on it was a demand to put on a pair of heels that she would find under the bed. The note went on to say that she was not to take them off, for whatever reason, unless explicitly told to do so. Failure to comply would result in severe punishment.

"What else is new." she thought as she read that last line.

Looking under the bed, sure enough, there was a pair of shoes. They were no ordinary heeled shoes. These were black pumps with four to five-inch spiked heels with straps around the ankle.

She had never worn shoes like this before. She was an outdoors girl, more comfortable in a pair of hiking boots than in stilettos.

"Crap! I can't wear these. I'll break my ankles."

Tossing them on the floor, she leaned back and lay down on her bunk. A few minutes later, a pair of guards came by, saw the heels on the floor, and Lara lying down on the cot. Enraged, they unlocked the cell door and entered.

Lara tried to speak, afraid of what they were about to do to her. They didn't give her a chance. Snapping at her about not wearing the shoes, they told her she would now have to suffer the consequences.

Screaming, Lara tried to fight them off. As healthy and toned as she was, she was no match for these brutes. By the time they finished with her, she was wearing her heels, crying and aching from the brutal invasion to her privates. They spared nothing, pinning her to the cell bars and fucking her to within an inch of her life. Later, Lara realized that they had done the deed against the bars so that the others would see and behave, putting on their heels before the guards came for them.

Lara laid on her bunk, crying and whimpering from the brutality of what they had done. Later, she checked herself to make sure she wasn't bleeding anywhere, including between her legs and her rectum. She was surprised that she found no evidence of blood anywhere.

She hurt all over. Her nipples screamed every time a piece of cloth dragged over them. Her breasts ached where the guards had ferociously grappled them, nearly tearing them from her chest. Her loins and ass screamed in pain as the memory of the vicious abuse vibrated throughout her body.

Eventually, she fell into a restless sleep, uncertain of what she would have to endure the next day, the man's words repeating endlessly in her dreams.

"You are now our property. You will never return to your former life. We own you. We will do with you whatever we please. In time, we will sell you at auction. We expect that your sale will more than cover our expenses. After that, your new owner will decide what to do with you. The sooner you accept this, the easier it will be for you."

"Robert, please help me." She lamented as she tossed all night long.

"Oh god, oh my god!" she grunted as his cock drove inside her, causing her to rise to new heights in her approaching climax.

On her back, Misty wrapped her legs tightly around the guy on top of her. As he pounded away at her, she lost all sense of what was all around her. All she could feel was the joy in her pussy, her legs hooked around his waist, trying to pull him deeper inside her.

"Oh my god!" she whispered, as her climax grew, deliriously happy.

She had given herself over to him, allowing him to control her body, knowing that the impending orgasm was going to be one of the very best ever.

"Oh ... my ... god," she grunted again, "oh my god ... YES!" she yelled, though uncertain whether the words truly escaped her lips. All she knew was that beautiful hard cock pounded her, nailing her to the bed, and she never wanted it to stop ... ever."

Driving into her, he leaned over her, pressed his hands against each breast, and pushed her against the mattress. Her tits flattened against her rib cage. She felt his strength entirely dominating her, crushing her while pile-driving into her pussy. She felt glorious and needed just what he gave her. His body was heavy on top of her. Crushing her chest, she found it impossible to breathe.

Just as her body demanded a breath, he released his death grip on her chest. As she started to gulp in air, he slid his hands up and wrapped them around her neck. With his hands around her throat, he dug his thumbs into that soft spot. That rush of air to her lungs halted, and she opened her eyes.

Seeing the bloodlust in his eyes, she screamed, only nothing came out. Pounding on his back, she struggled to push him off her. He was too heavy. Pinned to the bed, she watched him flex his arms, lean in, and shove. His hands tightened around her throat, his thumbs crushing her larynx.

In an instant, her building sexual euphoric state vaporized, replaced by the sudden fear and realization that she was about to die. He was strangling her. Struggling, she felt his climax, ejaculating inside of her, even as he throttled her, depriving her of her very life.

Pounding on his arms, she tried to break them free from their death grip around her neck. She felt tears well up even as her eyes popped out of her skull. Scared of dying, she clawed and scraped at him, still unable to push him off. As her need for air increased, so did her thrashing about, her legs flailing, looking for leverage to shove him away. She found none. Beating on his arms, all she saw was the determination in his face, even as it portrayed his orgasmic climax.

As a red haze fell across his face, her struggles weakened. Focusing on his eyes filled him with a determined need to kill. His face revealed what was happening. From the sneer in his smile, she knew just what he wanted from her. With a final thrust, he ejaculated inside her, his need to strangle her the impetus he needed to come.

Her mouth opened in a silent scream. She knew in an instant, he was determined. She was about to die.

"Oh my God, please don't. I don't ... want ... to ... die." She screamed in her head.

Jumping up, disoriented, and drenched in sweat, Misty realized it was all a dream, indeed a nightmare. Gathering her wits about her, she finally looked up from the thin mattress she laid on, remembering that while it had been a dream, she was living a nightmare. A nightmare began weeks ago when they sold her at auction, and she ended up in this place run by a cruel man and his woman. As much as she hated those early days, she couldn't forget them. They constantly replayed those awful days in her mind.

Naked and afraid, she looked around, trying to avoid looking at the bars encasing her in this small cell. Eventually, sounds from beyond the lined-up steel bars forced her to look up. Standing in front of her cell, a guard glared at her with a wicked look on his face. Immediately, she turned away from him as he laughed, taunting her before moving off.

"Oh my God, please help me." She prayed.

Somehow, she knew he would not answer her pleas. Long ago, she had forsaken him, so now why would he come to her rescue.

As best as she could tell, she had landed in this cell about two weeks ago, frightened and naked. Whoever they were, tormented her constantly, welding steel rings through her nipples, still tender to this day. Twice daily, they took her from her cell, forced her to learn how to walk a runway like some goddamn supermodel. Whenever she didn't walk just right, turn and flaunt her naked body, they punished her mercilessly. Not that she didn't like wearing heels, she did. Forced her to wear them day in, day out, even when she went to bed at night, was not something she appreciated. Already, she'd been assaulted, brutally fucked, and suffered beatings that didn't leave marks.

If that wasn't enough, just yesterday, they showed the depth of their depravity. In front of everyone, they hung a girl from a post in the cell block center. Unable to turn away for fear of recrimination, Misty watched them place a noose around the frightened girl's neck and crank her up off her feet. It was the most gruesome sight she had ever witnessed. As the girl dangled, her feet trashing, her head turned a deep shade of purple. With her hands tied behind her back, she was unable to reach up and claw at the rope wrapped around her throat.

Misty watched her struggle for what seemed like hours in her death throes, yet the execution couldn't have lasted more than a couple of minutes. Eventually, the girl lost her battle to keep her life, the noose having the final say as her struggling slowed. Seconds later, she was still, and her body relaxed in death. Urine seeped down her legs, her purple tongue languished out the side of her open mouth, the last of her saliva dangling from it and onto her chest. When it was all over, they left her hanging there for the rest of the day. Her head tilted at an awkward angle, her neck stretched by the weight of her body, and her toes pointing to the floor, still and unmoving.

"She was beautiful, and they murdered her?" She asked herself, still in shock by what she witnessed.

"Were they going to do that to me? Oh, God, please help me!"

Scared out of her wits, Misty kept asking herself the following questions.

"What are they planning to do with me? Are they really planning on selling me, to the highest bidder, to have some sleazy bastard?"

It was hard to understand why anyone would do such a thing. Still here she was, locked in a cage and tormented at the whims of those on the other side of the bars.

Misty hated to admit it, but deep down inside, she knew that was what was going to happen. Soon, any day now, they would make her walk the runway one last time and stand there, on display as others bid on her, determined to buy her and take her to their home. What came next frightened her even more.

Staring down at the floor, she didn't hear the guard approach her cell until she heard the lock turn.

"Come on, your turn," was all he said.

Resigned, she stood up, threw her shoulders back, and proudly walked to meet her fate.

"Fuck 'em," she thought, "if they're going to sell me, they're not going to take my dignity as well."

Minutes later, Misty heard her introduction, and she nervously stepped into the spotlight, shaking in fear. Walking the runway with all the dignity she could muster, she turned at the end, pirouetting as they taught her, and returned to stand under the auction board. As bidding got underway, Misty heard outrageous amounts as the audience, men and women alike, bid on her. In short order, the bidding slowed and came to a stop, and she heard the fateful words.

"Sold to bidder number ten. Congratulations!" as the gavel came down, and a round of applause rose among the darkened arena.

Since then, the living nightmare got worse. After being sold at auction, they did something and put her to sleep. Upon waking again, disoriented and unsure how long she slept, she discovered she laid in a narrow crate, bouncing around and jostled back and forth. From the movement, she figured she was on a plane, flying to who knows where.

Rope bound her hands and ankles, with another tying her wrists to her ankles, preventing her from scratching her nose.

She wore a large ballgag, pressed hard and deep in her mouth. Her jaw ached from being held open so wide. Spittle coated her mouth and cheeks, some of it dried and caked. It seems she'd been there a long time.

Holding her bladder, they landed, and she nearly lost control of herself. Barely managing to hold it, they moved her crate to a truck and drove off. As she struggled to control her bladder, the truck drove for what felt like hours over rough terrain. Squeezing her legs together, Misty was determined not to wet herself.

The truck finally stopped, and the overhead door opened. She heard the sound of several crates carried off the truck and dumped somewhere. Eventually, they moved hers, not too gently either, and dropped her on what she guessed was a trolley or rolling cart.

When they finally let her out of the crate and untied her hands and feet, they retreated with the box and slammed a barred cell door closed and locked the door. Misty ran for the stainless-steel toilet in the corner and emptied her bladder, sighing in relief as her water splashed below.

In time, she discovered why they took her and sold her at auction. She became the plaything for a pair of cruel people, a man, and a woman. Every day since, she lived in pain and agony, as they tag teamed her with torments of every kind. One day it was whips and floggers, on others, strapped to an odd piece of furniture and electrocuted. They nailed her tits to a table, crucified her, thankfully without using nails, and left her hanging by her wrists for days. They cut her, squeezed her, dislocated joints, and otherwise tortured her. Many times, she wished they just get it over with and kill her.

She found it odd that the woman seemed more like her, a prisoner suffering torments by the man's hand. She usually dressed as she was, naked and in heels. She wore a collar similar to hers and seemed subservient to the man. Yet, at times, her cruelty was worse than his. She didn't get it.

Time after time, day after day, it was the same thing. If she wasn't lying in bed wearing those fucking heels, moaning in pain, she was strapped to a post and beaten, screaming for their pleasure. What little sleep she got came slowly, filled with disjointed imagery that left her with little rest. By the time they came for her, she felt as if she hadn't gotten any rest at all. All she felt was pain and anguish.

It all started when they kidnapped her and sold her at auction.

Chapter Twenty-One

"Thank you, ladies and gentlemen. That concludes our auction for today."

A round of applause erupted around the room. Waiting patiently for the din to settle down, the MC stood smiling at the crowd. He knew that the Consortium had just made a killing on their latest sales, quadrupling their profits and the most successful in recent history. Even though it was a team effort, he and his auctioneers had made all the difference.

Putting his hands up, he said, "Thank you," not so much as accepting the crowd's appreciation, but more to help move the program along.

"Now, we proceed to the entertainment portion of the evening. We're going to take a twenty-minute break while we set things up. I'm sure you will enjoy yourself. Tonight's program will conclude in the new amphitheater arena. Thank you."

Finished, the MC left the stage. The crowd's din picked up again as everyone began talking to each other, comparing notes on their purchases and congratulating the winning bidders.

Meanwhile, off stage and exiting the auction room, the Chairman stopped for a time to look at the crop of products waiting in the wings for their owners to take them home. Each year, the auctions were growing bigger and bigger. They were running out of room to store the prey who managed to get caught by the hunters. If this kept up, soon he'd have to figure out how to keep up with the demand.

Moving on, he caught up with one of his assistants and asked. "Are we ready?"

"Yes, Sir, Henrietta is in the chute, anxious and ready. We're about to put the girl in the arena to join her."

"I'd like to see her up close before they do that."

"I figured. She's waiting for you just outside the arena."

"Very good, thank you," the Chairman said, already moving towards the amphitheater. Ahead, two heavy-set guards held a young, naked girl by her arms. She was young and petite, five-foot-one, and weighed barely one hundred six pounds soaking wet. She had short brown hair, decently sized breasts, and narrow hips. For the first time since she arrived, she was barefooted and looked tiny compared to the large burly men holding her between them. Her body was not to his taste, but then again, this was not about him, but rather the membership. He was determined to put on a good show for them. After all, he had made the Consortium and himself a lot of money because of this auction.

Stepping up before the three of them, he stopped and evaluated the girl.

"Yes, she will do nicely," he thought to himself.

Reaching out, he cupped one of her B-cups in the palm of his hand, feeling the soft, baby smooth, and tender skin. She tried to resist, but the guards held her in place. Using his thumb, he stroked her nipple, feeling it firm up under his touch.

"Getting a good feel, are ya Luv?" The girl's cockeyed accents revealed disdain and hate in her tone.

"What's your name?"

"What's it to ya?"

"What's your name? I won't ask again."

The girl stayed silent, at least until he backhanded her across the cheek.

"If it's anything to you, Luv, it's Penny, you prick."

"I may just be," the Chairman replied, as the two guards chuckled under their breath.

Pausing to reflect upon the handsome girl, he smiled at the mark his hand had left on her cheek. He loved seeing these passing marks. They filled him with a certain sense of satisfaction like no other. However, her usefulness to the training center was soon to end.

"Turn her around," he said while reaching into his pocket and pulling out a tailor's measuring tape. Turning her back to him, he measured the width of her shoulders and hips.

"Just right," he murmured.

Nodding to the guards, "She'll do," and turned away.

"Come on, girlie, let's see just how good you look after Henrietta gets a peek atcha," one of the guards told the girl. "You two are about to be excellent friends."

"Give her a kiss for us, Luv, why don't cha." The other guard teased.

Forcing the girl to follow, they led her to a short wall topped by a metal handrail. Picking her up, they lowered her feet first over the edge, holding her by her wrists. Leaning as far as they could, they dropped her the final six feet to the sandy floor below.

From a strategic location, the Chairman watched the girl as she dropped, content knowing what was about to happen. These first few minutes were precious, wondering if she would figure out what was to become of her. In all the years he did this, only one discovered their fate before it became a reality. Right now, he was happy to watch until the crowd gathered.

Bewildered, the girl crouched a moment, gathering her senses. Standing up, feeling very exposed and vulnerable, she started to look around.

She was standing on coarse sand, studded with modest-sized rocks scattered throughout the arena floor. A look of recognition came over her. That's what it was. She was in a circular arena, about forty-five feet across. There wasn't a single corner in which to hide. A sick feeling came over her, and she closed her arms over her belly. This wasn't looking good, not good at all.

Surrounding the field of sand were tall, glistening steel walls. Touching the wall next to her, she noted it was extremely slippery, with a glistening sheen. It was as if someone polished it with care and forethought. The wall towered over her, far above from where she could reach and climb out without a tall ladder.

The slick metal wall appeared flawless, without seams, hand grips, or protrusions she could use to climb. Except for the shape of a circle about three feet round to her left, the wall was pristine. Without assistance from above, she wasn't going anywhere. Not anytime soon, that is.

The obvious question on her mind was, "Why did they put me down here. What kind of fun did they intend for her?"

Questions were written all over her face for anyone to see if they bothered to look.

"What is it they want from me?" Few bothered to look. They were all waiting for her companion to join her.

Walking around, inspecting her surroundings under the bright lights that left no shadows, she investigated. In several places, she dug her hands into the sand, only to find more of the shiny stainless steel. It seemed to her she was in a large metal bowl. The sick feeling from earlier was getting worse.

It was about then that she heard the voices of multiple people approaching from above. She couldn't see any of them. It was as if they hid in the shadows behind the bright lights. However, she heard them plainly enough. They were laughing and, at times, taunting her, jeering at her. Apparently, they knew something, and the joke was on her.

Their voices were getting louder, and she tried to ignore them, dismissing them with the shake of her head. With nowhere to hide, she found herself standing somewhere in the middle of the space, slowly turning, holding her stomach to calm herself. Never before had she felt that she was in a precarious position, unsafe and unmistakably menacing.

She was still trying to figure out what to do when she heard someone start speaking over a public-address system.

"Ladies and gentlemen, may I have your attention, please? We have a special treat for you. Tonight, you are going to get to see something rather spectacular, something that is rarely seen by any human, and even rarer experienced. Something so entertaining that you will be talking about this for months, maybe years to come."

A cheer rose from the crowd above. Penny stood mute, uncertain as to what she should do.

"Penny, the girl you see below you, is about to meet Henrietta, who is very interested in meeting Penny. The two of them will soon become fast friends, at least for the next hour or so. After that, well, who knows? Perhaps one of them will fall out of favor with the other."

Laughter rippled through the darkness from above, as if they understood the joke that she didn't.

A look of concern appeared on Penny's face, as she couldn't fathom what she heard or what it all meant. Since she was taken captive, she had never once become friends with anyone in this horrible place. On the contrary, she hated them all. Since the day she was kidnapped and locked in a tiny cell, forced to wear those damned high-heels, they made her submit to treatments she wouldn't wish on her worst enemy. They had assaulted, beaten, and defiled her. No, she would never be friends with these assholes, and given the opportunity, she would do to them whatever they had done to her.

Still, though, they had left her alone for the past couple of weeks, allowing her injuries to heal. And now, she didn't have to wear those fucking shoes anymore.

"What was that, anyway? On top of it all, they were feeding me decently. Not great, but good." Penny thought.

At the time, she hadn't given it a second thought. However, now she did.

In her reverie, she almost missed the announcer's next words. "In just moments, we're going to let Henrietta join Penny in the arena for a playdate. This will be a contest of wits, wills, and determination." The announcer remarked, to more applause.

"Before we start, let me remind you, your tablets will display various wagers. Place your bets. Should you wish to bet on something besides those we offered, just key them in. I guarantee that someone will take you up on your bet. As soon as we let Henrietta join Penny, we will close the wagering window."

Pausing a moment, he continued. "All wagers will be paid off before you leave tonight, deducting and adding to your accounts as appropriate. As always, anyone unable to pay up on their losses will not be able to take home their purchases. If after three days and you're still unable to pay them off, you will forfeit your purchases, plus any money paid and a lien placed on you. So, please, bet wisely and within your means."

"We will begin shortly."

Penny heard a murmur from the audience, perhaps of acknowledging the announcement. Sounds of tapping followed as fingers banged screens. She assumed these were the tablets spoken about earlier. The announcer kept quiet for several minutes, presumably to let the wagering finish.

"So, then, they're betting on me. Maybe one of those bets will grant me freedom?" Penny wistfully wished to herself. "Or, perhaps, there is a chance I can get out of this mess with my skin intact."

As the conversation among the audience began to grow, the announcer continued.

"Okay, folks, are you ready? Are you ready for the fair Penny to meet Henrietta?" The announcer repeated his question, again and again, inciting the audience into a frenzy.

"Okay then, all bets closing in 5 ..."

"Wait, wait. Just a couple more bets," one of the members yelled out.

"Well, hurry up, old man. We don't have all day!" another member rebutted, much to the laughter of those around him.

"Okay, I'm done."

"Are you sure? I wouldn't want you to accuse me of making you miss a winning bet."

"Yes, I'm sure."

Fair enough. The betting window is closing in ... 5 ... 4 ... 3 ... 2 ... 1 ... 0. The betting window is now closed, success to the winners."

After a moment, the announcer continued.

"Are you ready? Can you feel the tension in the air? Should we wait a bit longer until Henrietta meets Penny?"

"NO!" a chorus rose among the spectators.

"Then, let the show begin. Gentlemen, open the door and let Henrietta in." He finally said after several seconds.

A sharp noise behind Penny broke her out of her bewilderment. Turning towards the sound, she could see the far wall's circular mark get darker and thicker before receding from the wall. Staring at it, she realized the circular pattern was actually a door.

"Please, let that be a door to freedom?" she briefly asked herself before realizing that escape was most likely not through that door. "No, that was the door from which Henrietta will enter, whoever she is."

The door began to slide to one side, and a black gaping hole appeared behind it. Taking a tentative step towards the door, Penny stopped when an anticipatory silence fell upon the crowd. It was almost as if the audience wanted her to step into the hole in the wall. Thinking better about it, she backed off, at least for now. She needed to know more before she went blindly in there.

In the silence of the crowd, she heard a new noise, one she could not quite figure out. It was a soft sound, barely perceptible, and it came from the blackness of the dark recesses of the door. Backing away, she looked left and right, irrationally hoping for another opening to appear. She was disappointed. None appeared.

Focusing on the sound, she tried to pinpoint where it was coming from. She couldn't quite place it, and it seemed to come from nowhere and everywhere. Looking around, the quiet anticipation from the crowd gave the impression to grow louder. The invisible people watching from above seemed to take in a single deep breath all at once.

Ominous dread enveloped her, and she shivered from the unknown. Despite the warm sand and the hot lights above, goosebumps appeared all over Penny's body as a cold shiver ran down her spine. Without realizing it, she took a slow deep breath inward and held it, waiting in anxious anticipation. A collective silence joined her, waiting to see what would emerge.

Peering deep into the darkness of the void, she thought she saw something, something moving very slowly. Still unable to place the sound, she turned her attention upwards, hoping that some clue would reveal itself. Twisting her head back and forth, she wanted to find something, anything to grant her freedom from this damned arena.

All at once, she heard a gasp from her audience. Turning, she could barely make out a figure in the opening.

"What was that?" telegraphing her question to the crowd.

Suddenly, she was feeling even more vulnerable and exposed. That dark cloud she felt grew blacker still.

After a long, pregnant pause, she identified the source of the sound and screamed. She screamed at the top of her lungs, enough to curdle one's blood, and backed away from the opening. What she feared most, the thing she dreaded above all, was staring at her right in the face. What had revealed itself in the door of the wall was the head of an enormous, monstrous snake.

Deathly afraid, she continued to shriek, backing away from the opening. Penny ran to the far side of the arena, trying to get as far away as possible from the ominous snake, slowly revealing itself. Concerns for her displayed nakedness evaporated, replaced with outright terror.

Turning towards the sheer wall, she desperately tried climbing it. As her arms and legs flailed, she kept sliding back to the sand. However, that didn't stop her from trying. She desperately needed to get as far away from the snake as possible.

"Of all the things in the world. Why a snake," Penny frantically whined.

Turning back towards the snake, in sheer terror, she stood frozen, unable to move. The snake appeared to be sniffing the air, its tongue flicking out and back in measurable beats. It began tilting its head back and forth, scanning for dangers beyond the door. Satisfied, it slowly slithered out of its lair. In short order, it revealed its full size to the crowd, taking up about a sixth of the wall of the arena.

"Ladies and gentlemen, I am proud to present to you, Henrietta, now entering the field." Pausing just a moment to gather interest in the crowd, he continued. "You're about to be treated to some wicked girl-on-girl action, as the two of them get it on."

"Henrietta is a wild twenty-four-foot-long reticulated python, originally from the Philippines. Yes, everyone, this snake is a girl snake. Female pythons are regularly more massive than their male counterparts. It's one reason we chose her. On an empty stomach, she measures forty centimeters across and one hundred thirty centimeters around. It's anyone's guess how much her body will grow after she eats. Perhaps we'll find out today."

The voice from above paused before continuing.

"With those gorgeous brown, black, and yellow markings crisscrossing the length of her body, she's a beauty. She's also an experienced hunter, as you will soon agree."

"Henrietta weighs in at three-hundred sixty pounds, massing a whopping one-hundred sixty-three kilos. She is a monster in both size and weight, and she's about to get much heavier. I'd say somewhere on the order of another one hundred ten pounds or so. Interestingly enough, that's just how much Penny weighs. Fifty kilos, imagine that?" He said with a bit of a laugh.

"Further, Henrietta hasn't eaten in a couple of months, so she's quite hungry. As with all snakes, she can unhinge her jaw and swallow significantly larger prey than her size would imply. There's no doubt she'll have any problems with the dinner we've presented here."

The MC paused to allow the ramifications of his announcement to percolate among everyone in attendance.

"Watch everyone, as Penny realizes the implications of what I just said."

Then, directing his comment to Penny, "Yes, Penny. Henrietta is very hungry, and she needs to feed."

Penny screamed all the louder, her fear resonating in the teeth of the audience. However, no one knew whether Penny heard him. She remained frozen to the wall, concentrating on the object of her dread lying opposite her.

Directing his commentary back to his audience, the MC continued. "Penny has been with us for several months. When we discovered that she was deathly afraid of snakes, we decided to keep her here at the training facility just for this day's entertainment. In the meantime, guards and administrators alike used her as play toys while we waited for today. After all, they have needs too. Don't they Penny?"

Laughter erupted from the crowd. They all knew what that meant.

"I turn your attention back to the pit. Henrietta is starting to get her bearings. Let's watch the fun and see what happens. Will Henrietta go first for Penny's feet or her head? Or, will she go for the immediate kill and wrap her body around poor Penny and crush her first before feeding on the body? It's anyone's guess. We've observed her doing all three in the wild. In the meantime, I will stop commenting on the events below. I ask everyone to remain quiet and hold off any applause until the end of the show."

"Have fun and *'Bon Appétit.'*"

Bloodcurdling screams filled the arena, eliciting further cheers and laughter from the crowd. Penny backed away from the snake, trying desperately to climb the slick walls to freedom. Despite her best efforts, she was unable to make any progress up the slippery walls. Her panic deepened, letting her fear control her actions.

Turning her back to the wall, she faced the massive snake after making its full exit from its lair, the door closing behind it. Uncertain as to what to do, she remained frozen, glued to the wall, while her screams echoed everywhere.

Penny, wide-eyed in fright, tried to dash to the closing door. However, unable to run fast enough, the door clanged closed, sealed tight before Penny could get halfway across the sands. Stopping suddenly and keeping perfectly still, Henrietta turned its head towards her. Realizing her perilous situation, Penny slowly backed away, fighting her panic to run.

The MC looked down and smiled, knowing the girl was doomed. If she had kept a cool head, she might have escaped through the open door. Her fear taking over, she guaranteed the outcome and her eventual death. There was no way she could escape. With the snake now getting its bearings, Henrietta knew where to find her next meal. Ever the patient hunter, she wanted to make sure there weren't any other dangers.

Once again, Penny's glued herself against the wall. The ever-patient Henrietta returned to inspecting its new surroundings. Initially, the snake sought to bask in the warm sands bright light. As she sniffed and tasted the air, she discovered something that would satisfy her hunger… a fresh meal.

Circling to the left, the snake slithered slowly along the edge of the wall. Like the girl, the snake was on its guard, using the wall as a level of protection. At times, the snake would slide up the wall, nearly seven feet, or so, before dropping back to the warm sands. Like Penny, Henrietta was a hostage on the sands of the arena.

With one eye on Penny and its other eye on the sands, the snake continued its circuitous route around the arena. Patient and observant, Henrietta needed to know what to expect when it finally finished its inspection of her surroundings. Satisfied, Henrietta began making inroads towards the center of the arena, straight towards the object of her hunger.

Screeching even louder now, Penny tried desperately to run from the approaching snake. Running backward now, she managed to stay three or four meters ahead of the massive snake. There was little Penny could do with the arena only fourteen meters across, and the snake was consuming much of the space. All she could do was dance, feigning in one direction before dashing off in another. Penny found it hard to stay ahead of the snake. The snake appeared to anticipate Penny's every move. Whatever Penny did, she knew that the snake always kept an eye on her. The snake's concentrated stare using its black vertical slit iris never once deviated from her. Penny shivered.

Unquestionably, the massive snake was an experienced hunter.

To Henrietta, the smell of her prey reeked. Its split tongue was tasting the air at an ever-increasing tempo. Hunger prompted her into action as she slithered faster towards Penny. Trying to get behind the gigantic snake, Penny ran as hastily as she could across the sands to the other side. Turning its head, Henrietta followed the girl's gait, teasing her, testing her, smelling her, and measuring her reactions to its composed movements. Everyone, except for Penny, could see that Henrietta was teasing the girl, playing with her until she made a fatal mistake.

Penny, for her part and in between screams, begged her audience for mercy. Almost like magic, someone threw a rope over the wall on the far side of the arena. Grateful, Penny tried to run for it and climb to safety. Darting at just the right time, she flew across the sands and jumped. Her hands found only air. Someone suddenly yanked the rope up and out of reach. Penny fell to the sand, her back against the polished metal wall, and stared at the approaching Henrietta.

Now, not only was the snake teasing her but so was her audience. Tears fell from Penny's eyes in torrents as she begged for her life. Her unsympathetic spectators cheered the snake's onward advance, sensing that time was growing short.

Looking left and right, Penny searched in vain for someplace to escape or hide. Facing the approaching monster, Penny once again began moving away from the threatening menace.

"Please, oh please, don't do this," Penny repeatedly whined, interspersing her begging with frightening screams. The only response she received was the excited sound of the audience cheering, urging on the snake.

"Oh God, please don't," Penny stammered as the snake got even closer. Moving slowly, Penny tried to find a way past the looming peril, barely looking past the concentrated stare from the snake.

The snake seemed to match her every move by now, adjusting its superior position, keeping its target in sight. Penny, still screaming in terror, continued to search for a way past the closing Henrietta.

Backing away, abandoning the wall's futile safety, Penny began crossing the open sand, so far untouched by the snake. Focused on its prize, the snake oriented itself towards Penny, slithering slowly over the sand. Facing the snake at all times, never shifting her gaze away from those deadly eyes, Penny didn't see the protruding rock in her path behind her.

Everything happened so incredibly fast. The next ten seconds turned into a lifetime for the doomed girl. As she backed away, Penny stumbled over the rock tossed about the sand. Down on her backside, she fell.

Henrietta, seeing the opportunity, moved in to strike. Crawling backward on her backside, Penny tried desperately to scramble away from the snake. Hands and feet churned the sand, pushing her body away from the looming beast. She crawled about a quarter of the way across the sand, on her ass. All the while, the monstrous snake grew ever closer to its prize.

Unrelenting and before anyone noticed, the snake's head appeared above Penny's prostrate body. In desperation, Penny began kicking at the snake, trying to fend it off. Kicking wildly, throwing bicycle kicks at the serpent's head, the snake smartly avoided Penny's feeble barrage.

For the briefest moment in time, Penny stared down the throat of the snake. It opened its mouth and provided her with a view of her destiny. The gaping chasm behind the teeth she saw seemed to stretch forever. Time slowed as that awful split tongue flicked the air overhead, brushing ever so delicately on Penny's face.

One would have thought that by now, Penny was beyond screaming any louder or more fiercely. They would be wrong. The scream that filled the air was far worse than anyone had heard so far.

Studying its prey carefully, Henrietta struck, timing its strike perfectly. Unlike Penny's inept attacks, Henrietta's first attack was anything but feeble. Unrestrained, the gallery erupted in applause, delighted in the gruesome events transpiring on the sands below. Henrietta engulfed Penny's feet above her ankles and snapped its jaws shut. Using her powerful muscles to suck and draw her prey further into her mouth, Henrietta began ingesting her meal.

Stronger than ever, Penny's screams of terror filled the arena and the surrounding hallways. Penny fought desperately for release, twisting and kicking, hoping to find her way out of the voracious atrocity.

Henrietta would have nothing of it. The snake was ravenous. Little by little, the snake nibbled at its prize, unwittingly assisted by the girl as she tried to free herself. Penny's feeble attempts to get away helped Henrietta devour more of her legs into its enormous jaws. Observers later reported that they could almost see the python smile as it started consuming its prey whole.

The flock of spectators leaned over the railing to get a better look at the spectacle. Everyone wanted to get the best view possible, as Penny began her trek down the gullet of the huge serpent.

Penny hadn't stopped fighting for her life. Lying on her back, she reached for anything that might disrupt the snake. First, she grabbed handfuls of sand and threw them at the snake. Henrietta ignored it, maintaining a firm hold on its dinner. Struggling, searching for anything, Penny tried desperately to escape the jaws of her fate. Feeling one of the rocks, she attempted to pull it from its sandy burial mound. It wouldn't budge even a bit. Penny seemed helpless. Grabbing more handfuls of sand, she threw it at the snake's head, hoping to get some of it in its eyes, and let her go.

Henrietta was too smart for that trick and continued sucking down on its prize. It didn't take long before swallowing Penny's legs up to her knees and start working on her thighs. With so much of Penny's legs engulfed, the snake took more and bigger gulps, leaving its long body to continue pulling its meal into its maw.

Screaming like there was no tomorrow, for there wasn't, Penny begged the audience again for mercy. No one offered her any. The good cheer of the crowd made it clear to Penny. They wanted her to disappear into the belly of the beast. No help was going to come – ever.

Pausing for a time when the snake had swallowed her up to her hips, it seemed to pause and ponder the girl's hips. Fortunately, she wasn't that hippy, and once again, the snake continued devouring its tasty meal. Sweeping its head back and forth, advancing its lips a bit at a time, Henrietta managed to get her jaws over Penny's hips.

The audience could see the snake's body's oscillating contractions, slowly advancing the girl's body down the snake's gullet. Unsurprisingly, those watching Henrietta's gaping maw consume her first meal in so many weeks felt it was the most spectacular event ever witnessed.

Powerless to do anything to stop the slow advance into the gullet of the beast, Penny shed torrents of tears, soaking the sand beneath her. She wished desperately for a tool or something to hurt or kill the snake before the snake could kill her. She found none.

Penny could feel its hot breath blowing warm rank air past her breasts and onto her face. Looking at its mouth, Penny noticed the edge of the snake's mouth engulfing her up to her waist. Her legs and feet swallowed beyond the monster's head, and feeling hot and grossly wet, felt the strong, undulating pulses contracted around them, pulling her deeper in the recesses of the huge snake.

Undeterred, Penny started pounding on the snake's snout and head, hoping to distract it and dislodge her from its mouth. Indifferent to Penny's attack, the snake merely continued feasting.

Envisioning an opportunity, Penny reached back to get as much power into her swing as she could, leveling a blow at the snake's delicate, fragile eyes. Swinging hard, Penny failed to realize that Henrietta was skilled at this sort of thing. Undeterred, Henrietta opened its mouth wide and caught Penny's hands in mid-swing. The snake's ambush caught Penny by surprise, trapping her hands inside powerful jaws. Ensnared, Penny began to accept that she was about to die, devoured alive by the beast doing the bidding of the monsters watching overhead.

"Please, don't do this. Please!" The young Penny shrieked, not wanting to die, at least not like this.

With the girl adequately secured, Henrietta once again continued feeding. Slowly, agonizing inch by inch, Penny disappeared down the gullet of the beast, doing what instinct and nature intended.

Looking down at the spectacle, observers watched Penny with bated breath, protruding half-swallowed from the snake's mouth. Buried up to her chest, Henrietta slowly advanced along the girl's body. It was a wonder how the girl could fit inside the snake's body. Amazingly, its body expanded to accommodate the struggling meal. Even more surprising, Penny continued to scream while Henrietta continued swallowing, unperturbed by the shrieking, shrill noise. With her hands and arms restrained inside the snake, Penny squirmed briskly, unknowingly assisting the snake in its quest. With every writhing movement, Henrietta inched her way along, further swallowing the tasty meal.

"Bastards," the doomed girl thought as her screams began to soften.

Increasingly, she had a harder time breathing. By now, the snake had ingested her up to her chest, and her breasts were about to disappear. As Henrietta clamped down, Penny could feel it compressing her body from all sides, squeezing the air from her lungs. Soon, she could barely suck air at all and hence, stopped her screaming. Half of her audience expressed disappointment, wishing the girl would scream to the very end. The other half applauded. No one was sure whether it was for relief from the loud, painful shrieking or whether it was for the gruesome live-action show portrayed on the warm sands of the arena.

Tilting her head, touching her chin to her chest, Penny watched the resolute dark, confident eyes of the snake slowly dine on her breasts. Little by little, she watched her nipples disappear into its jaws. As they vanished into the darkness, she felt the snake constrict her chest, making breathing impossible.

She tilted her head as far back as possible, in the wistful hope of getting any air into her lungs. Penny stared wide-eyed at the top of the wall, hoping to see, at last, her murderers. It didn't do any good. Darkness was the only image she saw. Her efforts, while comical, were fruitless. Gasping for air that never came, Penny stared up at the bright lights above, fighting to breathe to the end. Unrelenting, the snake squeezed tighter. Air refused to slide down her gaping mouth and fill her lungs. She was suffocating, and she knew it.

"At least I won't live to see the inside of the snake." Penny thought as she died.

Henrietta took its time swallowing the girl's shoulders. It could barely open its jaw wide enough to get around them. Slowly, Henrietta unhinged her jaw and stretched its mouth wider. With small, side to side motions, it advanced the girl's shoulders, slow but assuredly, disappearing into the mouth of the beast. Once devoured, Henrietta rested for several minutes, recovering her strength, preparing to finish its meal.

The sight of Penny's head sticking out of the snake's mouth drew smirks and high-fives to the observers. With the snake's jaw deliberately closing, Henrietta's nose touched the underside of Penny's chin. The image gave the impression that clamping down would separate Penny's head from the rest of her body with just a bit more effort. Observers later reported that they thought they saw a look of satisfaction and relief on the snake after it had consumed the girl's shoulders.

Several minutes later, Henrietta opened her mouth, grasped the girl's head, and slowly devoured its meal. Rested after the extreme effort of swallowing the shoulders, it didn't take long for Henrietta to finish Penny off. Thirty minutes later, everyone could see the outline of Penny's body stretching the snake's skin several feet well inside the length of its body. The faint outline of her tits, stabbing outwards against the snake's body, were right where they ought to be.

None of the observers knew just when Penny died. Was it when the snake swallowed her chest? Was it when the snake consumed her shoulders? Was it when it drew her face into its jaw? Was it after gobbling Penny's head and closed its mouth? Did she live for a time, consigned to the darkness inside the stomach of the snake? No one knew for sure. No one seemed to care.

"Ladies and gentlemen," the Chairman began, "the official results are in. We tabulated the times starting from the moment Henrietta made her appearance in the arena. Those results are now available on your tablets."

Official Results

- Duration until Henrietta made her appearance: 3 minutes
- Time until prey panicked: under 1 minute
- Successful strikes: 1
- Unsuccessful strikes: 0
- Time to initial strike: 19 minutes
- Time to successful strike: 19 minutes
- Time to swallow up to knees: 23 minutes
- Time to swallow up to the groin: 27 minutes
- Time to swallow the hips: 31 minutes
- Time to swallow the waist: 35 minutes
- Time to swallow the tits: 49 minutes
- Time to swallow the shoulders: 81 minutes
- Time to swallow the head: 93 minutes
- Total time spent screaming: 61 minutes

- Loudest scream: 93 decibels
- Highest scream frequency: 3,093 Hz
- Longest single scream without a breath: 37 seconds
- Longest silence between screams: 25 seconds
- Attempts to climb the wall: 21
- Cries for help: 33
- Begs for mercy: 13
- Kicks lashed out in futile attempt to escape: 79
- Time to kill: One hour, fifteen minutes
- Overall feeding duration: One hour, forty-five minutes
- Total overall time: One hour, fifty-eight minutes

"Attention Please: The house has completed tabulating the wagers." The Chairman said, speaking through the public-address system.

"We paid off the winners, depositing their winnings into their accounts. We've also collected the wagers from the accounts of the losing bets." Pausing for a bit, the Chairman allowed the attendees to check their bets' status before continuing.

"*La ragazza ha fatto una buona cena, non-pensi?*" The Chairman said in Italian. Repeating in English, "The girl made a good dinner, don't you think?" allowed more applause to erupt around the field.

"A thought occurred to me as we were tabulating the results. Most movies are about two hours long. Penny's dinner party lasted just about as long. I'm sure you'll agree. Tonight's entertainment was far better than any movie ever made."

"Thank you all, and this concludes the evening's entertainment."

A loud round of applause echoed throughout the room as the snake settled down to rest, content. The audience, utterly unconcerned about the young woman's horrendous death, began drifting towards the doors.

"It will be several days before Henrietta moves again. In that time, she will slowly digest the girl once known as Penny. When Henrietta is ready, we will entice her to return to her lair, to await her next meal. I trust you will all be here to witness the event."

"*Buon appetito.*"

Chapter Twenty-Two

"Brother, that was awesome.

A woman dressed in black leather crashed the door to the Chairman's office and strutted right in. Walking across the broad space between the door and the desk, she plopped onto one of the office chairs facing the Chairman and crossed her feet up on his desk.

"Sis, I gather you liked the show." The Chairman answered.

"Liked it? Are you kidding me? That was fucking awesome. I wish I had thought of it."

"Thank you, it was pretty spectacular, wasn't it?"

"Brother, I'd say it was more than spectacular. It surpassed anything you've ever come up with in the past. I can't wait for your next bit of inspiration."

"Well, sis, it will be a while. That particular stunt took years to put together, and only because we stumbled upon the snake. If we hadn't, we would have put on a standard show."

"Let me tell you. The membership will be talking about this for years, no, decades to come. How did you pull it off without the members getting wind of it?" she asked.

"It was hard. I have to admit. Only the executive committee knew about it, and even then, only in stages. It was only after we learned of the snake that the idea began percolating. For the longest time, we let the snake stay where it was, even though the locals were banding together to search and destroy it. You see, the snake was routinely taking their livestock and their children."

"You said, The Philippines, wasn't that?"

"Yes, one of our hunters was on vacation and heard stories about it. He investigated and decided there was truth in the folktales. The snake was foraging in the jungles, rarely being seen by people. It was a stealthy and an experienced hunter."

"So, what did you do?"

"Well, we approached the locals and promised to take care of the snake for them. Of course, they thought we were going to kill it."

"It's a magnificent creature. Killing it would have been a terrible loss."

"I agree. After we decided to capture it, we kept an eye on it and discouraged the locals from going after it themselves."

"They would have certainly killed it."

"Yes, I believe so. While we kept the locals at bay, we began working on building a facility to hold the snake here, as well as build an arena to put on the show."

"And what a show it was, brother. I'm still wet thinking about it."

"Yes, I can smell your need even from here." The Chairman said as she smiled at the thought, something written behind those eyes.

"It wasn't hard to talk the executive committee into funding it. I sold the arena as a blood sports arena, deathmatches, and so forth."

"That was clever," she interjected.

"Yes, I thought so. We're going to establish a deathmatch tournament shortly to help further pay off the facility. We've even begun collecting suitable men and women to battle it out on the sands. Before long, those sands will turn bright red, and we will fill the coffers from the wagers."

"But I digress. Keeping the arena under wraps wasn't too difficult. The holding pen we kept it in was hard to hide. It was easy at first since it was just a concrete and steel enclosure. Hiding it became more involved when we installed the environmental system, fake river, and finally, the vegetation."

"I have to admit, I did hear some scuttlebutt about that, but I knew who was running the project. Brother, I know this about you. You are one of the most creative people I know who can develop such elaborate mindfuck scenes that could scare even me to death. You came up with a good one."

"And we both know that didn't come easy," he chided her.

"No, it didn't."

After we had the pen ready, it was time to go after the snake."

"Tell me how many men did you lose?"

"Only two, they got careless. One was stupid enough to allow a viper to bite him. He was dead in minutes, nothing we could do. The other got too close to the snake, and it constricted him to death."

"Did the snake eat him?"

"No, he was too big. The snake reacted in self-defense and then moved off, right into the live-trap we set for it. Let me tell you, it wasn't happy but got over it when we fed it a deer."

"That kept her quiet."

"Yes, we noticed that after she ate, she slept while digesting it. She stayed placid for more than a week. In which time, we had her transported off the islands and into our facility."

"Without the knowledge of the Filipino authorities, I gather."

"Absolutely, and the locals are happy. Of course, they tried to talk us into killing it. When we didn't, they just walked away, shaking their heads."

"Stupid locals," Sis offered. All the Chairman could do was smile. "So, then what?"

"So, then we went on the hunt for the perfect victim to feed the snake. We found it in Penny. She was deathly afraid of snakes and the perfect size. According to research, a garter snake bit her when she was a little girl. She never got over it and never went anywhere near them."

"How did you go about finding the girl?" She asked.

"Well, we had all our usual sources. But we wanted someone who wasn't just afraid of them. We wanted someone deathly afraid. After all, we had a show to put on. If we found the wrong person to feed to the snake, and they turned out to be able to overcome their fear and do something about their situation, then that wouldn't have been very entertaining."

"No, I suppose not. And I don't suppose it would help to advertise for someone deathly afraid of snakes among the network."

"Definitely not! However, we did put out feelers among the hunters, putting out a story that didn't quite mention Henrietta. We didn't care what sex the candidate was, as long as they panicked when confronted by Henrietta. I suspected it would be a woman, but I didn't care. Eventually, one of them found a candidate in London. Apparently, someone in the network had submitted her name offhandedly, unrelated to the talent search we had underway. During her background investigation, we uncovered her fear of snakes."

"I suppose you didn't let it go at that?"

"Sis, what do you take me for? Of course not, we tested her. During her final exam, well, let me tell you, it was a lovely thing to watch. I still have the surveillance recordings of that night. They give me an erection every time I watch."

"Not after today, I'd say."

"No, today's spectacle far exceeds that recording by a long shot. Anyway, we wired her flat for sight and sound. After that, we confirmed we had a live feed we could record and placed a large harmless black snake, a little over a meter and a half long, in her bedroom closet. Then we sat back and watched the fun. It helped that she worked as a tavern barmaid. The day we did the test, she was working nights. Exhausted, she came home well after midnight, stripped, and tossed her laundry into her hamper in the closet."

Pausing a time to let his sister visualize the scene, he continued.

"The black snake, startled by the closet light or maybe something else, went on the move. After we heard the shrieking that came out of our subject's mouth, we knew we had our girl.

She ranted and raved about it for the rest of the night. She even called her boyfriend of the month. He didn't answer as he was busy sleeping with a couple of other girls at the time. Of course, he wouldn't leave his bedmates, leaving the girl to fend for herself.

In the meantime, with nowhere to go, she slept on the couch, one eye staring at her closed bedroom door all night, making sure the snake stayed in there. The following morning, she called animal control. Then it was only a matter of time to bring it all together. As soon as I saw the surveillance, I approved her taking."

"I presume that you set her boyfriend up so that he wouldn't respond?"

"Certainly, he was never going to leave the girls we sent him. They were the hottest tail he had seen in a year, and he couldn't believe his good fortune. No, he wasn't going to get out of bed and rescue his tail of the month. We paid the squeezes, of course, but he had no idea. They were out of town talent. To have two of them in bed with him was an undeserving gift. They tag-teamed him all night long. He tried to get their numbers, but they steadfastly refused. Penny broke up with the boyfriend the very next day."

"Penny, was that her name? Oh, never mind, I don't care. It's not important. What is important is that she put on the perfect show, shrieking her bloody head off, petrified by the snake and then, tried to outrun it. Stupid girl, but she put on quite a show."

"She did, didn't she? I was curious to see if she would entertain us. Even with testing the girl, there was a chance that it wouldn't come off as well as it did. I couldn't help myself but applaud along with the rest of you when Henrietta first caught her."

"Knowing you, I know you gave her a chance to escape from that thing. You love your mind fucks, playing with their emotions. What was it? What opportunity did you give her?"

"You're right. I do like playing mind fucks. The chance she had was while Henrietta was still entering the arena. With that twenty-four-foot-long body, she had a small window of opportunity to slip through the door and to safety. As you saw, the snake went left out the door as the girl watched from across the arena. If she hadn't immediately panicked, she could have carefully circled round to the snake's other side and slipped safely past the snake's tail to freedom. I doubt very much that the snake would have tried to stop her. I gave her less than a five percent chance of keeping her wits and saving her skin. I was right. She panicked and tried to climb a wall she already knew was impossible to climb. She was doomed the moment the door closed. I think even she knew it too."

"As in a snake dinner, you mean," she chuckled at her pun. "Well, brother, you did well."

"Thank you, Sis. Coming from you, that was sweet of you to say."

"Don't get too used to them. I don't offer compliments too freely."

"No, you don't. That much, I know. So, Sis, I must say, you came dressed for the occasion, even if you have your feet on my desk. Just don't scratch the wood with those deadly looking studs on those boots of yours."

"The studs? Oh yes, they have come in handy fending off those creatures your teams hunt and bring back to auction. Seriously though, you like them?"

"Yes, I do. The black leather looks very supple, especially how it climbs your thighs right up to your groin. Add that steel spike for a heel, and yes, I'd say I like them. Just don't use them on me. They look like they could punch a deep hole in unsuspecting flesh, which I assume you've already tested."

"Who, little ol' me?" she asked, feigning surprise. "What do you think about the rest of the outfit?"

"The rest of the outfit, oh forgive me, I didn't notice since you're pointing your pussy right at my face."

"My pussy? Oh, come now. I know you better than that. You noticed my outfit, alright. As for my pussy, we'll come to that later."

"I must admit, I like the outfit. It becomes you. That long black-leather topcoat that buttons down to just below your tits before the cut of the lapel frames your black corset and draws any curious eyes to your pussy barely hidden by your thong."

"Did it draw yours?"

"Ah, Sis, you know me better than that?"

"I'll take that as a yes. How about my tits?"

Laughing, he responded. "So now you're looking for compliments. You know I like a nice set, and you have one of the nicest pair in the family."

'You think so?" she feigned modesty, pretending to cover the ample flesh barely contained by the corset. "You're looking dapper yourself. I love the dark gray suit and that collar pin instead of a necktie. How radical?"

"Thank you."

"I do have a question for you, though, getting back to Henrietta."

"Yes?" The Chairman waited.

"That arena, if I didn't know better, it reminded me of a large version of one of Mother's mixing bowls from the kitchen."

"You mean that one?" He said, pointing to a bowl sitting on a shelf behind the woman.

Turning, she looked, and a smile appeared on her face. "Oh my, that is her bowl, isn't it?"

"Yes, it is, my dear sister. You're right. I did model the arena after it. It has the advantage of transferring heat and cold to the sands quickly, plus it makes it easy to replace the sand if it gets too blood ridden. I even set it on a track to rotate the door to a different holding pen not yet built. Again, I used Mother's bowl for the idea."

"Well, Brother, I could kiss you. That's the nicest surprise anyone has given me, except, of course, that spectacle out there in the arena. I never expected that. I knew you were up to something, you usually are, like when you stole Avril right out from under me."

"You're still sore about that?"

"Of course, not silly, I can still rub it in, can't I?"

"I'll think about it." The Chairman answered as a knock sounded from his door.

"Come," he answered.

"Sir ... Mistress." The Chairman's secretary stammered, not realizing that the Chairman had a visitor. "The membership is about ready to depart. However, many have asked for the opportunity to congratulate you on the show before they leave. Also, one member will be spending the night in his guest quarters. It seems his transportation is down for maintenance. He tells me that it should be airworthy by tomorrow."

"Certainly, he can stay, just not too long. We need to prepare for the next auction, and the longer he is here, the longer we have to wait. As for the rest of them, tell them I'll be along shortly. Give me an hour or so and have my plane ready for departure right after that."

Interrupting, the Chairman's sister said, "Make that three hours."

Looking to the Chairman for confirmation, he waited. After several seconds, he nodded his assent.

After the door closed behind the secretary, his sister asked. "What's the big rush to get home?"

"Oh, I left an experiment cooking that needs attending too."

"Ooh, cooking. Now you've caught my interest."

"No, not your kind of cooking. You know perfectly well I'm not into that sort of thing. Before I tell you about my experiment, how are your experiments doing?"

"Yes, Brother, I know you aren't. Right now, I'm trying to figure out how to keep them alive a lot longer after I put them in the oven. I'm not into those mind fucks that you are. I want them to realize that I am going to cook them alive. Currently, I'm using lower temperatures, hoping that will keep them conscious longer. I'm not too happy with the latest results. Even at two hundred degrees, they die way too quickly for my taste."

"But isn't three hundred fifty degrees the normal temperature to cook meat?"

"Yes, it is. But so far, they die within minutes in that heat, which won't do with my plans. I think it's because they can't breathe in the heat. I want them to stay alive as long as possible while cooking and knowing that they are cooking as it happens. It's why I bought so many low-cost walking slabs of meat today. There's no sense in throwing away good money."

"So, it's not working out too well, is it? Perhaps you need to do something different. Have you thought of giving them a respirator to help them breathe? That is, if the heat is keeping them from breathing, maybe that could be an answer."

"Brother, you may be onto something. I'll think I'll try that. You wouldn't know where I can get a high-temperature respirator, would you?"

"Come to think of it. It's already loaded on your plane along with the rest of your purchases."

Squealing, the woman clapped her hands in joy. "Oh, thank you, Brother. You knew, you dirty bum."

"Of course, I knew. I like to know what my little sister is up to these days. Just in case she gets into trouble and needs her big brother to swoop in and save the day."

"Well, thank you," she said, a bit more somber. "I'll let you know how it turns out. But enough about me, what's this experiment you're working on?"

"Oh, you're going to like this. Several days ago, I strapped a pair of my girls into cages, with an anal hook in their asses, and a pair of dildos stuffed in their mouths and twats, and then left them in the dark for three days without food and water."

"Hey, this does sound like fun. What are you hoping to come back to, finding both of them dead?" she asked.

"No, I'm quite confident that at least one of them will make it through. You know whom I mean. Avril," he answered. "You've fucked her enough."

"Oh, your love interest, the one you stole out from under me."

"That's the one. Can you believe this? She volunteered for the ordeal. I think she believes she can help the other one survive the ordeal. Personally, I'm giving that one only a twenty percent chance that she survives. I am expecting that she will panic, choke on her vomit, or suffocate from the dildo."

"And if she survives?"

"I'll let her recover and then give her a new challenge to overcome."

"And if she survives that one as well …?"

"I'll keep giving her new ones until she succumbs. I'm testing her willpower to overcome her fears and deal with the ordeals."

"You want her to die, of course?"

"Of course, it's all about mindfucks. I want to measure how long it takes to realize that I mean to kill her. When she does, will she give up and allow herself to die, or will she make me kill her?"

"Oh, brother, you are a true sadist and cruel too."

"Thank you, Sis. This coming from the most callous person I know, cooking her dinners while they're still alive."

"Thank you, dear. I love you too." She said, standing up and brushing off a corner of his desk.

Sitting up on the desk, she spread her legs and pulled her thong to one side, showing her brother her glistening, dripping pussy.

"Come on. You still have at least an hour before you have to meet those fools out there and let them pat you on the back. In the meantime, I want you to fuck me–fuck me hard like you do that redhead of yours."

"That's the thing about my sister," he reflected. "The bigger her bloodthirst, the hornier she is. Nothing could stand in her way when she was in heat, and she was always in heat. Sis, what would I ever do without you?"

"I don't rightly know. However, if I'm gone, I won't care. You'll survive. Now, give that to me." She said, reaching for his trouser fly and unzipping him. "You know I'm always in heat. There's never a day that goes by where I'm not. Now, what are you waiting for, a custom invitation branded on your chest."

"Yes, Ma'am." He said, splitting her dripping labia wide open, driving his erection on the first thrust. Taking a deep cleansing breath, she grabbed him around his waist and pulled him to her. Breathless with desire and wrapping her legs around his thighs, she locked him tight to her and didn't let go for some time.

Their respective insatiable thirst barely satisfied, it was well beyond an hour before they emerged and allowed the membership to applaud the Chairman on a good show. He gave them scarcely fifteen minutes before he dashed off to his plane. Frankly, he had been away longer than he planned. As it was, it was closer to four days since he had left them strapped in their cages. That wasn't something they didn't need to know.

Chapter Twenty-Three

Approaching his limousine, the Chairman stopped to look back at the facility. Over the past couple of days, Avril occupied his thoughts, almost to distraction. Frankly, he was worried. He had left her caged, strapped inside, immobile and in imminent danger. He had never done that with any of his properties. While she was capable of surviving the ordeal, there was still a chance of failing. Failure meant death. If she died, he would need to restart his search for his perfect mate.

So far, Avril stood up to the challenge, and in some ways, surprised him in her resilience. What's worse, she tormented him in ways that he tried hard to hide from her. There wasn't a day, nor an hour, in which this woman wasn't in his thoughts. He couldn't wait to get back to her and find out whether she lived or died.

"Sir?" his assistant gently broke his reverie.

"Huh? Oh, sorry. I was woolgathering."

"Sir, I just wanted to let you know that your purchases are packed and shipped. They will arrive shortly after the time you return home."

"Thank you. Very good. Is there anything else?"

"Sir, I just wanted to say that even though I knew what was going to happen after the auction, it was a privilege to see it in action. The way the snake took that girl, it was, well, spectacular. I'm not sure how you're going to surpass that."

The Chairman thought about it for a time, unable to find the words to respond. Eventually, he finished. "You could be right. But we can perform that stunt several more times before the membership gets bored with it. Besides, Henrietta still needs to feed regularly."

"Yes, Sir. Indeed, she does. How often do you think she needs to feed?"

"At least once a month, maybe a bit more."

"Sir, then we can repeat it at the next auction."

"We could, but we would quickly use up the entertainment factor. No, it would be better to alternate entertainments. Arrange for one of the standard entertainments."

"Yes, Sir."

"We can feed Henrietta a pig or something to tide her over. Besides, to be entertaining, we need to find the right victim who will die screaming, deathly afraid of Henrietta. Right now, we don't have a suitable candidate. However, start looking for another aspirant right away. Make sure you properly vet the candidates. I'll tentatively schedule a repeat performance within two auctions from now.

"Very good, Sir."

"Is there anything else?"

"Safe travels Sir."

"Thank you. I'm looking forward to getting home."

With that, the Chairman climbed into the limousine and sat back. Minutes later, the car pulled out and headed for the airport.

A half-hour later, he said, climbing aboard his jet, "Captain, let's get underway!"

"Yes, Sir. Please take your seat. I'll have us in the air within minutes."

"That will be sufficient. Thank you."

"No problem Sir." The jet's captain answered, finished his preflight duties, and spun up the engines.

Turning towards the cabin, the Chairman found his seat. His favorite flight attendant of the month was right there to hand his favorite single malt scotch chilled with two crystal clear ice cubes. Just two cubes, no more, no less.

"Thank you, my dear," he said, taking a long pull on the drink. "Be ready with another drink by the time you return. I'll be needing it and you too. Be right quick about it."

The attendant began to turn, feeling his demanding mood more intense than usual.

"On second thought, never mind the drink, get rid of that," he ordered, pointing to her flight uniform, "and bring a seat belt extender."

"Right away, Sir. The captain informed me that we are cleared for immediate departure. I'll be back and ready before we take off." She said, hoping to ease her owner's stress.

A minute later, she returned wearing only her heels and holding the seatbelt extender. Leaning over, dangling her tits for her master to ogle, she attached the extender and looked to Sir for instructions.

"Here, sit on my lap," he said, his trousers precisely folded on the seat next to him.

"Certainly, Sir," she said with a smile, seeing his erection already stabbing the air, ready for launch.

Sitting down on his lap, her back to him, his erection found its target and penetrated her. Snapping the seatbelt around the two of them, he pulled the belt tight, pulling her closer to him. With the woman cinched tight on his lap and cock deep-seated in her pussy, he growled, his passionate need escalating. Grasping her tits, he forcefully dug into them as the plane raced down the runway and leaped into the air.

With the increasing g-forces driving him deeper inside her, he locked one of his arms around her neck. His single-minded aggressiveness ignored the attendant's distress as he squeezed her airways shut. He didn't care what happened to the woman. His paramount need took precedence. As the plane came out of its climb and the powerful g-forces relaxed, he exploded several ejaculations into her core.

Taking the long-denied breath after he released her neck, she turned towards him and kissed him. She sensed the bloodthirst raging within him. She knew full well that, in his need, he might very well kill her. She knew that others had died by his hands in terrible, painful ways she couldn't begin to fathom. Knowing that he would kill her sooner or later, she would undoubtedly enjoy her final moments; what better way was there to die but in the heat of passion.

When the plane reached cruising altitude, and the captain turned off the seatbelt sign, she unbuckled and turned towards him, straddling his lap, facing him. Settling his unrelenting erection inside her, she fucked him hard, hoping to tame the savage beast.

His cock was still firmly planted inside her as the wheels touched down at his home runway an hour and a half later. Cum dripped from her every opening and coated her chest and tits, giving them a whitish sheen. After a final ejaculation, the flight attendant leaned in and cupped his face in her long-fingered hands. Smashing her lips to his, she expressed her deepest thanks with a long, drawn-out kiss.

Looking closely at her, speaking for the first time since they took off, the Chairman said, "Thank you, my dear. I needed that. As always, you were spectacular."

"You're most welcome, Sir. Glad to be of service."

"I'll be sure to tell your owner of your prowess and expertise." He teased.

"Why, thank you, Sir. However, I'm pretty sure he already knows. Don't you, my Master?"

"Yes, dear. You are right. I look forward to our next flight together. Get some rest. I may need you again at a moment's notice."

"Yes, Sir."

To Avril, it felt like years since she got secured inside this cage. After what seemed like an eternity, her jaw finally stopped feeling so sore. She couldn't feel it at all. It was numb. She hadn't slept either, concerned that she would aspirate to death if she drifted off. The damned dildo pressed against the back of her throat constantly threatened to suffocate her. She had to be careful, making sure she positioned it just right. It was one thing that it teetered on the verge of her esophagus. It was quite another if her airway got blocked by the fucker.

She had caught herself drifting off several times, only to rudely wake up when she choked suddenly, unable to breathe. In her near-sleep state, she could easily let the dildo slip down her airways. Staying alert was the only way she could stay alive.

"Damn, I'm so, so tired," she lamented. "Will this ordeal finally ever end?" Avril speculated for the millionth time.

The girl across from her had seemingly figured out the same thing. Like herself, she choked often enough, almost dying in the process. Still, Avril was worried. She hadn't heard the girl in some time. She could have perished hours ago, and she wouldn't have known it.

Not since Sir first came in and had someone wash them with a hose had she seen anyone. The utter darkness prevented her from even seeing poor Jenni. She could only hear the occasional utterances that seemed to escape past the dildos lodged in her mouth from time to time.

"Sensory deprivation," Avril realized.

It might have been a month or more since Sir had left her like this. She had no idea, and she was exhausted. Her body wracked in stiffness and pain from the strain of the foreign objects stuffed inside her took their toll.

Feeling air waft across her rectum was the strangest feeling she had ever felt. Still, there was nothing to be done about it except grin and bear it.

"Yeah, right," she bitched. "Grin and bear it. I've got a goddamn dildo stuffed down my throat. I've almost vomited and choked to death a dozen times. How am I supposed to grin and bear it?"

She had figured that the ass hook would be the worst, but she discovered her jaw complained the loudest. Having that dildo shoved into her mouth resulted in soreness that she never expected. She felt like she contracted a cold, complete with body aches, sore throat, and runny nose. Her histamine levels were up, filling her sinuses with junk, which despite her best effort, it made breathing that much more difficult. She often had to blow her nose to clear the snot and allow her to breathe normally. However, the mucus tended to land on the dildo and drip down her chin. She could taste it as it seeped past her lips and coated her tongue.

"Yuck!"

She also felt like she had drooled what little free moisture there was in her body onto the floor, water she could ill afford to lose and survive. She was looking forward to a drink of water. That perhaps was the worst part of her captivity. She could do without food, but not water. She no longer felt the need to pee.

"How long ago was that?"

Desperately wanting to sleep, the minutes and hours dragged on for what felt like an eternity. Putting aside her aches and pains Avril's mind was struggling to maintain its rationality. She couldn't remember when she had a single coherent thought. She felt as if she were slipping into insanity, despite knowing that Sir would never let that happen.

"Or would he?" she asked herself. "If I found this ordeal punishing, what about my companion? I can't remember the last time I heard a noise from her. Was that just minutes ago, hours or a day ago?"

Unable to do anything about her situation, her jaw was past screaming for relief. Plus, her pussy was tired of the cock facsimile stuffed in it and her asshole stretched by the steel hook opening her wide. She just wished for the millionth time for it all to be over.

"Please, God, let this end soon." she lamented. "I don't know how much longer I can take this."

Her mind ranted. Her lament lasted for, only God knows, how long, she had no idea.

"The worst part about it," she thought, "I can't even sleep anymore. At least then, time would pass, and I would be blissfully ignorant.

Instead, how many umpteenth seconds have ticked by?"

"This sucks," she groaned as best as she could, the words coming out more as garbled noise.

Caged in total darkness, all either of them could try to do was to survive and wait it out. Avril knew she was holding on, but what of her companion? There was no way to know or find out.

"Fuck!" she screamed in her head, as the two girls yelled past their stuffed mouths as blinding light filled the room. Avril squeezed her eyes shut to block out the burning to her retinas. Her eyelids did little to alleviate her distress.

"Hello, ladies. How is everyone today?" Avril heard through her anguish.

"Was the ordeal over; was Sir here to release them?" she asked herself.

At the same time, somehow, she knew her companion had also survived the ordeal. In her head, Avril responded to the query with a primal growl of discontent.

Sir walked in and squatted down between the two cages. With each hand, he stroked the foreheads of the two women, gently moving the wisps of hair dangling down over their faces. Avril had forgotten just when her hair started tickling her nose. Unable to do anything about it, she spent hours trying to ignore the urge to reach up and scratch her nose.

"Well, you two are a sorry sight." he added, "You're both a mess."

Snapping his fingers, another girl came in, as on the first morning, and hosed them down, cleaning away the smell of body odors filling the room. Avril had no desire to know just how bad it was. She just felt relieved to be cleaned by warm water, even if it came from a garden hose. When finished, Sir's helper departed, leaving them alone.

"It's a sorry mess the two of you got yourselves into," he teased.

"Let's get you out of there and properly cleaned up."

"Thank God" was all Avril could think of as Sir walked behind her and began freeing her. She was thankful that the first to go was the fucking anal hook.

In no time at all, he had removed all but her belly straps holding her up. The two dildos gone, all Avril could think of, was how weak she felt. In some ways, she dreaded removing the last strap, the one that kept her from collapsing on the floor of the cage. It seemed that Sir anticipated that as he came to her and supported from underneath. The girl with the hose, she presumed, silently unbuckled the last strap. Avril fell into Sir's arms, her body feeling the heaviest ever in all her life. He gently lowered her to the cage floor.

Sir lifted her from the cage and gently lowered her onto a gurney. It was a soft, comfortable gurney with a thick comfy pad, which Avril sunk into with gratification. The ordeal was over, and she instantly fell asleep.

Waking up, she discovered she was in what appeared to be a medical clinic. Getting her bearings, she noted that an IV stuck in the back of her hand. She was in a hospital bed, with the railings raised, so she didn't accidentally fall out.

Except for her jaw, she felt fine. The burning and stinging pain she had endured from the hook was gone. The dildo in her pussy, had it been in any other circumstances, would have been welcome. Now, she was glad it was gone. Her jaw bothered her the most. It was sore as hell, and she felt it would be a long time before she would even consider putting something in it. She only hoped that Sir would not insist. Although her runny nose cleared up and the feeling of having a cold gone, the experience left her throat scratchy and sore. In time, she felt confident that it would get better as well.

Tilting her head to one side, she noted that her ordeal companion was lying beside her. Her eyes were open, but she couldn't tell how long she had been awake.

"Are you okay?" Avril croaked, her voice hoarse from the ordeal.

Jenni nodded back in return. However, she didn't say anything. Instead, she slowly raised her arm and pointed at her throat. Avril nodded in acknowledgment and agreement, glad to see that the woman survived yet regretting it at the same time.

She knew Sir well enough that he would give her new challenges to overcome when the woman had recovered. The cycle would endlessly repeat until she gave up and succumbed to the ordeal, or Sir grew tired of it and put her down unceremoniously. Jenni was in a no-win situation. Avril was powerless to help.

Rolling her head back over and staring at the ceiling, she closed her eyes and waited for sleep to come to her. It didn't take long.

***

When she awoke, she found herself in her quarters and lying on her bed. She rarely slept here, and even though it was her room, it was strange to her. She felt more at home in the basement cell where she had spent more than a year. Since making her impossible choice all those months ago, she had slept mostly in his bed. It wasn't her favorite room, but it was where he was, so that was where she spent her nights.

He must have anticipated that she would soon awaken as he was sitting in his favorite wingback chair watching her while reading one of his many newspapers.

"So sleepy head, you're finally awake."

Nodding, Avril didn't feel like saying anything else.

"Hungry? You must be. You haven't eaten in almost a week." Sir said, walking over to a serving cart and lifting the lid on a crock. Grasping a serving spoon, he dished up a portion of the delicious soup that instantly filled the room with its enticing odor.

Suddenly, Avril felt hungry. The pleasant odors instantly triggered her to salivate, practically dripping drool from the side of her mouth. She sat up and leaned against the headboard as he approached with the soup.

"Here, this is a bit of broth with small chunks of chicken and vegetables. Your body is not up for a full meal right now, but this will get you on your way to full recovery. The worst is over."

Taking the bowl and the offered spoon, Avril waited until Sir placed a cloth napkin under her chin. As he finished, she dipped the spoon and attempted to put it to her mouth. She spilled most of the broth before it even got halfway to her lips.

"Here, let me," Sir offered.

Sir took the bowl and began feeding her, pouring small amounts of the soup into her mouth and wiping up any spills that leaked from the side of her lips. As he fed her, Avril couldn't help but relate his behavior as being romantic. Never before had she thought of him as a romantic? The revelation came to her as a surprise.

"Is everything alright?" he asked, noting her change in body language.

She nodded, 'Yes.'

As she ate, Sir filled her in on the damage to her body and her prognosis for recovery. As he concluded his report, the only thing of interest seemed that she might develop a UTI in the next week or so. If so, he would authorize an antibiotic to combat the infection. Otherwise, she came through the ordeal with flying colors. Avril nodded.

"Avril, I am very proud of you. You did well."

"Thanks … Sir," she uttered.

She was halfway through her second bowl when she felt she had eaten enough. Putting her hand up in a stop gesture, Sir put the soup down, removed the napkin, and cleaned up her chin.

"Avril," he started, "once again, you amaze me. Not that I didn't have all the confidence in the world that you could succeed in the challenge. No, it was that you even asked to participate in it. I never expected that."

Avril nodded, not in agreement this time, but rather in an acknowledgment of his comment.

"What made you do it? I've been asking myself that question ever since that day."

Closing her eyes, she tried to say, "I … I wanted to know … what it felt like," though she was barely understandable. Her jaw still hurt, and the back of her throat felt as if she had a cold.

"Avril, you survived many of my challenges and succeeded with each of them. Why did you choose to do this one?"

Putting a hand to her throat, she gently massaged it. "Sir … I wanted to help Jenni succeed. I … I didn't think … she felt she could do it … without seeing me survive it."

"You may be right. I had thought the bitch would fail the challenge. However, she's still with us."

"Back in her cell … I presume."

"Yes."

"Is she … otherwise okay?"

"Yes, she is. I have another one of my bitches watching over her. She didn't fare as well as you. Your instincts were right on to join her and give her strength. However, she's past the worst of it and getting stronger all the time."

"Will she have any long-term effects?"

"Long-term effects? That's relative. In the long term, she will be dead. Lasting effects might be a better question. No, she should not have any lasting effects. Like you, she was dehydrated and starving, achy, and depleted. I do believe she lost a lot more weight than you did by the end. Don't worry. She'll recover well enough for you to play with her and learn.

Avril closed her eyes as he spoke and pondered her next question. She was unsure whether she wanted to ask it but ended up deciding to ask.

"Sir …" she began, "… you're going to keep challenging her?"

"Of course, let's say that with this one, I'm curious. I want to find out just how much she can endure before finally giving up. I already know she is a survivor, but I want to test her resolve to overcome these life-threatening challenges."

"Until she finally fails one…"

"Yes, Avril, until she finally fails. It will be fun to see how far she takes it before she realizes it. Once she does, she will give up and die, or she will fight harder, just as you did. I may, of course, one day forego the challenges and let her live for a time. I do need the stock to serve and run the house. However, like the rest of my inventory, she will never leave here alive."

Nodding with the confirmation she had made some time ago, Avril just laid there, not trying to think about the girl. She couldn't. Ultimately, she asked one final question.

"Sir, what do … you think? Will she pass … your tests?"

"She just might. Time will tell. She's a real spitfire. I think in other circumstances, the two of you could have been good friends. Like you, she has had to overcome many childhood and early adulthood challenges. Fate made us aware of her presence. I believe strongly that one way or another, she was destined to end up here with me."

"I guess so." Avril croaked once more.

"Avril, when she first came here, I gave her to you. Now I want you to get closer to her. Bond with her, make her see you as more than her owner, but as a caring one, intent upon keeping her alive."

"What? I don't know what to say, Sir. You must know what you're doing, but I never expected you to ask me this."

"You earned her. Your performance in keeping her alive is outstanding. She will bond with you, lean on you for support."

"All the while, I will implement ... the challenges that she must survive?"

"Of course, the bitch will be a good training vehicle for you. I will help you with that. Together we think up new tests for her to overcome."

"And in the end ... I will be the one to kill her," coughing from her sore throat to cover up her anguish over the inevitability of her predicament.

"That should not be a surprise to you."

Avril closed her eyes and shook her head. "I guess not."

"We'll talk more about that tomorrow. Right now, get some sleep."

"Yes, Sir, I will," Avril muttered.

Rolling over onto her side and pretending to fall asleep, Avril fixated on what she would eventually have to do. She needed to find a way to postpone the inevitable. She liked the girl, and the idea of hurting her bothered her. To have to kill her, well, she didn't want to think about that. The more time she had to figure a way out of this mess, the longer Jenni would stay alive and perhaps, regain her freedom in the process.

Eventually, Avril drifted off into a restless sleep, half in and half out of consciousness. She found it difficult to shake her thoughts and fear that one day, perhaps soon, she would have to kill.

Chapter Twenty-Four

Tossing back the covers, Avril threw her feet over the edge of her bed. If there was ever a time, she desperately wanted a robe or coverall, as today was the day. A week after her release, the cage ordeal still haunted her. She continued to have a sore throat and body aches. While she didn't have any bruises, she felt agonizing pain everywhere. Tossing a throat lozenge into her mouth, she sat there trying to force herself to stand.

She was used to his treatment. If only she could do something to comfort the woman and let her know that she could endure what was to come. Rocking back and forth and not finding the energy to get out of bed, Avril wished she could lie in bed forever. She knew he wouldn't have it. Sir would soon demand that Avril get up and resume her duties, no matter how badly she felt. In some ways, she couldn't blame him. It made sense to her.

"Oh, shit!" she realized. Her hidden dominance was starting to blossom.

Pondering the thought, she sat there, her heeled feet planted on the floor, her hands clutched around her waist, holding her stomach. In her old life, the idea that she would control, no less dominate, another human being was utterly foreign to her. Now, it was apparent. Not only could she, but she also needed to.

"Am I walking a dark path to hell?" she wondered. "Is this my true destiny? Am I to burn for eternity?"

After several minutes of such thoughts and questions, she finally stood up, brushing imaginary dirt from her lap, and threw her shoulders back.

"Well, if I'm going to be her dominant, then it's time I start acting like her dominant."

After washing up, she touched up her makeup and made for the door. A couple of minutes later, she was standing in front of Jenni's door. Staring at it for a moment, she gathered her thoughts and took a deep breath.

Unlocking and opening the door, she walked in and surveyed the scene. Jenni's small cell was much smaller than the one she used to have. It was just big enough to have a bed, a small desk and chair, and a bathroom off to the side. There wasn't a closet or dresser as the girl didn't need clothes or anything besides her heels. Walking over to the desk, she pulled out the chair and sat down. Crossing one leg over the other, she sat back and watched the sleeping girl. She'd sit there as long as it took.

In the meantime, she reflected on her role as Jenni's dominant and owner. It was a strange life she found herself living. Two years ago, she worked for a dumbass who didn't know his ass from his elbow. She pulled him out of many scrapes, saving client after client, and he took all the credit. Now, he was dead, killed by the same man that held her captive. Was she his pet slave or something worse?

She only knew that she needed to find a way to escape. She had yet to discover a means that even if she did gain her freedom, she still needed a way to evade the Consortium. She did not doubt that they would find her, recapture, and kill her, thereby ending the threat against them. No, they wouldn't hunt her down. Instead, Sir would. However, he would use his considerable means within the Consortium to find her, return her, and then make her pay for her insubordination before brutally terminating her.

"Someday," she whispered under her breath. "Tomorrow might bring about the solution. In the meantime, stay alive," she thought.

Leaning her head back, she stared at the ceiling before closing her eyes. She wasn't sure how long she sat there with her eyes closed, but Jenni stared back at her when she next opened them.

Straightening her back, her hands on her lap, Avril looked back at the girl.

"So, you're awake. How are you feeling?" Avril asked her.

After a moment, Jenni answered. "Not too good."

"Yeah, I'm not surprised. That was quite the ordeal. I knew you could do it."

Softly, Jenni said, surprised. "Really? I didn't. I don't remember much after he came in – and cleaned us up. How long ...?"

"How long did he keep us caged?" Avril filled in Jenni's question. Jenni nodded.

"I don't rightly now. I'd say three or four days, maybe more. It's hard to tell. Sir likes to play games with time on his captives. Keeping us in total darkness like that, well, I have no idea. The important thing is that you survived, just as I knew you would."

"You did?"

"I did. Now, let's get something straight. I may be his property, but you belong to me. I own you, your body, and your life. I am your trainer, superior, may even be your executioner. You will refer to me as Ma'am. It would be best that you don't forget that."

"Do you understand?" Avril spoke sternly.

"Yes, ah, Ma'am. Then why?"

"Why did I join you in the cage?"

Jenni nodded.

"I'll tell you why. If I hadn't, you would be dead right now."

"Maybe that would have been better."

"Better, Ma'am," Avril spoke sternly.

Acquiescing, Jenni nodded, "Ma'am."

"This may surprise you, but I don't want you dead right now. I want you alive."

"Alive? Why?"

Avril looked at her rather sternly. Jenni got the message and added, "Ma'am."

"I'm going to train you. Sir is training me in learning how to train others. You are one of my first subjects I will train without direct supervision. The longer I keep you alive, the more I learn. Plus, staying alive is the first rule of escape."

"Escape? You told me there is no escape from here, except in death."

"Ma'am," Avril spoke sternly.

"Yes, Ma'am."

"I did tell you that there is no escape. However, there is always hope. If you can envision hope, you can find the resolve to stay alive long enough to escape."

Jenni closed her eyes. Avril looked at the reclining girl, knowing full well that she was thinking about her words.

"I had to remind you again to say, Ma'am. I'm getting tired of it. Keep that up, and I am going to punish you. You know that, don't you?"

Jenni nodded, ever so slightly. "Yes, Ma'am."

Putting her hand to her throat, she croaked out, "It hurts, Ma'am."

"It'll get better." Nodding, she agreed, knowing that Avril was right.

"Now, it's time you start learning the rules. There are a lot of them. I had the benefit of a rule book. You don't, but I will get you a copy. You will memorize the rules if you're going to stay alive. There are a lot of them. The sooner you learn them, abide by them, the better off you will be. There is one addition you must remember. Since he is training me, you will treat me as if I am Sir. He owns me, and in turn, I own you. You have no say in the arrangement and must answer to two masters. Is that clear?"

Avril paused to let that tidbit of information sink in.

"Suffice to say, anything you say or do, we will use against you. The main rule is this. Whatever Sir or I tell you to do, you do it without hesitation. No questions asked, and do not question either of us. Never ask questions unless we give permission first. Sir runs his life on giving or withholding permission for the behaviors of his property."

"Property? Meaning us, you mean, ah, Ma'am."

"Yes."

"What's with the high-heels, Ma'am?"

"I suspect that it's his way to control us. It makes it difficult for us to run. Control is his thing. Having us eat, sleep, and pee in them is his way to make us feel dependent upon him. He also uses them as a means of rewards."

"Is that, ah Ma'am, why your heels look so fabulous compared to mine? I mean, yours must have cost hundreds of dollars."

"Yes. Sir gave them to me as a reward for good behavior. Plus, he likes the way we look in his heels."

"I'll bet." Jenni sneered. "I mean, Ma'am."

"Be that as it may, the crystals on my heels denote status within the house. Most wear plain heels without crystals. Servants, housekeepers, and cooks wear a single crystal, and a couple more wears two. I wear three on each heel. I am the only woman in the house with three of them. In effect, I am the Lady of the house. Except for Sir, everyone in the house reports to me, and I report to him."

"Yet, all of you, I mean, all of us, will die sooner or later by his hands. That's his thing. Am I correct, Ma'am?"

"Yes, you are."

"You too," Jenni asked?

"Yes, one day. I expect he will kill me when he tires of me. He's promised me he won't, but with him, there are no promises."

"Except for the one that leads to death, Ma'am."

Avril nodded, affirming Jenni's opinion.

"What next, Ma'am?"

Quickly, Avril slapped Jenni across the mouth as hard as she could. The impact sent snapped Jenni's head back, cutting her lip and drawing blood.

"What was that for, Ma'am."

"You should already know. I will indulge you this time but understand. This is the last time. On several occasions, you did not use 'Ma'am' whenever responding to me, despite knowing in advance, you must use my title. That was a gentle reminder. The next time will be much more difficult for you, I mean."

"Yes, Ma'am." Jenni sulked.

"Next, I train you. You will learn, and you will suffer, but you stay alive. Right now, you rest and recover. Your next trial will be soon. For now, I will administer the ordeals you must suffer. There will be many, and all of them painful and difficult to endure. However, I am confident that you will get through them, enduring the very worse tossed at you."

Pausing a moment, Avril continued. "I don't know what he plans for you, but it is my job to get you ready for it."

Jenni nodded, closing her eyes.

"Get some rest. I'll send someone with some broth. Do you think you can handle that?"

Jenni nodded again.

"Good. Tomorrow, I'll get you back on solid food. Neither of us has eaten in some time. While I've endured many of his trials, you haven't. We both need to get our strength back. We'll do lunch tomorrow, which by the way, is not a request. Normally, I wouldn't even give you that much warning, so don't get used to it."

Jenni stared at the ceiling, offering a slight nod of acknowledgment.

"Good girl. Now sleep." Avril said as she walked out of the room and locked the door behind her. Falling back against the door, Avril breathed a sigh of relief, grateful that the session was now over.

She needed to de-stress. Despite her worn-out and achy body, a few miles on the treadmill followed by a soak in the hot tub were just the thing she needed. Turning, she made towards the gym at a brisk pace.

Chapter Twenty-Five

The air smelled rich with the scent of moisture and oxidizers rising from the waters in the pool. Sunlight streamed through the tall windows wrapping the pool deck on the south and west sides. The water was crystal clear and inviting.

Walking into the natatorium and grabbing a clean towel from the rack, she laid it out on her favorite chaise lounge and sat down. Staring wistfully for a moment at the scene beyond the windows, she bent over to remove her heels. About an hour later, after swimming lap after lap using various strokes, Avril got out of the pool and returned to the chaise lounge. Her chest swelled, drawing in much-needed air into her labored lungs. Even so, her breathing was almost normal, despite the vigorous exercise.

Putting two fingers on the inside of her wrist, she measured her heart rate. Satisfied at the count, Avril put her hands on her hips and stretched, bending backward as far as she could fold herself. Feeling refreshed, she sat down on the chaise lounge. After putting her heels back on, she stretched out. Water droplets beaded on her skin quickly evaporated in the warm afternoon sun. With her eyes closed, she almost fell asleep when she heard him walk onto the pool deck.

Squinting tightly, her hand shielding her eyes, she saw Sir walking softly towards her. Dressed in his typical day outfit around the estate, including a white button-down dress shirt tucked into dark grey trousers and polished black dress shoes, Avril admired the dapper man. In other circumstances, she would welcome his advances. Here, on the deck surrounding the swimming pool, he certainly looked out of place.

As he approached, he was already unbuttoning his shirt. Grabbing a towel and removing his clothing, he joined Avril in the adjacent chaise.

"Hello, Avril, enjoying the sun?"

"Yes, Sir, I am. Is there something I can get for you?"

"No, not just now. I thought I'd enjoy spending some time with you."

Avril nodded her acknowledgment but didn't add anything further. Side by side, the two of them laid back, soaking in the sun. It was hot, and Avril had already turned over a couple of times to make sure she didn't burn.

As they laid there, Avril couldn't help but think about the mission of the Consortium. She had been aching to learn more about them over the past many months. She didn't know just how to open the topic but had kept looking for the opportunity.

"You have something on your mind." Sir suggested.

"Always, Sir."

"Anything in particular …?" He asked.

"Yes, Sir. I do. I want to know more about the Consortium."

"Avril, that's a broad topic. Can you narrow it down a bit for me?"

"Oh … Yes, Sir, I see what you mean."

"Did I detect a slip? Did you almost apologize for something?"

"Ah, well, Sir, now that you ask, I did. I caught myself, though."

"Yes, you did. Go on."

"Thank you, Sir. It's about the reasons why the Consortium feels the need to kidnap people and sell them at auction. It seems to me that there is more to the Consortium than just the satisfaction of blood lusts."

"Such as …?" Sir prompted.

"Well, Sir. For the Consortium to exist for as long as you say, there has to be more to it than just kidnapping and killing people. In of itself, it's unsustainable. What you do is very expensive. There must be payouts to non-Consortium people to hide your footprints, so to speak."

Chuckling, Sir agreed.

"Sir," Avril continued, "I'd like to learn more about the finances. It seems to me, from my limited exposure to the goings-on within the Consortium, that it's run like a major business, operating on a global scale."

"I see." Sir confirmed. "You're correct. It is a global business and runs like one."

"Just not as a publicly traded business but similar to a private one. As I understand it, a private business does not have to file annual statements as public corporations. Doesn't there have to be a ruling body that handles the business side of things besides acquiring their prey? You have told me that you are very high up in the Consortium. Are you a member of this ruling entity?"

"What would you say if I wasn't?"

"Oh, Sir, I don't believe I could accept that, not for a moment. Observing you since I came here, I've come to understand that you know much more than you let on. A regular member who is in the Consortium just for the privilege of acquiring prey for their purposes wouldn't know as much as you know. That would be a lie, and to the best of my knowledge, you've never lied to me."

"That's very observant, my pet. You are correct in your assessment. I am a member of the ruling body, called the executive committee."

"Thank you, Sir. I appreciate the confirmation. I presume you are head of the executive committee."

Sir nodded in affirmation.

"I thought so, Sir. So, I gather you are privy to the financials of the Consortium."

"Which I will not discuss with you, remember, you are my property to do with as I please. Even members don't get to see the full financials. All they care about is whether their payments are sufficient to sustain their desires and needs."

"Yes, Sir, I understand that. I wasn't going to probe into the details of the finances. Rather, I want to know more about the driving forces behind them. I presume one of your duties is to keep the Consortium solvent, even flush."

"That's true, Avril. As Chairman, it is my responsibility to ensure the financial health of our group. There's more, of course, than just money. I am responsible for the integrity of all facets of the Consortium."

"I assumed as much, Sir. I assume you keep a lot of the details locked in your head. That is, many details would not be safe to commit to paper or electronic means."

"True, my dear. Just be careful. You're delving into areas that are none of your concern."

"Sir, I didn't mean to offend."

"You didn't. Just be careful. Too much information is not necessarily a good thing."

"Yes, Sir. I welcome your guidance in directing the conversation. If I may, can we talk about the process of deciding whom to snatch?"

"I suppose so. What would you like to know?"

"First off, Sir. How do you find your prey? Among the billions on the planet, how did you find me, for example?"

"Well, let's see. First off, we have a large network of operatives stationed all around the world. None of them know each other, nor do they ever come into contact with their handlers."

"So, they are not members of the Consortium?"

"More like paid contractors. They work in inconspicuous jobs that put them into direct contact with the public. They also have some limited access to the personal information of those they interact with. As for you, I'd have to look at your records to find out just how you came to our attention. At this point, it's safe to say that through your day-to-day activity, one of our operatives noticed you and submitted you as a potential candidate."

"Sir, do they know that their submissions eventually lead to our deaths?"

"No. Indeed not. Rather, most are under the impression that the submissions may lead to exciting job offers in exotic locations."

"So, whoever submitted me as a candidate, thinks that we get offered fantastic opportunities and travel the world to exotic locations?"

"I suppose so. I don't care what they believe. I only care that they use discretion in their submissions or don't get carried away with chumming the waters."

"Chumming, Sir?"

"Submitting too many candidates at once and risking exposing the Consortium."

"Sir, I gather that if those contractors get too ambitious or risk exposing your real intent, become prey themselves?"

"Sometimes, mostly though, we eliminate the threat making it look like an accident."

"I presume you pay a bonus to these contractors, Sir."

"Yes, we do, on a sliding scale based upon many factors."

"Sounds reasonable, Sir. You must have a substantial infrastructure to vet these candidates, kidnap them, and a transportation system to bring them to the training facility."

"Correct again, though I don't have all the details on how that works. I have a comprehensive understanding of those segments, but not everything."

"I presume, Sir, that most of those at these levels don't know each other and may or may not be members themselves."

"Avril, I fail to understand why you ask questions you already know the answer to."

"Yes, Sir. I understand. It just helps solidify my understanding. If I am to become a member, I want to know what I am getting myself into. As a member, outside these walls, I'm not just your property to do with as you please."

"Yes, I see what you're getting at. Very well, what else would you like to know?"

"Thank you, Sir. Do you oversee the training facility where I first brought to and trained in preparation for auction?"

"I do, though, like most executives, I have a facilities director that takes care of the day-to-day operations."

Nodding, Avril continued. "Sir, is he the one in charge of the guards? I presume you know and allow them their cruel, despicable acts upon the newly captured?"

"Yes. I am aware of the guard's behaviors. At times, I encourage them. It is important to train new prey that their old life is over and they must accept a new one."

"Including disciplining the unresponsive ones to their deaths."

"Yes. Tell me, when you saw that girl hang from the post during your training, didn't that make a lasting impression on you? Didn't it prompt you to follow the rules and accept the turn of events in your new life?"

"Yes, Sir, it did. I remember at that moment. I decided not to suffer her fate. Though, at the time, I did not know that our fates would eventually follow the same path. In some ways, she got off easy. I dare say. I prefer hanging from a post rather than roasting alive for that woman."

"I suppose I would too.

"Sir, all of this must cost a fortune."

Laughing under his breath, Sir agreed. "It does."

"And you recover your expenses at the auction?"

"In part, but that is not our only enterprise. There are others, many legitimate."

"Something I suspected, Sir. Tell me, which earns more profit, the legitimate or the illicit ones?"

"First off, we don't consider what we do as illegitimate. Clandestine is the more appropriate term for our activities. You see, in many parts of the world, what we do is not illegal. Many countries condone our activities as it keeps their populations from spiraling out of control and dragging down the rest. They strongly believe that if we don't cull their population, their economy suffers, and their remaining citizens go hungry."

"Sir, I find that hard to believe."

"You doubt my statement?"

"Not so much as doubt you, Sir. I find it incredulous. That's all."

"Be that as it may, it is true."

"Sir, going back to answer my original question, which of your enterprises earns the most profit?" Avril asked, still shaking her head in disbelief.

"Oh, they're about even. Though, for me and the rest of the membership, the auction is the highlight of the quarterly gathering."

"So, you auction off your prey every three months? I hadn't realized it was so often, Sir."

"Avril, sometimes, it's more frequent than that. The membership and our inventory guide us on how often we hold them."

"And the Consortium makes enough at these auctions to meet your expenses in hunting the prey, returning them to the facility for training and sale?"

"Yes, my dear, and very often earning a profit."

"Just from the bidding process, Sir?"

"Yes."

"How much does the membership know about those going up for auction?"

"A lot but not everything, it all depends. They know your physical attributes, your health, your abilities, what you like in and out of bed, and so forth. A little intrigue and mystery go a long way."

"Uh? Excuse me, Sir. They know what we like in bed?"

"Oh, yes. Take you, for example. I don't remember much about most of the prey we take. However, I do recall everything in your file. I know that during your vetting, you slept with several partners. Would you be surprised that a couple of them were our operatives?"

"Really? I had no idea, Sir. What did they report?"

"Oh, you were a firebrand in bed, a good lay, I think they call it in your country. Your bed partners also reported that you liked them controlling you during sex. That you seemed to get off on having a bit of restraint as they fucked you."

Thinking back, Avril agreed. "That's true, Sir, at least at that level. If I understand you correctly, some of the men who picked me up in the months before my taking were working for you?"

"Yes, in a way, though I don't know who they are, nor do I want to. I only read their reports."

"Sir, do you read the reports on all your prey before being taken?"

"Indeed, as Chairman, I approve the taking of all that we cull."

"Sir, you read my file and approved me?"

"Yes, I did. Reading your file intrigued me. I was anxious to meet you. When you arrived at the training center, still encased in your acrylic box, I inspected you as you slept. You fascinated me. Then, I closely watched your progress throughout your training. I only decided on the day of the auction that you had to be mine. Up until then, I was happy to let the market guide your sale. When I realized just how many others were hoping to acquire you, my competitive spirit arose, and I had to have you for myself."

"Sir, I'm not sure how I feel about that. After all, I'm now the property of someone else, a prisoner, and someone's property. I still struggle with that concept. Slavery is wrong."

"I understand. The fact remains, you are mine. I own you. You must either accept it or not."

"Tell me, Sir. Did you know more about me during that auction than the other members?"

"Of course, my dear. As Chairman, I must know everything about the prey to approve their taking."

"But you don't share all of that information with the membership, do you, Sir."

"That's true. That's very astute. I don't."

"Why? How can they make an informed decision?"

"That's half of the fun, Avril. They are gambling, hoping for a big return. Most times, they get enough to offset their purchase price. But for most of them, it's not about the money. They usually have more than enough. It's about their acquisitions. They buy what piques their interest."

"It's like when in your old life you see a cute guy that turns your head. You are interested in getting to know him and put yourself out there, in the hopes that they will bite. It's the same with the membership. They get focused on the talent before them, so they buy it, looking forward to whatever they want to accomplish. In my case, I want to inflict pain and hear screams. By the way, you scream very nicely."

"Thank you, Sir."

"In other cases, they have different desires. Some are not acceptable around the world."

"Such as the woman who bid against you in my auction, Sir, she wanted a roast for dinner."

"Well, yes. In that case, that member wanted something that appealed to her and would feed her guests. I suspect she knew that I wanted you for myself. She tried to upset me and steal you away."

"But with you, Sir, it's more than just the piece of meat up for auction?"

"Don't get me wrong. All of those things motivate me. However, with you, I saw something that made me want you. It had little to do with how much I was willing to spend for you. I see something in you that I have never seen before in any human, member, or property. I'm intrigued to see if that something, that spark I detected at the training center, can be fanned into flames. I am still intrigued."

"I suppose I should be grateful for that, Sir. Otherwise, I would have been that girl spitted, roasted alive, and fed to a bunch of hungry members."

"Yes, I suppose so."

"Back to the money, Sir, how did you make out with me?"

"Oh, alright, I suppose. I could have sold off your apartment, but I didn't. Rather, I transferred its ownership to me, through various shell companies, and I lease it out at a very nice profit."

"I want it back. I may want to go back there."

"Avril, you know that's impossible."

Nodding, Avril abandoned that line and returned to the previous conversation, "So, Sir, I am earning my keep."

"Yes, I suppose you could put it that way."

"Which gives you the incentive to keep me around, earning you a profit, Sir."

"No, that's not true. I could kill you now and still earn that profit you speak of."

"Yes, Sir, I see what you mean. I withdraw my last comment."

After a long pause, in which Avril processed what she had learned, a new thought suddenly crossed her mind.

"Sir, you said that some of the membership is not motivated by money but rather by other things. Is that what drives the auction entertainment? I mean, at my auction, the member who bought those three women, he hung them immediately. He spent good money for them and just as quickly, killed them for no reason."

"Avril, it wasn't for no reason. There is always entertainment at the auctions. Someone always dies at the expense of the enjoyment and pleasure of the crowd. Every member sponsors the entertainment on a rotating basis."

"Ah, I see. And in this case, this member chose to donate a pod of three women to torture and kill while others placed wagers as they died."

"Exactly right."

"And the crowd always expects to witness someone dying at these entertainments."

"Yes, they do. They also bet on various outcomes that one cannot predict. The wagering can get quite vigorous, and the donor and the house takes a cut on those bets as well."

"Ah, I see. Not only do you make a profit on the taking and selling of our bodies, but you also make a profit on our deaths."

"Splendid, my dear Avril. Right so … a splendid deduction."

Chapter Twenty-Six

"Central, seventeen checking in."

"Report."

"Subject spent the last two days searching for her sister without success."

"Where are her current whereabouts?"

"She's in front of her missing sister's apartment, sitting in her automobile, crying. She's been there for the better part of two hours."

"She's given up the search?"

"No, I don't believe so. Having run out of places to look, the subject is keeping vigil, hoping the sister will return soon."

"She's agitated?"

"You could say that, yes."

"Do you sense she will give up on the search?"

"No, definitely not. The subject is too invested in the sister. She saved the girl's life and feels beholden to her. No, she will search until she finds her. I get the sense that she will use every resource at her disposal to find her."

"Continue surveillance. Report any change. We'll send relief within the hour."

"Understood. Seventeen out."

The agent leaned back, keeping a keen eye on the distraught girl sitting in the car down the street. In many ways, she felt terrible for her. She knew what it was to love. The agent wondered at times if her masters knew. Still, she had a job to do. She would do it.

"Sir, the agent surveilling the sister of the girl who donated her heart just reported. We may have trouble with her."

"Explain." The Chairman answered.

"Sir, since we were not able to complete the background check before we took the girl, we continued it afterward. It turns out that it is likely that you would not have approved her culling. She has quite an extensive family. The sister was extremely grateful for the gift of life, and in the time after the donation, the two became extremely close."

"Understandable. In time, that should diminish."

"No, Sir. I don't think so. She's part of a large and powerful family in their home country."

"Which is?"

"America, Sir. The United States."

"Well, we've taken thousands from that country, perhaps millions over the decades."

"Yes, Sir. However, this family is well placed and powerful. They have the resources to make trouble for us."

"How so?"

The aide hesitated.

"Speak up. I don't have all day."

"Yes, Sir. It is now apparent that we may have been hasty in taking this girl. Her father is a high-ranking member of their legislative branch. Something called a Senator."

"We have agents in all branches of their government. In fact, one of our members is a Senator. We should be able to squash anything they could do to us."

"Normally, Sir, I agree. However, this senator is also a member of their Senate Judiciary Committee. He holds the title of Ranking Member."

"Shit!" the Chairman exclaimed. "How the hell did that escape our notice? That connection should have surfaced immediately."

"Unknown Sir."

"Do we have an agent in place?"

"We do, Sir, but I fear it may not be enough. The agent is not in a position to do much to prevent action. Agents positioned in these areas are there to observe and report. They are not trained to intercept or redirect courses of action."

"How soon can we get someone in place who can?"

"It's being looked into, Sir."

"Make this the highest priority, in fact, the only priority. Mark my words, I'm going to make our member pay dearly for his new heart."

"Yes, Sir, I understand."

"What's the current status of the subject?"

"The sister, Sir? We have her under constant observation. At last check-in, she's spent the last couple of days unsuccessfully searching for the missing girl. She is now camped out in front of the girl's apartment waiting for her return."

"It's going to be a long wait."

Chuckling, the aide went on. "Yes, Sir. Our analysis of the situation is that eventually, she will enlist the aid of her father to expand the search."

"So, we have to move fast."

"Yes, Sir."

"Options?"

"We are developing them. Currently, we are in the early stages of coming up with a course of action. However, the teams know the importance and the severity of the problem. They'll find the right approach."

"Soon, Mister, soon," the Chairman snapped at his underling.

"Yes, Sir."

"Dismissed."

"Yes, Sir."

As soon as the door closed behind his aide, the Chairman poured himself a drink and gulped the whole glass in one swallow. Preparing another, he walked over to the windows and stared out onto the scene. He usually loved the view. Today, he didn't notice the beautiful panorama beyond the glass. For the first time in his life, he had a quandary he could not resolve. He couldn't envision the future, nor an idea of what to do to control the situation.

"Fuck!"

His mind in turmoil, what he wanted most was to burn off some of his rage by going down to the cells and taking his frustration out on one of the recently procured prey. However, he knew that indulging in his favorite pastime, would not salve the savage beast inside him. For the first time in his life, he did not know what to do.

***

"Arrgggghhhhh," Heather screamed at her steering wheel in frustration. She had been sitting in her car for hours. Rachel had not yet returned, and Heather felt sure that something was wrong, terribly wrong.

Her mind racing, a course of action percolated. Picking up her cell phone, she dialed a number by heart.

"Mom, where's Daddy?" she asked.

"Heather, dear? Is that you? It's late, dear."

"Yes, Mom. Where's Daddy?"

"Your father? Why he's in Washington. Is everything alright?"

Before her mother could finish, Heather hung up, "Thanks, Mom, gotta go."

Starting the car, she pulled out and headed for the airport. She knew a phone call wouldn't do. Besides, she knew that Mom would alert Daddy that she was on her way. She wasn't worried about getting the next flight from Chicago to D.C. Multiple flights between them ran routinely every day.

At 6:40 a.m. the next morning, her United Airlines flight lifted off the runway and headed south-east. Somehow, she felt better, knowing that in a couple of hours, she'd be in Washington and with her daddy. He'd know what to do. By noon, they'd have a plan, and soon, they'd find Rachel.

"Central, seventeen checking in."

"Report."

"Subject is at the airport. She just booked a ticket to Washington, D.C., on the early morning flight. What are your instructions?"

"Relax, we'll have someone in D.C. pick her up. We know where she's going. We'll let you know when you can resume your surveillance."

"Is there anything I can do in the meantime?"

"Stand down and take the day off. Get some rest. We will contact you when we need you."

"Understood central, seventeen out."

Just before eleven a.m., having cleared security, Heather opened the door to her father's outer office.

"May I help you?" His secretary greeted her. "Oh! Hi Heather, what a surprise! Your father is expecting you. There's someone in there right now. He'll be with you in just a few minutes. Will that be alright?"

"Yes, thank you, ah ... Mr. Clark, isn't it?"

"Yes, Ma'am, you can call me Ben. He'll be right with you. You can have a seat right over there."

"Thank you, Mr., ah ... Ben." She said with a sweet smile and sat down to wait. Crossing her legs, she made sure she gave the handsome Mr. Clark a good view of her legs. After all, Daddy taught her that if she wanted something from the underlings, provide them something in return, and they would bend over backward to give you what you wanted. Not that she needed to in this case, but it was good practice.

A couple of minutes later, Daddy's inner office door opened, and her father escorted a gentleman out, shaking hands with the guy and patting him on his back before turning towards her.

"Heather, what a surprise!" he exclaimed as he kissed her on the cheek and escorted her into his office.

"Your mother called to tell me you were on your way. You were a bit abrupt with her."

"I know Daddy, I'm sorry. I'll make it up to her, I promise. Right now, though, there is something else that is more important."

"What, sweetie? What's wrong?"

"Oh, Daddy, it's Rachel," she said, starting to cry hysterically.

Wrapping his little girl in his arms, the Senator pulled the sobbing girl tight to his body and held her. He waited as she worked to get the words out between sobs. It took several minutes, and by the time Heather got control of herself, he got the gist of the message.

"Daddy, Rachel's missing. No one has seen her since she got back from her business trip last weekend. Daddy, she's been gone for days. I'm so worried. Daddy, something has happened to her, something bad, and something awful. I know it."

Senator Thomas Ladensen, a Ranking Member of the Senate

Judiciary Committee, waited until his daughter was composed and then moved into action.

"Heather, it's going to be okay. I'm going to call in the troops now. They're going to take your statement. It might get a little rough for a while, intense for sure. But together, we'll get to the bottom of this. We'll find your sister. You can count on it."

Nodding and feeling better, Heather agreed. Wrapped up in his comforting arms, she was feeling better, now that she came to him.

"Ready?" he asked her.

"Yes, Daddy."

"That's my baby girl."

Walking over to his desk, he picked up his phone and pressed a button.

"Ben, come in here, please."

In mere seconds, Ben Clark walked in.

"Close the door, Ben."

As soon as the sounds from the outer office died out, the senator came right to the point.

"Ben, Heather reports that my daughter Rachel is missing. She's been missing for nearly a week. Call out the troops and get the FBI involved. Her disappearance might be a way to compromise me. She was on a business trip across the country and may or may not have returned to Chicago. It's not like the girls don't talk to each other daily. They did. I want teams tracing Rachel's movements within the hour. I want to know what happened to my daughter. Find her now!"

"Yes, Sir, right away," Ben confirmed the matter of urgency and left the room.

"Heather, we'll find her. In the meantime, sit down." He said, pointing to one of his sofas. "I'll have them interview you here. At least it'll be a bit more personal. I'll be with you the whole way, right by your side."

Heather nodded and took a seat. Her father sat next to her and held her, comforting her as only a loving father could soothe a daughter. It didn't take long before a knock on the door, and it opened, revealing Ben Clark.

"Sir, the FBI is here."

Turning towards his daughter, he said. "Here we go. Are you ready?"

She nodded, and the Senator gestured towards Ben to send them in.

Whispering to Heather, as he kissed her cheek, "It'll be alright."

"I hope so, Daddy. I hope so."

Chapter Twenty-Seven

Grasping the key, Avril unlocked the door to the cell. Inside was her latest training victim, Misty. Avril found her sitting on her bunk, turning towards the cell door as she opened it.

"Get up," Avril commanded.

"Why should I? You're just going to beat me again," she retorted. "Look at me. I'm covered in nasty red welts, burn marks, and my mouth hurts. You've done enough to me. I'm not leaving this cell."

With a hard look on Avril's face, "I won't tell you again. Get up."

"Go fuck yourself. I'm not going."

"If that's the way you want it." Avril retorted, walking up to the girl and backhanding her across the cheekbone.

Misty's head snapped backward, nearly bouncing off the wall behind the narrow bunk. Tears instantly welled up in the girl's eyes. Grasping her by the upper arm, Avril pulled her up to her feet.

"Come with me," she commanded.

Sniveling and whining about the rough treatment, the girl nonetheless followed Avril. Pushed along, Misty's training heels clicked clumsily on the hard, concrete floor. This prey never had the opportunity to read or study the rule book. Instead, it took reinforcing punishments to make the girl leave them on her feet.

The cell she occupied was in the other wing of the property, opposite to where Avril spent her first year. It was the wing that Sir used to torture and ultimately killed his victims. Avril now had the task to lead the unfortunate girl to destiny, where she knew she would prove to Sir her resolve to submit her application to the Consortium. It was a short distance to their destination.

"Why? Why are you doing this?" Misty asked as she stepped towards the door.

"Because it pleases me, that's all you need to know," Avril replied sternly, pushing the girl through the door.

Misty turned to face her, ready to attack until she saw Sir standing off to the side. Changing her mind, she started to run the other way, only to be blocked by Avril standing in her way. Avril's hold on her arm turned her around.

"Not that way prey, this way." Avril sternly spoke, almost pushing her in the correct direction.

Misty, seeing Sir standing there, tried to pull away, but Avril held her steady. The girl glared at him as Avril led her past him and down the hallway. Sir followed silently behind as they made their way to their destination. The girl stumbled; hate directed in her eyes at Avril as she fell forward.

Silently they walked down the hallway and around a bend. Arriving at their destination, Avril led Misty into a large, brightly lit room. Almost blinding from the number of light fixtures spread around the space, it was evident that the lights directed their beams at the center of attraction.

Bewildered and tossing her head back and forth, Misty scanned for an exit and escape. There was none.

Only yesterday, they tied her wrists up high to the post and whipped her much of the day, rarely stopping to allow her time to rest and recover. She seemed to dance for them every time the tip snapped against her skin. Jumping up or to the side, Misty tried to avoid the punishing action of the whip. She failed and cried as they mercilessly flailed at her tenderized body.

As the day wore on, Avril grew tired of whipping the girl. Insisting that she continue, Sir pointed out techniques and suggestions to help Avril land the whip in just the right spot on the intended target. The target was usually less than a square inch in size. Misty wore hundreds of such 'targets' all over her body, each sporting a deep red welt or abrasion.

Over the past months, Avril had perfected her techniques using the whip. Months ago, Sir handed her the first whip she had ever held before. From handle to tip, it was about four feet long and made of extremely supple leather. Cradling it, Avril didn't know what she felt. Wielding it in her hands, she felt powerful. Avril was also confident and nervous at the same time. She hadn't guessed she would feel this way.

With Sir standing beside her, he showed Avril how to hold it. He demonstrated a simple flick of the whip using his own, which cracked the air with a resounding noise.

"Now, you try it."

Letting the whip unfurl, Avril held the handle and slowly dragged it across the floor. The sight mesmerized her as it tapered from a nice firm handle, perfectly sized for her hand, down to a narrow end with what appeared to be a short length of thin cording.

"Give it a flick."

Avril tried to duplicate Sir's previous demonstration. A moment later, not only hadn't she been able to make the whip crack the air, she managed to snap it against the back of her hand. It stung but otherwise did little damage.

"With practice, you'll get better. That's the business end of the whip. But first, let's talk about the parts of the whip."

"I think that would be good, Sir."

"The end you're holding, that's called the handle, obvious, isn't it?"

Avril smiled at the absurdity.

"After that follows the thong, a fall, and ending in the cracker. The main portion of the whip is the thong. It is what builds up the power from the swing of your arm and transports it to the fall. It is the longest part of the whip. It can range anywhere from a couple of feet to a couple of yards. It is usually made from braided leather, decreasing in circumference the closer to the tip it gets. Its structure is a bit more complicated than that, but you get the idea.

At the end of the thong is a small bit of cording called the fall. Its length is usually about one-quarter of the thong's size, and its purpose is to multiply the whip's power and direct it to the cracker at the end. That's that short bit of cording tied to the end of the whip. You'll notice that the very end is frayed. That's the business end of the whip."

"Sir, I notice that the cracker isn't leather, but a bit of nylon cording."

"It is. The cracker tends to need replacing with regular use. It's expendable, and as it wears out, I replace it with a new one. I tend to like using narrow, diamond braid nylon cording as crackers, as they tend to hold up better and deliver an awesome sound. Besides, due to their tight weave, they do a nice job as it snaps against the skin, leaving nasty red welts. I also have whips using leather crackers, but I don't favor them. They tend to cut the skin or do permanent damage. It all depends on how I use the whip. In the early stages of whipping a new subject, I like seeing the welts that don't break the skin. They often last for days or weeks. They are my marks, for which I am very proud."

Avril absentmindedly rubbed the back of her hand as he said that. Sir, observant as always, noticed, and smiled at the involuntary behavior.

"Now, let's try that again."

"Yes, Sir."

Over the next several weeks, Avril attended a lesson after lesson in the use of the whip. She practiced using several different kinds, but her favorite tended to be the first one he handed her. Eventually, he gave it to her, telling her it was hers. Besides, it was the wrong size and weight for his expert techniques. Not only did he teach her how to throw the whip, often learning painful lessons along the way, but he also taught her how to care for it. She never knew how much work it took to care for his toys, as he called them.

In the last month, she had moved from popping balloons to targeting live targets. While she rotated her training subjects, Misty was her first and practiced with it the most.

Over dozens of whipping sessions, Avril transformed the beautiful girl into a shell of a girl, covered with welts, bruises, cuts, and scabs. Avril rarely missed a day in perfecting her use of the whip on the unfortunate Misty.

Streaked with dried blood and sweat, Misty became little more than a quivering bag of human flesh, barely capable of standing on her own.

Standing in solitary guard, centered in a circle of light, stood a massive wooden post. It was a post that Misty had become intimately familiar with over the weeks.

Seeing the whipping post and envisioning what was to come, Misty wailed. "No, please, no more. Please don't whip me again. I can't take it anymore."

"Who gave you permission to speak?" A stern Avril reminded her. "You continue to ignore my commands. I'm getting tired of this – and you."

"Never mind that, now get up there," Avril commanded the

terrified girl, giving her a firm push towards the whipping post. Misty stumbled, only to try and turn away at the last moment.

"Uh-uh!" Avril uttered, grabbing the girl's hair and pushing her back towards the post.

"No, please, I ... I don't want to get up there." Misty sniveled, anxiously stepping up onto the platform where the post rested.

"Well, you're there now," Avril told the girl, grabbing a set of shackles and backing Misty against the post. Grabbing Misty's wrists, Avril securely bound them together behind the staff.

Whimpering softly now, Misty leaned her head back against the post and looked up at the ceiling. Sounds of fear mixed with prayers escaped her gaping mouth. If one could read Misty's mind, she honestly didn't know if she could withstand another whipping.

Taking another set of shackles, Avril secured the girl's elbows behind the post, just as she had done with her wrists. Tightly attached to the post against her back, Misty's elbows almost touched each other under the bindings' tension. Satisfied, Avril stared into Misty's eyes and smiled. Behind a false fascia, Avril hid remorse for what she was about to do.

"Please, whoever you are, please don't do this. I can't take it anymore." Misty begged, tears flooding her eyes and streaming down her cheeks.

Avril took a moment to inspect the girl in front of her. Making a decision, she picked up a large bundle of rope and tied the girl's waist to the post. After several tight wraps, she cinched the lashing and tied off the ends. She did the same to her thighs, calves, and finally, her ankles.

Misty was powerless to resist what was to come.

"Hmm, what am I going to do next?" Avril said to Misty.

Stepping up to Misty, she suddenly reached out and slapped the girl right on her left tit, eliciting a loud, welcoming response to the strike.

"Hmm, you still have feeling there. Good." Avril said as she added a second slap to Misty's right tit.

Misty begged in a feeble attempt for relief. Inspired, Avril rained blow after blow to the girl's breasts, making sure she covered the entire fleshy part with bright red handprints. Striking her prey, Avril made sure to pay attention to the girl's nipples. She wanted them super sensitive for the next act in the session. Avril only relented when her hands felt the sting of her slaps. Even then, she continued far beyond where she otherwise would have stopped. Today's session was a test. Sir was testing her resolve to dominate her subjects, control them, and to prove that she could take the torture to the end.

Avril stopped her onslaught with Misty crying profusely, rubbing her hands as she looked at the girl. Avril partly enjoyed giving Misty the beating, even as another part of her struggled with the idea of hurting a fellow woman. Despite the training that Sir had put her through, he could only train her in the physical and psychological techniques of torture. He could never change her fundamental outlook on life. But, if she were to survive and take down the Consortium in the process, she had to do what was necessary. May God forgive her?

Staring into the bloodshot tear-filled eyes, Avril gripped each of the girl's nipples between her thumb and forefingers and pinched hard. Simultaneously, she pulled them upwards towards the ceiling with such force that if the girl weren't bound to the post, she would have lifted her right off the platform. As it was, the strength of Avril's grip on her nipples stretched her breasts and turned the nipples white under the fierce compression. Avril never saw any of this. Instead, she just stared into the girl's eyes, watching pain telegraph from her breasts to her corneas, scrunched up behind eyelids.

Turning towards the table, Avril selected a hard rubber slapper and returned to her victim. Misty was still crying. Her tears ran down the length of her face and body in streams of salty water.

Misty looked up at her, her eyes begging for release. "How many times have you disobeyed me?" Avril asked the bound girl.

Downtrodden, Misty dropped her eyes and stared at the floor. A moment later, the wide hard rubber slapper smashed into a nipple on her chest, flattening her breast in an instant, delivering a whole new level of pain to the unfortunate girl. Focused on the target, Avril watched with interest the rippling across the fleshy gland.

Misty bellowed just as another strike of the heavy rubber slapper connected right on her other nipple. As before, her breast pancaked, and another loud bellow echoed throughout the chamber of torture.

Struggling inadequately, Misty tried to protect her soft and tender tissue from the onslaught. Avril would have none of it and beat her chest to a bloody pulp. By the time Avril ceased her assault, Misty's breasts were a bloody mess, barely recognizable as a woman's chest. Deep cuts seemed to leave her nipples dangling freely from the fleshy home where they once resided. The left one was missing the nipple ring that used to pierce it. The underlying breast tissue dripped fat and other body fluids mixed in with the blood.

Avril didn't stop there. She had moved onto the girl's belly and pubic region. In short order, her pubis mons mimicked the same bloody mess that used to be her tits.

After Avril finished, she dropped the slapper on the floor and stepped back, reviewing her handiwork. Throughout the assailment, she had never once looked back at Sir. Now, during the rest break, she felt an overwhelming desire to look for support. Resisting the urge, she locked her gaze on the girl, knowing that Sir would give her a down check for looking at him. He wanted her to do it all herself.

She had wanted to take her time with the girl. Never once had she seen Sir beat his victims without intermittent pausing. He had told her that the breaks allowed their misery to sink in, making it all the worse when they resumed. Plus, sitting back and taking a look at her handiwork felt somehow … good. A bloodlust had welled up inside her, and she couldn't seem to stop.

Staring at her victim, if it weren't for the ropes tying her to the post, Misty would have already fallen to the ground. As it was, her upper body leaned as far forward as possible with her arms shackled behind the post. Her head hung loosely while the girl forcefully whimpered. Her tears had stopped, though her crying continued.

Turning to the table of toys, Avril picked up a whip, her favorite one and one that Sir had given her early in her training. Stepping up to her victim, she held it out so that Misty could see it. Nodding in resignation, Misty could do nothing to prepare herself. She didn't have to wait long.

The first strike of the whip landed right on the center of her belly, leaving a four-inch scorch mark behind. Several seconds later, another flick of the whip left a second mark on Misty's ravaged abdomen. Ignoring Misty's whimpering, Avril rained strike after strike up and down her body, sparing nothing, marking everything.

Some indeterminate time later, with few pauses between strikes, Avril halted her assault. Obvious to any observer, the object of Avril's tirade was no longer generating the desired responses to the whipping. Misty seemed to be slipping into blissful unconsciousness.

Undeterred, Avril tossed a glassful of salty water onto the face of her victim. Misty screamed as the water refreshed her while the salt burned every one of her wounds. With Misty once again reactive, Avril set upon a second round of whipping the unfortunate girl. In much less time than before, Misty started to fail to respond to the strikes. She had given up.

Standing back, Avril reviewed the canvas in front of her, appreciating the paint strokes left behind by the whip's cracker. Satisfied, Avril replaced the whip on the table.

Pulling over a straight back chair from a nearby wall, Avril positioned it in front of the girl and sat down. Crossing a leg, one over the other, she leaned back and watched her prey suffer these final minutes.

***

Sometime later, with a crossed leg bouncing mildly at the ankle, Avril pondered about finishing off the girl. She knew Sir was waiting. As much as she wished she didn't have to do this, killing the girl would bring her one step closer to becoming a member of the Consortium, one step closer to taking it down from the inside, and with it, her freedom, plus freedom for all of the unsuspecting prey out there.

Months ago, after failing to find an avenue of long-term escape, she had stumbled upon the idea of taking down the Consortium from the inside. It was a fantastic, if not a ludicrous, idea. She had no idea about accomplishing it, but it seemed that she had a better chance of survival if she could eradicate this organization. She hoped that once a member, an opportunity would present itself.

"Just how to do it?" she muttered to herself.

"Avril, are you having second thoughts?"

"Uh, oh, Sir, I didn't mean to say that out loud. Uh, yes. I am considering two different methods."

"Oh, shit, he heard me. I have to be more careful." She thought to herself.

"Avril, whatever you do, make sure you make it up close and personal. You must feel her life slip from her, looking into her eyes as you do it."

"Yes, Sir. I understand."

Looking back at Misty, she realized that the girl heard the entire exchange. Without a doubt, the girl now knew she was about to die. Decided, she went over to her table and picked up a knife. Avril held the knife in her hand and looked down at it. It was a thin, shiny blade, about seven inches long. The room's lights reflected spots of light along the razor-sharp edge that narrowed to a sharp point. It was a deadly instrument, not meant to be used in the kitchen. No, it was a custom blade made especially for killing, the one Sir wanted her to use.

Fear flamed across Misty's wide-open eyes, and tears welled up in her bloodshot eyes. Her body began shaking, despite being bound to the post.

Her eyes were darting back and forth; the girl's mouth opened. "No, No, NO, Please, NO, don't kill me. I don't want to die! Please, don't do this to me. Please!" she screeched. "I'll do anything you want. Whip me, torture me, I don't care, just don't kill me. Please!"

Avril didn't answer her. She just stared at her prey, looking deep into her eyes.

"No, no, no, please, NO! Please don't." Misty yelled over Sir's commanding voice, her tears falling in streams down her cheeks and mixing with her bloody chest.

Avril stayed silent. She knew that she was sacrificing not only the girl but her soul for the greater good. She hoped that God would forgive her.

"No, no, no, please, no! I'll be good, I promise. Please don't." Misty yelled, tears flowing down her cheeks and onto her naked chest, painting them with a glistening sheen under the bright lights.

Avril looked at the girl begging for her life. Scanning her, she began with her feet, trailing upwards. Gazing up her legs and over her shaved genitalia, Avril realized the girl was so frightened that her bladder relaxed, coating her thighs with piss.

Without comment, Avril continued scanning upwards towards the girl's face. To Avril, the time it took to reach her eyes seemed to take forever. Time slowed to a crawl, and Avril tried to slow it even further. If she could stop time altogether, she would have, as it would save her from performing this deadly deed.

Time didn't stop, and eventually, her gaze fell upon the face of the girl.

'No, no, no, no ..." Misty rattled on. "No, no, please don't ...."

Misty's contorted face, red and glistening, spoke the request even louder than that of her mouth, yelling, "no, no, please don't do this. I don't want to die."

"I know," Avril told her in a soft, sympathetic tone.

"Oh, God, please don't. Please!" she shrieked as Avril began raising the knife.

By now, Misty shook her head back and forth, trying to dissuade and prevent Avril from getting access to her neck. "No, no, no, no!"

Grabbing a chunk of hair, Avril pulled her head back, exposing her throat. Settling the knife on the side of Misty's neck, Avril said so softly that only Misty could hear.

"I'm sorry, I really am sorry."

"Please, no, don't," Misty screamed.

"I'm sorry," Avril repeated quietly one last time to the unfortunate girl, moments away from dying.

"Oh, God, I'm sorry. Please forgive me." Misty prayed. Avril realized that the girl had found God in her final moments. Would she when her time came?

Looking at the blade pressed against the right side of her neck, Avril watched the pumping action of blood vessels just beneath the skin for the first time. Fascinated, she found that she couldn't take her eyes from the sight. The artery expanded and contracted at a fast rate, a visible sign of Misty's anxiety in her last moments.

Misty wailed, "No, no, no, noooo, please!" looking right into the eyes of Avril.

Avril noticed the lights reflecting on the glistening blade. Razor-sharp, a small line of red had already appeared under the edge. A cut Avril had not intended.

"I'm sorry." Avril mouthed as she drew the knife across the girl's neck in a slow, steady, and firm motion, slicing deep, cutting tissue and arteries.

Immediately, blood sprayed out from severed arteries, showering Avril in the thick, bright red fluid. Misty's cries of 'no, no, no' transformed into unintelligible gurgles, bubbles added to the viscous fluid streaming from the wound. Past the point of no return, Avril continued sawing and cutting into Misty's neck, forcing the blade to disappear into the delicate flesh. Slicing the knife across Misty's neck, the knife dug deeper, cutting tendons, ligaments, and blood vessels as if they didn't exist.

Misty's cries may have stopped, but her staring eyes still begged for mercy, transformed into something horrific as she saw her murderer's face drenched in her blood. Avril would never forget the look of surprise coupled with hate. Her eyes spoke volumes of blistering hostile thoughts.

'How could you?', 'Why?', 'I hate you,' and 'God will punish you,' were just some of the messages Avril detected in the dying girl's final moments.

Like suds erupting from an overflowing clothes washer, red bubbles percolated from the gaping wound, spilling down her chest and spraying Avril. Gurgling noises joined to the torrent of bubbles.

The knife slowly appeared on the far side of Misty's neck, severing her other carotid artery. The girl's heart, not realizing what was happening, continued to pump blood. Misty's brain, detecting a severe reduction in blood flow, sent panicky signals to the heart to send more blood, which was all too happy to oblige. More blood shot out of the severed arteries on each pulse, never arriving at its intended destination. It would take a minute or so before the heart ran out of fluid to pump before it finally stalled and shut down forever.

However, Avril forced herself to stare at Misty, looking into the girl's dying eyes.

She repeatedly mouthed to her victim, "I'm sorry."

Looking deep into the girl's eyes, she watched them slowly lose their ability to track her movements. The window to her soul receded into a deep chasm of infinity. A moment later, there was nothing in there, just a deep empty black hole and a blank stare.

With her partially severed head held fast by Avril's hand, the dead weight of Misty's body sagged, carving a gaping canyon between her shoulders and her chin. Her heart stopped spurting arterial blood and slowed to a stream, draining blood through the exposed wound, as gravity emptied her skull of its contents.

There was no doubt about it. Misty was dead.

However, that was not enough. Sir required her to sever the head. Grasping her hair and holding it up, Avril continued to cut, eventually finding the vertebrae. Finding the joint in the cervical spine, Avril sawed through her spinal cord and finally reached the back of Misty's neck. She made the final slice and lifted the head free from the body.

Holding the head in her hand, Avril let the knife fall, landing just to the side of Misty's feet. She refused to look at the decapitated head as it drained massive volumes of bright red blood onto the floor.

Like some horror movie ghoul drenched in the girl's gore, Avril's body was painted red, from head to toe. Avril merely stood there a long time, staring at the corpse. Blood continued to seep from the neck stump. She hated herself for killing the girl, knowing full well that she could never clean the black stain on her soul, no matter how much penance she did at God's behest.

If she wasn't already there, she was going to hell, and there wasn't anything she could do about it.

Chapter Twenty-Eight

Watching the monitor, Avril observed the woman sleep. She looked peaceful, lying there. Eyes closed, her face relaxed, and her arm tucked across her chest nicely under her breasts, she laid in bed halfway between her back and her side. Her slow deep breathing betrayed her restful state of being asleep.

The girl was beautiful. Under Sir's tutelage, Avril had been using Jenni to refine her skills. Leaning back in her desk chair, she pondered her next action. After she had murdered poor Misty, Sir had given her the monitor so that she could watch her training subjects covertly.

All during her captivity, she knew that Sir had ways of observing his acquisitions. Avril knew he had hidden cameras and other means of surveillance. She assumed that even now, he was watching her.

"Was there a way to use them to her advantage one day? She'd keep that in mind," she pondered to herself.

Staring at Jenni, she was somewhat envious. The girl's ordeal would soon be over, while Avril's would go on and on, perhaps for years. At least, a plan had started to form.

It was too bad that the girl had to die. Not only that, but Avril had to kill her by her own hands, using no tools nor weapons. Avril knew that she would have to kill poor Jenni face to face, with her own hands. She knew what she had to do, and today was the day.

She wished the monitor could do other things, but it only allowed her to watch over her subjects, no one else, just her trainees. She was down to two, and one was about to die, leaving her with only one left. In the big picture, she didn't worry about it. If all went well, there would be more. If it didn't go well, then she would be dead without needing more prey. There was no other option for her.

It was the middle of the night, and feeling hungry, she went downstairs and fixed herself an egg and cheese sandwich with a glass of juice. She knew she needed the strength for what was about to come. When she returned to her room, she sat down at her desk and kept vigil over the sleeping girl. A short time later, the girl got up and used the bathroom before returning to bed. She was asleep again within minutes.

"Soon, Avril, soon…" Avril spoke softly to herself.

Getting up, she went to her on-suite, put on a touch of makeup, and fixed her hair. Satisfied, she went to her dresser and opened a drawer.

From inside, she pulled out a double-ended strap-on with a harness. After inserting one end inside her vagina and adjusting the belt firmly around her hip, she walked over to her walk-in closet and draped a black embroidered cape over her shoulders.

Using her full-length mirror, she checked her reflection. Except for one thing, the cloak covered her completely, from shoulders to floor. The contrast of the facsimile cock protruding beyond the cape was just the look she wanted. It made a statement, alright. Jenni was going to have one hell of a send-off.

Retrieving one last item, she left her suite and headed for the prey's quarters where the sleeping girl waited.

Standing in front of Jenni's room, Avril stared at the door, committed to what she must do. She wished she didn't have to. Taking a deep cleansing breath, Avril unlocked the door and walked in.

Jenni was instantly awake and attempted to get out of bed and kneel on the floor. Avril stilled her with a gesture of her hand and a command.

"Stay."

Jenni laid back and watched her Mistress intently. Avril closed the door behind her and stood for several minutes, looking at the woman lying on the bed. Jenni was breathing fast and heavy now, fear apparent in her body language.

"Relax, Jenni. I'm just here for a good time. I'm horny, and well, you know what I like."

"Yes, Ma'am, indeed I do."

Unclasping her cape, Avril methodically folded it over the back of the only chair in the room.

"Move over," Avril told the woman in the bed. Sliding in next to Jenni, Avril kissed the woman full on the lips. Finding her breast, she encased it in the palm of her hand. Massaging Jenni's breast, they kissed, the passion between them quickly growing.

Before long, the two women were writhing on the bed. Hot for each other, the heat in their lips grew hotter in each passing second. Avril, a need building in her belly, reached over and picked up that last item she gathered as she left her room.

Jumping on top of Jenni, straddling her hips, and taking the superior position on top with the dildo pressing against the top of her loins, Avril whispered.

"I have something for you."

"That fake piece of meat between your legs, Mistress?"

"Oh, that. Well, yes, but not yet. No, something else," she said, holding a set of clover clamps linked by a silver chain dangling from her fingers.

"Oh, nipple clamps. Please, Mistress, may I wear them for your pleasure?"

"For my pleasure? Why not yours?"

"Oh, Mistress, I dare not presume. It is true. I do enjoy wearing them. I didn't think so before I came here, but I've learned to enjoy them."

"Yes, you do."

"You knew? Yes, I suppose you did, Mistress. Sometimes, lying in bed, before I get up in the morning, I pinch them, pretending that I'm wearing your clamps and that you're playing with me."

"That too, I knew."

"So, you watch me, even in here."

"You presume too much."

"Forgive me, my Mistress. I may have overstepped myself."

"Indeed, you have, my bitch," Avril said, as she pinched a nipple and roughly seated a clamp over it. Jenni let out an involuntary gasp as the crushing pressure closed over the delicate flesh. Seconds later, the second nipple joined the first in feeling the crushing pressure of the clamp. Leaning back, Avril took hold of the connecting chain and pulled. She watched in wonder as Jenni's breasts stretched skywards, extending, straining against the unceasing pull. Avril smiled and took her pleasure. Minutes later, after releasing Jenni, Avril fell upon her, crushing her mouth to hers.

As she did so, she took Jenni by pinning her to the bed with the strap-on with all force she could muster. Jenni took her pleasure, returning it in kind, measure for measure. Each fed off the other, and before long, Avril could tell that Jenni was getting close. It didn't take long before she made the first query.

"Please … Mistress, may, may I come now."

"No, you may not. Wait."

"Yes, Ma'am."

And so, they continued, writhing in bed, Avril forcing the passion in the woman to greater heights. At times, she let off before pushing her higher. Between roughly pulling on her nipple clamps and pinning her to the bed, Jenni continued begging to cum. Avril denied her and again.

"Mistress … I … I … beg you. I can't … hold it … much longer. Please let me come."

"You want to come, you say?"

"Yes, Mistress. May I … please come."

Ramming the double-ended dildo inside her, which of course, bottomed it out in both of them, Avril granted her permission.

"You may," she said with a bit of sadness. "Cum for me."

At that moment, Jenni threw her head back, rolled her eyes, which disappeared inside her skull, and seemed to melt away. As the girl climaxed, determined to maintain control, Avril kept her passion in check.

Feeling Jenni's climax rippling beneath her, Avril leaned in and kissed her mouth. Then, whispered into her ear.

"I'm sorry."

Jenni may or may not have heard her; she was in a different place. Her euphoria consumed her body, mind, and soul. It was the perfect moment that Avril had hoped to take the woman.

As if in slow motion, Avril looked at her hands as they gradually made their way forward and down. In what seemed like hours, before they found the sides and the back of Jenni's head, where she lovingly caressed it. Then, encircling the woman's neck with her fingers and crisscrossing her thumbs over the soft, delicate flesh under her chin, Avril squeezed. Leaning in, she deliberately closed off her airways and began strangling her.

Somewhere amid her ecstasy, Jenni must have realized what was happening as she seemed to return from her other place and focused on Avril.

Avril could almost have sworn that she was asking the question, "So, is it now? Is today the day I die?"

Avril nodded ever so subtly. Jenni nodded in return and closed her eyes.

Avril locked her arms, leaned her body in, and pressed her thumbs in harder, crushing the larynx. A moment later, Avril heard a soft snap of the hyoid bone, confirming the irreversible conclusion of Jenni's strangulation.

Unable to take in air, Jenni's resolving climax changed to one of bulging eyes, while red streaks appeared in the whites of her eyes. Jenni bucked, but with Avril sitting on her hips and already weakened by her orgasm, she couldn't move very much. A minute later, her body relaxed.

Jenni died when the light in her eyes went out forever.

Sitting up, several minutes later, Avril looked down at the dead woman. Caressing her cheeks, still warm, Avril hated herself. Staring at what should have been she, she mumbled, "I am sorry."

Climbing off, she quickly stripped herself of the strap-on, tossing it off into the corner of the room. She'd have someone else clean up the place. Right now, she needed to get out of there.

Six hours later, Sir walked into the workout room, where Avril had been all day. He had been watching her. After leaving her latest kill, she had come directly here where she had gotten on a treadmill and ran what must have been thirty miles, in her heels no less. Then, in a sweaty sheen, she moved onto the weight machines and worked out for another two hours, exceeding her limits, pushing herself, and straining herself. The numbers on the panel reported she had already gone another five miles on the treadmill. She was running at a steady pace.

Killing Jenni bothered her. He promised she would get over it. She wasn't so sure. He said he had many of the same feelings after his first kills. His kills of these later years were almost inconsequential compared to those earlier ones. He missed how he felt during those early kills. At least he felt something. Maybe that was what was now missing in his life. Perhaps that was what he hoped to regain in watching Avril travel her road of self-discovery.

Walking up to Avril, he stopped a short distance away and just watched her run on the treadmill. He did enjoy that one thing, watching her run. He loved watching her boobs bounce up and down, swing back and forth as her body shifted back and forth in her strides. Her legs were toned, and her calves, well, they could almost crush a person all by themselves. It was something he watched out for over the past year.

After observing her for several minutes, he said, "Avril."

She tried to shut him down by shoving a hand out in his direction, in a stop motion. He would have none of it.

"Avril, I require your attention."

Resigned, Avril pressed a button on the treadmill, and it slowed to a stop.

"Yes, Sir."

"Avril, you did well this morning. I wasn't sure you had it within you."

"Thank you, Sir."

"You planned that all on your own?"

"Yes, Sir."

"Tell me about it."

"Sir, I knew you were hedging about submitting my application."

"I was, but how did you know? I did not say anything about it."

"No, you didn't, Sir. I knew, anyway. I can't explain it. I just knew."

"What I can tell you is that while I was pleased with your performance with Misty, I still felt your heart wasn't in it. If I wasn't there to push you, I doubted you would complete the task. That left a bad taste, and as such, I withheld your application. The others who watched you that day did not observe your hesitation and would have signed off, but they did not have the advantage of knowing you the way I know you. Therefore, I decided to wait a bit more to see what you would do."

"And so, my Sir?"

"Well, I can tell you this. You sent her on very happy."

"I did, Sir indeed."

"I might have liked it better if she had been in agony, but there will be plenty of that in the future. Putting her down with your bare hands, without tools or weapons, was better. Getting close and look at your victim in the eye earning their trust as you kill them, takes cunning and skill. You seem to have that talent. Teaching you the skills to refine your abilities is only a matter of time."

He paused a moment.

"But you're still bothered by the killing."

"Yes, Sir."

"Would it surprise you to know that I am also and that one time, I felt as you do now?"

"Sir?"

"I am a cruel person, but each time, I feel for each of those I kill. With my first ones, I felt as you do now."

"Sir, I find that hard to believe."

"And yet, it is true."

"Sir, I don't know what to say."

"Don't say anything. There is nothing to say. I tell you this so that you know that you are not alone in these feelings."

Avril stayed silent for a time, uncertain and perhaps fearful as to how to respond.

"One more thing, Avril, I endorsed your application to the committee for membership. It'll take several months to go through the approval process, but I expect in the end, you will become a full-fledged member of the Consortium. Congratulations, Avril. I am very, very proud of you. Well done, my dear."

"I don't know what to say, Sir. Thank you."

"You remember, of course, you still belong to me, always and forever."

"Of course, Sir, my loyalties will always remain with you."

"Welcome to the Consortium, my dear."

Connect with the Author

website – RichardVerry.com

Facebook – richardverrywriter

twitter – @richverry

blog – RichardVerry.com/blog

Author's Notes

Thank you for reading this next chapter in Avril's story. If you enjoyed it, won't you please take a moment to leave me a review?

Telling her story preoccupied me for months, demanding to be let out of my consciousness and written down. With the success and demand for more, I came up with an idea for Avril's story's next few segments. In this next edition of her captivity,

'Perfect Prey' fills us in on what happened after Avril made the impossible choice in the first book, 'The Trafficking Consortium.' A choice made between a life of endless torment or choosing a quick death after a harrowing, torturous session. If she took a quick death, she would put her soul at risk for all eternity. Something her faith prevented her from accepting. Therefore, she felt obligated to take the long road to salvation.

Over the years, unable to find a long-term means of escape, she formulates a strategy that will betray her promise and her captor. Putting the plan into action requires that she make decisions and do things that she believes will forever damn her soul. However, in doing so, it will save thousands, if not millions, of innocent souls.

Does the mean justify the end? Will God ever forgive her?

I appreciate your sharing this book with your friends and acquaintances and posting a review.

Also, by the Author

Consortium
The Trafficking Consortium (Book #1)
Perfect Prey (Book #2)
UnderCurrents (Book #3)

Mona Bendarova Adventures
The Taste of Honey (Book #1)
Broken Steele (Book #2)
Lucky Bitch (Book #3)
Angry Bitch (Book #4)

Her Client Trilogy
Her Client (Book #1)
Her Overseer (Book #2)
Her Essentia (Book #3)
Her Client Trilogy (Books 1, 2, & 3)

Novellas and Short Stories
The Breakup
A Mermaid's Irresistible Curiosity

About the Author

Richard Verry is an Information Technologies Engineer who has coded and supported computer systems for decades.

He wrote many stories in his youth; all lost to history. He wrote his first short story as an adult in 2007. Over the next few years, he dabbled in writing stories, not expecting to publish any of them.

In 2012, he began writing full-length novels and novellas, where he is finally able to capture some of the ideas and story concepts steadily invading his mind.

Richard grew up and lives on the North-East Coast of America, where he lives with the love of his life, Janet. He enjoys skinny, sugar-free vanilla lattes and Kamikaze cocktails, red wine, single malt scotch, and a good steak.

Richard ponders, sometimes to the point of excess, the myriad of images and scenarios, mostly including the captivating nude female form, streaming through his consciousness. A rare few eventually come to life in his artwork and writings.

richardverry.com

Made in the USA
Las Vegas, NV
28 January 2022